OTHER NAN

Zoë Fairbairns was born in 1948. Her other novels include *Benefits*, *Stand We At Last*, *Here Today*, *Closing* and *Daddy's Girls*. She lives in south London and works part-time as a television subtitler.

OTHER NAMES

Zoë Fairbairns

MICHAEL JOSEPH
LONDON

MICHAEL JOSEPH LTD

Published by the Penguin Group
27 Wrights Lane, London W8 5TZ, England
Penguin Putnam Inc., 375 Hudson Street, New York, New York 10014, USA
Penguin Books Australia Ltd, Ringwood, Victoria, Australia
Penguin Books Canada Ltd, 10 Alcorn Avenue, Toronto, Ontario, Canada M4V 3B2
Penguin Books (NZ) Ltd, 182–190 Wairau Road, Auckland 10, New Zealand

Penguin Books Ltd, Registered Offices: Harmondsworth, Middlesex, England

First published 1998
1 3 5 7 9 10 8 6 4 2

Set in 12/15pt Monotype Sabon
Typeset by Rowland Phototypesetting Ltd, Bury St Edmunds, Suffolk
Printed in England by Clays Ltd, St Ives plc

A CIP catalogue record for this book is available from the British Library

Hardback: ISBN 07181 4327 2
Trade paperback: ISBN 07181 4340 X

The moral right of the author has been asserted

Author's Note

Thanks to everyone who helped, particularly Sara Fisher, Valerie Miner, Louise Moore, John Petherbridge, Michael Thomas and others who must remain nameless.

The Lloyd's of London insurance market is a real institution which has, over its 300-year history, comprised many thousands of underwriting syndicates, members' agencies and individual investors or names. However, the syndicates, agencies and individuals appearing in this book are entirely fictional. Any resemblance to reality is coincidental.

It was the biggest mistake of her life. She'll admit that if you ask her.

Are you going to ask her? Go easy if you do. She couldn't have known what a big mistake she was making.

She had enough on her plate. It was 3.30 on the afternoon of Christmas Eve 1983. In four hours' time, forty guests would begin descending on The Old Coach House for drinks and a buffet. She was working her way down her 'To Do' list. She was on schedule, more or less, but it was a tight schedule, and there was no space in it for unexpected and time-consuming telephone calls.

The call came from Olivia. 'I'm phoning to ask you a favour, Marje, which I know is a frightful cheek because you must be up to your elbows. How you manage to soldier on and throw open your doors as usual after the year you've had I simply cannot imagine. Have I ever mentioned Boniface Bennett to you?'

The name rang no bells for Marjorie, but that didn't necessarily mean anything, Lady Olivia Verlaine being the person she was. Is. You know what she's like – the habit she has, when addressing those whom she is pleased to regard as her social inferiors, of peppering her remarks with seemingly casual references to grand-sounding people whom she knows but her hearer does not. This has the twin effect of making Olivia sound democratic – as if she makes no distinction between her top-drawer friends and those who come from a little further down – and, at the same time, reminding the further-downs how out of touch they are with people who count.

'Jake's godson,' Olivia clarified. 'Annabel and Harry's youngest.'

Marjorie had never heard of Annabel or Harry. 'What about him, Olivia?'

'He's about to arrive on our doorstep. Not a word of warning, of course. Quite insane. Last I heard of him, he'd landed this super new job in the City and was on course to be a millionaire by the time he's thirty and keep us all in our old age.'

'How splendid.' Marjorie glanced distractedly at her watch.

'He was supposed to be flying down to Gibraltar for Christmas with some chums. That's what *you* should have done, Marje. Got that husband of yours to whisk you away for a holiday instead of letting you wear yourself out giving parties after the year you've had.'

Marjorie said nothing.

'Where was I?' said Olivia. 'Gibraltar. Boniface's firm has a yacht down there, for staff use. All right for some, I say. But when I phoned Ferdie this morning –'

'Ferdie?'

'I wanted to check whether the Havenfords had moved – I was surprised we hadn't had a card from them, but then I suppose they've got other things on their minds after what's been going on with the grandchild – have you and Robert had a card?'

'No.' Marjorie didn't know anybody called Havenford.

'Anyway, we were having a natter and the subject of Boniface came up and I said I suppose he's en route for Gibraltar now, jammy little sod, and Ferdie said, well, it's funny you should say that, because there's a bit of a mystery.'

Olivia paused for dramatic effect. In a moment of inspiration, Marjorie prepared to nip in smartly with *I'll look forward to hearing about it at the party, bye for now*. But Olivia was too quick. 'Apparently Vee and Toby Manio got a phone call this morning at the crack of dawn from Miles Candwell's boy, saying he was at Heathrow, Boniface hadn't turned up, the plane was revving its engines, and was Bon by any chance passed out on Vee and Toby's floor or if not had they any idea whose floor he might be passed out on?'

'And had they?'

'Well, of course not, darling. Why should they?'

Marjorie thought she had spotted where all this was leading. She made a dash for it. 'So Boniface missed the flight to Gibraltar, he's coming to you instead and you'd like to bring him to our party?'

'Not if it's a nuisance,' said Olivia.

'Bring him by all means,' Marjorie said, 'if you're sure he won't be bored.'

'Nobody's ever bored at *your* parties.'

'I mean there won't be anyone of his age. The girls aren't here. Just us oldies.'

'Then he'll be the centre of attention and he'll love every minute of it. Are you sure it's all right? Because we can just as easily leave him at home in front of the telly with a plate of mince pies.'

'Do please bring him. We'll look forward to seeing all three of you.' It occurred to Marjorie that anyone getting a crossed line at this moment might suppose that she was the one who was asking the favour, while Olivia granted it.

You get the picture? She could have said no, of course she could. But she didn't. So yes, it was her mistake. But her fault? You must be the judge, of course, but she didn't have a lot of choice. She was trying to get Olivia off the line, and this seemed the simplest way to do it.

If she had said no, she would probably never have met Boniface Bennett, and none of this would have happened. She would never have met me either, and I wouldn't be trying to explain what did happen.

My Christmas Eve was a bit different.

Not for me the delights of a des. res. in East Sussex with panoramic views of the South Downs. I was all alone and freezing cold in a bedsitter at the top of a tenanted house in south-east London, with views of Crystal Palace TV mast.

My cooking facilities consisted of a store cupboard with a tiny work top, a sink, a gas ring encrusted with soot and an electric kettle with a two-pin plug and a flex that looked like something out of a leaflet produced by the Royal Society for the Prevention of Accidents. So it won't surprise you to hear that I had no plans for inviting forty of my friends round for a Christmas Eve buffet. I hadn't got forty friends. I hadn't got four.

I spent most of the morning lying in bed smoking cigarettes. I was trying to keep warm, and to get my thoughts into some kind of order. I couldn't manage to do either.

At about two o'clock, a sour, scorching smell from the heater told me that it had run out of paraffin.

It was time to get up. It was time to do all sorts of things. Like Marjorie, I made lists of all the things I ought to be doing, and the order in which I would do them. But, unlike Marjorie's lists, mine remained in my head, and the things remained undone.

The sky darkened. My stomach began to rumble. I smoked my last cigarette and got out of bed. I put on three cardigans, my winter coat, thick socks, wellies and a woolly hat, and went out.

I went to my usual supermarket, the cheap one where they don't bother to unpack the stuff properly. Everything sits in the aisles in cardboard cartons, and you're expected to rip the cardboard apart with your bare hands to get what you want. If you can't manage that – because you've got arthritic hands or you're trying to hang on to a toddler – the supermarket's attitude is, tough. They know you can't afford to shop anywhere else. They don't give bags and they never have more than one checkout open. What they do have are a lot of smug notices explaining that what they call their down-to-earth approach is the reason why their prices are so low.

Another aspect of the down-to-earth approach that Christmas Eve was that most of the staff seemed to have gone home. The few that remained seemed mainly concerned with causing as much inconvenience as possible to shoppers. A guy in his twenties with bad skin and a Father Christmas hat on his head was chaining up the trolleys. To look at him you might think that, but for his vigilance, they would escape and start biting people. A girl of about my age was mopping the floor with an unnecessarily wet mop. A man in a suit advanced on the bakery shelves with a managerial look in his eye and a wheeled basket, and started hurling loaves into it.

I spotted the loaf I wanted. It was my favourite kind – sliced wholemeal, with grains of wheat stuck on the crust. It looked healthy, even though it probably wasn't. (The loaf itself might have been okay, but what had they stuck those grains on with?) It had a half-price label, and I made a grab for it. The man in the manager's outfit got there first, snatched the loaf off the shelf and slung it into his trolley. I took the next loaf, a white, spongy one, and skulked off with it.

Next stop was at the delicatessen counter. One thing I will say for this supermarket is that its pressed turkey roll is second to none in the annals of cheap meat. It's probably made from parts of the turkey that you wouldn't want to put anywhere near your mouth if you thought about them – feet and sex organs and those floppy bits of flesh that wobble under its beak – but the secret is not to think, just buy it and eat it. You'd never guess from the antiseptic-savoury flavour of the meat, or even its pinkish-grey colour, that it had anything untoward in it. With a quarter-pound, thinly sliced, and a loaf of bread, you've got all you need for a pile of cold turkey sandwiches. What could be nicer on Christmas Eve than cold turkey sandwiches, and what could be nicer on Christmas Day than more cold turkey sandwiches?

I asked the woman for a quarter-pound of turkey roll, thinly sliced. I noticed that the slicing machine was set to 'thick'. I waited for her to change it, but she didn't. She cut off a few thick slices and weighed them. They came to five ounces. 'Just over, all right?'

I took the slices and went to the booze-and-fags section. There at least I could be sure that no one would try to sell me something I didn't want, or stop me buying something that I did. I bought twenty cigarettes and two cans of strong lager.

While I was queuing at the checkout, I looked at other people's shopping. One old lady had nothing but a packet of out-of-date lemon curd tarts and a small tin of cat food. My own purchases came to more than I had expected, and I realized I could kiss goodbye to paraffin.

It was cold outside the supermarket, and getting dark. Shops were putting up their shutters. People were hurrying to their homes. I looked into their windows, at their front rooms, decorated for Christmas.

A car pulled up in front of me and a family got out – parents, children, a baby and a dog. They headed up the path of one of the houses. Their arms were full of suitcases and presents. The front door opened and another family rushed out to greet them with cries of joy.

Thick, blackish-blue clouds were gathering round the Crystal Palace TV mast. The mast flashed its warning lights to passing planes. I thought about Boniface flying down to Gibraltar. That was what I believed he was doing. I didn't know he had missed his flight. I didn't know he was on his way to Sussex instead, to stay with Lord and Lady Verlaine and to go to their friend's party. How would I know? I had never heard of any of these people.

I imagined him getting off the plane. I saw the bright Mediterranean sunlight. I felt the warm breeze and the softness of the sea. I could have been there with him. I was invited.

3

Robert emerged from the cellar with his arms full of bottles. 'Who was that on the phone?'

'Olivia.'

He gasped theatrically. 'You mean the Viscountess? In person? Not the butler calling on her behalf?'

It was a familiar routine. 'No, not the butler.'

'So you're telling me we've just had a titled person talking on our telephone?'

'Robert —'

'I hope you wiped the receiver with *eau de cologne* before you said anything.'

One of his bottles started to slip from under his arm. Marjorie watched him struggle to retrieve it, and did not assist.

'Was it to say that she and Jake can't make it tonight? They've been summoned to Sandringham to make up the numbers?'

'No, they're coming, and they're bringing one extra.'

'Oh, heavens!' He leaned against a wall for support. 'Where are we going to hang all the coronets?'

Another of his bottles was going. It looked serious this time, so she stepped forward and saved the situation. 'Don't ever get any new jokes, will you? I feel so comfortable with your old ones.'

'So who is this gatecrasher?' he asked. 'And how much is he or she likely to drink? Did Olivia say?'

'Jake's godson.' She helped him carry the wine into the library, where he was setting up the bar. 'A bright young man, from the sound of things, with a glittering career ahead of him.'

'As what?'

'Something in the City.'

'Hide the silver, then. Has he a name, this fellow?'

'Yes, a rather unusual one, but I've forgotten it.'

'Probably one of Olivia's toy boys.'

'Which would put your nose out of joint.'

'What's that supposed to mean?'

She laughed and did not bother to answer. Robert's alleged infatuation with Olivia was an ongoing joke between them. In truth, he could not stand the woman. His friendship was with Jake, and went back to pre-Olivia, rugby-playing days.

Marjorie located her 'To Do' list. Where had she got to? Most of the major cooking was either completed or in progress, but the salads, vegetables, sweets and canapés still needed attention. Her cleaning lady's two teenage daughters were hard at work in the kitchen. They were good, capable girls, but attention to detail was not their strong point, and an eye had to be kept on them. Flowers had just been delivered, and would need to be arranged. This morning's Christmas cards were waiting to be put up. The table needed laying. *Why not get that husband of yours to whisk you away for a holiday instead of letting you wear yourself out giving parties after the year you've had . . . ?*

She finished her tasks and went up to her bathroom. She took off her clothes and lay in the bath. My first Christmas as an orphan, she thought. It sounded like the title of one of those sentimental Victorian paintings. She gazed down at her body under the water. She didn't look like a Victorian orphan, or any other sort of orphan. She looked like a prosperous, middle-aged Englishwoman whose prosperity has gone to her hips.

Robert's parents were the first to arrive. They rang the doorbell on the dot of 7.30, making Marjorie wonder whether they had been waiting in their car with a stopwatch. She greeted them warmly, biting back the guilty irritation that she sometimes felt these days when she met someone of her parents' generation who was hale and hearty: *what are you doing alive? What's so special about you?*

The in-laws were followed by Robert's headmaster and his wife, and Addie Bernard, manageress of the charity shop in Eastbourne where Marjorie worked as a volunteer. New neighbours from down the road were next. The house filled up. By long tradition, Robert was the barman, Marjorie the meeter and greeter. In lulls between arrivals, she drifted amongst the guests, exercising her right as hostess to eavesdrop on interesting conversations without joining in the boring ones. A group of Robert's colleagues were conducting a staff meeting about the national curriculum. Marjorie broke them up and moved on to where Robert's father, Neil Fairfax, was laying down the law to Alexandra Purves from down the road about deteriorating standards of cabin service on transatlantic flights. Alexandra, a former air stewardess, was defending the industry. Jim Jessup from the cricket club was trying to find out how much the new neighbours had paid for their house. Elsewhere, a heated debate was under way on whether the miners really would go on strike in the new year.

The Verlaines were late. Perhaps they weren't coming. It was time to serve the buffet. She was on her way to the kitchen when she heard the purr of a car in the drive. She pulled back the curtain of the window by the front door and saw Jake Verlaine's silver-grey BMW gliding to a halt in the turning circle.

She waved, but the occupants of the car didn't see her. She waited for its doors to open, but they stayed shut. A light went on in the car. Olivia, in the front passenger seat, adjusted the driving mirror. She handed a comb to the figure in the shadows at the back.

Marjorie watched, fascinated, as the young man combed his hair under Olivia's supervision. Any minute now, she thought, she's going to make him lick his hanky, and wipe his mouth with it.

4

Light from the house shimmered on Olivia's silk stockings as she stepped elegantly from the car. She had on her musquash coat and very high heels. Diamonds glittered in her ear lobes. Even the patterns that her breath made on the air were delicately symmetrical.

She stood by the car while the young man got out. He wore a camelhair overcoat and leather gloves, which he clapped together against the cold. He towered over Olivia. Most men did.

Olivia picked her way up the drive like a fussy little pony. The men followed – first the stranger, then Jake in his sheepskin, with a wrapped bottle under his arm and his hands full of parcels.

Olivia stood on tiptoe to kiss the air somewhere behind Marjorie's left ear. 'Happy Christmas, Marje, darling. Sackcloth and ashes for being so late.'

'Not at all.'

'Blame Boniface. He got on the wrong train at Victoria.'

'Hasn't been his day,' Jake chortled. 'Missed planes, wrong trains . . .'

Marjorie looked sympathetically at the young man, who had, she guessed, been enduring this sort of banter all the way from Eastbourne. He was in his mid-twenties, tall, slim, with brown hair and regular features – probably quite handsome, though it was difficult to be sure when he looked so tired and disgruntled. He had bags under his eyes, and needed a shave. He stifled a yawn and stared round at the darkness.

'. . . great white hope of the City of London,' Olivia was saying, 'and he can't even read a platform alteration.'

The young man looked appropriately sheepish, and allowed

himself to be introduced. He said, 'I'm very sorry we're late, Mrs Fairfax. It's all my fault.'

She said, 'You're here now, that's the main thing,' and led the little party into the house.

Robert emerged from the packed sitting room. The warm hum of conversation rolled after him like a wave. He held out his arms. 'Olivia! Jake! At last the party can begin!'

'Robbie, darling!' Olivia kissed his lips and pressed herself against him. Her frailty looked sweet against his grey-bearded, comforting bulk.

When Marjorie considered their embrace had gone on long enough, she said, 'Darling, this is Boniface Bennett, Jake's godson.' She pronounced Boniface as she had heard it, to rhyme with lass.

Boniface stepped forward smartly. 'How do you do, sir?'

Olivia shrieked. 'You don't have to call Robbie sir, Bon.'

'He can call me sir if he wants,' said Robert. 'What are we all standing around here for? Olivia's got her tongue hanging out for her first gin of the evening.'

Jake sniggered. 'First?'

Marjorie helped Olivia and Jake to take off their coats. 'Does anyone want to go upstairs?'

Olivia said, 'Bon wants to tart himself up a bit, don't you, Bon.' It was not a question, and Marjorie led the young man up the stairs. His tread was heavy and weary-sounding. She was very conscious of him close behind her, and of her own awkward walk with her arms full of coats.

She took him to the guest room and pointed out the bath-room. She was tempted to offer shaving things and the use of Robert's trouser press, but she didn't want to sound like Olivia. 'Help yourself to towels and, er, whatever you need. Do you think you can find your own way down?'

'I expect so.' He didn't sound as if he cared.

'I'm looking forward to hearing about this super new job that Olivia tells me you've got.'

'She thinks it's so super, she can have it.' Boniface threw his coat on the bed and strode past Marjorie into the bathroom. He slammed the door and bolted it with great decisiveness. Soon she could hear him having a long, hard pee. On and on it went. It made her want to go.

She tidied herself up, then went downstairs to supervise the food. It wasn't until everyone had moved on to pudding that she remembered Boniface. Had he had anything to eat? Had someone given him a drink? Had he even made it downstairs? She peered through the crowds in the dining room and the sitting room, checked the library, the utility room and the downstairs loo. She felt flustered and foolish. She couldn't ask people if they had seen him: they wouldn't know who she was talking about. The only people who would know were Robert, who was gazing into the eyes of Nina Grassington from English Villages Preservation and obviously not to be disturbed, and Jake and Olivia themselves. She could hardly admit to them that she had mislaid their *protégé*.

She went upstairs and looked in the guest room. His coat was on the bed with all the others. The bathroom was empty. She looked along the corridor, and saw a light on in her daughter Caroline's room.

He was lying on her bed, fast asleep. He wore an old-looking sweater, clean but threadbare, and creased slacks. One arm was across his eyes; the other dangled over the side of the bed, the knuckles brushing the floor. He hadn't even bothered to take his shoes off. On the sole of one was a pink disk of chewing gum with bits of hair stuck to it. It looked like a squashed exotic insect.

She said his name. He buried his face in the pillow and waved her away in annoyance. She said, 'Boniface!' again, more sharply. This time he whimpered, and she felt sorry for him. He seemed so tired. Why should she disturb him? He wasn't doing any harm, though the shoes and the chewing gum might mark the bedding. Caroline wouldn't like that –

but Caroline wasn't here, was she? She had chosen not to be here.

The shoes weren't actually on the duvet, but he had only to move in his sleep and they would be. She sat on the end of the bed, untied his laces and removed the shoes. The left one came off easily, but the laces on the right had got themselves in a knot, like a schoolboy's laces. She struggled to disentangle the knot, trying not to breathe in the sweaty, leathery stink of the other foot. She looked at the sleeping young man and thought how vulnerable he seemed, lying unconscious on a strange bed in a strange house, while his shoes were removed by a strange woman who could smell his feet.

She left him where he was and went back to the party. Olivia accosted her at the foot of the stairs. She was tucking into a large slice of lemon cheesecake with extra cream. 'Super food.'

'I'm glad you're enjoying it.'

'I'll be drummed out of Weight Watchers,' said Olivia, who had never been anywhere near Weight Watchers. In the unlikely event of her ever needing to lose weight, she would take herself off to some 500-guinea-a-day health farm and do it among her own kind. In the meantime, Olivia ate what she wanted and never put on an ounce. Marjorie had decided long ago that it was something that went with blue blood. After generations of knowing that one would always be fed, always be warm, one's genes must get the message that they need no longer arrange for the laying down of reserves of fat. It could be burned off, like historic oaks in the ancestral park.

'Now, listen, Marje.' Olivia waited for someone to pass out of hearing range, then lowered her voice. 'I haven't had a chance to apologize.'

'What for?'

'Boniface.' She glanced round at the guests. 'Where is the wretched boy?'

'Oh . . .' Marjorie looked vague. 'Somewhere.' She doubted that Olivia would approve of his little siesta, and she felt protective of him. 'I saw him a few minutes ago. What is there to apologize for? I think he's rather a poppet.'

'The state of him when he got here.' Olivia speared a morsel of cheesecake with her fork and swirled it in the cream before putting it into her mouth. 'The dragged-through-a-hedge-backwards look.'

'He'd had a difficult journey.'

'Only from London, darling. Not from the outer reaches of Tibet. When I saw him getting off the train, my first instinct was to take him straight home and ask Bligh to drop him into the washing machine with the horse blankets, but we were late already.'

'Not to worry.'

'I've hardly spoken to him since we got here,' said Olivia. 'I still haven't got to the bottom of it.'

'The bottom of what?'

'The whole mystery. Why he missed his flight. Why he didn't simply get on the next one. And why, when I did manage to track him down, he was at his office, which was supposed to be closed.'

'A work crisis?' Marjorie suggested.

'That's what he tried to tell me, but it's nonsense, of course. The people he was going to Gibraltar with were from work. They'd have known if there was a crisis.'

'Good thinking.'

'I'll lay you any odds it's girlfriend trouble.' Olivia tapped the side of her exquisite little nose. '*Cherchez la femme*.'

5

There's no need for you to *chercher la femme*. You've already found me.

You've got me right here, telling you the story. And you've probably guessed already that I was the girlfriend trouble. I was the reason why he missed his flight to Gibraltar.

To explain how it happened, I have to say a bit more about the place where I was living, and how I came to be living there. To understand that, you have to know a few facts about my background. But I'll keep the CV brief. This is Marjorie's story, not mine. I am just the person telling it.

My name is Heather Julia Fox. And before you ask – *are you anything to do with* The *Julia Fox, author of* The Seven Demands and the Women's Revolution *and other trailblazing works on sexual politics?* – the answer's yes. She's my mother. Okay?

If you've read Mum's writings or heard her speak, you'll already know a bit about me. In case you haven't, I was born on 25 October 1964 in a hospital near Chelmsford. Twenty-four hours after the birth, a car came to collect Mum and me and take us back to the home for unmarried mothers.

She was eighteen. Her parents had sent her to the home. Her father, my grandfather, was manager of a tailor's and gents' outfitter's shop in central Peterborough. Respectability was important to him. There weren't many men of substance in the town whose inside leg he hadn't measured. He didn't want there to be any talk. My grandmother didn't want there to be any talk either. She was a big churchgoer.

The gents' outfitter and the churchgoer got together with the authorities at the home and decided what was going to happen. Mum would stay at the home for a couple of weeks to breastfeed me and give me the benefit of her antibodies. Then she could sign the adoption papers, hand me over to a social worker, and go back to Peterborough as if nothing had happened. Her old school wouldn't take her back, but another might be found where she could finish her A-levels and perhaps even get into university.

They had it all worked out. I marvel at it, I really do – even now, knowing the things I know. Quite apart from their small-minded cruelty, how could they have been so stupid? Having brought Mum up for eighteen years, they must have known something about her. There may not have been a women's movement in those days, but there was an awkward squad, and my mum was a fully paid-up member. If she hadn't been, she probably wouldn't have got into such a mess. Her parents ought to have known that there were some things they could get away with, and some they couldn't.

Night after night, Mum lay in the dormitory, listening to girls sobbing as they counted the days until their babies would be taken away from them. No way was she going to let that happen to her, to me. When they brought her the papers, she refused to sign.

The matron of the home went on and on at her about the difficulties we would face, and compared these with the many advantages and opportunities and comforts and luxuries that awaited me in my adoptive home – a father as well as a mother, my own room in a big house in the country, private education, trips abroad and a stable for my pony. Mum wept, but she wouldn't budge. The matron asked who she thought she was, to deprive me of the good things of life? Mum cried even more and said she was my mother, that was who, and she wasn't going to deprive me of anything. Whatever I needed, I would have; she would see to that. The matron said I might grow up to hate her for her selfishness. Mum said that was a risk she was prepared to take. And she was right to take it, because I haven't grown up to hate her – not for that, anyway.

She was afraid they might take me from her by force. So one Sunday morning when she was supposed to be at church with the other inmates, she put me in one of the home's carry-cots, packed a few things and walked out.

The home was out in the country, five miles from the nearest village. There were two buses a week, neither of which ran on a Sunday. It was early November, cold and windy. A sleety rain was starting to fall. I'm not describing this from memory, obviously. But I've heard the story so many times that it's as if I was there.

I *was* there, of course I was. But you know what I mean. I seem to remember much more than I could have known, or seen from my carry-cot. The towers of the home receded behind us, black against the grey, churned-up sky. Mum strode into the wind. She was five foot three and still sore between her legs from the birth. She wore a raincoat and a flowery headscarf. I lay in the battered, pee-smelling carry-cot, curled up and growing. She could feel me growing heavier by the minute. She didn't know where she was going or how she was going to get there but she walked purposefully and I bashed against her leg in rhythm with her strides.

A car slowed down and a man offered her a lift. She was scared to accept and scared not to. She got in. She was in luck. He was one of the good guys. He drove us to a Catholic convent where his sister was a nun. The nuns took us in and gave us food and a bed for the night. Next day, they started telling Mum that the best thing would be to have me adopted. She put her fingers in her ears. The nuns made her take them out again, but even when they were physically out, any sensible person could see that Mum wasn't listening. And the nuns were sensible. All those years of worshipping God had probably taught them that when you find yourself up against a will stronger than your own, you might as well give in. They suggested that Mum might like to telephone her parents and ask if she could take me home. They might feel differently, now that their grandchild was born. Mum doubted it, but she made the call. Her father said exactly what she expected him to say. She could come home any time she liked, her room was ready for her, but she couldn't bring me. He didn't want to hear from her again until I had been adopted, and neither did her mother.

The nuns phoned round and got us a place at a non-Catholic hostel. From there, we were sent to live with a family in King's Lynn who had agreed to take us in exchange for Mum being a mother's help. I have vague memories of that time. It was a big, draughty house, full of children, all of them older than I was, and very noisy. The girls treated me as if I were one of their dolls, fussing over me until they got bored and then strolling off to do something else.

Mum got sick of being a skivvy. There were rows, and the wife told her to look for alternative accommodation. A social worker found us a furnished bedsitter. It was cramped and badly lit and the air smelt of fish even though we never ate fish. We lived on supplementary benefit, handouts from a charity for unmarried mothers and, now and again, wages from jobs that Mum could do at home while looking after me. She addressed envelopes for catalogue companies, and made necklaces out of sparkling beads. I loved those beads. I thought they were probably magic, and this was the reason why Mum made me promise never to tell anyone about them.

There was no one to tell. Our only friend was a woman Mum had been at school with, called Dorothy Bridgewater. She visited us from time to time, bringing her new baby in a spotless carry-cot. She seemed a bit of a show-off to me, but Mum was glad to see her. The two of them sat for hours with cups of tea and cigarettes, ignoring me while they nattered on about their school days or about Dorothy's baby or her husband or her house. We were never invited to the house, of course, or introduced to the husband.

It was from overhearing Mum's conversations with Dorothy

Bridgewater that I first got to hear about Mrs Bloody Perfect, which was Mum's nickname for the woman who had tried to adopt me. Mum didn't know her real name, or much about her, beyond the fact that she was the sort of woman who would steal another woman's baby. That was enough. Mum hated her. So did I.

6

We never stayed long in one place. People were always complaining – about me crying in the night, or about Mum hanging sheets in the bathroom after I wet the bed. Nobody liked us. Either that or they liked us too much – like the landlord of one place who kept coming to our door in the middle of the night.

We found a cottage in the country, whose landlord lived hundreds of miles away. That might sound idyllic, but it wasn't. There was no electricity at the cottage, and the water supply came from a single cold tap next to the outside loo. The main road between Norwich and Great Yarmouth ran past the front door, so I couldn't play out. At the back of the house was a field full of animals – sheep and bulls. I knew they were bulls, and no attempt by Mum to point out their udders and get me to stroke their noses could convince me otherwise.

The cottage was larger than anywhere we had had to ourselves before – I had my own room – but that wasn't much use when I was too scared to go in it after dark. It didn't matter how many gas lamps and oil lamps and candles and torches Mum put in there; all I saw were shadows, and the monsters they contained. The carpet smelled of sick, and at night you could hear little paws scrabbling behind the skirting board.

The nearest village was a mile away. There were buses, but we always seemed to get to the bus stop too late and end up walking. One morning we were at the bus stop in plenty of time, both of us dressed in our best, and I realized I was going to school. I screamed and cried and begged Mum not to leave me there, but she did. The teachers tried to comfort me by lifting me up to a window and pointing out the tip of our chimney pot, which was just visible beyond a row of trees, but I went on crying. I didn't like being touched by anyone except

Mum. Mrs Bloody Perfect could be anywhere, waiting for her chance to try again.

I made a few friends at school, but when I discovered that this meant being invited to their houses I let the friendships drop. Mum encouraged me to accept the invitations, but I wouldn't go unless she came too. Even if she did come, I disliked being sent off to play in another room with the other children. I preferred to keep an eye on her.

Mum was determined that no one was ever going to have an excuse to say that I wasn't as good as the next child. Her way of ensuring this was to rule me with a rod of iron. I had to say please and thank you, wipe my feet, wash my hands, eat my greens and save out of my pocket money. Not that I got much pocket money, but if I did and if it contained six-pences, they all had to go in a cocoa tin for my future. 'One day, you'll be glad of it,' she said. Sometimes I thought she gave me sixpences on purpose.

I was never allowed to be late for school, and I had to be practically at death's door before I was permitted to miss a day through illness. After school, I had to do my homework before I did anything else. Bedtimes were strictly adhered to, and I had to fold my clothes and put them away properly, not leave them in a heap, which was all I thought they deserved, being for the most part second-hand. Mum said what did it matter, clothes being second-hand, as long as they fitted and were clean? She said it was just as bad for her, she never had new clothes either, but it wasn't as bad because she didn't mind. I did mind. Second-hand clothes made me think of Mrs Bloody Perfect – old things touching my skin, just as her wrinkled, witch's hands would have done.

A boy at school called me a 'little bastid'. I didn't know what it meant, but I knew I didn't like the sound of it, so I reported it to my mother. In the past she had always fended off questions about where my father was by saying he lived a long way away. Now she explained about mating and how babies were made. She said that most people were married when they mated, but sometimes people made a mistake and did it while they were still single, at a party, perhaps, when they were having such a nice time that they weren't thinking clearly; and then you had a baby born without a father.

This confused me. I was used to the idea of a father who lived far away. 'Far away' meant a foreign country, and that meant he was probably a spy or a secret agent. I had drawn pictures of him carrying a gun and a magnifying glass. Now Mum seemed to be saying that I had never had a father in the first place. That couldn't be right. Someone at that party must have mated with her. I wanted to know his name. Mum couldn't tell me. She said he had called himself Joe, but when she tried to find him after the party to tell him the good news that I was on the way, the people who gave the party said they hadn't invited anyone called Joe.

So 'Joe' was an alias. That was exciting. It seemed to confirm that he must be a secret agent. I was keener than ever to know what he looked like. A girl at school had a father who was dead, but at least she had photographs of him. I asked Mum if she had any photographs of 'Joe', but she said she hadn't. She had only met him once, and there hadn't been time to take any.

7

When I was about seven, she made friends with a man called Stan Haverstock. She told me she had got chatting to him in a bus queue and he had asked if he could see her again.

'Does that mean he wants to be your boyfriend?' I asked.

'What do you think?'

'I think he does.'

'He wants to take me to the pictures,' said Mum.

'Can I come?'

'I thought maybe you could be a big girl and go to Laurel's.' Laurel was a girl in my class whose mother had once said to my mother within my hearing, *you can dump Heather with us any time you like, Julia.*

I shook my head.

'You wouldn't have to stay the night,' said Mum. 'You could go to sleep there, and I would pick you up on our way home. I'd carry you out to Stan's car while you were still asleep. You'd wake up in your own bed.'

I shook my head even more emphatically. If she could steal me from a bed without me waking up, then so could anyone else.

Mum had another idea. 'You can stay at home, and we'll ask Judith to come and babysit.' Judith was Laurel's older sister. She was nice in some ways, but I knew she looked down on our house. She said things like, 'Such a dear little old-fashioned fireplace,' and 'It's lucky you don't have television because it means I can get on with my homework.'

I said to Mum, 'I want to go to the pictures with you and Stan.'

So the three of us went and saw Julie Andrews in *Mary Poppins*.

Stan was short and plump, with thick forearms. He had curly golden hair, and a round, smiley face. He reminded me of a lion. He wore workmen's dungarees, even though he wasn't a workman. He worked in a record shop and brought us free records. Mum and I couldn't play the records because we hadn't got a record-player, or any electricity to run one, but we enjoyed looking at the pictures and reading the sleeve notes. One day Stan drove up in his car with a portable record-player that ran off batteries. He said it was a sample and we would be doing the manufacturer a favour if we kept it and used it and reported to Stan on how well it worked. Another day, he brought a carpet, to replace the one in my room that smelt of sick. He said he had got it free from a friend of his whose warehouse had been flooded.

As well as carpets and records and record-players, he brought us autographed photographs of the stars – The Rolling Stones, Joan Baez, Carole King, Bob Dylan. I put them up in my room. He brought *New Musical Express* and *Melody Maker*, and he and I would sit for hours by the stove in the kitchen, tracking the progress of our favourite songs up and down the charts and making predictions for next week. He liked The Doors and Joe Cocker. I preferred David Bowie. Mum said she would always be loyal to The Beatles.

Stan did repairs around the house, cleared rubble out of the garden and planted things. He took me for walks in the fields and taught me not to be scared of the cows. I knew they wouldn't try anything with him holding my hand. He drove us to the shops to stock up on heavy things like potatoes and gas cylinders for the stove. He urged Mum to badger the landlord to put in electricity and other proper services. She said she didn't dare, because he would put the rent up. Besides, we were used by now to gaslight and candlelight. Even Stan admitted that it could be quite cosy. Sometimes when the three of us were sitting together in the evenings, he would hold Mum's hand. I climbed between them and sat across their laps.

Stan offered me a deal. He said that if I would agree to go to Laurel's once in a while, or to be babysat for at home, so that he and Mum could go out on their own together, he would take me to any film I wanted to see.

'Provided it's suitable,' Mum put in.

Stan winked at me. 'Provided it's suitable. What do you say, Heather? Is that fair?'

I nodded.

At first he kept his word. I let him and Mum go to see *If . . .* , and in return he took me to *Goodbye, Mr Chips*, which I liked so much that we stayed for the next performance. But sometimes he forgot when he owed me films. He seemed to forget us altogether. He would disappear for weeks on end. Mum pretended not to mind, so I pretended as well.

He came back. He said he had been in Paris buying dresses for the two beautiful girls in his life. Mum said, 'Paris, eh?' and looked at the labels, which were English. But she was pleased with her dress, and I was pleased with mine. It felt smooth and clean on my skin, and smelt of newness. Stan started staying with us on Saturday nights, and sleeping in Mum's bed. I knew what they were doing. I just hoped she wouldn't have another baby. I concentrated on looking forward to Sunday morning when the three of us would go out for a drive in his car. It was summertime, and Mum and I wore our new dresses. I saw how pretty she was. She had straight blonde hair which she wore with a feathery fringe like Marianne Faithfull, and a slim figure. She would step into the car like a film star, and be in a good mood all morning. We would stop for ice creams and newspapers, and I would be allowed to choose whichever comic I wanted. Sometimes Mum would read my comic with me and say how good it was. On the other six days of the week, comics were rubbish and a waste of time. That was the effect that having a boyfriend had on her. She throve on male admiration. She still does.

8

It was a Sunday morning in the summer holidays. We had had breakfast, and Mum and Stan were getting ready to go out. I had been ready for ages. I was waiting impatiently by his car.

Another car pulled up on the other side of the road, and two men got out. They looked at me and said something to each other. They walked towards me. I didn't like the look of them. Mum and Stan came out of the house, laughing at something. When they saw the men, they stopped laughing.

Stan went over and talked to them. Mum made me get into the back of the car. She closed the door on me and told me to wait. Then she went over and joined Stan and the other men.

I rolled the window down so that I could listen. I couldn't hear everything, but I heard the men say that they were special investigation officers. Special investigation officers sounded like secret agents. I wondered if one of them was my father.

They were saying that Stan was my father. From the way they said it, anyone would think that being my father was a crime. Even my mother was at pains to deny it. She kept saying, 'I've only known him six months.' She didn't want Stan Haverstock to be my father. Only I and the secret agents wanted that.

The secret agents sounded as if they wanted to put him in prison for it – and perhaps my mother as well. 'We've had reports of a fraudulent claim. You've been claiming supplementary benefit as an unsupported mother while cohabiting with a man as his wife.'

Mum looked amazed. Then she tossed her head. Sunlight made ripples in her hair. She was showing off her beauty and glamour to the men. She wasn't their girlfriend, she was Stan's. 'We're not married,' she said.

'No one ever said you was, darling,' said the secret agent. 'If you was married, you wouldn't need to live off taxpayers' money in the first place, now would you?'

'You call her darling, I'll kick your head in,' said Stan.

'Sh,' said Mum. She turned to the secret agents. 'He doesn't live here.'

'Oh, no?'

'Tell him where you live, Stan.'

Stan said, 'So he can make trouble for me, you mean?'

'Don't want the missus to find out, eh, mate?' said the secret agent, the rude one.

'You cunt,' said Stan. 'I live at 48a Blandford Avenue.'

'Satisfied?' said Mum.

The polite one said, 'We'll be making a report to our superior officer.'

Mum looked bewildered. 'A report *about what*?'

'You got your benefit book on you?'

She opened her handbag and brought it out. 'What do you want it for?'

The secret agent took the book and put it in the inside pocket of his jacket.

Mum's eyes widened. 'When do I get that back?'

'You don't,' said the rude secret agent.

Mum said, 'I've got a child to feed.'

The polite one jerked his thumb at Stan. 'Don't tell us, tell him.'

They drove away. Mum and Stan stared at each other, then went into the house. They seemed to have forgotten about me. I sat in the car for a while. I wished I knew how to drive it. Then I could go off for a Sunday morning outing on my own, and buy myself some ice cream and a comic.

I went into the kitchen. Mum was sitting at the table with her head in her hands. Stan was trying to give her a couple of pound notes.

She was saying, 'I don't want your money.'

He said, 'Treat it as a loan.'

She saw me and yelled, 'Heather, go to your room!'

I fled. I sat on my bed and read *Ballet Shoes*. I looked for the bit where Pauline loses the part in *Alice* and comes home and locks herself in the bathroom. It was my favourite bit. I stared at the picture of her lying on the floor, floppy as a doll, crying her eyes out.

I heard Stan leave. I wanted to go after him and ask when he was coming back, but I dared not leave my room until my mother said I could. It was very hot in there, and a wasp was flying round the light bulb with a mean look in its eye.

Eventually Mum came and said lunch was ready. Her tone was very bright. We had beans on toast and apples. We listened to *Savile's Travels*. I asked where Stan was. She said he had gone. I asked when he was coming back. She didn't answer.

After lunch, I went for a walk by myself. I crossed the field with the bulls in it. They stood in a circle and stared at me, swishing their tails. I was scared but I kept on walking. I wished they would chase me. Then Stan would appear and fight them off.

I came home and Mum gave me my tea. She sent me to bed early, which I didn't think was fair, but I didn't argue. It was too hot to sleep. I read *Ballet Shoes* again. I could smell Mum smoking. At about ten o'clock she started pacing instead, so I guessed she had run out of cigarettes.

I nodded off. Towards morning I heard her tiptoeing into my room. I watched her through my eyelashes. She was still dressed for going out with Stan. She had put a cardigan over her dress but she hadn't been to bed. She picked up my cocoa tin. It made a little clinking sound, so she wrapped it in the folds of her cardigan to muffle it. She went to the kitchen and there were more clinking sounds as she counted my money.

I went back to sleep. When I woke again the sun was up and

the cocoa tin was back in its place. I thought I might have dreamed her taking it away. But when I picked up the cocoa tin, it was empty.

I put some clothes on and went to the kitchen. She was asleep in a chair with my sixpences in piles in front of her. I started to take them. I knocked over one of the piles and she woke up. 'Who's that? What are you doing?'

'Taking my money back.'

'Leave it.'

'It's mine.'

'I said leave it.' She got hold of my wrist.

I fought to get free. I kicked her shin. She gasped with pain. 'You're a thief,' I said. 'You took my money. You're a thief.'

She let go of me and took a few paces backwards. She reached down and rubbed her leg, but never took her eyes off me. Her breath was coming in gasps. '*What did you call me?*'

'Thief, thief, thief!'

'Right!' She grabbed my wrist with one hand and her handbag with the other. She pulled me towards the door.

'Where are we going?'

'Wait and see.'

She dragged me along the street in the direction of the village. Cars whizzed past, hooting at us, drowning out the sound of my screaming. We reached a pub with a telephone box outside. She pushed me in and started dialling.

'Hello?' she said, in the posh voice she used for dealing with officials. 'Could you put me through to your adoption department, please?'

The word made my stomach rise to my throat and flop back down again. 'No, Mum.' I tried to take the phone out of her hand. 'Mummy. No. Please.'

'This is Miss Fox,' she said. 'It's about my daughter, Heather. She's decided she wants to be adopted after all.'

'I don't! I don't, Mum!'

'Is that same lady still interested? The one with the house in

30

the country, who was going to send her to boarding school?'

I tried to cut off the call but she was too quick for me. She held my wrist and went on talking into the phone. 'Heather doesn't want to live with me any more. She thinks I'm a thief.'

'I don't! I don't! You can have my money! All of it!'

'You'll send someone round in about half an hour, then? Fine. Thank you very much. I'll make sure she's ready.' She put the phone down and faced me. 'That's settled.'

I ran away from her and out into the road. A car came straight at me. I dodged and fell over. I lay on the ground with my eyes shut, pretending to be dead. I wished I was.

The driver got out, rushed round to the front of the car and squatted down beside me. She smelt of musty perfume. I peeped at her through my eyelashes. She was a bit older than Mum, tall with long dark hair folded back into a pleat. She wore a long purple skirt with a pattern on it, and a black top. She put one cool hand on my forehead and another on my wrist.

I heard Mum screaming, 'Heather! Heather!' There was another screech of brakes and the woman next to me drew a sharp breath. I opened my eyes and saw that Mum had come dashing out of the phone box, only to be nearly run over herself. The driver of the car was yelling at her and shaking his fist. She yelled back and ran towards me. She picked me up.

The dark-haired woman hesitated before saying, 'Maybe it would be better not to move her.'

Another car stopped. A man got out. 'Shall I call an ambulance?'

I didn't want to go in an ambulance. I broke free from Mum and tried to run for it. She grabbed me. The other woman opened the door of her car. 'I'll take you both to the hospital.'

We got in. Mum held me tight. She kept saying, 'Are you

all right, are you all right?' and examining me. She found a graze and a bruise. I wished there were more. Mrs Bloody Perfect was waiting. It was all arranged. But it might be dis-arranged, if Mrs Bloody Perfect found that I wasn't perfect myself. Maybe if I shut my eyes and opened them again, I would see a huge wound.

We reached the hospital and went to Casualty. A nurse asked Mum a lot of questions about me, and about what had happened. Mum told her that I had run out into the road. She didn't say why.

The nurse asked Mum to wait while she took me to be examined by a doctor. I screamed and clung to Mum's hand. The nurse said, 'Don't be a baby, dear,' and dragged me away.

The doctor made me lie on a table while he looked me over. He made me walk up and down and touch my toes. He said he couldn't find much wrong. He told the nurse to put plaster on my grazes and said, 'You're a very lucky girl, Heather. In future, you keep hold of your mummy's hand.'

The nurse took me back to the waiting room. I thought Mum would have gone but she was still there, talking to the dark-haired woman who had driven us. Maybe she was Mrs Bloody Perfect. She had been in such a rush to get to me and adopt me that she had run me over instead. Now that I was all right, she was going to take me away.

The three of us got into her car and drove towards central Norwich. I sat on Mum's lap with my head on her shoulder. We were having our last cuddle. She was talking to Mrs Bloody Perfect about Stan Haverstock and the social security men. Mrs Bloody Perfect listened with a serious expression. She stopped her car in a street with a market in it, and a row of small shops. Some of them were boarded up, but one had recently been painted. In the window was a big red fist in a circle with a cross. Underneath was written:

Women's Liberation: The Four Demands

1. *Equal pay.*
2. *Equal opportunities.*
3. *Free contraception and abortion on demand.*
4. *Free 24-hour child care.*

I didn't want to go into free 24-hour child care. I hung back, but Mum insisted that we go inside.

9

The place was called ROOOWC, pronounced like the bird or the chess piece. The Room Of One's Own Women's Centre.

The woman whom I took to be Mrs Bloody Perfect, but who was also called Madge, introduced us to a woman who definitely wasn't Mrs Bloody Perfect – she was much too scruffy. She wore patched jeans and plimsolls with her toes poking out. Her name was Viv. Viv made us a cup of tea, shared her cigarettes with Mum and listened to our story. 'Doesn't surprise me,' she said.

'What doesn't?' said Mum.

'Happens all the time. Men,' said Viv, 'want every woman to be either a wife or a prostitute. Not that there's much difference, of course.'

'There isn't?'

'The main difference between women,' Viv said, 'is between the ones who play these roles and the ones like you who have the guts to refuse.'

Mum didn't look like a person with guts. She was exhausted and tense and sad. But Viv's words lifted her spirits, and that was just the start. Viv got on the phone to the social security office and spoke to someone she seemed to know but not like. 'You people are way out of line on this one,' she said. She was fierce and unafraid. She quoted from acts of parliament and books of regulations and said we were going to appeal.

She gave Mum the name and address of a woman solicitor who would help us, and showed her how to fill in the forms to apply for an emergency payment to tide us over until the appeal was heard. Other ROOOWC women cooked us a meal, and bought groceries for us to take home. They gave me sweets and toys, and loaded Mum up with books, pamphlets and invitations to meetings and socials. Some of the women lent her money out of their own pockets. When Madge finally drove us home, Mum had a strange light in her eye. The light went on burning. It burns to this day.

We won our appeal and got our benefit book back. We didn't get Stan back, but we didn't care about that. Mum said we didn't care. She said she had received a letter from him saying that she was a lovely girl and so was I but he hadn't reached the time in his life yet for settling down with a ready-made family. Mum tore the letter up before my eyes and sang, 'Nobody asked you, sir, she said.' She waved her arms like a conductor. I did the same, and we danced round the room. I understood that I wasn't going to be adopted – not this time, anyway.

Mum said it was just as well Stan had gone off, because we wouldn't have had time for him. Not now. She was always at ROOOWC, and ROOOWC was a women-only space. I went there with her when I wasn't at school. We painted and decorated, and helped other single mothers with their benefit problems. We ran off copies of the Four Demands Newsletter on the Gestetner, and looked after toddlers in the crèche. Sometimes we went to consciousness-raising groups, or held them in our house. Even then, Stan wouldn't have been allowed. The only role men were allowed to play in consciousness-raising was taking the children out so that the women could raise their consciousness in peace. Mum tried to persuade me to go on these outings, but of course I wouldn't.

One day, Mum came home with a booklet about family life. It was glossy and full of advertisements for things like washing machines and disposable nappies. It had photographs of women in kitchens and men wearing polo-necked jumpers with children on their shoulders. When some of Mum's ROOOWC friends came round, she showed the booklet to them. She said it had been given to her free at a clinic and wasn't it disgraceful? They scoffed and hooted and said it was a rearguard action by the patriarchy against women who were going to change family life for ever. They read out bits in pompous voices: 'A growing girl looks to her father for a link with the outside world, a world in which she will, in time and with his guidance, take her place.'

I didn't see what was so funny. It might be nice to have a father to do those things. The only father I had was the women's movement.

Before the women's movement rescued us, I hardly knew there was an outside world. Our life consisted of surviving from day to day, moving from grotty accommodation at one end of town to grotty accommodation at the other. Now we started going to conferences.

We went to one in Birmingham, one in Leeds and one in Edinburgh. I particularly liked Edinburgh. Edinburgh was almost abroad. We drove through the night in a hired minibus. Madge Kennedy and her girlfriend Patience took turns at the wheel. Whichever one of them wasn't driving read the map for the one who was, gave her sweets and talked softly to keep her awake. Madge was dark and exotic-looking. Patience was short and plump, with blonde hair, blue eyes, pink cheeks and a jacket covered with badges.

In the back of the minibus, I snuggled against my mother. When I woke in the morning to the sight of the sun rising over Edinburgh castle, and the rocks on which it stood, I thought I had reached fairyland.

The conference was held in a school. Mum asked which workshops I wanted to go to. I liked the sound of 'Womyn's Self Expression: Please wear loose clothing and bring finger paints', but Mum said she preferred 'Women And Domestic Labour Under Capitalism', so we went to that.

I found the speeches pretty dull, but she sat rapt and fascinated. She gazed at the speakers as she once used to gaze at

Stan Haverstock. She wrote notes furiously, underlining things twice or three times. At one point I forgot where I was and said in a normal voice, 'Mum, this is really boring.' She came back to earth and looked annoyed with me, but everyone else laughed and applauded and said, 'Right on, sister.' Mum said, 'If you're bored, why don't you go and wander around?' so I did. I looked at the book stalls and the craft stalls and the food stalls. A woman leaned over a counter with a toffee apple in her hand. It looked delicious, but I knew not to accept sweets from strangers, so I walked away. I peered into classrooms and thought how funny everyone looked, big grown-up women with their knees crammed under tiny desks.

The women's movement fathered me in other ways too. It put a roof over our head. Some of the ROOOWC women were social workers. When they saw the conditions in which we were living, they pulled strings and hurried us up the housing list. We moved to a modern house on a new estate a few miles outside Norwich. I liked the house, although it worried me that, if Stan Haverstock ever tried to find us, he wouldn't know our new address.

When ROOOWC got a grant to employ an organizer, Mum got the job. So now the women's movement was our bread-winner too. The hours were flexible to fit in with my school day, and she did a lot of the work from home. The wage wasn't huge, but it was more than we used to get from social security, and it allowed us a few luxuries, such as new clothes. And the money was ours – hers – in the way our benefit had never been. She could now have boyfriends without fearing a repetition of the Stan Haverstock episode. She started making up for lost time.

10

You may be wondering what any of this stuff about my early life, and sexual politics in the 1970s, has to do with Boniface Bennett missing his Christmas flight to Gibraltar at the end of 1983.

I'm coming to that. I'm just trying to fill you in on the background of how I met him.

Growing up, I developed a habit of solitude. At school, I became skilled at spotting other loners. We understood each other and turned to each other when we were required to get into twos for some project or game. When the activity was over, we returned to our desks. We knew not to expect or offer anything else.

My mother in the meantime had a packed social calendar. She divided her time between women-only gigs at ROOOWC, and dates with right-thinking men.

She was becoming something of a local celebrity. As press spokesperson for ROOOWC, she was often quoted in the local papers. She wrote pamphlets which were published under the ROOOWC imprint and sold by mail order and at conferences. She gave interviews on Radio Norwich. That's how they found out where she was.

The letter said:

Dear Julia,

This is a very difficult letter to write, perhaps that is why it has taken your dad and me so long to write it. It is never easy to admit you have been wrong but we know now that we were wrong to send you away. Since then not a day has gone by without us wondering how you are and how little Heather is, although I suppose she is not so little now. We would dearly love to have news of you both.

Perhaps it is too much to ask that we might be reconciled and reunited as a family, but your dad says to tell you that if there is anything we can do to help you ever, you have only to ask.

God bless you,

Love from your mum and dad.

I looked up from reading the letter and saw that Mum's eyes were red. She turned away and blew her nose. 'What do you think?'

'Nothing. I don't think anything.' In fact, I thought plenty. I wanted to tear the letter up, drop it in the lavatory, and shit, piss and menstruate all over it. Mum put it away safely. Some time later, she wrote back. I never saw what she wrote, but the following weekend she went to see them.

When she came back she obviously wanted to tell me what had happened, but I wouldn't listen. I walked out of the room. Soon she was visiting her parents, not frequently, but regularly, two or three times a year. She tried to get me to go with her, but I refused to have anything to do with them. I despised their crocodile tears. It was easy enough for them to talk about reconciliation and regret now that Mum and I had a house and an income and a place in the community. Easy enough, now that I was in my teens, still in one piece, doing okay at school, and still on the right side of the law. No wonder they wanted to know us, now that people no longer fell down dead with shock at the idea of someone having an illegitimate baby. We were quite desirable commodities, Mum and I. Of course they wanted to be reconciled with us as old age crept up on them. I hoped they would live long enough to have to go into a home. I hoped it would be filthy and sordid, run by cruel attendants, the sort of place that there are scandals about in the papers. I hoped I would live long enough to be the one to put them there. As for their offer of 'help' – which I presumed meant money, I couldn't think of anything else they might have that we might ever want – they could keep it. They would need it for their incontinence pads and their anti-dementia tablets.

As time went by, it dawned on me that I was no longer in danger of being adopted. Even if something terrible were to happen and my mother were to die or abandon me for some other reason, I was getting to the age when I would be left to my own devices.

But by now I was used to my own company. Even if there had been anybody with whom I wanted to make friends, I wouldn't have known where to start. I preferred reading and going to films by myself and thinking my own thoughts.

As the time approached for me to leave school, every feminist in East Anglia had an opinion on what I should do next.

Mum wanted me to go to university. I applied and was offered a place, but I had to get an A and two Bs. I got two Cs and a fail, so that put paid to that.

Mum's friend Madge Kennedy thought I would make a good engineer. Don't ask me why, except that her niece Julie was training to become one. Patience, Madge's lover, recommended agriculture (she was a big fan of *The Archers*, Pat Archer in particular). Gill Hilaire from Lowestoft Reproductive Rights said that in her opinion no young woman should even consider starting out in life without a thorough grounding in computers. Mum's current boyfriend Clive, not to be outdone, favoured manual trades. He was a qualified carpenter. Three years from now, I could be one too.

Not one of them thought I should go away and live by myself in a room and be a writer. This showed how little they knew about me, and how successful I had been at keeping my secret.

11

I told Mum that I had decided to go to London to seek my fortune.

She looked worried. 'What fortune?'

'If I knew, I wouldn't have to seek it.'

'Who are you going with?' In Mum's world, whatever you did, you had to do it with someone else – a collective or an international network or your best friend.

'By myself.'

'But what will you do?'

'See some films.'

'I mean about money.'

'I'll look for a job,' I said.

'What if you don't find one?'

I helped myself to one of her cigarettes. 'I'll go on the streets, I suppose.'

'Heather!'

'If I don't find a job, I'll come home, okay?'

'You'll come home anyway. For weekends.'

'Mum, I don't know what I'll be doing.'

'Christmas, then. Promise me you'll come home for Christmas.'

'I promise.'

She wrote down the names of people she knew who lived in London and who she was sure would be only too happy to have me to stay. 'London can be a lonely place,' she said.

'I know.'

'And you'll need some money.'

'I've got my savings,' I reminded her.

'They won't last long.'

'I'll sign on.'

She gave me £200. 'I wish it could be more,' she began.

'Don't, Mum.' I put up my hand to stop her, because I knew what was coming next.

'Your grandparents would be only too pleased to –'

'Don't even mention them to me!'

I had been to London a few times, mostly to conferences with Mum when I was little. My most recent visit had been shortly before my A-levels, in a school party to see one of our set plays being performed at the Old Vic. We arrived early and were allowed to wander around. Everyone else went to coffee shops, but I found an Accommodation Vacant board and stared at it.

It was actually four boards, arranged in a square in a sort of courtyard surrounded by shops near Waterloo station. The four sides of the square faced north, south, east and west, with the accommodation arranged by area.

Tufnell Park, Comfortable bedsit with full facilities.

Earl's Court. One-room flat close to BR and tubes.

Elephant & Castle. Nice room for professional lady.

I could have stayed there all afternoon, imagining these places, imagining the people who would end up living in them and what would happen to them; but my teacher came and hauled me away to the matinée.

Now that I had left school and left home, no one could haul me away to anything.

I didn't need hauling away from some of the places I looked at. They were vile, and I speak as someone who is no stranger to sub-standard housing. And the prices made my head spin. But I noticed that rents were cheaper south of the river. I also noticed that if you went to the end of the underground, caught a bus and stayed on it until it reached the terminus, they were cheaper still. You were still in London, but only just. That's how I came to be living at Crystal Palace.

59, Blondin Gardens wasn't too bad. The house was dingy and decaying, but not filthy. It didn't stink or make your flesh crawl. My bed was clean. A clean bed counts for a lot, because it lets you rest easily. And breakfast was included in the price of the rent. Not your full English, of course; usually it was nothing more than a couple of slices of bread and marge wrapped in greaseproof paper and left outside the door, or a stale cake or an out-of-date yogurt in a plastic carrier bag; but it was free food. All contributions gratefully received, was my attitude.

Some of the other tenants looked a bit strange and down on their luck, but they probably thought the same about me. We didn't speak, anyway; just nodded at each other on the stairs.

The first thing I did after moving in was to re-read *The Outsider* by Colin Wilson. I had first read it when I was doing my A-levels. It wasn't on the syllabus or anything, I just read it.

The Outsider was my inspiration. You may have read it yourself. If you have, you'll know what I'm talking about, but if you haven't, don't worry. Don't feel you have to read *The Outsider* on my account. I wouldn't let you tell me what to read, so there's no reason why I should tell you.

(Of course, I'd like it if you would continue reading this.)

The Outsider is about alienation. It takes examples from literature of people who live solitary lives in single rooms, people who feel they are outside society – characters in novels by Camus and Sartre and Goethe and Hesse and Hemingway. They're all men, of course – the authors and the characters. Only men are allowed to be outside society. Women's job is to keep society going so that men can be outside it. That's according to a friend of my mother's who saw me reading the book. I'm not sure I subscribe to that theory, or conspiracy theories generally. I just think Colin Wilson wasn't very interested in female outsiders. He probably didn't know that we exist, but we do. I do.

12

When I went to the dole office to sign on, I was counting on them not having any vacancies; but they said they had just the thing. Soon I was standing outside Brixton station giving away free magazines.

It wasn't so bad. At least I didn't have to talk to anybody. I just stood there, thinking, and from time to time a commuter with a glazed expression on his or her face would take a magazine from my hand.

I cultivated a glazed expression of my own, so that my customers wouldn't know how closely they were being watched. I was trying to work out what they did for their living, and whether underneath their business suits they were outsiders too.

After a couple of weeks I got promoted from Brixton to the West End, which meant getting a free Travelcard. I had to work during the morning and evening rush hours; in between times I could please myself. It was too far to go home and come out again, so I went to cafés to write. It seemed a romantic sort of thing to do, but I found I could only concentrate for just so long. I felt exposed and bored, and longed to be back in my room with my things around me. I travelled round and round on the Circle Line like a vagrant, looking at people and making notes about them. One day, an inspector stopped me and seemed quite surprised that I had a valid Travelcard.

I went sightseeing, and window-shopped for clothes I would never be able to afford but which I might be able to find close imitations of on market stalls. I was quite good at spotting those, and sometimes even the real thing with the labels cut out. As long as they were new, I didn't mind.

If I had money I went to the pictures – I saw *The Lacemaker* at the Renoir and *The Lost Honour of Katharina Blum* at the ICA. If I was skint, I looked for free things: old war movies at the Imperial War Museum, afternoon concerts in the foyer at the Royal Festival Hall, poetry readings in bookshops. At one of the poetry readings, I found a leaflet advertising something called the Coates Clarion award, a prize for a first novel by an unpublished author under the age of thirty-five. The closing date was 31 January. It was October now.

As luck would have it, the magazine distribution work dried up and the dole office had nothing else for me, so I signed on. I sat alone in my room writing about a woman sitting alone in her room writing. I wished I could be out and about again, in the mainstream of life, but it was too cold. I took my work to the public library to save on paraffin. After a few days, the librarians started to recognize me, and occasionally said hello. On Sundays the library was closed, so I remained in my room with nobody to say hello to.

One Sunday evening in November, I was lying in bed for warmth, tired from writing but not tired enough to sleep. I was listening to a programme on Capital about Janis Ian.

When footsteps came up the stairs, I assumed it was someone to say I was wanted on the phone. I hoped it was. My mother usually phoned me on Sundays for a chat. I looked forward to her calls; I never got any others. She had been at a conference this weekend, but she ought to be home by now.

The footsteps went past my room. I was uneasy. Only one other person lived on my floor, an old woman whom I had never known to have a visitor. But it was too early for Mr Truscott, the landlord, to be bringing tomorrow's breakfast round – he usually did that late at night, lurching into the house on his way home from the pub to deposit provisions on our doorsteps.

I got out of bed, tiptoed to my door and made sure it was locked. I peeped out through the keyhole and caught a blurred glimpse of Mr Truscott's wife. She unlocked the door of the room next door to mine, which was vacant.

With her was a man with two suitcases. I could see more of the suitcases than I could of the man. They were large and looked heavy and expensive. He was obviously in the wrong place. Bona fide residents of 59, Blondin Gardens didn't have suitcases like that.

Mrs Truscott handed him a set of keys and went away. The man went into the room and closed the door. I heard him moving about, opening drawers and cupboards. He became silent, and I realized I was shivering. I went back to bed.

I woke up at around 5 a.m. I had acquired the habit of waking early during my magazine-distribution days and couldn't seem to break it, even though I would dearly have loved to sleep in. It would have made the days shorter.

I put the light on, got out of bed and lit the paraffin, then crawled back under the covers to wait for the room to warm up.

At 5.15, I got up again and went to the bathroom. I stopped on the way back to pick up my breakfast carrier-bag. I put it on the other side of the room so that I wouldn't be tempted to look inside until I had written a page.

I got dressed, made tea, smoked a cigarette, had a good cough and wrote the page. Then I looked in the bag. It contained a fruit yogurt. I ate the yogurt and wrote another page.

At seven o'clock, I heard a bleeping noise from next door. It sounded like one of those electronic watches that were becoming all the rage in circles I didn't belong to, and whose owners usually preferred to set them off in cinemas at crucial moments in the film. Ten minutes later, it bleeped again. The floorboards creaked and the door opened. There was an almighty clatter and the howl of a male in distress. I rushed to my door and opened it.

He was in his mid-twenties. He wore stripy pyjamas under a rather classy black quilted dressing gown, and he had fallen over his breakfast. In so doing, he had managed to pierce the foil top of the yogurt pot with his big toe.

It's amazing how much yogurt those tiny pots contain. You don't realize how much there is when all you do is eat the stuff. To get a proper idea, you have to see it splattered over the pyjama trousers of someone who has just gone arse over tip outside your door before they are properly awake. It was raspberry yogurt. Or possibly strawberry. It was definitely pink. Anyway, that's how I first met him.

I wiped the grin off my face and said, 'Are you all right?'

'Just about, thanks.' Even with three words, the voice gave him away as a public school type. He had light brown hair, blue eyes and one of those open, earnest faces that sometimes betoken a nice, if not very bright, guy, and sometimes appear on the news as belonging to someone who's been arrested for serial murder. The next shot shows his neighbours exclaiming to camera about how surprised they are.

He got to his feet. He looked shocked and slightly wistful, as if he was hoping it would all turn out to be a dream – not just the yogurt pot and the indignity it had inflicted on him, but the house, the room where he had spent the night, me standing over him in my cold-weather writing gear (track-suit bottoms, three sweaters, fingerless gloves, woolly hat), everything.

'No bones broken,' he said.

'So I don't need to call an ambulance?'

'Not for me, but when I get my hands on whoever left this here . . . What is it?'

'Looks like yogurt to me.'

'But why . . . ?'

I was cracking up. I hadn't spoken to anyone for days, and now this. I felt drunk. 'It's an initiation ceremony for new tenants.'

'Glad you find it funny.'

To make up for laughing, I fetched him a dish cloth. I rinsed tea leaves and noodles out of the cloth and squeezed it into a tight ball in the hope that he wouldn't notice that it was actually a pair of my old knickers.

I gave it to him, and he muttered, 'Thanks.' While he was

sponging himself down, I picked up the yogurt pot and put it in the carrier bag. I took the yogurty cloth off him and said, 'Okay now?'

'I suppose so,' he grumbled, as if it were all my fault. 'The bathroom's that way, right?'

I went back into my room and closed the door. I put the cloth in the sink and the rubbish in the bin, poured myself another cup of tea, and tried to get back to work. I reached for a cigarette but the packet was empty.

When he came back from the bathroom, I expected him to go straight into his room, but he didn't. I heard a rustling sound outside my door. I wondered if he might be some kind of pervert, rubbing himself up and down against my wall.

He knocked. I said through the door, 'Who is it?'

'Me again. Frightfully sorry to disturb you.'

'What do you want now?'

'I seem to have locked myself out. And I can't find my key.'

I opened my door. 'Not your morning, is it?'

'Well, I've met you,' he said. 'But there's not much else to be said for it.'

'How did you think I could help?'

'That rather splendid cloth that you were so kind as to lend me. I was wondering whether, when I gave it back to you, I might have accidentally handed you my key as well.'

I went over to the sink and shook my knickers. Nothing fell out. I looked in the bin where I had put the remains of his yogurt pot, but the key wasn't there either.

'I haven't got it,' I told him.

He looked despairing. 'What on earth am I going to do?'

'I don't know.'

'What time is it?'

'Nearly a quarter to eight.'

'I'm supposed to be in the City by nine.'

This was hardly my problem, but I reasoned that the sooner

he found his key, the sooner he was likely to stop bugging me, so I helped him search.

We looked along the corridor, up and down the stairs, in the bathroom and behind the loo. We found one or two choice items behind the loo, but no key. There were plenty of cracks between the floorboards to explain its disappearance.

He tried my key, but his lock wouldn't budge. I lent him a knife, a comb, a fish slice and a pair of nail scissors. The door held fast. He thought of something else. 'A credit card might do the trick.'

'I haven't got one.'

He looked as if he had never heard of anyone not having a credit card.

'You'll have to phone the Truscotts,' I said.

'Good thinking.'

'Don't expect to be their favourite person.'

'I don't think I'm anybody's this morning.'

I didn't contradict him. I wrote the Truscotts' number on a piece of paper and handed it to him, together with coins for the phone. He said, 'You're an angel. I'll pay you back when I can get into my room.'

'Don't worry about the money,' I said. 'But if you've got a cigarette in there . . .'

'I don't smoke. Sorry.' He went down to the payphone, taking the stairs two at a time. I tried to get back to work.

At about ten past eight, I heard the front door bang. Mr Truscott came stumping up the stairs, jangling his keys and muttering loudly to himself about 'some people' and 'there's always one'. He unlocked my new neighbour's door and let him into his room. Fifteen minutes later, the stranger (at this stage I still didn't know his name) was dashing along the corridor, hurtling down the stairs and slamming the front door with a crash that shook the house. I looked out of the window and saw him doing a four-minute mile up the street towards the station. He wore a dark grey suit and was trying to put an overcoat on and hold on to a briefcase while he ran. It seemed only a matter of time before he would fall over again. He needn't think I was going to come to the rescue.

I saw him again that evening. I was sitting in my room wondering why my mother still hadn't phoned me and wasn't answering her phone. I was also trying to decide what to have for my supper – tomato soup with a ham sandwich, or ham soup with a tomato sandwich. It was important to get it right. There's nothing worse than opening one kind of soup and then wishing you had chosen the other.

I heard a knock and went to the door. There he was, looking like a husband home from work. He had three newspapers under his arm: *The Times*, the *Financial Times* and one I had never heard of called *Lloyd's List*.

'Good evening, Heather,' he said.

'Hi.'

'Me again.'

'How did you know my name?'

'You must have told me.'

'I didn't.'

'You're right, you didn't. I remember now – thinking what a pity it was that you hadn't – so I took the liberty of asking that obliging fellow who came round this morning with the key. And I expect you've spent the whole day making similar inquiries about me.'

'I haven't, actually.'

'Then I'll save you the bother. The name's Bennett, Boniface Bennett.' He stuck his hand out and I shook it. He said, 'I wanted to give you this,' and reached into his coat pocket. He brought out a small package in a paper bag. The bag was grey and classy-looking, with royal blue writing and a crest. 'Farnham and Fortescue of Leadenhall Market. By Appointment. Purveyors of Fine Tobaccos since 1796.' Inside was a silvery box of fifty cigarettes, an upmarket brand that I had never heard of.

Another thing I had never done before was to see fifty cigarettes all in one place – let alone own them. I opened my mouth to thank him, but he interrupted. 'Don't tell me I shouldn't have. I know I shouldn't have, and you shouldn't.' His tone was kindly stern. The senior prefect was giving one of the younger chaps a wigging. 'But you're not going to stop smoking because of anything *I* say, and this is just to let you know how sorry I was that I hadn't any to give you this morning in your hour of need, when you were so kind to me in mine.'

'Was I?'

'Heather, you were an absolute trouper. If it hadn't been for you, I'd still be hopping around in my pyjamas, drenched in yogurt. Now, don't smoke them all at once . . .'

'I won't,' I told him. 'They'll last me ages. I'm not really a serious smoker.'

'No, I didn't think you were.' He glanced over my shoulder at the blue-grey haze that hung about my room. 'Well, I mustn't keep you from . . . whatever it is I'm keeping you from.' He got his key out and started to unlock his door. He paused. 'I don't suppose you know if there are any decent places to eat around here?'

I looked blank. I had seen a few restaurants, but of course I had never been inside them.

He said, 'Would it be a frightful bore for you to come out with me and help me find one? Or perhaps you've eaten already?'

'I was just about to open a tin of soup.'

'That doesn't sound very suitable,' he said. 'A girl like you should have her tins of soup opened for her.'

'Who by?'

'The finest chefs in . . . Where are we again?'

'Crystal Palace.'

'That's the one.'

'If you don't know where you are,' I said, 'why are you here?'

He frowned. 'That's a bit philosophical for the likes of me.'

'You know what I mean.'

'I'll tell you over dinner. Come on.'

'I can't,' I said. 'I'm expecting a phone call.'

'What, from your boyfriend?' I didn't answer. Boniface said, 'Surely he'd have phoned before now if he was expecting to see you this evening? Sounds to me as if he's taking you for granted.'

'You'd know about that.'

'Come out with me,' he coaxed. 'Make him jealous. My treat.'

14

I must have said yes, because the next thing I knew I was on my own, changing into a skirt and top and clean tights. He tapped on my door and asked if I was ready. I said I was, and off we went.

I got his life story as we walked up the hill. He was born in Singapore, where his father had business interests. He was the youngest of four brothers. All of them had been sent home to boarding school. That was the term he used – 'sent home'. To me it sounded like being sent away. His brothers got on fine at boarding school, he said, but he hated it. He missed his mother, which of course it wasn't done to admit, and he didn't like being cooped up with a lot of other yahooing males. He preferred female company, always had and still did. He turned his head and looked for my response. I kept on walking.

We went to the Taj Mahal Tandoori in Church Street. He was extremely polite, handing my coat to the waiter and holding my chair back for me to sit down. He took charge of the menu and ordered enormous quantities of food. I didn't care what he ordered, as long as it came quickly. I hadn't realized how hungry I was. Faced with the opportunity of eating in a restaurant with someone else paying, I could feel my stomach going into spasms of impatience. He asked if I preferred to drink beer with curry, or wine. I said I didn't mind, so he ordered lager – not just any old lager, but lager with a special foreign name which I didn't catch, but which he was most particular about.

When he had finished ordering, he went back to his life story, starting at the exact point where he left off. He finished school with one A-level, which was one more than anyone expected him to get. He messed around for a few years – delivering

54

parcels for a firm of couriers, trying and failing to be a landscape gardener, and going to Italy as a package holiday guide – then came home and went into insurance. 'Started out as second assistant office boy at a high street brokers just outside Carlisle, and now I'm with an underwriting syndicate at Lloyd's.'

This was obviously some sort of peak of achievement. Fortunately our lagers arrived, so I didn't have to say anything except, 'Cheers.'

'Your turn now,' he said.

'What for?'

'To reveal your innermost secrets.'

'I haven't got any.'

'I bet you have.'

'What do you want to know?'

He shrugged. 'Anything you want to tell.'

'I can't think of anything.'

'Then I shall have to interrogate you.' He frowned with great concentration as he thought up questions. 'Your name I already know. Your age I'm too much of a gentleman to . . .'

'I'm nineteen.'

'So you must be a student or something.'

'Hm.'

'At . . . ?'

'The London School of Economics.' It was the first thing that came into my head. I drank more lager.

'Studying . . . ?'

'Economics.' What else would you study at the London School of Economics? I hoped he wouldn't question me further. The London School of Economics might have been a bad choice. An underwriting syndicate at Lloyd's sounded like the sort of place where they might know about economics. I ought to have said I was doing art.

He said, 'You must be a clever girl.'

'I am.' I was getting quite tipsy. 'I'm brilliant.'

'Any more like you at home? And where is home, anyway?'

'Place near Norwich. You won't have heard of it.'

'Brothers and sisters?'

'No.'

'Parents?'

'My mother works at a women's centre.'

'A what sort of centre?'

'A women's centre.'

'And what does your father think of that?'

'My father's all for it. What's Lloyd's? What does an underwriting syndicate do?'

'That's a jolly interesting question, Heather. I wish I'd thought to ask it at the interview.'

'Are you new, then?'

'Today was my first day.'

'So that's why you had your knickers in such a twist this morning.'

'You're a fine one to talk about knickers in a twist,' he retorted, 'after what you gave me to wipe my pyjamas with.'

I drank more lager. 'You still haven't told me why you're living there.'

'Word of your charms reached me . . .'

'You promised to tell me.'

'Okay, okay,' he said. 'But the truth is a lot less interesting. I'd sort of fixed up to borrow a chum's flat, but it all fell through at the last minute. So I phoned an accommodation agency – so called – and said could they find me a small hotel within easy reach of the City – somewhere for me to lay my weary bones for a week or so while I sort out something more permanent.'

'Did they say, "Yes, sir, we've got just the thing. 59, Blondin Gardens"?'

He pressed his fingertips together. 'You always did find my discomfort amusing, didn't you, Heather?'

'You can call it discomfort. It's my home.'

'No offence meant. Anyway, I rang them this morning to

ask them what the hell they thought they were playing at, and it was all, "Sorry, sir, we got your file mixed up," and "May we recommend the following, with Jacuzzi in all rooms, and your own hair dryer?" I said, "Never mind all that – is there a fascinating woman living next door with a nice line in dish cloths?" They said they couldn't guarantee it, so back I came.'

15

We finished our meal and he paid the bill. Outside, the temperature had dropped. 'There's ice on the pavement,' he said. 'You'd better hold my hand.'

'I can't see any ice.'

'That's what makes it so dangerous.'

Hand in hand, we made our way back to 59, Blondin Gardens.

He opened the front door and I pressed the light switch. The brownish-yellow glare lit up a piece of paper on the table by the payphone. 'Heather Fox. Your mum rang. Please call back.'

There was no signature, or any other clue as to who had taken the message, which was written on the back of a KitKat wrapper. I didn't like that. It was too casual. What if whoever it was hadn't happened to be eating a KitKat? What if they had chosen a chocolate bar whose wrapper didn't have one blank side? Would they have bothered to look for something else to write on? How many other messages had there been?

Boniface read over my shoulder. '"Mum rang." Is that good or bad?'

'Neither, probably. She just wants a chat.'

'Mothers never "just want a chat". There's always more to it than that.'

'How many mothers have you got?'

'Just the one, but it sometimes feels like more. D'you need some change?' He brought a handful of coins out of his pocket and put them in a pile on top of the phone. 'I'll leave you to it.' He headed for the stairs and climbed them two at a time. I heard his door open and close, a bit too loudly, I thought, as if to make the point that he wasn't going to eavesdrop. Even so, and in spite of the fact that I had used this phone dozens of times before to talk to my mother, I felt exposed and nervous.

I dialled and spoke quietly. 'Hi, Mum. It's me.'

'Oh, hello, love. Are you at home? I'll call you back, shall I?'

'There's no need –' It was too late. She had hung up. Shortly afterwards the phone rang. She seemed to be in chatty mood. 'Have you been out?' she asked.

'Yeah.'

'Somewhere nice?'

'Mm-hm. How was your conference?'

'Great.'

'What was it about?'

'"Towards The Eighth Demand",' she said, and you could hear the capital letters.

This was a new one on me. The original four demands had grown to seven over the years, by the addition of: (5) legal and financial independence for women; (6) an end to discrimination against lesbians; and (7) freedom for all women from intimidation by the threat or use of male violence. And as if that wasn't enough, there was also an overall assertion about women having a right to define their own sexuality. I would have thought that just about covered it, but if they wanted an eighth demand, that was up to them.

'What is it?' I asked.

'We didn't get that far,' said Mum. 'But we did a lot of useful ground work. And guess who was in the men's group running the crèche.'

'Denis Thatcher.'

'Harry Wyatt,' she said.

'Who's he, one of your old boyfriends?'

'Just because I mention a man,' said my mother, 'doesn't mean he *has* to be a boyfriend.'

'Is he?'

'I went out with him a few times,' she conceded. 'I think it was when you were doing your exams. You were probably studying so hard that you didn't notice.'

'That sounds like me.'

'I'll tell you everything when I see you at Christmas.' This struck me as an odd comment – Christmas was more than a month away, and we would talk before then in any case. It was almost as if she wanted to slip Christmas subtly into the conversation without drawing attention to the change of subject. 'Talking of Christmas,' she said, 'when were you thinking of coming?'

The conversation was getting odder and odder. She was making it sound as if my Christmas visit was a vague plan whose details were yet to be finalized. But she had already bought my coach ticket and sent it to me.

'I'm coming on Christmas Eve, and staying till the 28th.'

'Christmas Eve to the 28th.' Her tone was thoughtful. 'I was wondering if you might like to make it a couple of days earlier – say on the 22nd?'

'What's so special about the 22nd?'

'We've been invited up to Scotland,' she said.

'Who has? Who by?'

'You and me. By Harry.'

'Hang on a minute, Mum.' I was beginning to see where this was leading. 'One of your old boyfriends wants you to go away with him?' I wedged the receiver between my shoulder and my ear, took a cigarette out of my bag and lit it.

'Us,' she said. 'He wants you to come too.'

'Oh, sure.'

'He *does*. He remembers you.'

'How come, if I was studying all the time?'

She didn't answer.

'Look, Mum. If you want to spend Christmas with him instead of me, be my guest. But don't pretend it's some sort of joint enterprise, okay?' I slammed the phone down and went to my room.

I was shivering. I drew the curtains and lit the paraffin. I paced up and down, smoking and thinking and trying not to feel so agitated. A rustling sound from next door reminded me that Boniface had lent me money for the call and I hadn't used it, I had left it downstairs on top of the phone.

I went back down to collect it, then knocked at his door and gave him the money. 'Thanks,' I said.

'Not at all.' He put the money in his pocket. 'Get through all right?'

'Fine.'

He looked at me closely. 'Was I right about mothers and little chats?'

I didn't answer. I didn't want to talk about it in the corridor; I wasn't even sure I wanted to talk about it at all. But he beckoned me inside, and I went.

His room was even bleaker and chillier than mine. There was no paraffin stove, just an electric fire with only one bar working. The overhead light was unshaded, and the curtains didn't quite meet across the window. 'Take a seat,' he said.

I perched on the wooden arm of the chair by the fire. On the floor was a fat textbook called *Principles of Underwriting*, full of pie charts, and columns of figures.

I said, 'I mustn't keep you from your work.'

'That's jolly mean of you,' he said. 'I kept you from yours this morning.' He was watching me closely. 'Are you going to tell me, or is it a case of "MYOB, Bennett"?'

I moved closer to the fire. 'It's freezing in here.'

'It is, isn't it? I bet your room is nicer.'

I shrugged and got up. He followed me out of the room, along the corridor and into mine.

16

I had never had a visitor before. I didn't know what to do. I asked him if he would like a cup of tea, and he said yes, please. I switched the kettle on and fidgeted with teabags. He roamed round the room admiring everything: my curtains, which Mum had sent from home, and my film posters, and my collection of necklaces which I kept hanging from a branch which had blown off a tree in Crystal Palace Park.

I could have made conversation in any number of ways. I could have told him that the glittery necklace had been made by my mother back in the days when she was a homeworker, and that the antique amethyst one, which had been an eighteenth birthday present to me from Madge and Patience, was one of the few second-hand things I didn't mind wearing.

I didn't feel like telling him any of those things. I wasn't ashamed of my background exactly, but I knew it was odd. Downstairs, the phone started to ring. I moved towards the door, but by the time I opened it, the ringing had stopped. I waited on the landing while footsteps came up the stairs. They stopped on the floor below mine. Somebody knocked on somebody else's door.

I came back into my room and busied myself making tea. Boniface said, 'What's going on, Heather?'

'Nothing much. I was supposed to be going home for Christmas. Only now one of her old boyfriends has turned up and wants to take her to Scotland.'

He looked startled. 'Hang on a minute. What about your father?'

'I haven't got a father.'

'But I thought . . .'

'I made that up. I haven't got a father. I'm a little bastid.'

He nodded as if to show that he had registered the information but it wasn't very important. 'So you don't fancy going
up to Scotland as part of a threesome?'

'Would you?'

'Maybe not, but I'd love it if *my* mother found herself a
boyfriend. Might keep her away from the gin bottle.'

I resented him bringing his mother into the discussion. I
imagined an aristocratic old soak with thinning hair and
diamond-encrusted fingers. I felt like throwing the contents of
my mug into her face. I picked up my mug and went to sit in
the armchair. I left him to help himself.

He wandered over towards me, stirring his tea. 'Your mother
isn't one of these feminists who hates men, then?'

'You can say that again.'

'That's a relief.'

'Why? What difference would it make to you?'

'You might have inherited it, and it would be such a waste.'
He bent down and kissed me lightly on the lips. He seemed to
be testing me, so I tried not to react. I didn't know how to
react. His lips moved to the side of my nose, and my nose stud.
'Fascinating,' he said. 'I can't keep my eyes off it. Did it hurt,
having it put in?'

'Have one yourself and you'll see.'

'Go down a treat at the office, that would.' His eyes gleamed.
'If you don't want to go to Scotland with your mother and her
swain, why not come to Gibraltar with me?'

I stared at him. 'Gibraltar?'

'Rocky place, down at the bottom of Spain.'

'I know where it is.'

'Firm's got a yacht down there,' he explained. 'Some of the
chaps are flying down on Christmas Eve with their wives and
significant others. There are a few seats left on the plane.'

'And you're going?'

'At first I thought probably not,' he said. 'Wouldn't be much fun, being the new boy, *and* being the only one on my own. But if you came too . . .'

'We hardly know each other,' I reminded him.

'What better way to get to know each other?'

'I'm broke.'

'So? You'd be my guest.' He gave me a teasing look. 'Or are you a bit too conventional for that?'

'You're the one who's being conventional.'

'Don't you believe it. The conventional thing would be to take you down there as my girlfriend. Show you off in the daytime, and share a berth at night.'

'Isn't that what you had in mind?'

'Of course it is, but we wouldn't have to do it that way. We can be like brother and sister if you prefer.'

'I've never had a brother or a sister.'

'Then you haven't lived.' He sat at my feet. He looked up at me with his big, earnest, greenish-brown eyes and said, 'It's a serious offer, Heather. Why don't you think about it? Then if you decide to say no, fine, but let it be for a good reason, such as that you've already been to Gibraltar three times this year, or you think I'm a crashing bore. Don't let it be because you think I'd put pressure on you to do something that you wouldn't dream of doing otherwise. That would be a very crude approach, and whatever else I may be, crude I am not.'

'Aren't you?'

'Look at me now, for instance.' He put his cup down and turned round to face me. He sat back on his heels and kissed the palms of each of my hands in turn. 'I don't suppose it'll come as a huge shock to you to know that I'd much rather spend the night in here with you than sleep by myself in that grim chamber next door. But I'm not going on and on about it, am I? I'm not making a nuisance of myself. I'm not waving our restaurant bill in your face. And I'm not even mentioning the fact that while I was paying it you ate both the chocolate mints and I didn't get a look-in. I'm just sitting here, basking

64

in the warmth of your heater, breathing in the health-giving fragrance of your fags, and waiting for you to make up your mind.'

17

'Okay,' I said.

He looked into my eyes. 'Is that okay to Gibraltar, or okay to . . . ?'

'It's okay to.'

He laughed and kissed me hard on the mouth. The kiss went on for a long time, blocking my breathing and turning into a bite. I moved my face away. He pulled me down on the floor. Something was pressing between my shoulder-blades – a teaspoon or a biro, I couldn't tell which.

He put his hand up my skirt and fiddled with the waistband of my tights. I wriggled free and rolled away. I knew I was making a fool of myself. What had I thought I was saying okay to, if I wanted to keep my tights on?

'Heather,' he said, 'you have done this before?'

'I haven't, actually.' I tried to sound casual, as if it were purely a matter of chance that I had never taken part in this particular activity.

'For heaven's sake!' He looked upset. I didn't see why. I thought men liked women to be virgins. To hear the way some of Mum's friends talked about men, you might think they insisted on it, as a way of establishing property rights.

Boniface said, 'You should have said.'

'Why?' I didn't mean *why?*, I meant *how?*. How do you tell someone something like that? At what point do you tell them? What words do you use – *be gentle with me*? I squirmed.

'A man likes to know these things.'

'Even if a woman doesn't want to tell him?'

'Why wouldn't you want to tell me? This should be a special occasion for you. And for me too, of course,' he added. He took my hand and raised me to my feet. There was no more rolling around on the floor with cutlery digging into my back. He undressed me with great courtliness, kissing as he went and finding complimentary things to say about each newly uncovered part of my body, from my nipples ('like fresh raspberries') to the stubble in my armpits ('new-mown hay').

He led me to the bed and pulled back the covers. He was like a chauffeur, opening the door of a Rolls-Royce for some fine lady to get in – except that I didn't think the chauffeur would take all his clothes off, climb in after the fine lady and start kissing her between her legs.

It was cold without our clothes on, but we soon warmed up. We kissed and cuddled and he stroked my breasts. He called my vagina my pussy, kissed it and said how pretty it was and how fine it tasted. He pressed his lips on mine and told me to lick them and tell him if I didn't agree. I wasn't sure.

He guided my hands to his penis and showed me how he would like me to stroke it. 'And feel free to kiss it,' he murmured. 'If you get the urge, I mean. Don't let me stop you.'

After I had kissed it a few times, he put his lips to my ear and whispered, 'Guess what I want to do now.'

'What?'

'I want to come inside you. Very slowly and carefully. I think you'll like that. What do you think?'

'I don't know.'

'Let's find out, shall we?'

At first it was quite difficult, and I could see exactly why some of Mum's friends called it penetration, and advised against having anything to do with it. But after a while it got easier and nicer.

When we had finished, he said, 'I can't believe no one's ever wanted to do that to you before.'

I smiled mysteriously. 'I didn't say they hadn't *wanted* to.'

'Oh, I see. You've been besieged by suitors.'

'Of course.'

'But you told them you were saving yourself for someone who knew what he was doing?'

'Yeah. Someone modest.' I kept having to remind myself that this was me trading bawdy wisecracks with this stranger and generally behaving in an uncharacteristic fashion.

We lay still for a while with our arms round each other. The silence was broken by the sound of my stomach rumbling. I didn't know why, I wasn't aware of being hungry, I thought I was full of curry. But he said, 'I'm starving too.'

'We just had dinner.'

'A lot's happened since dinner.'

'I suppose it has.'

'Uses up thousands of calories, this business. Better than a five-mile run. You haven't got any rich fruit cake stashed away, by any chance? Or fresh oysters?'

'I could do you bread and jam?'

'Bread and jam would be perfect.'

I made tea and jam sandwiches. By the time I got back to bed, I was freezing cold. He rubbed me all over to warm me up. 'When we're in Gibraltar,' he said, 'we'll be able to walk around stark bollock naked all day.'

My body tensed up. I didn't say anything. I couldn't.

'If we're going,' he said, 'I ought to book the tickets tomorrow.' He glanced at my alarm clock. It was just after three. 'Today, I should say.' He looked at me expectantly. 'What do you think?'

For an answer, I crawled down the bed and started playing with his nice curly hairs. First I used my fingers, then my tongue. I didn't really know what I was doing, but the effect was miraculous, and it soon put a stop to all the talk about Mediterranean holiday resorts.

18

I woke up alone. I guessed it was around ten. The daylight was harsh and cold, showing up marks on the sheets, and little heaps of my clothes, and unwashed dishes from our late-night snack.

I found the box of cigarettes he had given me last night, lit up, lay back and blew smoke into the air. As I relived everything that had happened, I felt a stupid grin spreading itself across my face.

A piece of paper was lying under the door, looking as if it had been there for some time. I picked it up.

Heather, darling. What can I say, except that you're beautiful, and thank you for sharing your beauty with me. What kind of world are we living in when I have to leave you and go to work? But I do. Will phone around midday to get your answer re Gibraltar. Please, please, please make it yes. Besottedly, B.

I shuddered, as if someone had put an icicle down my neck. Of course I couldn't go to Gibraltar and stay on a boat with a bunch of people I didn't know. Once we had cast off from shore I would be trapped. I would be so frightened that I would probably end up throwing myself into the sea.

I turned the radio on and found that it was later than I thought: 11.15. I dressed hastily and went out. I didn't want to be in when he phoned.

If he phoned. Once he got into his office, he might think better of the whole Gibraltar idea. In the cold light of day, he must realize that a person like me couldn't mix with his posh friends. Perhaps I couldn't even mix with him. He might have done a runner. I almost wished it.

Almost, but not quite. My whole body remembered how he had touched me. It wanted to know when it would happen again. I had no answer. Were Boniface and Gibraltar a package deal, or could I have one without the other?

I went to the library, but I couldn't settle to any work, so I wandered round Crystal Palace Park. I looked at the Victorian dinosaurs by the lake, and the empty plinths where statues had once stood. I tried to get a cup of tea, but the café was closed for the winter. I sat on a bench to smoke a cigarette, then went into the Ladies to warm myself. A sign on the wall gave the address of a Youth Drop-In Centre where you could get advice on contraception.

It was a bit late for that. I simply hadn't thought. I tried to imagine what my mother's reaction would be if a few weeks from now I had to tell her that I was carrying on the family tradition of getting pregnant at awkward times.

I copied down the phone number, then went to a greasy spoon for a bacon sandwich. Back at the library, I wrote a sex scene for my novel. It ended unhappily. My eyes started to burn.

I stayed in the library till it closed at six o'clock. The supermarket was still open, so I bought some tins of soup. Back at 59, Blondin Gardens, I walked past the phone with my eyes straight ahead so that I wouldn't see if there were any messages.

I climbed the stairs, wondering what I would do if there were a light under his door. I needn't have worried. There was none. Obviously he wasn't coming back.

I changed the sheets on the bed and listened to *The Archers*. Footsteps came up the stairs. Knuckles knocked at my door. I opened it, and we were in each other's arms, hunting for each other's mouths.

When we stopped for breath, I thought he was going to tell me off for not being in when he phoned, but he just said, 'Have you missed me?'

'Yes, but there's something I have to tell you.'

'That sounds ominous.' He said it cheerfully, as if he couldn't believe that anything I had to tell him could be bad. 'I've got something to tell you as well. Shall we flip a coin to see who goes first?'

We flipped. I won. I thought that should mean I could choose whether I went first or second, but he said no, it meant I had to go first. He opened his briefcase and brought out a bottle of wine. 'Have you got a corkscrew? I'll open this while I listen.'

'I'm not really a student at the London School of Economics.'

'I can live with that,' he said. 'Where *are* you studying?'

'Nowhere. I didn't get in.'

'Join the club.'

'My A-levels weren't good enough.'

'Become its president. What *do* you do?'

'Nothing. Nothing much. I'm unemployed. I'm trying to write something. That's why I can't come to Gibraltar with you.'

He opened his briefcase again. This time he brought out a booking form and pretended to study the terms and conditions. 'As I thought. There's nothing here about people who are trying to write something, not being allowed to go to Gibraltar.'

'It has to be finished by January 31st,' I explained. 'I don't have time to go on holiday.'

'Rubbish. Everyone takes time off at Christmas. Even you. Have you got a corkscrew or not?'

I found it and gave it to him. He looked at it as if it wasn't the kind of corkscrew that he was used to, but he was prepared to be a sport and give it a go. 'Now listen, Heather. Do you remember what I said when I first broached the subject of Gibraltar? I said it's up to you whether you come or not, but if you decide not to, I want it to be for a proper reason. I think I'm entitled to know what that reason is.'

'I've told you.'

'No, you haven't. What you told me was a lie. You had time

to go to your mother's, you've got time for this. And it wasn't your first lie. You lied to me yesterday about your father and you lied about being a student. Maybe you had a right to do that. Maybe I was coming on too strong with my questions. I thought I was showing polite interest, but there you go – one man's polite interest is another, er, person's third degree. It was none of my damn business. But this is my business, and I have rights too. If you're not coming to Gibraltar I want to know *why*.' He abandoned the uneven struggle with the corkscrew, and gave me a stern look.

I said eventually, 'I'm not very good at meeting new people.'

'You managed yesterday. The way you met me had a lot of style.'

I didn't say anything. He slapped himself on the wrist. 'Shut up, Bennett. Listen to the girl. Go on, Heather. You're saying you feel shy?'

I didn't answer. Of course I was shy, but that was only part of it. *Shy* was such a short, everyday word.

'I'm shy myself,' he said.

'I've noticed.'

'You can mock.' He returned to the wine. 'But beneath this brash exterior, the unending flow of wit and badinage –' the cork came out with a soft, wet popping sound. 'It's all an act. Inside, I'm a shrinking violet . . .' he put his arms round me '. . . longing to be plucked.' We kissed. 'Don't you want to be plucked, Heather? Come with me to Gibraltar and we'll pluck each other like harps till our strings drop off.' He looked into my face. I turned away. When he spoke again, he sounded irritated. 'All right, sweetie, forget it. I'm not going to drag you on to the plane against your will. Got any glasses?'

We sat far apart and drank our wine. I got out my cigarettes, but he gave me a pained look so I put them away again.

He broke the silence by saying politely, 'Have you had a good day?'

I nodded. 'And you?'

'Excellent, thank you.' He drained his glass and stood up. 'Well, I'm sure you have things to do.'

'Didn't you have something to tell me?'

'What?' He looked puzzled. 'Oh yes, that. Remember I told you I was supposed to be borrowing a chum's flat? Well, he's got his act together, and I can move in at the weekend.'

I went cold. 'Is that what you're going to do?'

'Might as well.'

'Had enough of slumming, have you?'

I didn't mean to say that. It just came out. He looked at me in amazement. '*Now* what are you talking about?'

'Move out to your yuppie pad. See if I care.'

'Now, hang on a minute, Heather.' He stood in front of me and got hold of my shoulders. 'I think it's time to get a few things straight.'

'They're straight already.' I was nearly crying.

'Not to me,' he said. 'You've got me wrong. I'm not scared of living in accommodation that's a bit basic. I've been to an English public school, don't forget. That prepares you for anything a slum landlord can throw at you.'

'Don't call my home a slum.'

'It was a figure of speech. And anyway, you used the word before I did.'

I couldn't deny it, or stop myself smiling a little. He kissed me and we sat down again.

'Maybe we should start this evening again,' he said. 'I'll come in and say, "Guess what, that flat's come up again, what do you think I should do?"'

'I don't want to tell you what to do.'

'And I don't want to tell *you* what to do,' he said. 'I want us to discuss things, and come up with solutions that will make us both happiest.'

'Okay.'

'I certainly don't want you thinking that now that I've had my wicked way with you, I'm hopping it.'

I thought for a few moments. Then a voice that didn't sound like mine said, 'You can't hop it. You're taking me to Gibraltar.'

19

I rang my mother and told her that it was fine with me if she wanted to spend Christmas in Scotland with Harry Wyatt. Then I told her why.

She listened in stunned silence. '*Gibraltar?*'

'Rocky place,' I explained. 'Down at the bottom of Spain.'

'I know where it is.'

'His employers have a yacht down there.'

'Oh, a yacht.' She was laughing with disbelief. She had always hoped that one day I would spread my wings and have an independent social life, but she had not envisaged this. 'What do they do – import diamonds?'

'Insurance. Lloyd's.'

'*Lloyd's?* Aren't they all millionaires?'

'I don't know,' I said. 'Shall I tell him you asked?'

'No, but you could ask him if he's got a friend.'

'What happened to Harry Wyatt?'

'What happened to Little Miz I-Vant-To-Be-Alone?'

She knew the answer. So did I. I was changing. I was trying something new, I was being someone new.

Boniface and I went to see his friend's flat in Docklands. It was like something out of a colour supplement, ultra-modern, with pale, fitted carpets, every gadget you could think of, and a water bed. The development of which it formed part had its own private gardens, leisure centre, bar and swimming pool. I could see Boniface comparing it with Blondin Gardens. To be honest, I was making a few comparisons myself.

We bounced on the water bed and agreed how nice it would be to try it out properly. We also agreed that it was too early for us to start thinking about living together, but we could have the next best thing. He would give me a key and the phone number of the cab company with whom his syndicate had an account, and I could come over whenever I wanted.

The other reason why he moved was that, nice though it was to live under the same roof, we weren't getting enough work done. We just had sex all the time, which was all very well, but it wore us out, and each of us had a deadline approaching – for me the Coates Clarion closing date, for him *Principles of Underwriting*. He had to be word-perfect in time for his three-month appraisal in February. 'It's a long book with a lot of long words in it,' he said. 'So I must ask you to keep your appetites in check.'

'What about yours?'

He clasped *Principles of Underwriting* to his heart. 'My only appetite is for learning.'

We agreed that I would spend weekends at the flat, but that during the week we would not sleep together. I met him after work and we went to the cinema, or to restaurants. Sometimes we just sat in pubs and talked. He told me funny stories about his day at the office, doing all the voices until I felt I knew the people. I told him some of the stuff I've been telling you about my early life. The feminist part made him uneasy, until he realized that I didn't take it as seriously as Mum did. He was fascinated that we knew lesbians socially. He asked about what I was writing, and I tried to tell him about being an outsider. I offered to lend him *The Outsider* by Colin Wilson.

He said he would like to read it, but I had a feeling he was only being polite. And when I brought him my copy, he turned it over in his hand and gave it back. 'Not really my kind of thing,' he said.

'How do you know?'

'I'm more a *Principles of Underwriting* man,' he joked. 'That's what I call a good read.' I found his self-mockery disconcerting, as if he thought I were some kind of great intellectual trying to force books on him, which, as I've already said, is not something I would ever do.

One evening we went to have a drink with some of his friends from work, people who would be on the holiday. We met in a wine bar: a man called Oliver, another called Charles, and one called Roger. The women were Naomi, Fliss and Antonia. Oliver and Naomi were, like Boniface, trainee underwriters. Charles was a solicitor, Fliss was a secretary. Roger worked in the press office. I didn't catch what Antonia did. They were all in their twenties, apart from Charles, who seemed older. They wore expensive clothes and talked in posh voices, but they were friendly and polite. They said how pleased they were to meet me and that Boniface had told them a lot about me. I didn't know what to say to that, so I just said that he had told me a lot about them too. They said, 'He was lying,' and we all laughed.

Naomi asked if I had ever been yachting before. When I said no, she said jolly good because neither had she, but she had already warned Charles that if the sea got too rough she was going to bail out by parachute.

Soon the talk became shop talk. Boniface did his best to divert it, or keep apart from it and talk to me himself, but he was drawn in, and I was left on the edge. I didn't mind. I was enjoying my third pina colada and my little dish of spiced nuts. Not so long ago, I had been alone in my room with no idea that a world like this existed. Now a stranger looking at me would not know that I was not part of it – not if the light in the wine bar was dim enough to conceal the difference between their authentic fashions and my imitation ones. In the past the idea of being drawn into something that I didn't understand among people I didn't know had been a matter for horror, but now I was discovering something new about it. It could be fun. It could make me laugh inside. I could move away in my mind and watch from afar.

This world was so unlike anything I was used to that there

was no danger of my being swallowed up by it. I could leave whenever I liked and go back to my room. But I didn't want to go back. I wanted to stay here and drink pina coladas and listen to these people who traded in risks. I tried to imagine what risks might look like, being traded. Were they smallish, like potatoes, and sold by the pound? Or did they come pre-packaged, or in slabs? These people made their livings by taking bets on the likelihood of disasters happening, but they didn't make them sound like disasters. They made them sound like minor inconveniences, or slapstick jokes. For them, jumbo jets didn't collide in mid-air, killing everyone on board – they bashed into each other. Buildings didn't collapse, they fell over. Nuclear power stations went phut. It was shocking in a way, but I couldn't be shocked. It was funny, but I didn't want to laugh. It was too magical for that. They couldn't see that they were magical. They sat perched on bar stools in their fashionable suits and elegant skirts, bought each other drinks, lit each other's cigarettes and spoke in numbers and initials and jargon. They didn't know that they were like fortune-tellers, soothsayers, poets.

20

Our flight was scheduled to leave Heathrow at 11 a.m. on Christmas Eve. Rather than have me haul my luggage over to Docklands, Boniface was going to pick me up in a taxi at about 8.30.

I packed and went to bed. I set my alarm clock for seven and lay in the darkness thinking that this time tomorrow I would be in a foreign country. It was no big deal. I had been in a foreign country for weeks.

Everything felt unreal. I put the light on and opened my suitcase. The sight of my new swimsuit reassured me. My mother had sent it to me as a Christmas present. She wouldn't have done that if she hadn't believed that all this was really happening and it was okay.

I got up at about seven and opened my door. The plastic bag was there as usual. Inside it, I found a chocolate biscuit wrapped in foil with a reindeer design, and a sealed envelope addressed to me.

I assumed it was a Christmas card from the Truscotts. I was sorry I hadn't thought to give them one. I opened the envelope and took out the sheet of paper. It had an amateurishly printed letterhead, with 'Fifty Nine, Blondin Gardens' spelled out as words.

Dear Guest,
Kindly note that Fifty Nine Blondin Gardens will cease trading as a guest house one month from today on the 24th January next.
I hereby give you notice of termination of our bed and breakfast agreement with you. Please ensure that you vacate your room by that date. Any personal property left behind will be disposed of.
Yours faithfully,
E J Truscott (Prop.)

I didn't know what to do. I ran downstairs and phoned Boniface. 'Bennett,' he said, as if he were at work. He sounded sleepy.

'It's Heather.'

That woke him up. 'Darling! What time is it? Have we missed the plane?'

'I'm about to be evicted.'

'You *what*?'

I read the letter aloud to him. It seemed a nice, easy, mechanical way of dealing with the situation. When I got to the end, he said, 'That's not so bad then.'

'Isn't it?'

'I thought you meant the bailiffs were there now this minute . . .'

'No, but . . .'

'. . . and you were barricading yourself in with your furniture.' He made it sound like slapstick, something he had to deal with at the office. Tragedies were jokes, and evictions were scenes from a Marx brothers movie.

'Bring the letter,' he commanded. 'You can show it to Plater on the plane.'

'Who's Plater?'

'Charles Plater. Solicitor. You met him. Top man. He's more maritime law, but he'll probably be able to give you a few pointers.'

I looked at the letter with its phony letterhead and rough-and-ready typing. I had a sudden vision of it being passed along the plane, from one well-manicured hand to another. Drops of expensive booze were spilt on it. Eyebrows were raised. Opinions were given, but not as if they mattered. It was an interesting problem. Perhaps not even that. The letter was handed back to me. I put it away with a feeling of shame. It was out of place, and so would I be.

'Rotten thing to happen,' said Boniface. 'I wish I were there to give you a big hug. But I'm on my way.'

'Don't,' I said. 'I can't come.'

'Rubbish,' he said. 'Darling, I know you're upset, and I don't blame you, but we've been looking forward to this trip . . .'

'And now I'm looking forward to living on the street.'

'Of course you're not going to live on the street. D'you think I'd let you live on the street?' His tone took it for granted that he had the power to prevent it.

'Read that letter again,' he ordered.

I obeyed. When I got to the bit about January 24th, he stopped me. 'See? Nothing's going to happen for a month at least. We can deal with it when we get back. Even then, he can't throw you out just like that.'

'Can't he?'

'I should say not. I've got friends who've had the devil of a job getting rid of tenants.'

I waited for him to correct himself, but he went blithely on. 'They had to go to court, get injunctions, God knows what. It takes months.'

'Your poor friends,' I said. 'It must be a real drag for them to have to deal with people like me.'

'You know I didn't mean it like that.'

It was the *you know* that finished me off. If he had just said, *I didn't mean it like that*, things might have been okay. I might have been able to dismiss what he had said as one of those stupid, tactless remarks that everyone makes from time to time, and which they go cold thinking about for the rest of their lives. But *you know* implied that he could tell me what was in my mind. He could tell me because our minds were the same. Our minds were the same because he had taken me over. He was like the people who had tried to adopt me. They had tried to bribe my mother with promises of big houses and ponies and posh schools. It had got them nowhere. So they had lain in wait and sent Boniface along, with gifts and food and sex and promises of trips of Gibraltar, and now they thought they had turned me into the sort of person who takes the landlord's side.

'I heard what you said and I know what you meant!'

'Heather, I simply meant that time's on your side.'

'Well, it doesn't fucking well feel like it!' I banged the phone down, went back to my room and locked the door. There on the floor was my suitcase, packed and labelled and ready. I tore off the labels and ripped them up. I upended the suitcase and tipped everything out on the floor. I kicked my swimsuit in the belly and knocked over my necklace tree. A thread broke, and beads scattered. I got into bed and pulled the pillows down round my ears. I didn't know what was going to happen. I was frightened. I wanted my mother, but she was in Scotland with Harry Wyatt. I heard a thudding sound, which might have been Boniface knocking, or somebody to say he was on the phone, or one of the other tenants wanting to talk about the letter. Whatever they wanted, they weren't going to get it from me. I lay very still. I might have shouted to them to go away. Eventually the thudding stopped.

I've already described how I spent the rest of Christmas Eve, lying in bed in a depressed state, smoking cigarettes, mooching around the supermarket and assuming that Boniface was on his way to Gibraltar, when in fact he was going down to Sussex, to Marjorie's party.

Speaking of Marjorie, I've just realized that of the twenty chapters you've had so far, only three have been about her. The rest have been about me.

This from the narrator who promised to keep her CV as brief as possible. This from the person who said, 'This is Marjorie's story, not mine. I am just the person telling it.'

It is, I promise you, and I am. I will now back off, bow out and get on with it.

21

The party started to break up at around 11.15, when the midnight communion crowd set off to commandeer the best seats in the village church. Next to leave were Robert's parents. They would be back again for lunch tomorrow, and, as his father cheerfully remarked, 'If we use up all our conversation now, we won't have anything to talk about over the turkey!'

'It's been lovely seeing you both,' Marjorie murmured.

By about 12.30, the only guests remaining were Olivia and Jake. It could no longer be concealed from them that Boniface was fast asleep upstairs, and had been for the entire evening.

Olivia was indignant and apologetic, but allowed herself to be calmed down with Armagnac and chocolates in front of the sitting-room fire. 'No need to ask what Marje and Robbie's new year resolution's going to be – no more uninvited guests at parties!'

'He's not doing any harm,' said Marjorie.

'He is. He's a bloody embarrassment. Let's go and tip a bucket of water over him.'

'Let's try coffee first, shall we? Does anyone else want any?'

No one did. Marjorie went to the kitchen, stopping on the way to let Castor and Pollux out of the utility room. The two red setters were always locked away during parties because of their tendency to become so hysterical with joy at the sight of visitors that they wet themselves. Olivia and Jake, being old friends, did not have this effect.

She made coffee in the individual-size cafetière and took it upstairs. She was startled to find that the lights were off. She had left them dimmed but still on, so that when he woke up he would know where he was. But he showed no sign of waking up. On the contrary, he seemed settled for the night. He was under the duvet. His clothes were in a heap on the chair.

'Boniface.' She switched on the overhead light. 'I think it's time for you to wake up now.'

He groaned and covered his eyes. 'Leave me alone, for fuck's sake.'

'What did you say?'

'Bugger off.'

'This is my home, Boniface. You're the one who has to bugger off.' He slept on. Marjorie put the coffee where he could reach it, and went back downstairs. Olivia had kicked her shoes off and was curled up prettily on the hearth rug, tickling the dogs' tummies. Jake was lolling in an armchair, musing on Boniface's sleeping habits. 'Extraordinary fellow. He'll go for days without sleeping at all. Then he has to sort of store it up again, like a camel.'

'And is he usually so sweet-tempered,' Marjorie inquired, 'when he's storing it up?'

'I say, Marje. I hope he hasn't been rude to you.'

She shrugged. 'It wasn't Jane Austen.'

'Right.' Jake looked grim. He set down his drink and his cigar and rose to his feet. 'We're not having that.' He headed towards the door, his jaw set.

Marjorie, Robert and Olivia followed him up to the bedroom. The four of them stood looking down at the young man's inert form.

Jake prodded his shoulder. 'Wake up, man. This won't do.'

Boniface grunted and covered the shoulder with the duvet.

Olivia said, 'Boniface, I'm going to count to three. And then I'm going to . . .'

'She's going to get in with you, Boniface,' said Robert. 'Be warned.'

Marjorie said, 'I don't see why there has to be all this fuss. He can stay the night.'

Robert's eyebrows shot up. 'He can?'

'I won't hear of it,' said Olivia. 'He's made enough of a nuisance of himself as it is. Boniface, I'm counting. One . . .'

'The poor boy's exhausted.'

'Two. Two and a half . . .'

'Robert or I will drive him over to you in the morning.'

'Nonsense,' said Olivia, walking towards the door. 'Phone us when he wakes up, and we'll send Skeate.'

22

The tail lights of the Verlaines' BMW disappeared down the drive and out into the wintry darkness. Castor and Pollux followed, barking joyously. They had never grasped the point that you weren't supposed to express as much enthusiasm at guests' departure as you did over their arrival.

Marjorie and Robert waved from the porch. The night was cold and clear, smelling of frost and salt. There were thousands of stars. If you kept absolutely still, you could hear the sea.

She said, 'How do you think it went?'

'I think people enjoyed themselves,' said Robert. 'Apart from him.' He nodded up in the direction of Caroline's window. 'What on earth possessed you to let him stay?' He wasn't angry, just amused at his wife's eccentricity.

'Ssh,' she said. 'He'll hear.'

'Fat chance of that.'

She lowered her voice. 'What choice did we have?'

'The four of us could have carried him down and put him in their boot.'

'Not without scraping the paint. Anyway,' she added, 'I liked him.'

'Liking him isn't the point.' Robert whistled for the dogs, who ignored him. He walked back into the house. 'I might have liked him myself if I'd had the chance to exchange more than two words with him before he passed out. Was he drunk?'

'I don't think so. He seemed very tired.'

'And emotional?'

'Preoccupied,' she said. 'Depressed. Olivia seems to think he's in *lerve*.' She squeezed his hand.

He returned the squeeze, then spotted some glasses hidden

under the hall table and went to pick them up. 'Those were the days, eh? Bonking till you can't stand up.'

There's no law against it, even these days, thought Marjorie, looking at her hand.

She went to the kitchen. Most of the clearing-up had been done: Sandi and Mandy had loaded the dishwasher, wiped down the surfaces, mopped the flagstone floor and wrapped the leftovers before setting off for their home in the village on their two-seater moped.

A few glasses remained to be washed, ashtrays to be emptied. By the time Marjorie had done all this, finished off the leftover cheesecake and made a pot of tea, Robert was in bed asleep.

She got in beside him and closed her eyes. She dreamed of strangers, intruders in the house. She woke to reassure herself that there was no intruder, only Olivia's young man.

Her next dream had him in a starring role. It was set in a foreign holiday resort – Gibraltar, it must be Gibraltar. She recognized the outline of the Rock. She was in Gibraltar with Olivia's young man. He had whisked her away for a winter holiday. Somebody had missed their flight, but it wasn't either of them. Perhaps it was his girlfriend.

She opened her eyes. It was still dark. Robert lay on his back with his mouth open. A faint trace of saliva gleamed on his beard. She hoped that he would sleep late, and that Boniface would wake up early.

She knew what was expected of her. Olivia had left clear instructions: her chauffeur was to be sent for. But Olivia couldn't expect always to have things her own way. Fancy expecting your chauffeur to work on Christmas Day. Fancy *having* a chauffeur.

Marjorie was in no hurry to get rid of Boniface. She had hardly exchanged two words with him. Wasn't she entitled to get to know a little about him, after welcoming him into her house, covering up for him, pleading his cause? What else had she to look forward to this Christmas Day? Clearing up, going to church, cooking the turkey, eating it with the in-laws.

She would offer Boniface a shower and shaving things. She would lend him a dressing gown – the white towelling one from the guest room. He would look gorgeous in it.

While he was in the shower, she would put his shirt and underclothes through the washing machine. She would press his trousers and jacket, and polish his shoes. When she finally returned him to Olivia, he would be in better condition than when Olivia brought him to her.

She would offer him breakfast, and talk to him. Or rather, she would let him talk. She would sit quietly at the table with him and listen, the way she used to with Caroline and Di in the days when they used to tell her things. Soon she would know more than Olivia knew about Gibraltar and the girlfriend trouble.

She dozed off. She woke again at 5.20. The bedroom was still dark and Robert was still comatose, but she was as alert as if an alarm had gone off. Perhaps some bird or animal had made a sound in the garden. If it had disturbed her, it might have disturbed Boniface. She was concerned for him. There was nothing worse than waking up in a strange house, not knowing where you were, or where the bathroom was, or what was expected of you.

He might be hungry. He might go looking for food. He might try to leave the house, and set the burglar alarm off. He might encounter the dogs. They wouldn't hurt him, they would adore him, but even that could be disconcerting to the uninitiated.

She crept out of bed and into the bathroom. She looked at the two dressing gowns hanging from the hook and considered which to wear. The quilted print was fresh from the laundry, but the blue mohair, with its high neck and elegant waist, had a more slimming effect. She sniffed the armpits of the blue mohair. It seemed all right so she put it on, brushed her teeth and checked that there was no sleep in the corners of her eyes.

She ran a comb through her hair, then made her way along the dark corridor.

Outside Caroline's room she stopped and listened. Boniface's breathing was deep and regular. Each inhalation ended with a faint and squeaky snore, like the snuffling of a baby. She pushed the door open and looked at him. All she could see was the dark shadow of his hair on the pillow, and the mound of his body moving rhythmically as he breathed. He wasn't ready to wake up yet, and might not be for several hours.

She was annoyed with herself. She ought to have stayed in bed. What was she going to do now? If she went back, she might wake Robert. And wouldn't it be just her luck to have him decide that this would be one of his let's-get-up-early, this-is-the-best-part-of-the-day mornings?

She went to the spare room and got under the covers. She looked towards the window. Faint smudges of pre-dawn light were beginning to appear in the sky. She hoped he would want breakfast. She would enjoy cooking him a proper breakfast. He hadn't reached the age when he needed to worry about his heart. She and Robert never ate a cooked breakfast, but she had had the foresight to lay in supplies of bacon and sausages in case any of the party guests took a sudden fancy to a late night snack. And she had oats left over from making flapjacks for the Christmas fair at Robert's school. She wondered if Boniface liked porridge. It was years since she had made por- ridge. Try giving porridge to teenage girls. She imagined stirring the porridge with a wooden spoon, watching it thicken in the pan. She poured it into a blue pottery bowl and set it before Boniface as he sat at the table in the warm kitchen.

She yawned and stretched, savouring the prospect of the morning ahead. The dogs would be asleep in their basket by the Aga. Beyond the leaded window with its holly-lined sill, the sky would be brilliant, wintry blue; blackbirds, robins and chaffinches would be hopping about on the bird table, gobbling up bits of bacon rind. Across the frost-tipped lawn there would drift the sound of Christmas church bells. Boniface would be wide awake, cheerful, chatty and appreciative of everything, particularly the porridge. He hadn't had porridge since he was at school, and then it had been tepid, grey and lumpy. Nobody made porridge for him these days – not even his girlfriend. Particularly not his girlfriend. She wasn't the porridge-making type. Much too good for it. Little bitch.

23

It was light when Marjorie woke up again. Robert was standing over her, dressed in cords and a sweater, with a cup of tea in his hand. He bent down and kissed her cheek. 'Happy Christmas, darling.'

'Same to you, darling.'

'What are you doing in here?' he asked.

'I couldn't sleep. I didn't want to disturb you with my tossing and turning. What time is it?'

'Nine o'clock, and Little Lord Fauntleroy's still dead to the world.'

'Oh, good. That means he's had a comfortable night.' She drank her tea, then went for a shower. She put on brown tailored slacks and a fawn cardigan. The cardigan was long enough to cover her worst bulges, but she was dissatisfied with the overall effect. She would have preferred Boniface to see her wearing something more feminine, but it was her habit to wear loose slacks to perform her morning chores. If she dressed up this morning, Robert was bound to notice. He might even guess the reason. She would then be on tenterhooks, waiting for him to make some unfortunate remark.

She went downstairs, stuffed the turkey and prepared breakfast for Robert and herself – half a grapefruit each, with low-calorie sweetener. Robert was out on the lawn, throwing sticks for the dogs. She wished they would make less noise. It was 9.30 now. If Boniface could just manage to stay asleep for another hour, that would be perfect. Robert would have to go to church without her.

They exchanged presents. He had bought her a book about English gardens and some French perfume. She gave him something called a Master Organizer 5400Z. Apparently all the boys at his school had them. She had had to make a special trip to Tottenham Court Road to look for it.

He was delighted with it, and gave her an immediate demonstration of how it would enable him to check his bank statement, remember people's birthdays, look up wine vintages, and find out what the time was in any major city in the world. She said, 'I hope you'll be very happy together.'

The sound of a throat being cleared made her turn her head. Boniface was standing in the doorway, with a diffident, uncertain expression on his face. He appeared to have found the white towelling dressing gown. She had been right about it suiting him.

'Good morning,' he said. 'Er, Mr and Mrs Fairfax, isn't it?'

She smiled into his eyes and pulled out a chair. 'Marjorie and Robert.'

'Sleep well?' Robert asked.

'A bit too well, I'm afraid, sir.'

'Nonsense,' said Robert breezily. 'The sleep of the just.'

'I don't know about that. Or where to start apologizing.'

'Have a cup of tea instead.' Robert glanced vaguely towards the kettle, as if he expected it to switch itself on.

'Jolly kind of you, but I won't have anything, thanks. I was wondering whether you had such a thing as a Yellow Pages.'

'Why? Has a pipe burst?'

'Not that I know of, sir, but if I could call a cab, I could get myself out of your way.'

'Taxis on Christmas Day? You're not in London now, you know. You're trapped with us, I'm afraid.'

'I can't think of a nicer place to be trapped, but I wouldn't want to outstay my . . . I *say*.' Boniface had spotted the Master Organizer. His eyes lit up. 'That's a fine piece of kit.'

'Christmas present from my wife.'

'Lucky you, to have such a nice wife.'

To hide her blushes, Marjorie got the Brussels sprouts out of the vegetable box and started to peel them. Robert and

Boniface, in the meantime, were explaining to each other how the 5400Z differed from earlier models. Neither of them appeared to be listening to a word the other said, but they seemed perfectly happy.

They were too absorbed to hear the phone ring. She went to the hall and answered it. Olivia's voice said, 'Don't you want to get rid of that frightful boy yet?'

Marjorie reached out and quietly closed the kitchen door. 'He's still asleep.'

'Well, wake him up,' said Olivia.

'We tried that last night. Don't fuss, Olivia. He's not doing any harm.'

'He may not be to you, darling,' said Olivia. 'But he is to me. This is damned inconvenient.'

'What's the problem?'

'Do you know the Horrockses? Of course you do, they were in our party at Glyndebourne.'

Marjorie suppressed a sigh. 'What about them, Olivia?'

'It's not so much *them*, darling. It's that poor old mum of theirs, over in Shoreham. Nancy Horrocks. She was a Skeffington. I take their word for it that she can be a difficult old bat, she's always charm itself with me, but really! Decamping *en masse* to the West Indies for Christmas and leaving her all on her own with that spooky housekeeper. So of course I said she must come to us, and it was all fixed, only she's just phoned to say she's having one of her dizzy spells. Not so dizzy that she can't come, mind you, oh no, that would be much too simple, but too dizzy to drive herself over. Afraid she'll have a blackout.'

'Ah,' said Marjorie.

'A taxi's not to be had for love nor money, of course, and the housekeeper's still *hors de combat* thanks to our friend the breathalyzer, so there's nothing for it but for us to send Skeate for her and I'll come for Boniface. As Jake says, he always knew we were running a branch of the social services out here,

93

but he didn't realize it was a minicab company as well. He's involved in a three-act drama with one of the mares at the moment, so it's down to me. And the thing is, Marje, I'd like to come for Bon sooner rather than later, before the hordes descend on us and things get completely out of control. So if you *could* wake him . . .'

'You think I haven't tried? But listen, Olivia. You've obviously got a lot on your plate. Why don't we leave him to wake up in his own time, and then I'll drive him over to you?'

'Because we've imposed enough on you already,' Olivia said. 'I won't hear of us imposing any more.'

24

'Got everything?'

'Yes, thanks.'

'Orf we jolly well go, then.' She started the car. At her side, Boniface was clean-shaven, damp and sparkling from his shower. He hadn't let her wash his clothes, he hadn't wanted any breakfast, but she was allowed to drive him to Olivia's.

On the road into the village, they passed Robert, who was walking to church. She tooted her horn and he lifted his hat.

She drove past the church. People were starting to gather. She was disappointed not to see anyone she knew. But there might be someone who recognized *her*, and who might notice her with her glamorous passenger.

Boniface cleared his throat. 'This is jolly kind of you, Mrs Fairfax.'

'Please call me Marjorie. And it's no trouble. Olivia seems to have her hands full.'

'Olivia always has her hands full. Usually with things that are none of her business.'

Marjorie raised her eyebrows but made no comment. She kept her eyes on the road and the greyish-green, frosty hills rising gently on either side. Boniface said, 'I shouldn't have said that. She's a friend of yours. She's a friend of mine, for that matter.'

'I'm very fond of her,' Marjorie said slowly, 'but I know she's not perfect. Which of us is?' she added.

'She means well,' Boniface said. 'But . . .'

'But at the moment, you wish you were going somewhere else?'

'Almost anywhere,' he admitted.

'Gibraltar, for example?' Her lack of tact horrified her. She probably wasn't even supposed to know about Gibraltar.

'Gibraltar,' he repeated. She couldn't tell whether it was an affirmative answer to her question, or whether he just liked saying the word.

He didn't appear to mind her knowing about Gibraltar. She decided not to push her luck by letting him know that she knew about the girlfriend as well. 'Was it something to do with your work that made you miss your flight?'

'Not exactly.' He stared straight ahead.

'Sorry. None of my business.'

'It is really. You've had to put up with the aftermath.'

'If you want to talk about it,' she said, taking a chance – after all, what had she to lose? – 'it won't go any further.' They both knew who she meant by *any further*.

There was a long pause. The car started to climb the road towards the cliff. Traffic had thinned out; it was just the two of them up on the hill with a few sheep.

'Stupid argument with this girl I know.' His tone was carefully bored. It suggested that the only reason he was telling the tale was because he might as well. To keep the matter secret would be to give it too much importance. 'Not *girl* – *woman*, I should say.' He sounded as if he had been trained to make the distinction but couldn't for the life of him see why it mattered.

'Someone you're fond of?'

'You could say that.'

'And does she feel the same?'

'I think she finds me, you know, not too objectionable.'

Marjorie smiled.

'That is,' Boniface said, 'until I opened my mouth and inserted both feet.'

'We've all done that.'

'It was my fault. We were under starters' orders to fly down to Gib together, and then at the last minute she got word that she might be turfed out of the place where she was living.'

'You mean because of something you did?'

'Good Lord, no.' He looked surprised. 'What makes you say that?'

'You said it was your fault.'

'Not in that sense. The way I reacted. You know how it is. You've only just woken up, you try to be helpful, you say the first thing that comes into your head, it's wrong, you try to put it right, you make it worse. She bangs the phone down. I go bombing round to her place, she won't answer the door . . . pretty bloody childish, really.'

'And in the meantime, you missed your flight?'

'Yep. So I said to myself, well, Bennett, you're going to have a lousy Christmas whatever you do. So why not make the best of a bad job, go to the office and see if you can catch up with some work.'

'Which you were doing until the phone rang and it was . . .'

'. . . the fairy godmother herself.' He picked up a pen from the dashboard and waved it like a wand. ' "You *shall* go to the ball!" '

That's your lot, Marje, she thought. For the rest of the journey, he asked polite, bland questions about herself and Robert and the family, and she answered with equal politeness, to show that she understood and accepted the prohibition on any further questioning about his private life.

'I suppose you'll be taking things easy today,' he said, 'after last night's extravaganza.'

'Don't you believe it,' she replied. 'My in-laws are coming.'

'Well, don't jump for joy about it. You might crash the car.'

She laughed. 'Am I that transparent? They're not so bad, I suppose.'

'But a little of them goes a long way?'

'We had them last night, you see,' she said. 'They come every year. I say to Robert, "Do they have to?" And he says, "They'll be so hurt if we don't ask them." ' She heard herself whinging to this near-stranger, but she didn't stop. 'It seems so unfair. *My* parents, they're dead now, but –'

'Yes, Olivia said. Quite recently, wasn't it?'

'My father died two years ago. My mother –' she swallowed '– last October.'

'My sympathies.'

'Thank you. But what I was saying was, Mummy and Daddy had their own lives. They never expected to live in our pockets. Last year was different, Mummy was ill, but in their day they were always gadding about, going on cruises, whatever. Same applies to my daughters. Not cruises, but you know. If I can accept that they may not always want to spend Christmas with me and their father, why can't his parents accept the same thing about us?' She stopped. She had said too much.

Boniface said, 'I can't believe you've got children old enough to spend Christmas on their own.'

'I'm a grandmother.'

'No!'

'And *you* are a flatterer.'

'Never.'

They pulled into the drive of Cliffhead Lodge – a listed building with a long history and a Gothic silhouette, dramatic against the seascape. Olivia appeared at an upstairs window.

'There she is,' said Boniface. 'Cruella De Vil.'

Olivia waved. Boniface moved to open his door, but Marjorie wanted to keep him for a few more moments. She wanted to sit with him under Olivia's gaze, and let Olivia wonder what they were talking about. She continued with her potted family history. 'The baby was only born in November, so I can't blame Di and Tony for not wanting to travel hundreds of miles. They live in Newcastle.' The front door of the house opened, and Olivia emerged, beaming and waving. She wore a tweed skirt, a fluffy pink angora jumper and court shoes with very high heels. 'My other daughter,' Marjorie continued, 'is spending Christmas in my parents' old flat in London, with some university friends.'

Boniface waved at Olivia. He opened the door of the car.

'Well, Marjorie, this looks like the parting of the ways.' He took her hand in both his, and half-shook, half-squeezed. 'Thank you for everything, and have a wonderful Christmas.' He looked as if he couldn't make up his mind about something. Suddenly, with the air of throwing caution to the winds for the sake of a moment of pleasure, he leaned forward and kissed her left cheek, just above her jaw bone. He smiled into her face with amused defiance. He got out of the car, strode across the yard, flung his arms round Olivia and kissed her on the mouth. He scooped her up and carried her into the house. Olivia kicked and protested prettily, and gestured back towards Marjorie about how impossible he was.

25

The flowers arrived early in the new year – a delicate arrangement of irises, freesias and Asian orchids, with winter ferns and foliage, wrapped in cellophane with a lilac silk bow.

The card read, 'To Marjorie, with renewed apologies, and many thanks for your kindness. Best wishes for 1984, Boniface Bennett.' She pressed the card to her lips. She realized what a fool she must look. Fortunately, she was alone in the house. Robert had gone to the station to meet Caroline off the London train.

She slipped the card into the pocket of her skirt. She carried the flowers to the utility room, and selected a vase. She took her time arranging the flowers, touching them and enjoying their subtle fragrance. She put them on the hall table.

She went into the sitting room, sat at her writing desk and took out a sheet of headed notepaper.

My dear Boniface,
I am writing on Robert's behalf and my own to say a most sincere thank you for the beautiful flowers which have just arrived. They are in the Chinese vase on the hall table, looking very cheerful and reminding us that spring isn't too far away.

She frowned at what she had written. She had no confidence in her ability to put things down on paper. Was it necessary to say 'on Robert's behalf and my own' in that *my husband and I* fashion? The flowers had been addressed to her personally, not Robert. Was 'cheerful' the right word for such a delicate bouquet? And as for the flowers being a reminder of spring – might that sound ungracious, suggesting that the flowers were not enough in themselves, but must be a foretaste of something better?

I am writing to say a most sincere thank you for the beautiful flowers which have just arrived. It was most kind of you to send such a delightful gift, but quite unnecessary. It was a great pleasure – albeit rather an unexpected one – to be able to put you up over Christmas, and, far from expecting you to apologize, I take it as a compliment that you felt so relaxed in our house that you were able to sleep so deeply and for so long!

She wasn't sure about the exclamation mark. Caroline had once told her that she used too many exclamation marks in her correspondence. *They're gauche, Mummy.* Gauche or not, they offered protection against being taken too seriously, and Marjorie was reluctant to abandon them altogether.

Still dissatisfied with the letter, she tried again. Three drafts later, she reverted to the original. She was becoming impatient with herself – it was only a thank you letter, for heaven's sake. It hardly mattered what it said.

She got on the phone to the Verlaines to find out Boniface's address. Olivia was out, so Marjorie spoke to Jake. She would have preferred to tell Olivia directly about the flowers, but with a bit of luck Jake would report back. Marjorie took care to describe the flowers in detail, and to say how surprised and delighted she was to have them. Jake said it was the least the little devil could do.

He gave her Boniface's address – 15, Barbados Wharf, Rope Street, E1. She wrote it into her address book, then copied it on to the envelope. She put her coat on, called to the dogs and walked down the road with them to the post box. She was just about to drop the letter in when she stopped. Was this all? Thank you for the flowers, best wishes for the new year, end of story?

She returned the letter to her pocket and walked back to the house. In her head, she was drafting a new paragraph. *Your sending the flowers gave me an excuse to get your address from the Verlaines, and, now that I have it, I hope it won't be too long before I may write again and invite you to visit us properly, perhaps one Sunday for lunch* . . . Would he want to come all the way from London for lunch? He probably preferred to spend his weekends with his friends, with his girlfriend. Then let him bring her along. *I also hope that you have by now reached a happy resolution with the friend with whom you had the 'tiff'. If so, then of course the invitation will include her.*

Marjorie hoped nothing of the kind. She hoped that Boniface and his girlfriend had been put asunder once and for all. Nevertheless, it seemed like a good move, to mention her in such a benevolent way. What on earth would they talk about if she came to lunch? Presumably she was one of these clever young women who were doing so well for themselves in the City these days, hard as nails and beating the men at their own game. Marjorie hoped she wasn't quite beating Boniface at his game. She wasn't even sure what his game was. She would have to bone up on it before he came to lunch. She didn't want to look a complete ignoramus in front of his girlfriend.

She arrived back at the house in a dead heat with Robert and Caroline. The dogs went crazy. Caroline stepped out of the car in her tailored jeans, high-heeled boots and Afghan jacket. With her glossy, chin-length hair and light make-up, she looked like a fashion model on her day off. Marjorie waited in line behind the dogs to kiss her daughter and escort her into the house. Robert followed with her luggage.

'Did you have a good time, darling?' Marjorie asked.

'Super, Mummy, thanks. And before you ask – no, we didn't leave Granny's flat looking as if a bomb had hit it.'

'I believe you. Thousands wouldn't.'

Robert took Caroline's luggage up to her room. He came back down and the three of them sat round the kitchen table drinking tea, eating slices of Christmas cake and discussing their plans for the next few days. Caroline had an essay to write. She also wanted to go riding, and to invite some old schoolfriends for dinner. Robert had some colleagues coming round for an informal staff meeting and lunch. No one asked what Marjorie would be doing.

Caroline said, 'I hear you've had a houseful of hunky young men staying.'

'It's true.' Marjorie cleared away the tea cups. 'We've been packed out.'

'When's he coming for Sunday lunch?'

Marjorie stared. 'Who said anything about Sunday lunch?'

'You always invite people to Sunday lunch. How about next weekend?'

'I think that's a bit soon, darling.'

'But if you leave it too long, I'll be back at Cambridge and I'll miss him.'

'So you will.'

26

On second thoughts, it might not be such a bad idea to have Caroline present at the lunch party. At least then Boniface would have someone of his own age to talk to. And if the girlfriend came too – well, she and Caroline could compete with each other over which of them was the more glamorous. This would leave Boniface dazzled and confused, and in the mood to appreciate someone who might have more to offer than mere youthful beauty.

But if Caroline was to be included, the occasion would have to be postponed until the Easter holidays. It seemed like a long time to wait.

The dilemma nagged at Marjorie all day. In the night, another idea came to her. She got out of bed quietly, in order not to wake Robert. She found pen and paper, and wrote,

You mentioned that your friend was having some difficulties with her accommodation. I don't know if *I* mentioned that my late parents' flat in Chelsea is currently unoccupied. We are planning to put it on the market later in the year, but if in the meantime it would be of any use to your friend – perhaps to tide her over for a few weeks while she looks for something more permanent – I hope you will get in touch.

She was impressed. She didn't normally think of herself as a clever person, but this time she had come up trumps. Never mind 'hoping' that Boniface would get in touch; he would have to. Even if the girlfriend had solved her housing problem by now (and Marjorie hoped that she had), good manners dictated that Boniface should write or phone to tell Marjorie this.

It was so much better than the lunch party idea. Not that it was either/or. The offer of the flat didn't rule out the lunch invitation – on the contrary, it made it more likely that the invitation, whenever it was issued, would be accepted. Marjorie would by then have established herself as a friend: a kind and resourceful person who paid attention when Boniface talked about his problems, and was prepared to put herself out to help solve them.

She added, 'I feel sure that we will be able to come to a mutually beneficial arrangement,' thus making it clear that she was not offering the flat to the girl free of charge. That would look naïve, and Boniface would not respect her if she were naïve. She would expect a sensible rent – but a girl like that, with a high-flying job in the City, would be in a position to pay one.

Two days after she posted the letter, he rang. She was shocked, and yet not shocked at all. She felt like a teenager. She pretended to be a friendly, middle-aged woman. 'How are you, Boniface?'

'All the better,' he said, 'for hearing your voice.'

She glowed.

'Marjorie, thank you for your letter, and for the very generous offer of your flat.'

Her spirits fell. She didn't want that girl anywhere near the flat. But she forced warmth into her voice. 'Is your, er, friend interested? I'm sorry, I don't know her name.'

'It's Heather.' His tongue seemed to linger on the *th* sound, as if he liked the taste. 'Heather Fox. And yes, she is very interested. It was passing on your offer that got me back into her good books.'

'I *am* pleased.'

'Perhaps the three of us could have lunch and sort out the details.'

'Splendid,' said Marjorie.

He suggested Rees's in Flood Street, just round the corner from the flat – the day after tomorrow, if that wasn't too soon. It was much too soon for Marjorie, who had a dental appointment arranged for the day after tomorrow; but it was only a check-up, and could easily be postponed.

There was no time to lose weight, or to linger over choosing a new outfit. But she spent half an hour phoning round letting agencies in Kensington and Chelsea to find out what the market rent would be for a flat like her parents'. Five hundred pounds a week seemed to be the most popular figure.

She arrived at Rees's just before one. She saw Boniface and the girl straight away, chatting over aperitifs at a table for three. The girl was smoking and eating bits of bread.

As Marjorie studied her, she realized that her expectation of the girl being a brash yuppie was off the mark. She was small and pale, thin with hollow cheeks and short, blonde hair tucked behind her ears. She wore a skirt made of a purple patterned fabric, with a matching top and a wide belt. The belt emphasized her slender waist; such a pity that the belt was plastic. The fabric of the skirt and top was also synthetic, and she wore cheap beads. She wasn't unattractive – being so young and so slim, how could she be? – but she had no idea how to dress.

The waiter led Marjorie to the table. Boniface stood, clasped Marjorie's hand, kissed her cheek and performed introductions. Marjorie said, 'How do you do?' to Heather. Heather shook hands awkwardly, as if she were unaccustomed to formality. Close to, her lack of grooming was even more apparent. The strap was coming off her handbag, her shoes were scuffed, her fingers were stained with nicotine. Worst of all, she had a silvery stud in the side of her nose.

'Do you work in the City, Heather?' Marjorie inquired, when drinks had been ordered and menu items chosen.

Heather smiled. It was quite a pretty smile, but Marjorie couldn't look at it for long because of the nose stud. 'Me? No way.'

'We wouldn't have her,' Boniface teased.

'Couldn't afford me, you mean,' Heather retorted.

They gazed fondly at each other. Marjorie wondered if she was going to have to spend the entire lunch watching the two of them flirt. What was she *doing* here?

She knew what she was doing. She was playing the part of Heather's prospective landlord, as a pretext for spending some time with Boniface. She was, in other words, a complete and utter fool, but she didn't mind that, as long as she could be with him and as long as he did not discover how much of a fool she was. In order to prevent him discovering, she must continue to play the part.

What questions would a landlord ask? *Where are you living now?* That sounded a bit bald. *What references can you supply?* Even worse.

Heather saved her the bother. 'I hear you've got a flat to let.'

Marjorie bristled. What right had this girl to bring up the subject? She should wait until the flat was offered to her – which it wasn't going to be. 'I do have a place, yes.'

'Where is it, exactly?'

'A short way from here.'

'What sort of size is it?' Boniface asked.

Marjorie gave him a warm smile. She didn't mind *him* asking. 'A good size. Mummy and Daddy loved entertaining, and having people to stay. It has three bedrooms, a dining room and a sitting room. Two bathrooms, and a utility room. It's furnished, and . . .'

'Sounds great,' said Heather.

'Thank you, dear. Are you not happy with your present accommodation?'

'It's not a case of her not being happy,' said Boniface. 'Her landlord's playing silly Harrys. He wants to sell the place to developers, so he's given Heather and the others notice to quit.'

'Has he indeed?' Marjorie gave a light laugh. 'I think he'll find it's not as simple as that, getting rid of tenants. I've known people . . .'

Boniface said quickly, 'Quite. Chap hasn't a leg to stand on, of course. Even so, it's not a very happy situation for Heather to be in. What sort of rent would you be looking for, Marjorie?'

Marjorie opened her mouth, then closed it again. However deep her dislike and suspicion of this unkempt waif, she couldn't quite bring herself to ask her for £500 a week.

'No need to be coy, Marjorie,' said Boniface. 'We all under-stand that this is a business arrangement.'

The way he said *business arrangement* made her realize what she ought to have known all along – that the rent would not be a problem for Heather, because she wouldn't be paying it.

Heather was his kept mistress. Marjorie didn't know why that disturbed her so much. She had known all along that he had a girlfriend, and she had taken it for granted that they slept together. But taking such a thing for granted is one thing; being brought in on the financial side is quite another.

How would it work? Would Boniface send her monthly cheques, or would he think it more delicate to have her supply him with her banking details so that he could set up a standing order? Or would Heather pay the rent to Marjorie, each of them pretending that Marjorie did not know where the money was really coming from?

How could Boniface do this to her? She was resigned to the fact that he did not like her as she liked him, but must he wipe her face in it? She wished she had the courage to get up and leave. But they might guess the reason. Anyway, she had a better idea. Two could play at this game. Two could take Heather under their wing. 'I was wondering,' she said, 'whether Heather would be able to see her way to doing me a small favour.'

Heather looked suspicious. 'What sort of favour?'

'The flat is only available for a short while; we're planning to put it on the market soon.'

Boniface nodded. 'That's understood.'

Marjorie addressed herself directly to Heather. 'I'll have to have someone round to value it. I always think it's best to get three valuations, don't you, and take the middle one? And then there'll be the business of showing potential purchasers round. If you wouldn't mind moving in for a few weeks, Heather, it would save me journeying up to town every five minutes. There would be no question of payment, of course – either way.'

27

Boniface said, 'That's an extremely generous suggestion, Marjorie.'

'Not at all.' Marjorie didn't feel generous, just incredulous at what she had just done. This was her first meeting with the girl. Until two days ago, she hadn't even known her name. She had never intended that she should live in the flat, even at a fair rent. Yet now she had offered it to her rent-free.

'Oh, but it is. Isn't it, Heather?'

'Very.'

Gloomily, Marjorie ate her lunch. She considered ordering more and more items, to postpone the moment when she must take Heather round the corner and show her the flat. With a bit of luck, the girl might suddenly remember another appointment.

In answer to some conversational question from Boniface, Marjorie began to talk non-stop. She heard herself babbling about Robert and the girls, about the Old Coach House and the village and her work in the charity shop in Eastbourne. She knew she was being a bore, that the things she was saying were inconsequential, but she didn't care. Let Heather and Boniface form the impression that she was a chatterbox who said things without thinking. Then they might have the tact to disregard her earlier offer.

Boniface paid the bill. 'I'd be happy to sit here all afternoon,' he said, 'but I'm sure Marjorie has more important things to do. Can we ask you to show us the flat now, Marjorie?'

They walked round the corner – it wasn't worth taking a taxi. She wished she had checked the flat. Caroline had assured her in don't-fuss-Mummy tones that she had left everything clean and tidy, but the words 'clean' and 'tidy' meant different things to different people. If there had been any lapses or oversights, Marjorie didn't want Heather's sharp little eyes seeing them.

A cold wind blew off the river. A huge brown barge was going by, sunk low in the water by its unidentified cargo. Three seagulls circled above it, looking lost and out of place. Marjorie opened the garden gate of the mansion block, and stood aside for Heather and Boniface to precede her up the path. Boniface took the gate from her and insisted that she go first. She brought the keys out of her handbag, opened the front door and ushered Heather and Boniface into the lobby.

The smell welcomed her and hurt her. She had known it would be here: the familiar mixture of the wool of the stair carpet, beeswax polish on the bannisters, oil in the mechanism of the lift, and central heating. It was the smell of coming home. No – that wasn't right. She mustn't over-sentimentalize. This had never been home to her – just a place to visit, sometimes with the family, sometimes on her own, but always to be spoilt with huge meals and fattening cakes, and drinks served with a generous hand. Always to be made to feel special. Even after her father's death, her mother had kept up the tradition of spoiling, until, with her own illness, it became impossible. Marjorie had measured the early stages of her mother's cancer in the dwindling standards of her hospitality. Out went the roast beef dinners, the elaborate home-made puddings; in came the convenience foods which her mother would once have despised. Towards the end she was too listless even to offer a cup of tea. By then there were other smells – medicine, broth, flowers, and an antiseptic soap used by the visiting nurse.

The memories were as raw as skin under a blister. When Caroline had suggested holding a Christmas party there, Marjorie had initially been shocked, not by the idea of a party as such – her mother had always enjoyed parties, and would have said, 'Let the young people enjoy themselves' – but by Caroline's wanting to bring strangers into the flat while her grandmother's things were still in place and before the proper formalities had been observed.

But Caroline's strangers had been friends, and at least Caroline had remained on the premises to supervise them. What would Heather get up to if left to her own devices? Had Marjorie been told the whole truth about why her landlord was trying to evict her?

Marjorie pressed the button for the lift and immediately wished she had suggested taking the stairs instead. The lift was too small for three people to occupy in comfort. The lift arrived and they got in. Boniface's elbow pressed against Marjorie's back. She pretended to be somewhere else.

She opened the front door of the flat. At first glance, everything seemed to be in order – carpets hoovered, washing-up done, furniture not too far out of place. Closer examination revealed a trail of pine needles leading to the front door, a toilet roll out of its holder, ashtrays emptied but not wiped, and a dozen empty wine bottles clustered in the corner of the kitchen. The beds had been stripped, but the sheets were still in the linen basket.

But at least there was an air of life about the place – not like before. She had been here perhaps six times since her mother was taken to the hospice for her final days – to fetch items that she needed, and then, after her death, to make lists of her effects for the solicitors. She had arranged for the delivery of some tea-chests, but she hadn't got very far with filling them. She had put all that off until the new year. It was the new year now.

She led Heather and Boniface from room to room. She didn't know what she was supposed to be saying. 'This is the dining room.' 'This is the bathroom.' What else would these rooms be? She sounded like an estate agent. Ought she to be pointing out special features – the original fireplaces, the conveniently fitted kitchen, the Regency chandelier found by Daddy in an auction room in Hatton Garden? Why should she? More to the point, ought she to be thinking about putting away the ornaments and silverware, in case Heather had a tendency to be light-fingered? 'This was my parents' bedroom.' She opened the door briefly to reveal the king-sized brass bed, the carved mahogany wardrobes, then closed it again. 'You might prefer to sleep in the guest room, Heather.'

'Fine. Whatever.' Heather's tone was vague, her manner fidgety, almost as if she had lost interest in the flat. Boniface made up for it, admiring everything, asking interested questions about the fittings and furnishings, the wall mouldings and ceiling roses, about Daddy's antiques and Mummy's paintings.

Heather cleared her throat. 'Look, er –'

'What, darling?'

'I've just remembered another appointment.'

Marjorie wondered why she couldn't have remembered it before.

'Thanks for showing me the flat, Marjorie.'

'It's been a pleasure.'

'But I'm afraid it's not quite right for me.'

Not quite RIGHT? Marjorie felt like slapping the girl's face. 'What's wrong with it?' she demanded.

'Nothing wrong with it at all,' said Boniface stoutly. 'It's a super flat.'

'Oh, it is,' said Heather. 'But it's just, you know, not right for me.'

Marjorie said icily, 'You must please yourself.'

'Thanks. I hope you find someone else to let your estate agents in.'

'I'm sure I shall.'

Heather headed towards the front door with an unmistakable air of relief. Anyone would think she had been detained in the flat against her will.

28

I'd better explain.

If you're going to understand what's going on, and what happens next, there's something you need to know.

You're probably a bit confused anyway. The last you heard of me, I was refusing on principle to go to Gibraltar with Boniface because he had shown a callous attitude to the problems of low-income tenants. Then I was back with him again, apparently only too willing to let him set me up as a kept woman in sole occupancy of a family-sized residence in leafy S W 3. Now you see me turning up my nose at said residence.

What's with her?, you're wondering. I hope you are wondering. I trust you haven't written off my behaviour as yet another example of me being my normal weird self. Just because I've said that this is Marjorie's story and not mine, it doesn't mean I want you to ignore me altogether.

I've already described my Christmas Eve. Christmas Day was much the same, except that it was colder and no shops were open. I was out of paraffin, so I stayed in bed.

Occasionally I got out to eat something or to try to work on my novel. But the words wouldn't come.

Half-way through Boxing Day, a knock came at my door. I thought it might be Boniface, miraculously returned from Gibraltar, but it was the elderly woman who lived in the basement. She said her name was Kath Baker, and she was organizing a tenants' action group. Did I want to come to a meeting in her room? I hesitated; I wasn't a meetings person at the best of times, and this wasn't the best of times. She said there would be tea and mince pies. I said I had flu. She noticed my typewriter and asked whether, once I was feeling better, I would type the minutes. To get rid of her, I said okay.

From the minutes I learned that Kath Baker had a friend who had a grandson who was a Legal Aid solicitor, specializing in housing rights. He was away for Christmas, but Kath planned to contact him as soon as he got back. Someone else was going to ring up Shelter and ask for their advice. It all seemed quite business-like and sensible, and I started to believe that Mr Truscott had bitten off more than he could chew and I wasn't going to be homeless just yet.

There was some consolation in this. I might not have a lover any more, but at least I had a home. I started to write again.

I worked steadily. Then the day dawned when Boniface was due back from Gibraltar. I waited for him to phone me or come round, but he did neither. I tried to phone him but he was never in. I left messages at his office.

I sank back into depression. My room was full of reminders of him: empty wine bottles, bread and jam, pills from Croydon Youth Drop-in Centre. Every morning I had to decide whether to take one or not.

Maybe he was right to blame me. Maybe it was all my fault. All right, he had been tactless in his response to my eviction letter, but tactlessness isn't a crime. Maybe this wasn't about tactlessness at all, but my own fear. Maybe I had never meant to go to Gibraltar in the first place. The eviction letter had provided me with a let-out, but if it hadn't come I would have found something else.

All my preparations, my excitement had been self-delusion. I was too scared, too hooked on the idea of myself as an outsider to dare to behave like an insider for once.

He came round one evening when I was heating a tin of soup for my supper. He knocked and I answered.

He looked the same as ever, wearing his suit, briefcase in hand, newspapers under his arm. He didn't look particularly happy to see me. He didn't smile or try to touch me. He just said, 'Hello, Heather,' in a flat voice.

'Hello,' I said.

'Thought I'd pop round and see how you are.'

'I'm all right.'

'Mission accomplished, then.' He turned away. 'I'll be off.'

'Don't.' I put my hand on his sleeve. He looked at it with a sort of distaste, as if I had no right to touch him. But he came into my room. He gazed around, as if he were trying to reorientate himself. He took in my unmade bed, my overflowing ashtrays, the paraffin heater, the heaps of paper round my typewriter. Something gleamed in his eye – relief, perhaps, that nothing had changed? Or disgust that I was such a slob? 'You haven't been kicked out, then?'

'No.'

'So I was right.'

'How was Gibraltar?'

'Stupendous.' He threw his briefcase and newspapers at my bed and flopped down in my armchair. 'Brilliant. Sun shone every day, a fair wind blew, and there was carousing and fornicating far into the night –'

'Thanks for telling me.'

'If I could finish my sentence? I was going to say, ". . . or so I am reliably informed."'

'You mean you didn't go?'

'Of course I didn't fucking well go.'

My chicken soup rose in the pan and boiled over. It poured on to the hot gas ring, where it started to burn and bubble and form a crust. Shreds of chicken stuck in the vents. Smoke filled the air.

I cleared up as best I could. Boniface opened the window and flapped the curtains. He said, 'Was that supper?'

''fraid so.'

'God, Heather. You are so hopeless.'

'Not so hopeless that I wouldn't phone someone back if they took the trouble to phone me.'

He went on flapping the curtains. 'I didn't want to phone

you back. I wanted to make you suffer, like you made me suffer.'

'I haven't been suffering,' I said.

'Neither have I.'

The room was getting cold and most of the smoke had blown away, so he closed the window. He turned, put his arms round me and said, 'What fibbers we both are. I've been through hell.'

'Me too.'

'Funny I didn't see you there.'

'I was in a different bit.'

We threw stuff off the bed and made love. It wasn't one of our long, drawn-out sessions, it was more like something we had to get done. But it was good. I was so happy afterwards that I didn't even want a cigarette.

He lay next to me and said, 'Oh, by the way. I may have found somewhere for you to live.' He explained about the woman whose Christmas party he had slept through and who had written him a letter offering me the use of a spare flat that she happened to have lying around in Chelsea.

'Why?' I asked.

'Why not? She's a nice lady.'

'She doesn't even know me.'

'No, but she could tell from the way I spoke about you that you're multi-talented . . .' he kissed my mouth '. . . sweet-natured . . .' he kissed my navel '. . . and perfectly formed.' He kissed me again.

Sometime later, I said, 'What's the rent on this flat?'

'Don't know. We can ask her when we meet.'

'*Meet*?'

'You'll have to meet her if you're going to live in her flat.'

'I haven't said I am.'

'No, but it's something to think about.'

'Thanks for the thought,' I said. 'And please say thanks to her. But I think we're all right for the time being.' I told him about the tenants' action group.

He listened with polite interest, but said, 'Let's go and see it anyway.'

'Why?'

'Why not?'

I propped myself up on my elbow and looked down at him. 'What are you up to?'

'I'm not "up to" anything. I just want to see her flat.'

'Why? You're not thinking of moving again, are you?'

'No,' he said, 'but I'd like to see what it's worth. What *she's* worth.'

'Oh, I *see*. You're thinking of proposing to her.'

'No, she's married already,' said Boniface. 'But we might sign her up as a name.'

29

What's a name? I hear you ask.

Or perhaps I don't. You probably know already what a name is. There's been enough about them in the papers.

But you may not have read it, or taken it in. You may have got the general drift, but not bothered with the details. You may have thought it was nothing to do with you. It would be an easy mistake for you to make.

I'd better explain what a name is, as otherwise the rest of this story won't make much sense.

A name is a kind of investor, a backer for the underwriting syndicates at Lloyd's. But unlike ordinary investors, names don't actually put up any money. They just have to have it available if it's needed. Since most of the time it isn't needed, they can in the meantime invest it in something else.

'It's a way of making your money work twice,' he said.

'Oh, right,' I said. 'Can I be a name? Then my money could work twice.'

'Er –'

'Go on. Say it.' I got him in an arm-lock. 'I'm not rich enough, right?'

'We do look for people who can show a level of wealth somewhat greater than the resources you currently have at your disposal.'

So I understand what a name was. What I didn't understand was why, in order for Marjorie Fairfax to become one, I had to go and see her flat.

'Because I can't just ring her up and say, "Hi, Marje. Fancy being a name?" '

'Why not?'

'Because, Heather, that's not the way it's done.'

'How *is* it done?'

'To be honest, I don't really know,' he admitted. 'Recruiting new names isn't my responsibility. If we meet any likely prospects, we're supposed to refer them to a chap called Tim Kenilworth. He's what we call a members' agent. They look after the names on a day-to-day basis.' He made them sound like children with special needs. 'I don't want him wasting his time – or her wasting hers – if she turns out not to have the necessary. There's obviously family money there – they didn't buy that house out of a school teacher's salary – and I have a hunch it's her family rather than his. But it could be more complicated than that. I'd like the chance to check her out before I hand her over to Tim Kenilworth and let him work his charm on her.'

'Oh, I *see*.' I rolled over on to my back. 'That's "the way it's done". Male charm. What if she's immune?'

He smirked. 'She's not.'

'What do you mean?'

He looked mysterious. 'Nothing.'

'Fancied you, did she?'

'I think she found me . . .' he searched for a phrase '. . . not too objectionable.'

'Can't think why,' I said.

'But I said, "Unhand me, madam. I am promised to another."'

'Can't think who.'

'I suppose,' he said after a while, 'now that you've burned your soup and had your way with me, you're expecting me to take you out to dinner.'

Outside the house was a slinky white sports car. He unlocked the passenger door and held it for me to get in. The seats were leather and the dashboard looked like something from the cockpit of a jumbo jet. Speeds on the speedometer went up to 170 m.p.h. 'I'm probably mad,' he said. 'I should at least have waited until I got my appointment confirmed. But I needed cheering up.'

'Are you cheered up now?'

'Totally.' He kissed me and fixed my seat-belt. He started the engine and we swooped smoothly forward, heading towards the West End. He turned on the stereo, and Bruce Springsteen came at us from all sides. I was so happy that I thought I was flying. I closed my eyes to hold on to the moment. 'Am I allowed to smoke in here?'

'Only if you agree to be my Trojan horse.'

'Your what?'

'My cover story for getting into Marjorie's flat. Once we're there, you can make your excuses and leave me to it.'

So that's what I did.

30

Marjorie and Boniface stood by the window, watching Heather walk along the road towards Battersea Bridge and the bus stop. She looked small and forlorn against the darkening January sky. No one would guess what a spoilt bitch she was, Marjorie thought.

'*What* a charming girl.'

'She can be,' said Boniface. 'But she's a bit . . . direct.'

Marjorie decided to be conciliatory, and so earn points for herself. 'There's no point in taking a flat out of politeness. If you're going to live in a place, it has to feel right.'

'It's nice of you to see it that way,' said Boniface. 'But I'm the one who doesn't feel right.'

She looked at him with concern. 'Are you ill?'

'Ill, no. Embarrassed, yes. I agree with every word you say about a place having to feel right, and I know it's not always possible to put your finger on why it doesn't. But she could have shown a bit more sensitivity. You're not some commercial letting agent, and this isn't just any old flat. It's been – it still is – part of your life.'

Marjorie lowered her head. 'Yes.'

By now, Heather had disappeared into the shadows. Marjorie drew the curtains together, switched on the wall lights and the standard lamp and turned off the overhead light. She felt a thrill of excitement, quickly followed by alarm. Ought she to have done that with the curtains, the lights? Wasn't she jumping the gun by assuming that he would stay?

She said, 'Would you like some tea?' If he said no, she would have to pretend that she had been planning to spend the evening here in any event.

'That would be lovely,' he said.

She went to the kitchen. He followed her, offering to help. 'I *think* I can manage,' she joked. 'But you can talk to me while I do.' She waved at her father's breakfast chair and he sat down in it.

'What did your parents retire from? If you don't mind me asking.'

'I don't mind at all. They were in the hotel business. Started out with a guest house in Portsmouth just after the war. Gleneagles Lodge, it was called.' She smiled. 'Rather a grandiose name, I'm afraid – it was mainly just navy people, and travelling salesmen.'

'Not grandiose at all,' he replied. 'Great oaks, little acorns, and all that.'

'I don't know about great oaks, but by the time I'd grown up, they had quite a little chain going – a hotel in Lymington, a larger one at Shanklin on the Isle of Wight, and the Gleneagles had doubled in size. They worked for it, mind you.'

'I don't doubt it. And you as well, I expect.'

'I was at school most of the time.'

'Even so, I expect you had to pull your weight. You and your brothers and sisters.'

'I was an only child.'

He looked at her. 'You sounded very sad when you say that.'

'Did I?' She felt self-conscious and made a special effort to perk up. She made the tea and picked up the tray. He took it from her and carried it into the sitting room. She tried to remember whether, as a child, she had minded being the only one. Perhaps when she first went off to boarding school she would have liked to have had a big sister to show her the ropes. But in the holidays, she had enjoyed having her parents to herself – what little was left over from their work. Later, when Daddy died and Mummy became ill, she might have wished for someone to share the worry and the sadness. She poured the tea. Boniface was saying, 'Didn't you want to take over from your parents?'

'Good gracious, no. I have no head for business.'

'But you must have picked up a lot.'

'I helped out in the holidays,' she said. 'Some of it stuck. I can clean a room with the best of them, and when it comes to folding table napkins into the shape of a peacock, there's nobody to touch me. But the management side, the high finance – all that was way above my head.'

'How about Robert?'

'He's worse. Can't even keep track of his bank account. I'm chancellor of the exchequer in our household.' Boniface was watching her over the rim of his tea-cup. Their eyes met. Quickly she went back to talking about Robert. 'He's only ever wanted to teach.'

'Where does he teach?'

'He's head of English at St Aelfrid's in Hastings. You probably won't have heard of it.'

'Heard of it?' said Boniface. 'We used to play them at cricket. And a right old pasting they used to give us, from what I remember.'

She felt a proprietorial pleasure. 'They do rather pride themselves on their sport.'

'Would you think me very greedy if I asked for another cup of your delicious tea?'

'Of course,' she said, pouring it.

'You were telling me about your parents.'

'Where was I? Ah, yes. Well, they were getting on in years, a Canadian firm made them an offer and they decided to accept it. Let someone else have the headaches, was their attitude. They owed themselves a few years of doing their own thing . . .'

'In this lovely flat,' Boniface said softly.

She smiled. 'People thought they were mad, retiring to London. Their friends all talked about living at the seaside. But Mummy and Daddy had had enough seaside to last a lifetime.'

'I can believe it.'

'They wanted bright lights and shops and galleries, and a chance to see all the theatre shows they'd missed. Mummy was passionate about the theatre. "Imagine," she used to say, "going to the theatre six nights a week, each time to a different show." And when she discovered there were lunchtime theatres as well, she thought she'd died and gone to heav– oh, dear.' Hot tears rolled down Marjorie's cheeks.

Boniface walked over to her and gave her a clean white handkerchief. She sobbed into it. It was warm from having been in his pocket, close to his body. He returned to his seat and waited.

He said quietly, 'Your mother sounds like a super person. Both your parents do.'

'Oh, they were.'

'I'm sorry I never met them.'

Marjorie was sorry too. Her moment of weepiness had passed, and she enjoyed imagining how her mother would have fallen for Boniface's charm and good looks. Her father would have liked him too, though it would have been a while before he admitted it. He would have huffed and puffed behind Boniface's back about nancy boys who spent their days moving pieces of paper round desks, rather than rolling up their sleeves and doing an honest job of work.

'What will you do?' Boniface asked. 'Look for another tenant?'

'I don't know. I've been a bit lazy about it. I suppose that would be the sensible thing. The rates and the service charges are fairly steep. I can't seem to make up my mind yet about whether to sell it or not.'

He said, 'You'll probably get a better price if you wait.'

'That's what the accountant says, but . . .' she couldn't finish the sentence.

'But there's more to it than that.'

'Yes.'

'May I guess what it is?'

Marjorie nodded. She didn't think there was much chance of Boniface understanding the complicated feelings she had about the flat; she didn't fully understand them herself; but it was nice of him to try.

'Does it seem like a sort of betrayal?' he asked. 'To get rid of the place where your parents were so happy?'

'You've got an old head on young shoulders, Boniface.'

He shrugged. 'My mother was the same when my father died in Singapore. The obvious thing was for her to come home, but she said it would be like walking out on him.'

'What did she do?'

'She came home eventually. Settled in Cambridge, near one of my brothers.'

'Do you see her often?'

'When I can.'

'Do you think she regrets coming home?'

'No more than she regrets anything else.'

Marjorie smiled. 'I don't suppose she regrets having had *you*.'

'Not a lot she can do about it if she does. But look here, I wasn't intending to inflict my life story on you, or start probing into yours. All I meant was – at the risk of sounding like someone on "Thought For The Day" – go easy on yourself. You've had a bereavement. Two. You're not over them yet.' He looked at her with concern. Tears burned the backs of her eyes at the realization that he knew how she felt. He knew better than Robert, better than the girls. How could Robert or the girls know? All three of them had both parents still living.

Boniface said gently, 'Don't rush to make a decision. About the flat, or your parents' estate generally. There'll be no shortage of people offering you bright ideas – some brighter than others. Listen to them by all means, but don't lose sight of the fact that it's none of their damn business. It's up to you – you and Robert – to decide.'

She said cheerfully, 'Robert won't be any help.'

'Oh?'

'He'll say it's my inheritance and it's up to me what I do with it.'

'Is that what he says?'

'We haven't really discussed it,' she said. 'But that was his attitude with the house.'

'Your house, you mean?'

'Mummy and Daddy bought it for us. They put it in my name. At the time I was quite annoyed with them. They seemed to be saying that Robert was good enough to marry me, but not good enough to be trusted with a half-share in our home. They said it wasn't that. They said they couldn't have wanted a better son-in-law, but you never know what can happen. Robert took their side. He said if he had daughters he would do the same thing, because there are some scoundrels about.'

31

Lloyd's of London. How grand it sounded.

Much of his explanation went over her head. That didn't matter. He could tell her more at a future date. There would have to be future dates, wouldn't there, if she became involved with Lloyd's of London?

He looked at his watch. It was gone six. 'Good Lord, have I really been haranguing you all this time? You must be bored to death.' He stood up.

'Not at all.' She stood with him and picked up the tea-tray. 'Supposing I was interested. What would be the next step?'

He took the tray from her and carried it into the kitchen. 'I'd introduce you to a colleague of mine.'

She frowned. That wasn't what she wanted. 'Who would that be?'

'Chap called Tim Kenilworth. Works for a members' agency called Kenilworth Snell.'

'And what's the difference between him and you?' *Apart from all the difference in the world*, she thought.

'All the difference in the world. We write the business, Kenilworth and his cronies watch over us on your behalf and make sure we're writing it properly. Make sure we haven't got too many lines on fireworks factories built next door to oil refineries, or Liberian-registered tankers with holes in the side. If they don't like what we're doing, they'll take you away from us and put you with someone more prudent. On the other hand, if we're too cautious and end up not making you any money, they won't like that either. It's their job to see to it that you get a nice fat cheque at the end of the year. If you don't, they don't. That's roughly it. Tim can explain better than I can. He'll give you a damn good lunch as well.'

'I don't know that I want to take up Mr Kenilworth's time at this stage.'

'You wouldn't be taking up his time,' said Boniface. 'That's how he spends his time – taking charming ladies out to lunch. And charming men too, of course, but like most of us he prefers the ladies. Can I help you wash this lot up?'

'No, really. I can manage.'

'Can I get you a taxi, then?'

'No, I've got a few little jobs that I need to do here. But don't let me keep you, I'm sure you've got things to do.' *Like telling Heather off for being so rude to me*, she thought with satisfaction.

Two days later a large parchment envelope arrived in the post at The Old Coach House, addressed to her. Robert picked it up. 'What's Kenilworth Snell? Cruises to the Caribbean for the over-fifties?'

'Something like that.'

She waited until she was alone and opened the envelope.

My dear Mrs Fairfax,

My colleague Boniface Bennett tells me that you have very kindly agreed to allow me to write to you, sending you introductory information regarding underwriting membership of Lloyd's.

I hope that the enclosed materials will be of interest to you. Do please take your time over reading them, and show them to your professional advisors, if you wish. If you would like to take the matter further, I will be very happy to hear from you, and to arrange a meeting over lunch.

Kind regards,

Yours sincerely,

Tim Kenilworth.

She eyed the signature with distaste. She didn't like Tim Kenilworth. She started to thumb through the brochures. Two were syndicate reports – pages of figures which meant nothing to her. The other brochure looked more interesting. At least it had pictures. It was more like a museum catalogue, or the guide book to a stately home.

Lloyd's of London, 300 Years of Excellence. An old woodcut showed men in wigs sitting round a table, drinking from tiny, steaming cups. Through a window behind the men, old-fashioned sailing ships were tacking to and fro across the Port of London. Silhouettes of the Tower and Tower Bridge could be made out.

The text explained that this was the origin of Lloyd's: a seventeenth-century coffee house where merchants, financiers and seafarers met to make private arrangements to insure their vessels and cargoes. These days, Lloyd's provided insurance for a great deal more than ships; but present-day names remained the proud inheritors of the traditions of the men in the coffee house.

She sipped her own coffee from her Oxfam mug and turned the page to a facsimile of a medieval legal document.

'By means of which Policies of Assurance,' it read, 'it comethe to passe, upon losse or perishinge of any Shippe, there followethe not the undoinge of any Man, but the losse lightethe rather easilie upon the many, than heavilie upon fewe.'

Marjorie thought how beautifully that was put. It was like something out of Shakespeare. It made her want to cry.

32

Tim Kenilworth was a brisk, efficient host and an excruciatingly boring conversationalist. He covered much of the same ground as Boniface had, but whereas Boniface had brought his subject to life, Tim Kenilworth killed it stone dead.

Boniface's words had had a tang of salt to them – salt and glory. He had evoked a past when Britannia had ruled the waves and taught the world a thing or two about how to set up financial institutions. He had made it seem entirely credible that part of the heritage of that time was a secure and comfortable financial future for Marjorie Fairfax and family. Tim Kenilworth, on the other hand, chuntered on about tax years and accounting periods, premium limits and unlimited liability, marine syndicates, non-marine syndicates, and concessions from the Inland Revenue.

He insisted on showing her round the Lloyd's building, a low-slung, colourless structure which from the outside looked like a grey ship dry-docked in the heart of the City. Inside, it was more ecclesiastical than nautical, with marble floors and stained glass windows. 'This is the Room,' said Tim Kenilworth, as if the Lloyd's underwriting room were the only room in the world. To Marjorie's eyes it was a dreary place, huge as a railway terminus but lacking its air of purpose. Hundreds of men and a few women sauntered between clusters of desks with bits of paper in their hands.

She endured it all with fortitude and politeness, and escaped at around three, hurrying towards the main business of the day: tea with Boniface.

It was a matter of great frustration to her, the way she could only see him by sitting through lunch with someone else. She had phoned him to ask if she could see him before seeing Tim

Kenilworth, so that he could brief her on what would be the right questions to ask. Boniface had been reluctant; it wasn't the done thing, he said, for one chap to nobble another chap's names. Marjorie had said she understood that, but it hardly applied in this case, since it was Boniface who had introduced her to Tim Kenilworth in the first place.

'True.' Boniface had thought it over. 'Tell you what. Fix up your date with Tim, then give me a call and tell me when it's to be. If you're not in too much of a rush to get home afterwards, you could pop round to my office in Cotton Square for a cup of tea and a debriefing.'

It was a cold, cloudy afternoon. Snow, forecast for later in the week, looked as if it was coming early. She consulted her *A–Z*. The Lloyd's hinterland was a maze of little streets and squares with odd, mercantile names. They all seemed to have subtly altered their location and relationship to each other since the map was printed.

She spotted a sign – 'Cotton Lane, leading to Cotton Square'. Cotton Lane was narrow and cobbled, like something out of Dickens. At the far end was a locked-up Victorian church with a notice advertising lunchtime concerts from last August. Next to the church was a terrace of houses converted into offices.

She found the one she wanted. The front door was not locked. She climbed the carpeted stairs to a reception area where she was greeted by a Sloane Rangery type of girl with silky hair, a smile to match and a skirt so short that Marjorie wondered why she bothered to put it on.

'I have an appointment to see Mr Bennett.'

The smile faltered. 'Boniface Bennett?'

'Yes.'

The girl looked embarrassed. 'What name is it, please?'

'Marjorie Fairfax.'

'I'm afraid he's not here, Mrs Fairfax.'

'But I have an appointment.'

'May I ask what it was in connection with?'

'It's a personal matter.'

The girl seemed relieved that Marjorie was nobody important. 'Boniface doesn't work here any more.'

Marjorie stared. 'Since when?'

'Since yesterday.'

'So where is he working now?'

The girl shrugged. 'Nowhere, as far as I know.' Her manner
was most unfortunate, Marjorie thought: offhand to the point
of rudeness. Someone ought to have a word with her about
the way she communicated with visitors to the office. She could
give quite the wrong impression. To hear her, anyone might
think that Boniface had been sacked.

She said dismissively, 'I'll contact him at home.'

'Good idea,' said the girl. 'Tell him everybody sends their
love.'

Marjorie left the building. Something was wrong. She hailed
a taxi. It stopped and backed towards her. She brought out
her address book and looked up Boniface's address. She
remembered obtaining it from Jake Verlaine shortly after
Christmas so that she could write to Boniface, thanking him
for the flowers. What a stroke of luck that was. Without it she
would be unable to go to him now when he needed her.

The taxi crawled eastwards through thickening traffic. Everyone seemed to be trying to get out of town before the snow
started. Robert would be back from school soon, making
himself a cup of tea and turning the central heating up. She
was moving further and further away from home.

Why had Boniface lost his job? Why hadn't he told her? Had
he eaten since it happened, or had he been too upset? She would
offer to cook him a meal. She still hadn't cooked for him. She
tapped on the driver's window and asked him to stop at a shop
where she could buy provisions. 'A supermarket,' she said. 'Or
a corner store.'

He seemed amused. 'You'll be lucky, love. They haven't got round to shops yet.'

She could see that they hadn't. The main road seemed to be passing through acres of building site. Cranes swayed in the wind. Earth-movers and heaps of rubble lurked in the shadows alongside brand new, half-lit office blocks, and ancient ware-houses transformed into flats. In the dark gaps between the buildings, the river glittered. The driver stopped outside one of the warehouses. She paid him and he drove away.

The red brick building was part of a stylish, expensive-looking complex. A sign pointed the way to a swimming pool and leisure centre. An estate agent's board proclaimed that three units of phase three remained for sale; phases one and two had sold out. She approached the bank of doorbells and pressed one.

A voice barked, 'Yes?'

'Boniface, it's me, Marjorie Fairfax.'

'*Marjorie?*' He sounded neither pleased nor displeased; merely incredulous.

'You weren't at your office . . .' She heard reproach in her tone and stopped.

'Come on up.' The doorbell buzzed. 'Fourth floor.'

She stepped into the paint-smelling lobby. A decorator's ladder leaned against the wall, with overalls draped across the top step. She entered the lift and pressed 4. The lift went up, then stopped. She got out. Before her were three identical front doors made of new, unvarnished wood. There were no numbers. She felt like a character in a legend who has to choose between three doors or paths or jewelled caskets: two of them would lead to destruction, one would give her her heart's desire.

33

The middle door opened. He wore a dressing gown and smelt of whisky. He didn't smile, but stood aside for her to enter the flat. It was over-warm, open-plan and untidy. Newspapers and dirty crockery littered the floor; the sink was full of dishes. The television was blaring out rubbish.

'Butler's day off,' he said.

'Don't worry,' she replied.

'Shall I take your coat?'

'I'm not staying.'

'You haven't been invited.'

She considered walking out, but decided that that would be to attach too much importance to what was really only a minor piece of rudeness, and quite understandable in the circumstances.

She said, 'I came to say how sorry I was to hear about you losing your job.'

He glared. 'How did you know about that?'

'They told me at your office.'

'What were *you* doing *there*?'

'We had a date, Boniface.'

He looked bewildered.

'An appointment,' she corrected herself. 'For tea. After my lunch with your Mr Kenilworth.'

He rolled his eyes. 'Hell's teeth. Forgot all about it.'

'Don't worry.'

'I do worry. Whenever our paths cross, I seem to end up behaving like an oaf. Do please take your coat off and sit down.' He hung her coat on a hook. She would have preferred a hanger, but made no comment. He turned off the television and gathered up his dirty plates. He closed the curtains, blocking out the raw, gloomy evening. He adjusted the lighting to a gentler glow. She started to pick up newspapers, but he said, 'Leave them.' She realized that they were all open at the Situations Vacant pages.

'When did this happen, if you don't mind me asking?'

'Yesterday,' said Boniface. 'So yes, I could have let you know.'

'Was it completely unexpected?'

Boniface said, 'D'you fancy some tea?'

'If it's no trouble.'

'I was thinking I might trouble *you* to make it, while I put some clothes on.' He went to the bathroom and closed the door. She boiled a kettle and washed the dishes in the sink. She was relieved to find that there was only one of everything. Two would have suggested Heather's presence. Why should she do Heather's washing-up?

He came out of the bathroom, having shaved and washed, and wearing clean grey slacks, a fawn sweater and slippers with no socks. 'That's better,' he said. 'I was a pretty revolting sight before, wasn't I?'

'Yes,' she said playfully. She gave him his tea and said in a bright voice, 'So how is Heather these days?'

He muttered into his cup: 'No idea.'

'But I thought . . .'

'Didn't you know she's given me the old heave-ho as well? It's getting to be a trend.'

She wondered why he would expect her to know. Did he imagine that she and Heather were confidantes? 'I'm sorry to hear it.'

'I don't know why I bothered with her. I ought to have known I was playing outside my league.' Marjorie thought that if anyone was playing outside their league it was Heather. 'How can I compete,' Boniface was saying, 'with a Trotskyite lawyer with his hair in a pony-tail?'

'I don't think you should try.'

'I did try. I lost.'

'Perhaps she'll change her mind,' Marjorie suggested.

'Perhaps pigs will fly.'

'Did you have a quarrel, or –'

'Look, first he saves her from being evicted. Then it turns out he's read all the books she's read. I mean, where does that leave me? Nowhere. No fucking where. No job and no woman.'

Marjorie's throat was tight. When she spoke, her voice was a whisper. 'Was there a connection?'

'Between what and what?'

'Between you losing your job and breaking up with Heather?'

'What sort of connection?'

I don't know, she thought. *Why ask me? I'm asking you. I'm talking to you. I'm trying to get you to talk to me.* 'I meant . . .' she tried to think of what she could have meant. 'Were you thinking about her, and did that perhaps lead you to make a mistake, or speak – I won't say rudely, but perhaps a bit sharply – to someone you shouldn't –' *The way you sometimes speak to me.* 'Perhaps if you explained the circumstances to your boss . . .'

Boniface picked up the whisky bottle and waved it at her with an inviting expression. She shook her head. He poured himself a large one. 'You're half right, Marjorie, but only half. I *was* pretty cut up about Heather, and it didn't do much for my efficiency. I made a cock-up of an excess-of-loss calculation. It's quite important to get all the noughts and decimal points in the right places. I didn't, and it all had rather an unfortunate effect on the bottom line.'

'But did you *explain*?'

'"Sorry I nearly lost the syndicate a million quid, sir; my girlfriend dumped me"? No, I didn't think to say that. I was given a right bollocking by the boss, during which he saw fit to point out that this wasn't the first time he'd noticed that maths weren't my forte. "Pocket calculators are wonderful things, Bennett. A boon to mankind. But traditionalists like me still think there's a lot to be said for underwriters who can count beyond ten without taking their socks off." Sarcastic bugger. Should have been a school teacher. Er – no offence to your husband, Marjorie.'

'None taken.'

'So I took the much-maligned calculator out of the aforesaid pocket, shoved it at him across the desk and suggested where he might like to put it.'

'Oh, dear.'

'"Oh dear" indeed,' he mocked.

She knew she ought to go home, but she hadn't drunk her tea. It was still too hot. It seemed to be taking a long time to get cool enough to drink. She hoped he didn't think that she had made it extra hot on purpose, in order to spin out her time with him.

She put down her tea-cup, walked across to where he was sitting and sat down next to him. She put her arms round him and kissed his mouth.

He let her do it. She felt relieved and euphoric. She was doing this outrageous thing, but he was not angry with her. He was not repelled.

She moved her mouth on his mouth. His arms went around her. His hands moved down her back towards her buttocks. He squeezed them tight. She wondered if he could feel the bulge where her pantie girdle ended and her thigh began. He was forcing the lower part of her body towards him. His groin was hard. She was making that happen.

Her exhilaration didn't last. It was taken away by the advance of his tongue which pushed rudely past hers and on towards her throat. She coughed. He took back his tongue, grasped her shoulders and held her away from him. He looked as if he were about to give her a good shaking. 'Marjorie. What are we doing?'

'Don't you know?' She sounded coquettish, although

coquettish was not a word she would have associated with herself.

'Are you sure?'

She nodded and handed herself over to him. He put his hand up her skirt and pulled down her tights, then struggled with her pantie girdle. Firm Control, it had said on the box, but Boniface was equal to it. Anyone would think he had struggled with a Firm Control girdle before. He was rougher than she would have liked, but she enjoyed the excitement, the novelty and her sense of power. As he entered her, she remembered how glum and lethargic he had been when she arrived at the flat. Now he was enthusiastic. She had revived him.

34

He rolled off her and looked at her. 'Well, Marjorie. That was rather . . .'

She waited humbly to hear what word he would use.

'. . . unexpected.'

'I'm sorry.'

'What on earth for?'

'Coming round here like this, and . . .'

'Seducing me? No need to apologize. I wish it happened more often.'

'I ought to be going,' she said.

'Ought you?' He moved to let her stand up. He pulled his trousers on.

'Robert will be wondering where I am.'

He made no comment on Robert. 'I'd offer you a lift,' he said, 'but I'm in no fit state.' He nodded at his whisky glass.

'Of course.' She headed for the bathroom. 'But if you would be kind enough to call me a taxi . . .' She bent down to pick up her jacket. As she straightened, her breasts made a soft slapping sound against her spare tyre. She didn't care. *He* hadn't minded their pendulousness, so why should she? He hadn't minded her stretch-marks either, or her darkened nipples, or the way her greying pubic hairs encroached down the insides of her thighs. He wished it happened more often.

From the bathroom, she heard him phoning. 'Victoria station. One passenger, Mrs Fairfax. As soon as you like.' She heaved herself into her pantie girdle.

When she was dressed, he escorted her downstairs and out into the cold night. A light snow was falling. A flake stung her eye. He opened the door of the taxi, pressed his lips to her hand and waved her off.

She sat back. Between her legs, she was wet and warm and pleasantly sore. The taxi made its way westwards at a cautious pace. The snow was getting heavier. At the same time, it couldn't seem to make up its mind whether to settle or not. There were thick white drifts on one side of the road, melting grey puddles on the other. She tapped the driver's window and asked him to take her to Cheyne Walk.

The taxi reached its destination. Marjorie got out and paid. She opened the garden gate and walked towards the block. She had only ever been here as an adult, but now she felt like a teenager whose parents would insist on knowing what she had been up to. She went up in the lift and entered the flat. The central heating thermostat was on low and the air was chilly. She turned the heating up and switched on the lights. The phone began to ring.

She smiled. Boniface had guessed her change of plan, known intuitively where she would come. They were that much in tune.

'There you are,' said Robert.

'Oh. Hello, darling.'

'I've been worried. It's blowing a blizzard down here. I met three trains and you weren't on any of them.'

'I'm all right,' she said.

'Where have you *been*?'

Her jaw went up and down like a fish's jaw, but nothing came out. She had to say something, but what? In the nick of time, a memory came to her, of a jokey article she had read in a magazine, on the theme of how to have an adulterous affair without your partner finding out. Tell the truth as often as possible, was the advice; save lying for emergencies.

'I was at Boniface's.'

'Is that that poncey bistro on the King's Road?'

'Boniface *Bennett*, darling. You remember. Olivia's toy boy.'

'What on earth were you doing with him?' Robert asked.

She said amusingly, 'Wouldn't you like to know?'

'I don't know whether I would or not.'

'He wasn't at his office so I popped round to his flat,' she explained. 'We got snowed in.'

'But you're not snowed in now?'

'No, it stopped, but I didn't want to risk the trains, so I thought I'd bed down here.'

'You might have let me know,' he grumbled.

'I'm letting you know now. How has your day been?'

Luckily he had some good news which he was keen to share with her: a colleague had approached him about contributing a chapter to a teacher-training textbook entitled *Comprehension and Communication in the Classroom*. They talked about that for a while, then said goodnight.

She ran a bath and took off her clothes. She squatted down and splashed water between her legs and her labia. She told herself that she had nothing to worry about. She washed herself out again, then lay down for a long soak. Still the anxiety gnawed at her. It wasn't unheard of. Next time she would wear her Dutch cap – if she could still find it. If not, she would go to the Family Planning and get another. They would be surprised to see her. Never mind next time – what if the damage had been done this time? Or was being done now as she thought about it? Her mother used to have a douche bag. Was it still here somewhere? Could she find it? Could she use it? Would she be able to bring herself to try? She got out of the bath and padded around the flat, leaving wet footprints on the carpets, opening drawers, but her dead mother's douche bag was nowhere to be found.

35

She woke up at about eight with the sun shining in her face. The snow had gone, but, beyond the window, a row of silver icicles hung melting from the gutter. The garden was crisp with frost, golden and purple with early crocuses. Sunlight sparkled on the river.

She got out of bed and dialled his number. 'It's me, Marjorie.'

'Oh, Lord.'

She said lightly, '*That's* not very flattering.'

'Now you know I didn't mean it like that.' He didn't say how he had meant it.

'I didn't go home last night.' Her voice sounded husky. It wasn't put on, it came out that way.

'You didn't?'

'I'm at Cheyne Walk.'

'Well.'

'Just a few miles away.'

'Yes.'

'And I was wondering if you'd like to meet me for breakfast.'

After a short pause, he said, 'That sounds like a lot of fun, Marjorie. I can't think of anything I'd rather do. But I've got this damned interview to go to this morning.'

'You didn't say anything yesterday about an interview,' she said.

'Didn't want to talk about it. Makes me nervous.'

'I'm sure you have no need to be. How about lunch afterwards?'

'Sounds fabulous, but the interview goes on all day. It's an American bank, so of course it'll be all psychometric testing —'

'What sort of testing?'

'Oh, you know. What do you make of this ink-blot, and did you have a traumatic experience at the age of four?'

Had he? She wanted to know all about it so that she could comfort it away. 'This evening, then?' She would tell Robert that the central heating had gone on the blink and she had to wait in for the engineers. 'Come for a drink around six.'

'I wish I could,' said Boniface. 'But I haven't got a moment to call my own this week. Or next. Finding a job is a job in itself.'

She got dressed, took a taxi to Harvey Nichols, and browsed among the lingerie. A saleswoman asked if she could help her. She looked as if she were eating a lemon.

'I'm just looking,' said Marjorie, wondering what would happen to the lemon if the woman knew *why* she was looking.

She selected a long, silver-grey nightdress with a matching silk negligee. The assistant asked if she wanted to try them on, but she hadn't the nerve so she said, 'No, I'll take them now.' She got out her card, then stopped. Another piece of advice in that article had been, *always pay cash*. Funny how it all came back to her.

She said, 'I'll be back,' and fled. That was the last time she would ever be able to shop at Harvey Nick's.

She took cash out of a cashpoint machine and went to Harrods instead, where she bought another, similar, nightie and some high-heeled, furry slippers. She went to Bedding and Linens and bought silk sheets, pillowcases and towels. She moved on to Bathroom Accessories and stocked up on soaps, men's and women's fragrances and bath oil. Her final destination was the Food Hall. She chose chocolates and other non-perishable luxury foods: game soup, rich fruit cake, mangoes in Grenadine, water biscuits, Gentlemen's Relish, a Stilton in a pottery jar and vacuum-sealed caviar. She bought wines, and a bottle of brandy, and took a taxi back to Cheyne Walk.

She was aware of her parents' disapproval as she furnished her love nest in their home, but it meant nothing to her. They had lived in a different world. She stripped naked and tried on the nightie and the negligee. She paraded from room to room, from mirror to mirror. She tried out various poses. She wished she could assess herself objectively. Was the nightdress sexy or mumsy? Was it elegant, or was it mutton dressed up as lamb? She wished she knew more.

She would find out. He would teach her. *I wish it happened more often.* She wondered how he was getting on at his interview. He would probably phone tonight with the good news. She hoped she would be close to the phone when it rang, but it wouldn't matter if Robert took the call. Boniface would know exactly how to handle the situation – not because he was practised at having love affairs with married women, but because he had such beautiful manners.

She caught a late-afternoon train from Victoria and arrived back in Eastbourne in the early evening. In the station car park, she found a surcharge sticker on her windscreen. How petty the world was. She drove out towards the country road. Lights gleaming from Waitrose reminded her that she hadn't given a thought to supper. She could always take something out of the freezer, but . . . She stopped and bought fillet steak, new potatoes, Tunisian strawberries, and a bottle of Robert's favourite claret.

As she entered the kitchen, she smelled cooking: pork chops, she guessed, with some sort of sauce – one of his own concoctions with too many onions in it. She had told him before about putting too many onions into things. For a moment he didn't notice her. He had his old grey sweater on over his work clothes, and slippers, and was taking sips from a whisky and soda while he stirred his sauce. The radio was tuned to Radio Four for a programme about the government's education policies. A junior minister was holding forth. 'Bollocks,' said Robert.

The dogs dashed towards Marjorie, yelping with joy. Robert turned round. 'There you are, you dirty stopout.'

'I'm sorry, darling.'

'Not at all, not at all, nice of you to call round.'

She calmed the dogs. 'That smells nice.'

'Well, someone has to keep the troops fed, we can't all go gallivanting off to London every five minutes. How did you get on anyway? You didn't say.'

'I don't know, it's all a bit complicated.' She tasted the sauce. 'Onions?'

'One or two.'

'Any messages?'

'Olivia wants you to organize a garden party for one of her causes.'

'Which one?'

'Something she's patron of. National Organization of the Brain-dead, would it be? She's putting the bumpf in the post. And Di rang. She didn't sound too chipper.'

Marjorie gritted her teeth. Di never sounded chipper, particularly when talking to her father, who could be relied on for sympathy long after Marjorie's ran out. 'She'd like you to phone her,' said Robert. 'I think she needs a mother–daughter chat.'

Marjorie went to the downstairs loo. Of course Boniface hadn't phoned yet. She wouldn't have expected him to. He had probably gone for a celebratory drink with his new employers. He would phone later this evening. She washed her hands and combed her hair. She didn't look as if she had been up to what she had been up to. She looked like a cross housewife. She was entitled to be cross. She had just got back from the biggest adventure of her life, and what did she find waiting for her? Orders from Olivia and a sauce with too many onions in it from Robert. And emotional demands from Di. All right, post-natal depression was a nasty thing to have – if it really was post-natal depression. Marjorie sometimes suspected that Di's woes came from nothing more complicated than the discovery that new babies generated a lot of work. Did it never occur to Di that a mother–daughter chat ought to be a two-way thing? Sometimes it might be the mother who had something to confide – something that would turn the daughter's eyes into saucers and have her gasp in tones of shocked admiration, *Mummy! You didn't!*

36

The following day, she was due to work a morning shift at the charity shop in Eastbourne – ChildPeril, it was called, a name which had irritated Marjorie ever since it was introduced four years ago. The old name – the National and Colonial Association for Aid to the Children of the Destitute – may have had a somewhat old-fashioned ring, but at least it meant something and kept its capital letters in the right places rather than sticking them in the middle of made-up words.

Her starting time was 9.30, and her normal routine was to leave the house at around nine, having seen Robert off to work and cleared away the breakfast things. But this morning, her chores seemed to be taking longer than usual. Nine o'clock became 9.15, 9.20, 9.25, and still she did not go out.

She was waiting for the phone to ring. She was sure that it was just about to. She knew how Boniface's mind worked. He would be awake by now, and rested after last night's celebrations. He could be confident that Robert would be out of the house. Now was the perfect time.

So why didn't he ring? It was most annoying. Did he think she had nothing better to do than wait around for his call? She picked up the receiver and started to dial the number of the shop to explain that she had been delayed. A family matter, she would say. No one would inquire further. Everyone knew her circumstances, and how much there was to do after a death.

The phone rang and rang. She drummed her fingers; all this time while she was not getting through to ChildPeril, Boniface was not getting through to her. He might give up, resolving to call later. Which would be fine if she knew about it, but how could she know? It would be ChildPeril's own fault if she didn't go in today.

The phone clicked. A young man answered. Her heart flipped over, even though she knew who it was: one of the regional fund-raising managers who toured the ChildPeril shops to check the accounts and issue the latest edicts from head office about how the goods were to be arranged on the shelves and the precise wording on the price tickets.

Marjorie stammered out her apologies. The young man listened without comment, then said, 'When can we expect you?' Marjorie had no answer. She hadn't thought it through that far. She said, 'I'll be in as soon as I can.' The young man said, 'Thank you for letting us know.' He wasn't actually rude, but he managed to give the impression that he had had it up to here with unreliable volunteers.

She put the phone down. It gave a little tinkle, which for one sweet moment she believed was the beginning of a proper ring. But silence followed. What did they expect, for goodness' sake? Volunteers were human beings with human problems. Anyone could have a domestic crisis. If only Boniface would phone now, she would tell him about the brusque young man. This, she would say, was the way things were going in the charity world. He might not know much about the charity world; it would be something *she* could inform *him* about instead of it always being the other way round. It would be nice to have something to talk to him about that wasn't to do with their relationship. It would reassure him that she wasn't going to be demanding or clingy or neurotic. She was too happy to have his love to want to go on and on about it, dissecting it, digging it up to see if it was growing.

She busied herself with household tasks and tried to think of something other than the silent phone. The dogs were having a pretend fight on the stairs, snarling theatrically and flashing their teeth. She remembered Boniface's teeth, how white and even they were. She remembered how they had felt on her tongue during that first kiss, so strong and young. Did teeth feel young? Could you tell? Could you guess a person's age from the feel of their teeth on your tongue? The question was absurd. Touching someone's teeth with your tongue was an intimate act. You wouldn't do it to someone whose age you didn't know.

She had nearly lost one of her own teeth last year, because of an abscess. Her dentist had drained the abscess and saved the tooth. Next time, she might not be so lucky. Both her parents had had false teeth when they died. The day would come when she too would lose her last tooth – unless she died first. In either case, she would never again know the feel of living ivory. She felt oppressed by a presentiment of death, her own and everybody else's.

What if Boniface had had an accident? It could happen. How would she find out? Casually from Olivia, weeks later? *Oh, by the way, Marje. I've been meaning to tell you. Remember Jake's godson? Frightful business. We were at the funeral yesterday.*

The phone rang. She rushed to it.

'Mummy, it's Di.'

'Hello, darling. How are you?'

'Oh, you know,' said Di. 'Up and down.'

And down now, from the sound of things. Marjorie waited.

Di said accusingly, 'Didn't Daddy tell you I phoned last night?'

'Um, he might have.'

'Well, I wish you'd called back.'

'I'm sorry. It slipped my mind.'

'Because I need to talk to you.'

'Shall I phone you back this evening?'

'I need to talk to you *now*,' said Di. 'I wanted to ask if it's all right for Tony to stay in Granny's flat for a couple of nights.'

Marjorie froze. 'When?'

'Tonight, actually.'

'*Tonight*?'

'I did try to ask you yesterday,' Di pointed out.

'I know, dear.'

'Tony's got a couple of job interviews, and it seems silly to waste money on a hotel.'

'Yes, I suppose it –'

'When you didn't call back, I sort of assumed it would be okay and told him to go ahead, but then I thought I'd better just check that you haven't got Caroline in there giving one of her parties.'

'That was a special occasion.'

'So is this. It is okay, isn't it?'

Save lying for emergencies. Was this an emergency? Marjorie moistened her lips. 'Tony's very welcome to stay there if he needs to, but I need a bit more notice. How am I going to get a key to him?'

'Not a problem,' said Di. 'I've given him mine.'

'*Yours?*'

'Granny lent it to me.'

Somehow, Marjorie got off the phone. She grabbed her coat, dashed out to the car and drove like a bat out of hell up the A22. She reached Chelsea before her son-in-law did, and so was able to remove the evidence.

After that, she drove slowly round the streets of west London, her car loaded with lingerie and linens and luxury foodstuffs, wondering what to do with it all.

At first she thought she would simply hide everything in a left-luggage locker somewhere and put it back when Tony had gone. But what if he came back? What if somebody else turned up? How many other spare keys had her mother distributed amongst family and friends?

She could always change the locks, but . . . Marjorie went cold, as if someone had dropped an icicle down her spine. In that moment she knew that there was no need for her to change the locks or find a home for the accessories of her love affair, because she had no love affair. What had happened between her and Boniface was not a love affair, and it was not going to happen again.

The pain of this knowledge took her breath away: she had to stop the car. She closed her eyes and wept. The tears relaxed her and made her realize how foolish she was being. Of course she had not lost him. Hadn't he said *I wish it happened more often*? He was probably trying to reach her now.

37

How To Stop Thinking About Him – When He's All You Can Think About.

She was waiting at the hairdresser's when the headline caught her eye. Listlessly, she picked up the magazine and flicked through its pages.

It's over. The last harsh words have been said and you've gone your separate ways.

Or perhaps it wasn't an acrimonious break-up. You sat down together, talked things through and agreed that it was time to part. You've shared out the record collection and made amicable arrangements for custody of the cat.

Now comes the difficult bit – getting used to being without him.

It took months, or perhaps years to get into this relationship. Hopefully it won't take quite as long for you to ease yourself out and become your old self, ready to start dating again and enjoying life.

Our Nine-Point 'Forget Him' Action Plan will help you make the process as fast and painless as possible.

A shampooist was advancing on Marjorie with a smile and a cape. Marjorie assumed an expression of absentmindedness and slipped the magazine into her bag, before allowing herself to be led away. Soon she was leaning back over the basin with a folded towel under her neck. She tried to enjoy the sensations of the warm, scented water washing over her head while the girl's skilled fingers massaged her scalp. She tried to relax. But she had forgotten how to relax and enjoy things. She couldn't remember a time when she hadn't felt tense, bereft and guilty.

She was aware of the stolen magazine in her bag. Not that anyone would say anything. She was a regular customer, and it was an easy enough mistake to have made. But what if they guessed why she had been interested in the magazine in the first place?

They wouldn't guess. They would assume she had been looking for recipes or knitting patterns. Anyone could see that that article wasn't aimed at menopausal matrons with guilty secrets. It was for sensible youngsters with moral codes and stable relationships – people who owned cats together and built up record collections, which they then shared out after reasonable discussions.

Nik, her stylist, asked how she wanted her hair. She gave an answer that was both vague and precise. They both understood the ritual. Nik would decide how to do her hair, as he always decided. She would express satisfaction with the result, as she always expressed it. In the old days she used to mean it, but these days nothing could satisfy her – not food, not hair-dos, not charity work, not touching herself in the night while Robert slept at her side.

He was wiser than he knew, avoiding sex with her. She might be diseased. An item on *Woman's Hour* had been aimed straight at her. Nowadays it wasn't just homosexuals getting it, it could affect normal married couples too. The husband goes away on business, has a fling and there you are. They didn't say anything about wives going away on business and having flings.

She had no symptoms, but she drew no comfort from that, or from the impossibility of imagining Boniface doing any of the things that lead to infection. She didn't think he was infected, she only thought she was.

Robert was avoiding the risk. But he had been avoiding making love to her for longer than there had been any risk. It was two and a half years now. At first she had thought it was just a phase he was going through. There had been times in the past when they had both lost interest. It had always come back. This time only her interest had come back.

Was that why she had done it? Was that all it was? An

appetite needing to be satisfied? Was she like men who went to prostitutes, or who bought rubber dolls for themselves, with holes in them? Had Boniface sensed this and thought, *she only wants me for one thing*?

She didn't only want him for one thing. She wanted him for everything. She wanted to see him and talk to him, cook for him, go out with him, laugh with him, hold his hand. She wanted to listen to his troubles – even his girlfriend troubles. She didn't mind his girlfriends. Of course he had girlfriends. She didn't mind if he never made love to her again, as long as she could see him, be with him once in a while.

She paid for her hair-do, left the salon and hurried to the car. She felt anxious and guilty and light-headed, as if she were about to go on an eating binge. She opened the magazine.

Action Point One. Rearrange your life. It took on a particular shape and rhythm when you were together. Change that shape. Change that rhythm.

Do you still sleep in the bed where the two of you once made love? Burn it.

Are you living alone in the flat or house that you shared? Move.

Do you run into each other at work? Change jobs. Still have friends in common? Ditch them.

Sounds drastic? Well, we never said it would be easy.

It didn't sound drastic at all. She had already got rid of all the treats and luxuries that she had bought for her and Boniface to share in the flat. She had cut the linens to pieces amid a bout of weeping. She had poured the wine down the sink. She had taken the foodstuffs to a charity shop in a distant town. She couldn't bear waste. She had walked in, dumped the carrier bag on the counter and walked out again. She wondered what they thought. If such a thing were to happen at ChildPeril in Eastbourne, the speculation would continue for weeks.

Against all that, the thought of setting fire to the sofa where she and Boniface had made love was nothing.

She hated him. She would strap him to the sofa and watch him burn. Why did he treat her like this? Why had he said he wished it happened more often, if the truth was that he wished it hadn't happened in the first place, and he was determined never to let it happen again? He had moved out of his flat. There was no forwarding address. She knew because she had phoned and a strange man had answered. If he was a strange man, and not Boniface doing a different voice. She wouldn't put that past him. She wouldn't put anything past him in his campaign to belittle and humiliate her. Why did he bother? Did he not realize that she was already as deeply humiliated as it is possible for a woman to be?

Do you still have friends in common? Ditch them. Ditch Olivia? If only I could, Marjorie thought. Olivia got on her nerves at the best of times; seeing her these days was torture, and not just because of her blasted garden parties. She and Jake had known Boniface all his life, and must surely have his current address. What else did they know?

The Nine-Point 'Forget Him' Action Plan advocated enrolling in an evening class, joining a dating agency, or sponsoring a child in the Third World and counting your blessings.

If none of that did any good, perhaps you should consider counselling or psychotherapy.

Then again, you could splash out on a top-to-toe makeover and invest in a glamorous new outfit. After that, you could ring up all your old boyfriends and get them to take you out on a morale-boosting date.

Oh, there were hundreds of things you could do.

38

Rearrange your life, the article said. Marjorie's was rearranging itself whether she wanted it to or not.

Di was pregnant again. Marjorie guessed that it was an accident. It was happening at the worst possible time. Tony was being made redundant. That was why he had come to London for the interview. He hadn't got that job, but he and Di were still planning to move back down south. An old college friend who had a software business in Mortlake had offered Tony a partnership. Marjorie liked the idea of having her grandchildren living closer by, but the job situation sounded insecure and worrying.

She told Di and Tony that they would be welcome to bed down at Cheyne Walk while they were sorting out the sale of their Newcastle house. The offer was accepted with gratitude but a certain lack of surprise, making Marjorie wonder whether they had been assuming all along that this would happen.

She suggested that Di might like to drive down ahead of the move to sort out which of her grandmother's furniture she wanted moved out to make room for her own. Di said it would probably be simpler if it were all left *in situ*, and their own stuff stored; it wasn't as if they would be staying at Cheyne Walk for more than a few weeks, or months at most.

Marjorie drove up to Newcastle to assist with the move. It all helped to keep her mind off things. She believed that a time would come when she would no longer wake up in the morning with his face before her eyes, and spend the whole day on a rollercoaster of longing and bitterness, sadness and self-reproach. She had to believe that. In the meantime, each day had to be got through.

During the drive back down, Tony casually mentioned that

he and his partner were looking for new backers for their company. He casually mentioned this several times. Marjorie became so irritated at his devious hinting that she casually mentioned that probate had not yet been granted on her mother's estate, and it might be quite some time before it was.

It took until the autumn. Everything came to Marjorie, as she had known it would. What she had not realized until the solicitor started going into details was the size of the legacy. Marjorie had been expecting to inherit the flat and its contents, a few thousand pounds in savings, and the share portfolio that her father had built up over the years as a hobby. Some hobby. The shares, she now learned, were worth nearly £100,000. As if this were not enough, her mother had £47,000 in various building society accounts and £5,000 in premium bonds.

Marjorie stared at the documents. She felt sad, excited and bewildered. She didn't want all this money, she wanted her mother back, advising her what to do with the money. The money felt like a person to whom Marjorie had obligations. She must do right by it.

She wished her mother had placed some sort of restriction on the money, earmarking a certain proportion for the girls and the grandchildren, something else to be put aside for Marjorie and Robert's retirement; something for charity, something for a rainy day, and some fun money. Don't forget the fun money, she would have said.

'Be able to push the boat out at Christmas,' Robert said, his head bent over the proofs of his chapter for *Comprehension and Communication in the Classroom*.

'We always push the boat out at Christmas,' she replied.

'Course we do.' He did not look up from his work.

'Even last year.'

'Last year was great.'

'Great, was it?' Her voice was tense, quiet.

He looked at her. 'What's all this about?'

'My mother died,' she said desperately. 'And you expected business as usual.'

He looked genuinely bewildered. '*I did?*'

'It never occurred to you, did it, that I might want to do something different? Go away, or – or something?' What a luxury it was, to blame him for last year's party and for everything that had happened since.

He said slowly, 'Is that what you wanted?'

'I might have.'

'Well, I'm sorry,' he said. 'You should have said. My memory is that we were hardly back from the funeral before you were looking up menus, making guest lists –'

'So you're saying I was disrespectful to my mother's memory.'

'On the contrary,' he said. 'I thought you saw it as some kind of memorial to her – something of which she would have wholeheartedly approved.'

It was true. She remembered: in the days and weeks after the death she had wanted nothing so much as to get back to normal, and so had clung to the reassuring rituals of the year. *But he could have stopped me*, she thought.

39

So there she was with her two problems. One was the sort of thing that happens to most of us at one time or another – loving someone who doesn't love us. The other is something we might wish (to borrow Boniface's phrase) happened more often: having more money than we know what to do with.

While she struggles and writhes on the horns of her dilemmas, I'd just like to set the record straight about something.

A few chapters ago, Boniface told Marjorie that the reason why I had split up with him was because I had met someone else, a lawyer with a pony-tail, who had read all the right books.

Did you believe that? I have a feeling you might have. If you did, it shows how little you know about me.

But then you might reply in your own defence, *I don't need to know about you, Heather. This isn't about you, it's about Marjorie. You've said that often enough. You're just the narrator . . .*

All of which is perfectly true. But even narrators have rights, and I have the right to place it on record that I am not the sort of person who turns against another person just because they haven't read the right books. I'd be turning against myself, because I certainly haven't read them. Ask the examiners who marked my A-levels.

It's true that there was this solicitor. His name was Ronnie Zermatt, and he did have quite long hair which he sometimes tied back from his face with a rubber band. If you want to call that a pony-tail, go ahead. He was the grandson of a friend of Kath Baker, the woman who had set up the tenants' action group at 59, Blondin Gardens.

Ronnie laughed his head off when he heard about Mr

Truscott's free breakfasts. He said he hadn't realized that scam was still being tried. He said it would take more than a few pots of out-of-date yogurt and a bogus registration with a city slickers' accommodation agency to convince a court that 59, Blondin Gardens was a *bona fide* guest house. As far as Ronnie was concerned, we inmates were tenants with full Rent Act protection. He wrote an official letter to Mr Truscott, warning him that any further attempt to get us out would be treated as harassment and a criminal offence. With a bit of luck, Ronnie said, that would be the end of the matter.

And so it seemed. The date for our eviction came and went. Kath Baker organized a collection round the house to buy Ronnie a pair of winter gloves as a thank you present.

The day he received the gloves, he came round to thank Kath. He got no reply from her bell, so he rang mine. I went down. He said how pleased he was with the gloves, and that we really shouldn't have bothered because he was only doing his job. He asked if I would pass on his thanks to everyone in the house, and I said, sure. And then, partly because I had made a new year resolution to be more sociable and less frightened of people, and partly because I was at a bit of a loose end now that my Coates Clarion entry was finished and posted off for judgement, I invited him up for a cup of tea.

I was quite shocked with myself, but he said yes, so I couldn't get out of it. He followed me to my room. My table was strewn with drafts of an erotic poem I was writing about Boniface. I put them in a drawer. Ronnie in the meantime was looking at my posters and prowling along my bookshelves. 'I see you like Camus.'

I don't know why people assume that if you like a particular book by a particular author, you like everything they wrote, you like *them*. I didn't like everything by Camus – I particularly didn't like *La Peste*, which was on my A-Level syllabus. The only good thing about reading *La Peste* was that it introduced me to *L'Etranger*, which wasn't. I said, 'I like *L'Etranger*.'

'What do you like about it?' Ronnie asked.

I put the kettle on. 'I like the way he doesn't let anyone tell him what to think or how to feel.'

'You don't think that's too individualistic?'

I shook my head.

'You don't think society has a right to demand certain standards of behaviour?'

'I don't think anyone's got a right to tell anyone else how to behave when their mother dies.'

It was all quite friendly. This was what I imagined it would be like to be at university: having to have opinions, and give reasons for them.

Ronnie tried another tack. 'So you think his murdering the Algerian was a noble act? An assertion of his existential freedom?'

'No, but that's not what they guillotine him for, is it?'

'Isn't it?'

'That's just their excuse,' I said. 'They don't give a damn for the Algerian. All they care about is the way Mersault behaved when his mother died – smoking, and drinking white coffee, and not crying enough. There was no reason to bring any of that up in court, but they went on and on about it.' This was the answer I would have given in my A-levels, if *L'Etranger* had been on the syllabus. I had all the references off pat.

I made tea and toast and we talked a bit more about Camus and about other books, and about Ronnie's work and my work. I told him about going in for the Coates Clarion award. He asked what my entry was about, and I tried to explain. I forgot about the time until suddenly it was six o'clock and in walked Boniface.

Ronnie and I were sitting on the floor. There was no special significance in this, apart from all my chairs being covered with junk as usual and the floor seeming like a convenient place to put our mugs and plates. We were nowhere near each other.

The paraffin heater was between us. But the sight of Boniface made me feel guilty, and I stood up.

He put down his *Financial Times* next to *L'Etranger* and gave a sarcastic little bow. 'A thousand pardons. Should have knocked.'

'This is Ronnie Zermatt,' I said. 'Our solicitor.'

Boniface lifted his eyebrows as if to say that he had met a few solicitors in his time and Ronnie didn't look like any of them. Ronnie hitched up his jeans and rose to his feet. The jean-hitching gesture was entirely innocent, he just happened to have rather a large stomach, possibly from eating too much toast and jam with his clients, but I could see Boniface reading all sorts of things into it and comparing Ronnie's bulges with his own flat belly.

The two men shook hands. Boniface noticed my copy of *L'Etranger* and picked it up. Ronnie said, 'Heather and I were talking about Camus.'

'I don't doubt it,' said Boniface. 'Heather and *I* talk about little else.'

'I'll be on my way,' said Ronnie. 'I've got a meeting to go to.'

'Then don't let us keep you from it.' Boniface tossed him his coat and held the door open.

I went downstairs with Ronnie and saw him out. He gave me a comradely peck on the cheek and said, 'Sorry if I've caused problems for you.' I said, 'You haven't,' and went back upstairs.

40

He had taken his coat off and was flicking through *L'Etranger*. Mimicking Ronnie's pronunciation, he said, '"We've been talking about Camus."'

I said, 'I'll talk to my friends about whatever I like.'

'Be my guest. I suppose you have to find intellectual stimulation somewhere. Can't expect anything like that from a pig-ignorant insurance man.'

'If that's what you think of yourself, that's your problem.'

'You're probably right.' He smiled in a way that made me think the quarrel was over. He put his arms round me and we stood hugging for a few moments. He moved his lips to my ear and murmured, 'But what about the other kind of stimulation, Heather? Any good at that, is he?'

'Oh, for heaven's sake.' I pushed him away.

'Does he know what you like? The way I know?'

'Piss off.'

'I was going anyway. I shouldn't have come. I was forgetting myself, dropping in without a written invitation.' He picked up his coat. Half-way to the door, he seemed to change his mind. He said in a wheedling voice, 'How would you like it if you turned up at my place and I had another girl there?'

I gave him an icy look. 'Do you mean "woman"?'

'Woman, then.'

'I wouldn't mind, if she was your solicitor.'

'You would if you loved me,' he said.

He was looking at me steadily. He had never said that he loved me. Not in so many words. I had never said that I loved him. He seemed to be saying it now. It was obvious what I was supposed to say. But I'm like the man in *L'Etranger*, I don't like being nudged into saying what I'm supposed to say even if it is what I feel, and I wasn't even sure that 'I love you' was what I did feel about Boniface at that particular moment, so I kept quiet.

'If you loved me,' he went on, 'you wouldn't believe she was my solicitor. Or you'd think, "Okay, she's his solicitor, but what else is she?"'

I listened to him telling me not what I thought, not what I had thought, but what I *would* think in a situation that had never arisen. I said, 'Let's drop it, okay?'

'I don't want to drop it. I want to know if that fellow is your lover.'

'I don't have to answer that.'

'You don't, that's true. But I'd like you to. Just a straightforward yes or no, please, Heather, and then we'll say no more about it.'

'Who do you think you are?'

'Nobody,' he said quietly. 'Nobody at all. Just your lover. One of your lovers.'

I had never seen him like this. Not that we hadn't fallen out before — of course we had. You wouldn't expect us not to. You've seen the kinds of people we were, and the different sorts of backgrounds that we came from. You've heard how we quarrelled about Gibraltar, and about my eviction letter. And we had differences of opinion galore: he admired Margaret Thatcher as a politician but hated her as a woman; I admired her as a woman but hated her as a politician. We often argued about that sort of thing, but the arguments usually wound down into jokes, flirtation and bed.

He wasn't joking now. He was very pale. Even his eyes had gone pale. He was like a stranger. To calm him, and myself, I said clearly, 'Ronnie Zermatt is not my lover.'

'Good,' said Boniface. 'At last we're getting somewhere. Has he ever touched you?'

'You said you wouldn't ask any more questions.'

'Has he?'

'Mind your own business.'

'That means he has.'

'If you know, why ask?'

He paced up and down, clenching and unclenching his fists. 'You've shaken hands with him. Of course you have. That's what you meant by touching, isn't it? Nothing wrong with that.' He was talking to himself. 'It would be a funny sort of solicitor–client relationship that didn't involve the odd handshake.' He turned his eyes on me. They were burning like searchlights. 'It's not as if he's kissed you or anything. Has he?'

I knew what I ought to do: lie. Deny it. Calm him down. Wait till he was himself again. But the lie stuck in my throat. I hadn't done anything wrong, so why should I behave as if I had?

'He has kissed me, as a matter of fact.'

'Whereabouts?'

'Downstairs.'

'Don't get clever. *Whereabouts?*'

'Guess.'

'Heather,' he said. 'Don't push me too far.'

'Or what?' I jeered.

'Or this.' He slapped my face. It didn't hurt. I hardly felt it. I only knew he had done it because of the noise. He looked as if he might be about to do it again, so I moved out of range.

He grabbed my wrists. 'What sort of kiss was it? Show me. Give me a demonstration. No, you don't need to. I know how wimps like that kiss women. They don't know the first thing about it. It was like this, wasn't it?' He made his lips go soft and rubbery, and planted a wet, ineffectual kiss on the corner of my mouth. 'That's how he kissed you, isn't it? Not like I kiss you.' He forced his tongue into my mouth and bit my lips. 'Sweetie, I've got the most enormous erection. What are you going to do about it?'

'Nothing.' I tried to get free, but he was nudging me towards the bed. The nudge became a push. He was using all his force. He was laughing. It wasn't a sexy laugh, or even a nice laugh.

It was a sly, hedging-your-bets kind of laugh, as if he wanted to keep open the option of pretending that this was all a joke. But I wasn't laughing. I was fighting. I kicked out. My foot caught the paraffin heater. Over it went. I thought we were both about to go up in flames, but the heater's safety catch snapped down and there weren't any flames, just a puff of sour-smelling smoke and paraffin leaking out all over my carpet.

He tried to say something, but I told him to go and he went. That's how Boniface and I split up. That's why. It was nothing to do with who had read which books and who hadn't.

41

I mopped up the paraffin as best I could, but it had soaked into the carpet and I couldn't get rid of it all. The air was thick with fumes, and I spent a sleepless night. In the morning, I packed my things and went home to my mother.

I didn't tell her I was coming. I didn't want to talk about it over the phone. I wasn't even sure I wanted to talk about it at all. I just knew I had to get away, and this was the only place to go. I caught a train up to Victoria, a coach to Norwich and a bus out to our estate.

It was February, a bitterly cold afternoon. The east wind cut between the houses and through my clothes, making me shiver. I found the key in its usual place under the flower pot by the back door and let myself in.

It was an ordinary 1960s council house, semi-detached, two up, two down. From time to time during my childhood, various women's carpentry collectives had hammered their way through the rooms, erecting shelves and cupboards and storage units. But even the most cunningly designed and spacious had always been defeated by the sheer quantity of Mum's possessions – her books and pamphlets, her wholesale consignments of stationery, her poster- and banner-making equipment, her ornaments and knick-knacks. Everywhere you looked there were ashtrays embossed with images of the goddess, some full of ash, some providing homes for pins and paper clips; double-axe fobs hanging from leather thongs; mugs with slogans on the side crammed with biros with other slogans on their sides. Posters adorned every wall, from 'Free Angela Davis' to 'Don't Do It, Di'. There were paintings, paperweights, tapestries, dried flower arrangements, candles, leatherwork – a thousand souvenirs from a thousand conferences, or else gifts from friends or lovers.

I dragged my luggage up to my room. There was a computer on the bed, so I came back down again. I made some tea, turned the TV on and smoked a cigarette. I watched children's programmes and then the news. Most of it was about last-ditch negotiations to try and prevent a miners' strike. At about six I heard a key turn. I stood in the sitting-room doorway and watched her come in. She hadn't seen me yet.

Her hair was short and fair like mine. She was wearing her navy blue duffle coat which was older than I was, and a long woollen tapestry skirt, thick blue tights and black lace-ups. A bluestocking in sensible shoes, she would call herself. To me she looked more like a cross between a pixie and a bag lady. She had devised her own portable filing system consisting of supermarket carrier bags. Each of the seven demands had its own bag: Equal Pay went into Tesco's, Equal Opportunities into Safeway's, Free Contraception And Abortion On Demand into Shoppers' Paradise, and so on. There was a bag for fund-raising, another for correspondence with the council, another for the Seven Demands Newsletter. Sometimes, if you searched through the bags diligently enough, you might find groceries.

'Hello, Mum.'

'Hello, stranger.' She looked surprised to see me, but pleased. She hugged me. 'What brings you here?'

'Oh, you know.'

'Felt like a bit of mother's home cooking? I'm afraid you're out of luck.' From one of her bags she produced an individual frozen lasagne. She looked at it doubtfully. 'There's probably enough for two.'

'I'm not hungry.'

'I'm in and out this evening, I'm afraid.' She went into the kitchen and put the lasagne into the oven. 'Policy meeting. We'll catch up with each other later. This *is* a nice surprise. How long are you staying?'

'Not sure.'

'Love, is anything wrong?'

You can't hide anything from her. I burst into tears and told her what had happened. She listened calmly, then said, 'The shit.'

'Yes,' I sniffed.

'The fucking slimeball.'

'I know.'

'What did the police say?'

I ought to have known she would ask that. I ought to have been ready for it. 'I haven't been to the police.'

'Why not?' my mother asked.

I didn't answer.

She persisted. 'Why not, love?' Her voice was gentle but firm. You could tell she had made this speech before. 'You say he hit you, he tried to rape you, he nearly set the place on fire. He sounds dangerous.'

I could only agree. The man she described did sound dangerous – but he didn't sound like Boniface, so how could I report Boniface to the police?

She ate her lasagne and talked to me about how I mustn't fall into the trap of thinking I must protect him. A key turned in the front door and a voice called out, 'Hi, Julia. It's only us.' Madge Kennedy swept in with Patience in her wake. Madge was wearing an elegant dark red velvet cape with matching hat. Patience looked more like a middle-aged rebellious schoolgirl, with her pink cheeks and blonde curls and her array of badges.

They smiled to see me. Madge said, 'I didn't know you were going to be here.'

'It's a surprise visit,' said Mum, thin-lipped.

Patience said, 'I was only saying the other day – wasn't I, Madge – it's a shame we never see Heather. How's the big, bad city?'

'Big and bad.'

'You're enjoying yourself, then?'

Mum said to her friends, 'I might give the meeting a miss.'

At first they looked surprised. Then they glanced at me and the penny dropped. 'Okay,' said Madge. 'We'll let you know what happens. See you, Heather.'

I hissed at Mum, 'You can go.'

She shook her head. 'I'm not leaving you on your own.'

'He's not going to turn up.'

'How do you know?'

'He doesn't know where I am.'

'Are you sure? They're clever, these violent men.'

'Mum, he *doesn't know*.' I finally convinced her, and off she went. I washed up her lasagne dish, smoked and watched TV. It was nice having a TV to watch. Boniface had one at his flat, but we hardly ever used to watch it.

I watched a game show, followed by a sitcom about milkmen. It was quite good, and I resolved to watch it again next week. I watched the late-evening news, which was the same as the early-evening news, and went upstairs. I moved Mum's computer off my bed and lay down. I listened to cars going along the road. I waited for a sound I might recognize. It wouldn't be that difficult for him to find me. A door banged. Footsteps approached. I went to the window in time to see someone going in next door.

It was after midnight when Mum got home. The car that brought her was full of women, all sounding quite drunk. It took at least ten minutes for Mum to get out, kiss them all goodnight, finalize arrangements to see them again and make her way into the house.

42

Over the next few days, she went on and on at me about going to the police. I said there was no point. She tried a different tack, urging me to make an appointment with the doctor to make sure I hadn't sustained any hidden injuries. I told her I had no injuries.

'What about counselling?' There was a free service at ROOOWC for survivors of domestic violence. Women only, absolutely confidential.

'I don't want counselling,' I said. 'I'm not the type.'

'There's no *type*.'

'I'd hate it.'

'How do you know when you've never tried it?'

'Have *you* tried it?' I asked her.

'No,' she admitted. 'But I haven't just been beaten up by my so-called boyfriend.'

'Neither have I.'

'Oh? What do you call it, then?'

'It was an accident.'

She was quiet for a few moments, then said, 'Don't you think it would be a good idea to talk to someone about this "accident"? If ROOOWC is too close to home, they could easily refer you somewhere else.'

I walked out of the room. She was missing the point. It wasn't the location of the domestic violence survivors' service that bothered me. It was my complete inability to feel like a domestic violence survivor.

I did think about going to the doctor, to get some sleeping pills. I wasn't sleeping. Some nights I didn't get off until four or even later. It was really boring, being awake all the time. Sleeping pills would have helped, sleeping pills would have been great. But I knew our doctor and I had a feeling that she wasn't the type to hand over sleeping pills just like that. She would want to know why I wasn't sleeping.

Most days I woke up at around ten, after Mum had gone to work. I went downstairs for a coffee and a fag and a look at yesterday's newspaper. Mum always took the current one to work with her. She had to be up-to-date with the news, but for me it didn't matter if I was a day behind.

After I had read the paper, I would go out, either to pick up some groceries if she had left me a list of what she wanted, or, if not, for a walk. One day I walked all the way into Norwich, a distance of about six miles, and all the way back again. It took the whole day. I was trying to wear myself out so that I would sleep. It didn't work, because the only part of me that got tired was my body, and it wasn't my body that was keeping me awake, it was my mind. Walking was quite boring, and I thought about getting a dog so that I would have someone to talk to.

I walked across fields and farmland. I didn't realize where I was going until I got there. I found myself near the cottage where Mum and I had lived when I was little. I hardly recognized it with its new roof and double-glazing and tidy front garden. This was where Mum had been accused of cohabiting with Stan Haverstock. I wondered what had happened to him, and the social security inspectors. They must have rued the day they had ever dared to tangle with Mum, because when they stopped her cohabiting with Stan she had started cohabiting with feminism instead, and became a much bigger thorn in their side than ever she would have been with Stan to keep her happy. I tried to remember what he looked like, to reconstruct his face, but the only face I could get was Boniface's. I shook my head to get rid of Boniface's face and wandered along the road towards the place where the phone box used to be, the one where she had pretended to ring up social services to say that Mrs Bloody Perfect could have me after all. I wondered if it was still there. It was, but in a slightly different place, and modernized. I imagined how telephones might keep echoes within themselves of all the conversations that had ever gone on in them. I picked up the receiver, but I couldn't hear anything.

I walked back past my old primary school. The children were being met by their mothers. I was glad I hadn't got a dog, because it might have barked and frightened them. I wondered if they noticed me, or imagined that I had ever been where they were. They probably thought I was immensely old. I didn't blame them, I felt old, I felt worn out, as if I had had my life, made a mess of it, and come home to die of old age.

That couldn't be right. You don't go home to your mother to die of old age. Maybe she wasn't really my mother, maybe I was hers. I couldn't remember giving birth to her, but that didn't prove anything. Perhaps I had adopted her.

She asked me a few times what my plans were, but I never had a sensible answer, so she gave up. One thing I did do was to write to the organizers of the Coates Clarion award to give them my change of address. They wrote back thanking me for the information and saying that unfortunately my entry had not been shortlisted. If I cared to send them a stamped, addressed envelope, as specified in Section 10 of the Conditions of Entry, they would return the manuscript to me.

A couple of weeks later, another letter arrived with a Coates Clarion postmark. I became quite excited, thinking they must have changed their minds about my entry, but the letter said,

Dear Heather,

I hope this reaches you. It was the only way I could think of to get in touch. You mentioned going in for the CC competition, so I thought they would probably have your new address and be kind enough to forward this.

I was concerned to find that you had moved out of No. 59, particularly as no one in the house seemed to know where you had gone, or why. None of their business, of course, and certainly none of mine, but I just wanted to say that I hope nothing is wrong. If there is a problem, and if you think it is something I can help with, I hope you will get in touch.

Kind regards and best wishes,
Ronnie Zermatt

43

The letter depressed me – not for what it said but for what it demonstrated. Ronnie had shown initiative, imagination and knowledge of what was important to me, and tracked me down. Boniface could have done the same, but he hadn't bothered.

Mum asked about the letter. I couldn't be bothered to explain, so I gave it to her to read. She said Ronnie sounded like a nice man, unlike some, and was I going to write back?

'What for?' I said. 'It only says to get in touch if there's a problem, and there isn't.'

She sighed and went off to a meeting. Controversy was raging at ROOOWC about the miners' strike. Some of the women wanted to set up a solidarity group. Others like my mother couldn't see any reason to show solidarity with a bunch of men in a men-only job. She thought ROOOWC should concentrate on the nuts and bolts of equality, by which she meant the seven demands. She remembered the early years, as she was fond of reminding people who didn't, and the struggle for a sex discrimination act. 'Who opposed it? Who demanded exemptions for themselves, along with the Church of England, the Church of Rome and the armed services? The miners, that's who. That's who they were shoulder-to-shoulder with then. Why should we stand shoulder-to-shoulder with them now?'

Her fierce, unforgiving attitude to the wrongs committed by groups of men she had never met was in striking contrast to her passion for individuals. When her boyfriend Harry Wyatt came to stay for a weekend, you could feel her spirits rise, see the spring in her step, hear the lilt in her voice. Whoever made up that saying about *post coitum omne animal triste est* had never seen my mother with a morning-after gleam in her eye.

It deepened my misery. I wrote to Ronnie, thanking him for

his letter. I told him that nothing was wrong, I had just decided to visit my mother for a while. He wrote back saying what a coincidence it was that my mother lived so close to Norwich, as he quite often came to Norwich on business and perhaps next time he was there we could get together for a drink. I didn't reply, but he obviously took this as a yes and rang up to make a date. We met in a pub near the cathedral. He told me about the case he was working on, something to do with rights for part-time workers. I told him about not winning the Coates Clarion award. He said, 'Better luck next year.' Then he asked if I wanted to go back to his hotel.

We lay on the double bed and kissed and took each other's clothes off. I remembered my first time with Boniface, and how disconcerted he had been to discover that I was a virgin. I had thought he would be pleased because I wouldn't be able to compare him with other men. Ronnie showed no interest in whether I was a virgin or not, and didn't seem to be comparing me with anyone. He was too nice for that. I wished I was nice. I couldn't help making comparisons. My body made them, even as my mind was telling me that it shouldn't. The things Ronnie did weren't that different from the things Boniface had done. But they felt different.

He said, 'Do you mind if I use a condom?' I said, 'Please do.' It made a wet, sticky sound as he took it out of its packet and put it on. He rubbed gel on to it from a tube and slid himself inside me. I wondered when he had bought the condom and the gel, or whether he carried them with him at all times. That would be sensible, especially if you were in the habit of asking people on the off-chance. I wouldn't have thought Ronnie was the off-chance type, but you never know. Perhaps anyone could be an off-chance type in the right circumstances. I wasn't sure whether my mother was an off-chance type. I thought she liked to have relationships with them first, but I also knew that Madge worried about her and urged her to be careful. Mum laughed and said she had always been careful, she had invented being careful. After me, she presumably meant. She wouldn't have wanted a repetition of me. You couldn't blame her, really, particularly now that I was back from my adventure, cluttering up her house. I had tried growing up but it was too hard for me.

I wondered whether all the rooms in this hotel had double beds, or whether he had requested one specially. Then I wondered why I was wondering. I never used to wonder about things like that when I was making love with Boniface. I never used to wonder about anything.

44

She said, 'I suppose I'd be wasting my breath if I told you I was going to see your grandparents tomorrow.'

'You wouldn't be wasting it at all,' I replied politely. 'Thanks for the information. Now I won't wonder where you are.'

'I meant, would you like to come with me?'

'No, thanks.'

'You're really determined never to meet them? Never even to lay eyes on them?'

'It's no more than they were determined to do with me,' I reminded her.

She sighed. 'That was half a lifetime ago.'

'A whole lifetime, actually, Mum. Mine.'

She said slowly, 'Those were the times they lived in. That was how people thought.'

'These are the times I live in. This is how I think.'

'What – vengeance for ever?'

I thought she was a fine one to talk about vengeance, she who wanted me to report Boniface to the police. But I didn't want to use his name in a conversation like this. 'It isn't vengeance, it's indifference.'

She said, 'Isn't it rather tiring, being so angry for such a long time?'

'Not as tiring as it would be to go.' I looked at her. 'Don't *you* find it tiring – having to be polite to them after what they did?'

She laughed. 'What makes you think I'm polite?'

'Aren't you?'

'I am now. More or less. I wasn't to start with.'

'So why are you now?'

She shrugged. 'I suppose I've come to see that they were just as much victims as I was.'

179

'Oh, bring on the violins.'

'All right, Heather,' she snapped. 'I shouldn't have mentioned it.'

She obviously wanted to end the conversation, but I didn't see why she should get out of it so easily. 'What was he like, anyway?'

She smiled. 'He's a cantankerous old sod sometimes. But he can be very kind.'

'I didn't mean your father,' I said. 'I meant mine.'

She stared at me. 'Yours?'

'Yes. Mine. What was he like? Seems a perfectly fair question.'

'Of course it's a fair question. That's why I've answered it – lots of times.'

'What, he was just some guy you met at a party and you never even knew his name?'

'You sound as if you don't believe me.'

'Oh, I believe you,' I said. 'I've always believed you. I just don't think it's very fair. I mean, I've never had a father. Ever. Not even a cantankerous old sod. I couldn't care less, but you know. Maybe I'd have liked some say in the matter. You didn't give me any say. You dropped your knickers at some sleazy sixties rave-up and here I am. No one ever says anything about that. I'm not saying anything about it. It was "do your own thing", wasn't it? That was your thing and you did it. But when I say my thing is to have nothing to do with my grand-parents, you treat me as if I'm all twisted and neurotic.'

When Mum got back from her visit, I was watching TV and eating crisps. She switched the set off and stood in front of it.

I protested. 'I was watching that.'

'We have to talk.'

'We've talked already.'

'Not about that,' she said. 'Well, yes, it is about that. They want to give you some money.'

I ate a crisp noisily to show my indifference. But I couldn't help asking, 'Why?'

'I don't know, frankly,' said Mum. 'I said to them, "Have you considered the cats' home?" But Dad retires at the end of the year, and he has a choice between a full pension or a smaller pension with a lump sum. He and Mum reckon they can manage on the smaller pension and give you about five grand.'

I didn't say anything.

Mum went on, 'There are no strings attached, in case you're wondering. They'd like you to use it to get yourself started in a career, but that's up to you. They don't like the idea of you wasting your life any more than I do.'

'You've been discussing me, have you?'

'Yes, Heather. When I go to see my parents, if I've got something on my mind that's worrying me sick, I talk it over with them. That's what parents are for.'

I didn't answer. She said, 'You wouldn't have to collect the money personally. They'd put a cheque in the post.'

Even so, I sensed a bribe. It was an interesting idea, being bribed to be a granddaughter. I probably wouldn't be the first. 'I don't want it,' I said.

My mother's temper snapped and she stormed out of the room, yelling, 'No, I didn't think you would. Why lower yourself to accept money from them when you can live off me?'

45

I got the message. I went out and found myself a job as a waitress in a burger bar. The wage wasn't very good, but there were tips and I did a lot of overtime. It kept my mind off things.

What with the job and seeing Ronnie, I was hardly ever at home except to sleep. Relations improved between me and my mother. Next time she went to see her parents, she did so without comment.

She was curious about Ronnie. She kept asking what he was like, and about the work he was doing with the union. I tried to answer, but I couldn't always go into as much detail as she wanted. It wasn't that important to me. One day, partly to tease her and partly to shut her up, I said, 'Why don't you ask him yourself?'

'Love to,' she said. 'When am I going to be introduced?'

The three of us met in a pub. She took to him at once, and proved it by getting into an argument right away. He, trying to create a good impression, made the mistake of saying that his part-time workers' campaign would be of particular benefit to women.

'Why's that, Ronnie?' Her voice was innocently conversational. I had heard that tone before, and I trembled for him.

He walked straight in. 'Because of their domestic responsibilities.'

'Oh, I see. Domestic responsibilities are all down to women, are they?'

'Good point,' said Ronnie.

'I know it's a good point. Answer it. If even people like you take inequality in the home for granted, something to be worked round rather than changed, when will it ever change? You think about that while I get some more drinks. Same again, everybody?'

She went to the bar. He turned to me in mock terror. 'What do I say?'

'Whatever you like.' I lit a cigarette. 'You got yourself into this.'

She came back with the drinks. Ronnie was ready with his speech. 'In the past, domestic responsibilities have always fallen to women –'

'They haven't fallen,' Mum corrected him. 'They've been pushed. By men. And women haven't always had the sense to get out of the way in time.'

As one of Mum's domestic responsibilities myself, I said nothing.

Ronnie said, 'Part-time work is of particular benefit to *people* with domestic responsibilities. Okay?'

Obviously it was okay, because shortly afterwards she invited him to one of her spaghetti Bolognese evenings. Also on the guest list were Harry Wyatt, Madge and Patience, a woman called Anita, who was staying with Madge and Patience (ex-ROOOWC, now a women's studies lecturer in London), Anita's former husband Bernard, and Bernard's current partner Alan. All in all it was quite a little family gathering, with my new boyfriend being paraded for my father's approval.

When everyone had finished praising Mum's cooking, be-moaning the awfulness of the government and reporting on the love-lives of people known to everyone except me and Ronnie, they moved on to the good old bad old days at ROOOWC: the time when someone rang up to ask whether women's lib gave tips on skin care, the time when the collective wrote to the Hoover Trust asking for a donation and got offered a free vacuum cleaner instead. Mum kept saying, 'This must be very boring for Ronnie.' Ronnie said, 'No, honestly, Julia, it's fascinating,' and back they would go to discussing the cranky old duplicator which was donated by the Gay

Centre when the Gay Centre got its first computer and how everyone thought it would only be a matter of time before the Gay Centre would be begging for its duplicator back because computers were never going to catch on. This led to memories of how the duplicator used to spray you with ink when you were trying to run off copies of the Seven Demands Newsletter.

'The seven *demands*.' Anita sighed nostalgically. 'I can't believe how naïve we were – to think it could be that simple. Make demands of the patriarchy, and it'll cave in.' She tinkled with laughter.

'It's caved in a bit,' said Mum.

Anita didn't hear. 'I don't suppose any of us can even remember what the seven demands were. Let's go round the table.'

'We don't need to go round the table,' said Mum briskly. 'We're still campaigning for them.'

'Oh, *are* you?' Anita made it sound as if she had just heard that the ROOOWC women were spending their time developing a circular invention with spokes that would make it easier for vehicles to move along the ground. 'I thought the general feeling around the movement was that the seven demands are out of date.'

'What, you mean because they've all been achieved?' Mum's sarcasm was veiled under a hostess's politeness. 'Or because they weren't worth fighting for in the first place?'

Madge intervened, obviously not wanting an argument to break out between the guest she and Patience had brought along and Mum. 'So what are you doing in your group, Anita?'

'Well, obviously you have to look at the miners' strike, the effects of Thatcherism on –'

Mum started to clear the plates. I helped her and we went out to the kitchen. She winked. 'What is it with academics? You ask them what they're *doing* and they tell you what they're *looking at*.' She took a swig from a glass of wine and checked to see that the pavlova was properly defrosted.

Back round the dining table, Anita was still holding forth about '. . . the Miners' Wives Support Group.'

Mum started to slice the pavlova. 'Whose support group was that, Anita?'

'Miners' Wives. What you have to look at is –'

'I wasn't asking who they were married to,' said Mum pleasantly. 'I was asking who *they* are.'

Anita didn't answer.

'Or to put it another way,' said Mum, 'why is a feminist group making common cause with women who choose to define themselves in terms of their marital status and their husbands' jobs?'

There was a general rustle round the table, as if someone had farted in church. Anita snapped, 'Don't you read the papers, Julia? Don't you know what's going on in the pit communities? I think those women have enough on their plates without some middle-class outsider barging in and telling them they've got the name of their group wrong.'

Mum nearly dropped the dish of pavlova that she was trying to hand to Ronnie. He rescued it. 'Middle-class?' she said. She pointed the cake slicer at Anita. 'You've got a tenured lectureship. I –' she pointed the slicer at herself '– am an underpaid gofer and Jill-of-all-trades who has to put on discos to fund her own salary. And *you're* calling *me* middle-class?'

Patience said quickly, 'Anita didn't mean it like that, Julia.'

Harry Wyatt said, 'This pudding is terrific.'

'Certainly is,' said Madge.

Ronnie said, 'Julia, I'm interested in what you say, but don't you think class is about more than what job you do? Don't background and attitudes come into it?'

If he thought this was his chance to get revenge for the way she had wiped the floor with him in the argument about domestic responsibilities, he was out of luck. I could have told him he would be out of luck. '*Background and attitudes?*' she repeated. We were eating by candlelight, but I saw her face go pale above her black top with silver threads on it, between her silver earrings. 'Listen, Ronnie. When you've been thrown out of your home and your school because you're eighteen and pregnant, then you can talk to me about background and attitudes.'

He put up his hands. 'Yeah. All right. Sorry.'

But there was no stopping her. 'When you've practically had to kidnap your own child to stop her being taken away from you, when you've lived in one run-down sleazy dump after another, where people walk past you on the stairs without speaking to you. When someone's suggested to you that your best plan might be to wear a wedding ring and call yourself Mrs in the hope that people might treat you and your child like human beings – and worst of all, you find out that they do, *but only* because you're wearing a wedding ring and calling yourself Mrs –' her eyes were glinting in the candlelight, though whether with anger or tears, I couldn't tell. 'When you've been told you can't be moved up the housing list any faster because it wouldn't be fair to married couples, when you've been threatened with destitution because you dared to have a boy-friend and *that* isn't fair to married couples – when you've done all those things, Ronnie, Anita, all of you, then you can talk to me about who's middle-class and who isn't. All right?' Mum tossed her fair hair and smiled brightly round the table at all the concerned faces. 'Now – does anyone want cheese?'

After the party, Ronnie said to me, 'I hope I didn't offend your mother.'

'Offend her?' I laughed. 'She's crazy about you.' I had had rather a lot to drink, and I added, 'My dad liked you too.'

'Your dad?' He was surprised. 'Which one was your dad?'

'All of them.'

He couldn't work it out. 'You mean you were artificially –'

I was getting tired of the conversation so I kissed him to shut him up. 'Artificially, yes.'

46

I'm doing it again, aren't I? Banging on about myself when I'm supposed to be telling you about Marjorie.

I was only trying to set the record straight about why Boniface and I split up. Then I got a bit carried away and told you more than I meant to – perhaps I was trying to show you that Marjorie wasn't the only woman who could get into a state over Boniface Bennett.

You might like to bear that in mind when you come to judge her.

It never occurred to Marjorie, as she pined for him, that I might be pining too. As far as she was concerned, I had given him the push and that was it. If I hadn't given him the push, he might never have lost his job, and if he hadn't lost his job she would have had no reason to go to his flat. It was all my fault. Bitterness choked her. She had tried to do me a favour, and this was how I had repaid her.

But she knew in her heart that it wasn't my fault. She knew she was responsible for her actions.

She reflected on the word *responsible*, which sometimes meant the exact opposite. *Who's responsible for this mess?* should surely be, *Who's irresponsible for this mess?* She would be responsible now: responsible for rebuilding her life, responsible for maintaining her marriage.

She brushed aside the temptation to tell Robert everything. It might give her some short-term relief, but at what cost to him? He would never be able to trust her again.

Yet still the idea of talking to him – really talking – had enormous appeal. Not that they didn't talk. They talked all the time, about the family, the house, what was on the news, who they had seen, what she was doing, what he was doing.

They did not talk about intimate things – perhaps because they had always assumed that intimate things were things shared intimately between them and so in no need of discussion.

Another reason for not telling Robert was that, if she did, it would mean that she could never, ever raise the question of why he himself no longer made love to her. To combine the two subjects would be to imply that there was a connection between them, that Robert was responsible for what she had done. It was either one subject or the other.

It seemed better to talk about her and Robert's life together – which at least had a future – than to dwell on the past. She thought about how she might broach the subject. She would be tactful, gentle and loving. She would let him know that she had read in a great many magazine articles that this was not a not-uncommon problem in men of his age, and that it could be solved. She imagined it being solved, and him turning lustfully towards her in the night. Her mind blanked out. She couldn't remember how it felt with him. She only remembered Boniface.

She met him again at Olivia and Jake's New Year's Eve party at the end of 1985, two years after their first encounter. She knew he was going to be there – Olivia had cracked a little joke about it when she issued the invitations: *if you can bear to see him again after what happened last time*. Marjorie froze; but Olivia made it clear that she was only referring to the way Boniface had so amusingly passed out and had to stay the night.

Marjorie went through the motions of accepting the invitation, but planned to be struck down by a migraine at the last minute and so prevented from going. But as the day drew closer, she became defiant. *Why SHOULDN'T I go? Why should he be allowed to come between me and my friends? He is dirt under my feet, and here's the way to let him know it.*

She treated herself to a new cocktail dress, made of dark blue Italian velvet. It was dignified, yet had a touch of mystery.

That was how she would present herself. That was how she would behave.

She took her time over dressing for the party. Robert watched the final stages. He seemed to like what he saw. 'You look . . . what's the word?'

'I don't know, dear. What are you trying to say?'

'Majestic,' he said. 'In command, but in the nicest possible way.'

She nodded, satisfied. They went out to the car. It was a cold night, the sky glittering with thousands of stars. The drive through the downs to Cliffhead Lodge took about twenty minutes. They turned off the main road on to the drive. The lights shone out from the restored medieval turrets. The place had started life as a monastery and been sacked by Henry VIII. It had lain in ruins for more than a century, after which some ancestor of Jake's had acquired it and done it up as his country seat.

Robert said, 'Whose turn is it to drive back?'

'Yours, but I'll do it. I won't be drinking tonight.'

The front door was open. They walked straight in. A maid directed them to the cloakrooms. Marjorie left her coat but kept her titivating to a minimum. She was nervous, and wanted her first encounter with Boniface over and done with.

Robert was waiting for her in the hall. Together they entered the drawing room. It had once been the monks' refectory. The stone walls remained, painted white – the only trace of monastic austerity that had been preserved. Successive generations of Verlaines had insisted on comfort, fine furnishings and works of art. The central heating was more than efficient as it backed up the log fire in the wrought-iron grate. The glow of the fire lit up one end of the room; a huge Christmas tree dominated the other, decorated with delicate silver baubles and white light. In between, the guests were mingling – about a hundred of them. Marjorie only saw one.

Olivia came forward, clad in a low-cut, black silk dress and a white stole. She kissed Marjorie and Robert and stopped a passing waiter to give them drinks. She introduced them to a QC, whose wife Marjorie already knew through ChildPeril, and someone who worked at the Foreign Office. 'And you already know Boniface.'

'Yes, indeed.' Marjorie extended her hand. 'How are you, Boniface?'

'Very well, thank you, Marjorie.'

'He's managed to stay awake this evening,' Olivia quipped.

'So I see. You remember Robert, Boniface? My husband?'

'I certainly do. Nice to see you again, Robert.' The two men shook hands. My love and my ex-lover shaking hands, she thought, as she fixed a smile to her lips and made her way to the far end of the room.

47

If it had been any other kind of party, she might have avoided him altogether. But at midnight, after the chimes of Big Ben had died away and a piper in a kilt had played the new year in, there was 'Auld Lang Syne' and indiscriminate kissing.

She tried to cling to Robert, but he was determined to have his annual statutory snog with Nina Grassington from English Villages Preservation. Marjorie allowed Jake to paw her and breathe whisky over her before he too set off after other quarry. She stood by the Christmas tree and tried to blend in.

'I won't if you don't want me to,' a voice said in her ear.

She turned and faced him. 'You made me jump.' Of all the things she could have said, she came out with that.

'I'm sorry.' He lowered his head. 'In fact, I'm sorry for a lot of things.'

She blushed, and hoped her face was hidden by the shadows of the Christmas tree. 'There's nothing for you to be sorry for.'

'I wish that were true.' He looked awkward, hesitant – sorrowful, even, against the background of festivity. 'I won't embarrass you.'

'Thank you.'

'But how about this as a compromise?' He took her hand and raised it to his lips. 'Happy new year, Marjorie.'

'The same to you.' She looked round for an escape. A man she didn't know was heading her way with bits of food in his moustache.

'Have you had a pleasant Christmas, Boniface?'

'Yes, thank you. And yourself?'

'For God's sake, you two.' Olivia was walking unsteadily towards them with a bottle of champagne in her hand and a

Christmas tree bauble down her cleavage. 'Stop standing aloof and come and join the fun. People will think you're having an affair.'

'We are,' said Boniface.

'Don't give me that, you little wretch. I know what you're up to, and I've come to put a stop to it. This is a party, damn it, not a Lloyd's recruitment drive. He's trying to make you sign up with his bloody agency, isn't he, Marje?'

'What agency?'

'That's what he's been doing with everyone else in the room. Anyone would think this was one of those what do they call them? Parties where everybody has to buy a plastic sandwich box.'

Boniface raised his eyebrows. 'I didn't know you were into Tupperware, Olivia.'

'But where's the free gift for the hostess? That's what I want to know.'

Boniface put his arm round her. 'You'll get more than a plastic sandwich box if you sign up with me, Olivia, my sweet.' He bore her away to dance. But as the party wound down, and Marjorie and Robert started making *are you ready to leave?* signals with their eyes, Boniface appeared out of nowhere with Marjorie's coat and helped her on with it.

He murmured in her ear, 'Are you still living in the same place?'

She assented in casual tones, as if she could not imagine why he would need to know.

'Of course you are,' said Boniface. 'Why would anyone want to move from such a beautiful house?'

She smiled in gracious acknowledgement and swept out on her husband's arm.

A week later, Boniface phoned her and asked her to meet him in town for lunch.

She took her time before answering. 'I don't know, Boniface. I'm a bit tied up at the moment.'

'I can wait,' he said. 'When could you be free?'

'I don't want to sound rude,' she said, 'but it's only fair to tell you that I have no interest whatsoever in joining your agency.'

'I don't want to sound rude either,' he replied. 'But *I* have to tell *you* that it isn't even an option.'

'Oh.'

'I wouldn't allow it.'

'Fine.'

'Not after . . .' he paused. 'Marjorie, are you alone? May I speak personally?'

'By all means.'

'I want to see you.' His voice was urgent. 'I have to see you. It's nothing to do with work. Forget work. Would it be more convenient for me to come to you?'

'No,' she said in alarm. 'No, it wouldn't.'

'Then suggest somewhere else. Please, Marjorie. I'll meet you anywhere. You can spare me fifteen minutes, surely?'

They met for tea at Laird's in Piccadilly. He seemed happy to see her, but ill-at-ease. She chatted to relax him. 'So you're back at Lloyd's?'

He smiled. 'We said we weren't going to talk about work. But yes – I had a stroke of luck. Some chums of mine were setting up a new outfit.'

'And they asked you to join them?'

'Couldn't get anyone else. Now look, I hope you're going to help me eat these cakes.' He passed the plate.

'Just one, thank you. Are you doing the same sort of thing as before?'

'Er, no,' said Boniface. 'I think it's generally agreed in informed circles that I'm not one of nature's underwriters. I'm more of a Tim Kenilworth figure, if you can imagine such a thing.'

She couldn't. 'How *is* Mr Kenilworth?'

'He retired last month. But Kenilworth Snell's still going

strong. They're the people I'd probably refer you to if you *were* still interested, but you're not.'

'You're right, I'm not,' she said. 'But – just as a matter of interest – why would you refer me to them? What about your own agency – what's it called?'

'Perryer de Park.'

'Why not refer me to Perryer de Park? Olivia said you were looking for people.'

He said with disgust, 'Olivia was pissed.' He took a gulp of tea. 'What does she take me for? Of course I'm looking for people, that's my job, but that doesn't mean I have to spiv about at my godfather's parties.' He put down his tea-cup and looked at the tablecloth. 'And it doesn't mean I have to start putting pressure on people who I've been as close to – as you and I have been close, Marjorie.'

She said quietly, 'That was a long time ago.'

'It doesn't feel like a long time to me. It didn't feel like a long time on New Year's Eve when I saw you and realized you were avoiding me. Not that I blame you. There have been times over the last couple of years when I've felt so bad about what happened that I've wished I could avoid myself.'

'It was never my wish,' she said slowly, 'for you to feel bad.'

'The number of times I've come close to picking up the phone and calling you . . .'

'Why didn't you, then?' Her voice was louder than she had intended, and full of pent-up pain. She hadn't wanted him to know about the pain, but now she was displaying it to the entire restaurant.

'I didn't know how to begin to apologize,' he said.

'There was nothing to apologize for.'

'Wasn't there? Abusing a friendship? Taking advantage of a kindness . . .'

'We're both adults,' she began.

'Indeed,' he said. 'Responsible for our actions – and the consequences.'

'There haven't been any consequences.'

'You don't think your husband suspects?'

'No.'

'Then at least,' said Boniface, 'I have the consolation of knowing that I did the right thing.'

'You did?'

'By staying away from you,' he explained. 'Resisting the temptation to try and see you again. I'd never have forgiven myself if something I did caused problems between you and Robert. You two have been together how long?'

'Twenty-eight years,' she said.

'Twenty-eight years.' He sounded wistful. 'I don't think anyone would put up with me for that long.'

'Of course they would. You just haven't met the right person yet.'

'Oh, I have,' he said.

'You have?'

'I'm always meeting women who seem to be right. Attractive, intelligent, sexy.' He grimaced, then shrugged. 'But they're always with someone else.'

48

Higley & Higley was a family firm, established shortly after the war. It had looked after Marjorie's parents' hotel business from the beginning, and had grown with it.

In the bewildering days following the settlement of her mother's estate, Marjorie had gone to the senior partner, Frank Higley, to ask what she should do.

He was in his seventies, sharp and alert. His initial advice, since she had no immediate need for the money – no outstanding debts, no mortgage to pay off – was to do nothing. The share portfolio was performing well, so she might as well leave it as it was; and the premium bonds represented a pleasant little flutter. Savings he advised her to reallocate around different types of account, some fixed-term, some with easy access. Then, if she got the urge to do some home improvements, or give the family a holiday, or make a charitable donation – which were the sorts of things people tended to do with legacies – the money would be available.

Mr Higley's advice was sound and solid and she had acted on it; but now, listening to Boniface, she remembered that she had found it somehow unsatisfying. It didn't resolve the puzzlement she felt about having the money in the first place: money that she had not earned or won or even found lying about in the street, but merely received in the post, for no better reason than that she was herself.

Boniface seemed to be aware of that puzzlement. 'There's no point in having money if it doesn't make you happy. I don't mean that naïvely – I know it can't *buy* happiness, but –'

'You can be miserable in comfort?' Marjorie quipped.

He did not smile. He looked politely shocked at her levity. 'On its own, it's nothing. In the old days, at least it was a bag of gold or a pile of notes, something you could see and touch; now it's just numbers, electronics. What it is, is potential. Potential for doing things, having things, potential for letting others do things and have things. Making people's lives better, making your own life better. But how many people have the wit to realize how to do that? Not many. I run into quite a lot of rich people, and believe me, wealth is wasted on them. You know why? Because they don't know what makes them happy. They wouldn't know happiness if it jumped out from behind a hedge and mugged them.'

Soon they were discussing what made Marjorie happy. She talked about the holiday she had treated the family to last summer: she and Robert had rented a villa in Crete for a month, and Di, Tony and the children, and Caroline and her boyfriend had flown out to join them. That had made her happy. She was happy to have Cheyne Walk, to be able to help Di and Tony out by letting them live there while they sorted themselves out. She was a bit less happy at the way they continued to drop hints about her investing in Tony's business – she felt that a free flat ought to be enough – but that was families for you. She had enjoyed helping Caroline to buy a car, and giving Robert a state-of-the-art computer for his birthday. And she had made a donation to the ChildPeril Foundation.

'All things to make other people happy, Marjorie,' Boniface remarked, looking into her eyes. 'What about *you*?'

She wanted to say, *YOU made me happy once, Boniface*, but it might embarrass him, and anyway it wasn't even true. That had been an exciting time, but not a happy one. It had been too full of anxiety, of scheming, and ultimately of hurt. This was better: the two of them sitting openly together in a restaurant, talking business.

'So tell me about your work,' she said.

'Nope.' He shook his head, boyishly defiant. 'Sorry. The word "Lloyd's" shall not pass my lips. We've already established that you're not interested, and that's just fine.'

'Of course I'm interested, Boniface. In your work. Your life.'

Later, she was to remember doing *Othello* at school. Desdemona had fallen in love with Othello after listening to his tales of derring-do. *I loved him for the dangers he had passed.* Something like that. Boniface's was a different type of derring-do, but no less thrilling. He spoke of marine risks and non-marine risks: aviation, space travel, pharmaceuticals, telecommunications, information technology, lasers. He spoke of smaller, idiosyncratic transactions involving actresses' teeth, cancelled papal visits, the Loch Ness Monster. It was a strange business, he admitted – a mixture of hard-nosed commerce (Perryer de Park names were enjoying average returns of up to forty per cent per annum at the moment), ancient customs (a three-year accounting period, dating back to the time when it took three years for a sailing ship to make a trading voyage round the world, the origin of the expression *when my ship comes in*) and almost magical clairvoyance – *the computer printout may tell the underwriter one thing, Marjorie; but if the pricking of his thumbs tells him something else, a lot of our best chaps will go by the pricking of their thumbs.*

She decided to talk it over with Higley & Higley. Frank Higley had retired, and her affairs were now looked after by a new partner called Rajiv Chaudhery. He was in his late twenties, slender and immaculately groomed. He wore a dark suit and dazzling white shirt. Framed photographs of his wife and young children hung from the wall alongside his professional certificates. 'Good morning, Mrs Fairfax. How nice to see you again.'

'You too, Rajiv. And I've told you before – it's Marjorie.'

'Thank you.' He smiled shyly. 'Do please sit down ... Marjorie.'

She sat, and so did he. 'Thank *you* for making time to see me.'

'It sounded urgent on the phone.'

The comment disconcerted her. Had she made it sound urgent? 'It isn't urgent at all.'

Rajiv Chaudhery inclined his head.

'I wanted to ask your advice about something,' she said.

'May I arrange some tea for us first?'

She couldn't wait. 'I'm thinking of becoming a name at Lloyd's.'

Rajiv looked startled. 'I see.'

'Lloyd's of London,' she clarified. 'The insurance market.'

'Yes, I am aware . . .'

'But you don't approve?'

Rajiv spread his immaculate brown hands. 'Mrs Fairfax, it is hardly for me to approve or disapprove of such a venerable institution.' He buzzed for his secretary and asked her to bring tea. He remained silent for a few moments, thinking. When he was ready to resume the conversation, he said, 'May I ask what has given you this idea?' His tone was gentle. He might be responding to some hare-brained scheme dreamed up by one of his children.

She said defensively, 'It was suggested to me by a friend.'

'Someone who works in the market, perhaps?'

'He's with the Perryer de Park members' agency.' She felt proud saying it.

'I am not sure that I know that one.'

'It's new.'

'And therefore is on the lookout for new clients?'

'Don't get the wrong idea, Rajiv. He hasn't been doing a heavy sell on me.'

'I am pleased to hear it. What does your husband think?'

She laughed. 'I've told you before about Robert and money.'

'But surely you intend to discuss it with him?'

'How can I, when I hardly understand it myself? That's why I've come to you – for more information. Of course, if you're saying you don't know anything about it . . .'

'I am not without knowledge.' Rajiv's tone was brisk. 'We

do have clients who are names, and in fairness it must be said that their syndicates' results have, over the past few years, been satisfactory. More than satisfactory, in some cases.'

She glowed. It was like getting a favourable report from her child's school. 'Underwriting,' Rajiv continued, 'can be an excellent thing for the right person, but . . .'

'But I'm not the right person. Is that it, Rajiv?'

'I have not said . . .'

'Why not? Because I'm not a peer of the realm?'

He smiled. 'Mrs Fairfax, the English class system is a great mystery to me, and I would not be so incautious as to form an opinion on how it operates. I am not concerned with who you are, I am concerned with what you have and what you might lose. In my opinion, you are somewhat undercapitalized for Lloyd's membership.'

'But Boniface says –'

He would not let her interrupt. 'You may know all this already. If so, forgive the repetition. For my own peace of mind, I would like to be sure that you understand that underwriting at Lloyd's is not like an ordinary investment. It is not like the ICI shares that your parents left you, for example, or unit trusts. It is not even like gambling on horses. If you were to put your life savings on the favourite in the 3.15 at Aintree and it fell at the first fence, that would be very sad for you. But at the end of the day, you could not lose more than your original stake.'

'Of course not,' she said, with some impatience.

'You say "of course not", Marjorie, but if you were on a Lloyd's syndicate that suffered a substantial loss, you would have to make good that loss. You personally, and the other names personally. You would have what is called unlimited liability.' He paused. 'Lloyd's syndicates,' he went on more gently, 'specialize in predicting the unpredictable – and paying up like English gentlemen when they get it wrong. You would have to pay up like a gentleman, Marjorie – to the full limit of your resources. Your savings. Your parents' shares. Your car. Pictures, jewellery. Perhaps even your house. Did your friend mention that to you?'

49

'Marjorie. Me.'

'Oh, hello, Boniface.' Three weeks had gone by. She was very cool.

'I was wondering,' he said, 'if you'd had a chance to have a look at the bumf I sent you.'

'I have.'

He waited. So did she.

'I'm not supposed to do this, you know,' said Boniface.

'To do what?'

'Pursue you.'

'Is that what you're doing?'

'I'm supposed to bung the literature in the post and let it speak for itself. We don't need to chase people. They're queuing up. If someone isn't interested, then they aren't interested.'

'Why would they not be interested, Boniface?' She made the question sound unimportant, a casual speculation.

'Search me,' he said. 'I suppose there'll always be people who don't know a good thing when they see it.'

'I suppose there will.' As if changing the subject, she said, 'I had a word with my accountant.'

'Jolly good.'

'He told me something that surprised me rather.'

'May I guess what it was? He warned you about unlimited liability.'

She was taken aback. 'How did you know that?'

'They always do. At least, they should. If he hadn't mentioned it, you'd be well advised to sack the fellow.'

His audacity made her jaw drop. 'So why didn't *you* mention it?'

'Why should I? You said you weren't interested.'

'You were starting to make me interested.'

'Was I? All right, but I don't think I'd exactly twisted your arm behind your back and said "sign here", had I?'

A *frisson* went through her as she imagined how that might feel.

'That's next time,' he joked. 'Seriously, I knew you'd take advice, and I knew your advisor would tell you everything. I thought it would sound better coming from him. Anything *I* might say on the subject might sound like special pleading.'

'Oh.'

'And to be honest with you, Marjorie, I can think of a few people who'd be pretty surprised to hear me being accused of not mentioning unlimited liability. I bore for England on the subject – as you will discover next, wait a minute, Thursday. Are you free on Thursday – say 2.30 at Embankment tube?'

Why this location, he did not say; perhaps he would be on his way to another appointment. This, and the time he selected, seemed to indicate that he did not have a long meeting in mind. Certainly not lunch, or afternoon tea.

Just as well, she told herself. The time for lunching together had passed. They would have a coffee, he would say his piece and she would listen. It was the least she could do, after having doubted him. And then they would go their separate ways.

It was a bitter March day, too cold even for snow. A sharp wind nipped at her face, at her fingers through her gloves and her toes through her boots. Vagrants clustered in the station forecourt, too demoralized even to beg.

He came pushing through the crowd, a few minutes late, well turned-out as ever, but slightly pale and tired-looking. He shook her hand and said how pleased he was to see her. He led her out through the Embankment exit and towards the pier, where pleasure boats were moored. One, headed for Greenwich with about four passengers, was starting its engines.

'Fancy a boat trip.' It was not a question. He stood aside

for her to walk up the gangway. She hoped they would go below with the other passengers, but he seemed already to have decided that they would sit alone on the upper deck. For privacy, she supposed. In other circumstances this might have been romantic; but the gusts of wind were like buckets of cold water thrown over them. 'Forgive my childishness,' he said. 'I love boat trips.'

'I'm very fond of them myself.'

The boat backed out into the middle of the river, turned and headed eastwards towards the City. Old warehouses and wharves brooded over the grey river, some derelict, some converted into sparkling new blocks with landscaped walkways. 'What troubles me most,' he said, raising his voice above the throb of the engine, 'is that you should have had a moment's unease on my account.'

'I haven't,' she said quickly. 'I never –'

'Not even after talking to your accountant? You haven't been wondering what sort of crook you've got yourself involved with?'

Involved, she thought. *Are we involved?* It was just his manner of speaking. 'Rajiv never said you were a crook, and I never thought it.'

'Who?'

'Rajiv Chaudhery. My accountant.'

'Where's he from?'

'Kingston-upon-Thames.'

Boniface paused before saying, 'I'm sure he's a first-class chap.'

'I think so.'

'He certainly got it right as far as Lloyd's is concerned,' said Boniface. 'It *is* unlimited liability. It has to be, because that's the nature of risk. Look at it from the policy-holder's point of view – from *your* point of view as a policy-holder. That super house of yours. Presumably that's insured, and presumably you pay through the nose for it.'

'We certainly do,' said Marjorie.

'If, heaven forfend, something happened to it one day – have one of these, it'll keep you warm.' He brought out a small box of liqueur chocolates. She took one with Cointreau in it for warmth. 'Suppose your cleaning lady left her fag burning and the place went up in flames. What would you think of your insurers if they turned round and said, "Frightfully sorry, Mrs Fairfax, there've been rather a lot of house fires this month, we've reached our limit and we can't pay out any more"? I think your attitude would be, "Who are you to have a limit? I've paid my premiums, you jolly well pay my claim."'

She nodded. The Cointreau was warming her chest. Perhaps in time it would reach her toes.

'So that's how it is,' he said. 'Lloyd's always pays legitimate claims – and if that sometimes proves expensive for the market, tough.'

'Tough for the names, you mean?'

'Not really,' he said. 'It doesn't work like that. It couldn't. Some of our names are . . . well, I mustn't be indiscreet, but think captains of industry, think landed gentry, think the great and the good, think some of the canniest business people in the land – not to mention a small but growing circle of financially sophisticated Americans. Think film stars, sporting personalities, high court judges, members of parliament. Think not a million miles from Buckingham Palace. Would they stick around – would their advisors let them stick around – if they thought they were going to come down to breakfast one morning and find a bill beside their Weetabix – "One flood, one fire, one pestilence – 500 million quid, plus VAT. Kindly send your remittance within twenty-eight days"?'

Marjorie smiled. 'Probably not.'

'A syndicate doesn't take on an entire risk. Five or ten per cent is more usual. The rest is shared round the market and reinsured. So an individual name wouldn't find himself liable for a whole ship.' He glanced round at the deck. 'You'd be insuring the glass in the third porthole on the starboard lower deck, or the toothbrush-holder in the captain's bog. And you wouldn't even be doing that if it was a high-risk vessel and you'd made it clear to your agent that you only wanted to be on low-risk syndicates.'

'I could do that, could I?'

'What – take an interest? I certainly hope you will. Hey, Marjorie, you look freezing. Do you mind sitting up here? I hate having all those people around. Wear my scarf.' He put it carefully round her neck. 'I warned you that I bore for England, I didn't tell you I was going to give you hypothermia as well.' He tucked the scarf in.

'Do please go on, Boniface. I'm not bored at all.'

'Where was I?'

'You were saying you like names to take an interest.'

'Lord, yes. Nothing we like more. It's a very personal relationship. You'll always get some who just hand the whole thing over to us, and we don't get a peep out of them unless they decide that the fat cheque we've just sent them isn't quite as fat as they'd hoped. But we prefer the ones we can be friends with, the ones who ring us up from time to time for a chat, pop in and see us when they're in town.'

Membership formalities took several months. Boniface said they might take all year. When you have been doing something for three hundred years, the word *hurry* doesn't appear in your vocabulary.

She didn't mind how long it took. She enjoyed the attention – not just from Boniface, but from Rajiv too. Once Rajiv had satisfied himself that this was what she really wanted, he hid his disapproval and was helpfulness itself. He worked with Boniface to prepare statements of her assets and other documentation. He referred to Boniface as 'Mr Bennett'. Boniface referred to him as 'that chap of yours'. She enjoyed having two young men beavering away on her behalf.

By autumn, everything was ready. She had to attend an interview with three senior members of the insurance market's governing council. Boniface accompanied her. He said there was absolutely nothing to worry about, but he seemed more nervous than she was as they waited in a long, hushed corridor. A door opened and an elderly couple came out, shepherded by a man in a suit. The man and Boniface nodded at each other, but did not speak. Marjorie and Boniface were next. The room was vast, with a dark red carpet, a chandelier and a polished table with three men sitting behind it. They were polite and charming, but this took nothing from the seriousness of the occasion. They asked about her journey up from Sussex, and whether Boniface had given her a good lunch. Then they went straight into unlimited liability. Had Boniface told her about it? Did she understand what it was? She was proud to be able to say yes. She had the feeling that if he hadn't told her, he would now be in quite serious trouble. It was reassuring, that they were so meticulous. A few weeks later, she received her membership papers. Her first year of underwriting began on 1 January 1987.

50

The wind woke her at 2.50 a.m. Having lived most of her life near the coast, she was no stranger to autumn storms; but this eerie whine, combined with savage force, was unlike anything she had ever heard.

A branch slammed against the side of the house. For an instant she saw twigs against the window, like grasping fingers. They fell back into the darkness.

Robert slept at her side, undisturbed. She snuggled against his back. Without waking, he gave her a little push and rolled away from her embrace.

Shaking, she got out of bed. The curtains were billowing into the room like sails. She closed the window, then tried to put lights on. Nothing happened. More flying debris clattered against the outside wall.

Robert sat up. 'What's going on?'

'How the hell should I know?'

Down in the kitchen, Castor and Pollux were howling with terror. Robert put on his dressing gown and went downstairs to comfort them.

She followed. 'That's right. Look after the dogs.'

'*What did you say?*' He was shouting to be heard above the rattling of the doors and windows. She shouted back, 'Are you having an affair with someone?' The question flew out of her, like something on the wind. The question she had never dared ask for fear of what the answer might be, the question she had no right to ask.

A deafening thump came from the other end of the house, followed by a crash and tinkle of glass. Perhaps he had not heard the question. They rushed to the sitting room to investigate. The patio doors had blown in. They had only had them six months.

One had fallen across the settee, ripping the fabric. The other door hung dangerously from a single hinge. Rain and melting hailstones were soaking into the carpet. Marjorie's mother's carriage clock had fallen from the mantelpiece and shattered into pieces, along with several ornaments.

They shored up the patio doors as best they could, Robert shouting instructions. How masterful he was in an emergency, she thought sourly. They moved furniture out of range of the rain and hail, rolled back the carpet, put breakable objects in safe places, collected up pieces of the ones that had already broken. Robert located the guarantee for the patio doors. They did a quick tour of the house to check that the remaining doors and windows were intact, then went back to the dark kitchen and looked for candles.

The wind had an intermittent quality; it shook the house, then paused as if to gather its strength for another go. During one of the pauses he said, '*What* did you ask me before?'

'When?'

'Just now.'

'I don't know what you're talking about.'

'You asked me if I was having an affair with someone.'

'Are you?'

The wind was picking up. Out in the yard, tiles were raining down from the roof. The back door was rattling as if the hounds of hell were hurling themselves against it. Robert struggled to wedge it with folded newspaper. 'What a thing to ask at a time like this,' he said.

'When would be a better time?' she snarled, lighting candles. 'And why won't you answer?'

'I'll answer. The answer's no, but I have to say I think it's a hell of a question.' An airborne object thudded into the side of the house. Castor and Pollux whimpered. Robert patted them. 'What's brought this on?'

'You pushed me away.'

'I did? When? Where?'

'In bed. I was frightened and I cuddled up to you and you pushed me away.' She sounded like a child. Embarrassed, she moved her face out of the candlelight.

'I must have been asleep.' He held out his arms. 'Come and have a cuddle now, to make up.'

'No thanks. I'm not your car, needing to be serviced.'

He raised his eyebrows. 'Who am I supposed to have been having an affair with? Do tell.'

She hadn't thought it through that far. In her fantasies about his adultery, the woman was always a shadowy figure. She said the first name that came into her head. 'Olivia?'

'Spare me.'

'Nina, then.'

'Nope.'

She believed him. Her heart sank. It wasn't that he found another woman more attractive than he found her. It was that he didn't find her attractive, full stop.

She fetched her radio and moved the dial from station to station. The news was piecemeal. No one seemed to know what was really happening. All they had was rumour and anecdote about the freak winds that were sweeping across the south-east of England. There were no proper newsreaders – just sleepy, late-night disc jockeys trying to rise to the occasion. They reported in bemused tones that buildings, bridges and other structures were collapsing. Sea defences were being breached, causing serious flooding. Ships were in difficulty in the channel. Lifeboats going to their assistance had been forced to turn back. 999 switchboards were jammed with calls, but the winds were too strong to allow emergency vehicles on the road. Official advice to the public was to stay indoors, keep away from windows and remain calm.

'What is it about those words "remain calm",' Robert mused, 'that tells you that things are serious?' He obviously thought their earlier discussion was closed. He tapped at his battery-driven lap-top while the screen shed its greenish glow on his lined, hairy face. Following the success of *Comprehension and Communication in the Classroom*, he was now working on an article entitled *Speaking and Listening Tasks for Third-year Pupils – An Overview*.

Towards morning, the wind eased and the proper news-readers turned up at the radio stations to take over from the disc jockeys. Grown-up, solemn-voiced and systematic, they assembled facts and statistics and located experts to interview. Staff from the London Weather Centre confessed themselves baffled. Nothing like this had happened in three centuries. Officials at Kew Gardens were wringing their hands over fallen trees. A senior dignitary at the Stock Exchange announced that trading would be suspended today in order to avoid panic selling of shares. He was followed by a spokesman from the insurance industry.

The spokesman was calm and avuncular. 'Most house-holders,' he said, 'can take comfort from the knowledge that storm damage is usually included in standard buildings policies.'

Robert scoffed. 'Listen to those weasel words. "Most" house-holders. "Usually" included. "Standard" policies. They'll find a way to get out of paying, you mark my words.'

She eyed him coldly. 'You think so?'

'They'll try. Otherwise, this little lot is going to cost someone a fortune.'

51

The garage was badly damaged, but the cars had somehow survived. Robert set off to try to drive to school.

Marjorie attacked the yard with a broom and a shovel, clearing up bits of garage, broken tiles and splinters of wood from the shattered dovecote. Where the doves had gone, heaven alone knew.

She was keeping an eye on the time. At nine o'clock, she hurried into the house and dialled Boniface's office.

The line was engaged. She made a face. The dotty duchess had beaten her to it.

She had heard about the dotty duchess a few weeks ago, when she happened to be in town and had called in at Boniface's office for a chat. She couldn't remember how the subject came up – perhaps he was apologizing for not having time for more than a quick cup of tea with her. He had spent the whole morning on the phone, pacifying the dotty duchess. He hadn't revealed her full name or where she was duchess of – *even I'm not that indiscreet, Marjorie. Suffice it to say she's a lady of leisure who fancies she knows a thing or two about underwriting. She goes through the papers every morning with a magnifying glass in one hand, tot of gin in another, red biro in another* – he demonstrated.

She could hardly stop laughing. *THREE hands, Boniface?*

A remarkable woman. If she spots anything that looks as if it might give rise to an insurance claim, she puts a big red ring round it, then gets on the blower to us demanding to know what her exposure is. We've tried telling her it doesn't work like that, but you know. In one ear and out the other.

What a pest the woman sounded. Marjorie would never pester him. She just wanted a quick word.

She kept dialling the number, but it stayed engaged. Robert came home unexpectedly and she slammed the phone down. 'Those wretched patio doors people,' she said. 'Engaged all the time.'

'Let me have a try.' He put out his hand for the phone and the number, but of course she hadn't got the number. He gave her a funny look and went to look for it. When he eventually found it and dialled it, he got straight through. Afterwards he said, 'I shall start to think you're the one who's having the affair,' in light-hearted tones.

His school was closed, pending a safety inspection by structural engineers. He and Marjorie spent the day contacting repair people, making appointments with tree surgeons and fending off phone calls from Olivia, who was conscripting people into an emergency task force.

The next day was Saturday. Robert was sent out on to the by-pass as part of a team equipped with chainsaws to cut fallen trees into firewood and so clear the road. Marjorie's orders were to report to the village hall where accommodation was being provided for those whose homes had been rendered uninhabitable, along with hot meals and advice from the local bank manager on how to fill in insurance claims. Before setting out, Marjorie considered phoning Boniface at home. She had his number. It was on the back of a special business card which he gave only to his names. Even so, she was hesitant about using it. If someone was at home, you couldn't know what else they were doing when they were talking to you. They could be in a roomful of people you had never met, making faces about you.

He could be in the bath. He could be in bed with Orlanda. She had met Orlanda on another of her visits to the Perryer de Park office. Boniface had taken her round, introducing her to everyone. Most of them were men, but there was this marmalade cat of a girl. Marjorie had known at once.

She didn't mind. This was the great thing about her being a

name and Boniface being her agent – it meant that other things were out of the question, in the same way that they were out of the question between a doctor and his patient. So you didn't mind so much.

On Monday morning, the phone lines were clear and Marjorie got straight through to Perryer de Park. Orlanda took the call, informing Marjorie in her gushy, over-the-top way that Boniface was in a meeting. Could she help? Marjorie thanked Orlanda for the offer but said she would like to speak to Boniface personally.

Orlanda promised to pass the message on, but she must have forgotten, because Boniface didn't return the call until Wednesday.

'Marjorie,' he said. 'You've been on my conscience.'

She loathed that expression, and was sorry to hear him use it. She couldn't understand why anyone used it. Did they imagine that their conscience was a desirable place to be?

'How are you, Boniface?'

'Extremely well, extremely busy – which is why I've been neglecting you. That's a reason, not an excuse.' His tone was brisk. 'What can I do for you?'

'I just wanted a quick word about the hurricane.'

'Cat 87J,' he said.

'I'm sorry?'

'Catastrophe No. 87J. That's what we call it.'

'Do you?'

'Name them, number them and file them away, Marjorie. Cut 'em down to size. Stop the blighters getting an undue sense of their own importance.'

Marjorie hadn't noticed any diminution of the event's importance in *her* eyes, but she said, 'Yes.'

'I expect it hit you pretty hard,' said Boniface.

'Has it?' she said in alarm.

'You and Robert. Being on the coast.'

'Oh, I see what you mean. Yes, it *was* rather lively.'

'All mopped up now?'

'Oh, yes.'

'Jolly good.'

'But, you see, Boniface, I was wondering –' she put laughter into her voice '– at the risk of sounding like –' ought she to mention the duchess over the phone? His colleagues might not approve of the special relationship she and Boniface had, in which he felt free to pass on office gossip. 'I don't want to be a nuisance, but I wondered whether the, er, whether my syndicates –' she didn't know how to phrase her question. This world she had entered had its own language and etiquette, and she had no grasp of either.

'Nothing to worry about,' he said. 'Just a little blip.'

'It didn't seem like a blip to us, when our new patio doors went sailing over the horizon.'

'No, I don't suppose it did. But you see, Marjorie, what may be perceived by the general public as a huge disaster is pretty much routine for us.'

For a chilling moment, she thought he was classifying her as a member of the general public – the one thing she thought that she had ceased to be when she became a name. A sharp comment rose to her lips; but she bit it back, realizing in the nick of time that he had not meant that at all. She wasn't included among the general public, she was included among *us*. Us in the business. We who understand these things, as opposed to the general public, who do not.

52

Since she was so worried, he said, he would look into the matter, and let her have a full report on her exposure to the catastrophe. He insisted that she had no cause for concern. 'I wouldn't have put you on those syndicates in the first place if I wasn't confident that the chaps running them know exactly what they're doing. They'll have a good spread of risk, and they'll have reinsured everything a hundred times over.'

'Boniface, forgive me,' she said. 'I've never really understood about reinsurance. You've tried to explain it to me, I know, but I'm a bit dim. Could I possibly come and see you about it?'

'Can't think of anything I'd like more,' he said. 'But –'

'When you've had a chance to look it up.'

'Look what up?'

'My, er, syndicates.'

'I will, by all means,' he said. 'And I'll give you a call towards the middle of next month.'

It seemed a long time to wait, but this must be a busy time for him. She mustn't be a pest.

Next day she went up to London, to Cheyne Walk. She had promised to babysit while Di went to an exhibition at the Royal Academy with an old school friend.

She took a taxi from Victoria and reached Cheyne Walk at around 11.30. Men on scaffolding were repairing the roof. Another insurance job, she thought. She let herself into the building with her key, but when she reached the front door of the flat she rang the bell. She wasn't one to go barging into her daughter's home as if she owned it, even if she did.

Di called, 'Come in, I'm on the loo.' Marjorie opened the door. Four-year-old Emma was sitting on the antique oak chest in the hall, kicking the wood in time with a song she was singing as she looked at a picture book. It was a charming sight, and Marjorie tried to be charmed by it. She tried not to see the scuff marks on the carvings of the chest. She tried not to wish for the umpteenth time that she had moved all the good furniture out before letting the family move in.

Emma slithered off the chest and rushed towards her. 'Granny, Granny, Granny!'

'Hello, darling.' Marjorie picked her up and hugged her. 'Where's your mummy?'

'Bathroom,' Di called.

Oliver came crawling across the greying Axminster of the hall with his hands coated in chocolate. 'My precious little boy, what *are* you eating?' It was one of those chocolate cream egg things. 'I don't think that's such a good idea, do you? You'll spoil your lunch.' She took the egg away from him. He fought for it, but Marjorie triumphed. Oliver howled. Marjorie went to the kitchen and made space for the chocolatey slime in the overflowing swing-bin. She rinsed her fingers under the tap. The double sink was full of dishes.

Oliver was still crying. Marjorie wiped his face and hands, then chose an apple from the fruit bowl and looked for a clean knife. There being none, she chose a dirty one and washed it. She peeled the apple, cut it into quarters and gave him one. He threw it on the floor and stamped on it.

Rolling her eyes, she caught a glimpse of a scrap of paper pinned to the notice-board near the fridge. It bore the words 'Heather Fox', and a telephone number.

At first it hardly registered. It was just a piece of random family information, among the dental appointments and special offers and bills. But the name was familiar. That girlfriend of Boniface's was called Heather. And now that Marjorie thought about it, the surname could well have been Fox.

Di appeared in the kitchen doorway in a navy blue dress, matching coat, and make-up that had been too hastily applied.

Her recently announced third pregnancy hardly showed. She frowned at her screaming son: 'What are you bellyaching about? Do try and be good for your granny or she won't come again.' She turned to Marjorie. 'Lunch is spaghetti hoops for them and a piece of smoked mackerel for you in the fridge with horseradish if you can find it. And yogurts.'

'Di, who is Heather Fox?'

Di looked blank. Marjorie pointed at the notice. Di said, 'Oh – her.'

'Do you know her?'

'Hardly,' said Di. 'She said she knew you.'

'But how did you meet?'

'Long story.' Di kissed her children and headed for the door. 'I'll tell you when I get back.'

53

It's not all that long, not really, but you might as well hear it from me.

The alternative is to tell it as Di told it to her mother, but I would then have to come along afterwards and correct the bits she got wrong, as well as putting in the bits she couldn't have known about. And you might start to lose patience.

Mooching around at my mother's, I at last decided that there must be more to life than working in a burger bar and sleeping with Ronnie Zermatt when he came to Norwich on business. So in the autumn of 1984, I enrolled part-time at the local poly to try and improve my A-levels.

I read all the books on the syllabus, which went against the grain, as you can probably imagine, but I had set my heart on trying again for university – in particular the University of South Bermondsey in London, which had recently been featured in the education section of the *Guardian* as one of the few universities in the country to offer a creative writing option to undergraduates.

To make up for having to read people like D. H. Lawrence and E. M. Forster and Milton, I devised an alternative syllabus of my own, consisting of novels about women living on their own in rooms. There were quite a number of them if you really looked – books by Jean Rhys, Lynn Reid Banks, Muriel Spark, Rosalind Belben, Elizabeth Taylor. Inspired, I set to work on another novel of my own. I thought I was inspired. The judges of the 1985 Coates Clarion award took a different view, and back my entry came.

My mother and Ronnie tried to persuade me to send it to publishers, but I was too disheartened. I decided to put off any further literary endeavour until I was safely ensconced in the

English Studies department at the University of South Bermondsey. They at least had not completely spurned me – I had sent some sample chapters with my application, and they had offered me a place, subject to my getting at least Grade Bs.

Ronnie took it for granted that I would get them, and started making plans. 'When you come back to London, shall we get a flat together?'

'Well, I don't know,' I said.

'All right, Heather,' he said. 'I won't push you.'

When my exams were two months away, I told him that I wouldn't be able to see him until they were over.

He looked upset. 'What, not at all?'

'I've got to get good grades,' I said. 'This is important to me.'

'It's important to me as well, but you can't study all the time. I come all this way to see you –'

'No, you don't,' I reminded him. 'You come to Norwich on business and you fit me in.'

He looked embarrassed, and I wondered whether his work in Norwich had really necessitated his presence quite as often as his frequent visits suggested.

'Is that the way you see it?' he asked.

'It's not a question of the way I see it,' I replied. 'It's a question of me not being able to see you again until after my exams.'

The day after my last exam, Mum said, 'Will you be seeing Ronnie again now?'

'Possibly.'

'Only possibly?'

'Oh, you know,' I said. 'I might meet him now and again as a friend. He's a nice guy.'

'But nothing more?'

I looked at her closely. 'Why are you so interested?'

She went pink. 'He's coming to Norwich this weekend for a party. He wants me to go with him.'

I stared at her. '*You?*'

'Yes.'

'How long's this been going on?'

'Nothing's "going on".'

'You mean he's just asked you to a party, out of the blue?'

'No,' she admitted. 'He rang up a couple of weeks ago, but I told him I didn't want anything to happen that might upset you while you were doing your revision.'

'It wouldn't have upset me.'

We were quiet for a few moments. She offered me a cigarette, and I took it. I said, 'What about Pete?'

Pete was her current man. He had replaced Harry Wyatt about a year ago.

'Pete and I,' said Mum, 'have reached the end of the road. We were never right for each other. It was a rebound thing, after Harry.'

I thought this was a bit rich, considering it was she who had finished with Harry, rather than the other way round. But this was Mum all over. When her lovers became exes, she always talked about ends of roads, partings of ways, about never having been right for each other. She made it sound as if their splitting up had been inevitable from the beginning, nobody's fault, one of those things. She never admitted that she just became restless and had to move on.

54

They refrained from sleeping together in the house, but I knew it was only out of kindness for me, and some kinds of kindness are almost as bad as their opposite. When Mum went off for the night and came back with a certain look in her eyes, I felt lonely and cast off and sad.

I waited in dread for my exam results. If they weren't good enough, it would be my third rejection in a year – Coates Clarion, Ronnie and university. I might never get over it, never get away.

My fears were unfounded. I got what I needed, and in the autumn of 1986 I left home again and began my course at the University of South Bermondsey. This would have been round about the time when Marjorie was going through the final formalities of becoming a name.

I discovered that the creative writing module in the English course didn't begin until the second year. This was because the lecturers were under pressure from the university authorities to prove that the writing course wasn't just a soft option for weak students who couldn't handle the rigours of Anglo-Saxon and literary theory. So I had to endure a year of Anglo-Saxon and literary theory.

Lectures were given in huge halls to audiences of several hundred. Tutorials were few and far between. I lived in a basement bedsitter not far from the Elephant & Castle, found for me by the university accommodation office. It was expensive, but the alternative would have been a shared student house or flat, and I didn't want that. I worked part-time to supplement my grant, at first in a burger bar and then, at the beginning of my second year, for a company called Eavesdroppers.

I found the Eavesdroppers job through one of the creative writing tutors, Alice Lott, novelist and big favourite of my mother's friend Patience. I didn't mention this to Alice, though perhaps I should have – it might have made her more merciful. I hardly dared say anything to Alice, except 'Thank you' when she tore my work to shreds. She had a fund of depressing statistics to prove that the chances of any of us ever making a living from writing were infinitesimal, regardless of how talented we were – and she never gave the impression that she thought any of us was particularly talented. She urged us to investigate other employment, particularly the kind that involved words and documents. She reminded us that Dickens had worked in a legal office, Kafka in insurance, Stevie Smith in the civil service and Fay Weldon in advertising. None of them had been any the worse for it, she declared briskly in the tone of one who was in a position to judge, and neither would we be if we found jobs that helped keep our writing muscles active. If she heard of opportunities, she drew them to our attention.

Eavesdroppers monitored radio and TV broadcasting on behalf of clients such as government departments, pressure groups, foreign embassies and publicity-hungry TV stars. That may sound glamorous, but it wasn't. Eavesdroppers was based in a cluster of prefabricated huts in a business park behind the Old Kent Road. It employed people with fast, accurate keyboard skills and an up-to-the-minute grasp of current affairs (I'm quoting here from the job description) to turn up at the prefabs at strange times and spend the next six to eight hours listening to the radio or watching TV and writing a précis of what we heard.

The hours were irregular, often involving nights. But the wages were reasonable, and paid in cash at the end of each shift. I fitted in well, because at Eavesdroppers a reclusive personality was a must. A gregarious, party-going type would have been miserable. Not only would all the night work have made it difficult for them to go to parties, but even when you were at Eavesdroppers you couldn't talk to other people. This was partly because of the equipment – at any one time at least a third of the computers would be down, their places taken by old-fashioned manual typewriters, which looked as if they had been acquired in a job-lot circa 1972 and made the most tremendous racket. Another reason why there wasn't a lot of chit-chat was the shift system. Everyone was employed on a casual basis, so you might see someone on one shift and never again. There were no set breaks. If you wanted a break, you had to wait for pauses between programmes, otherwise you might miss something important. People who needed to go to the loo would sit with their legs crossed and agonized expressions on their faces. The more crude among them would enact what was likely to happen if they didn't go soon, with sound effects. The rest of the time, my fellow Eavesdroppers were just faces in the gloom, with headphones clasped round their ears and pens and cigarettes between their teeth, shouting out in anguish, 'How the fuck do you spell Reykjavik?' Their hands thundered across the typewriter keys, making the building shake. The walls were that flimsy, the foundations that fragile. So you can imagine what it was like on the night of the hurricane.

55

It happened in the second or third week of the first term of my second year. My shift began at 11.30 p.m. As I waited for the late bus, I sensed that something was not quite right. The wind had an odd, damp quality and a strange taste and smell. It wasn't nasty so much as disturbing, like the first time you taste a foreign food or someone else's bodily fluids.

I didn't think much about it. I was thinking about the creative writing module, which had just started, and wondering how I had ever got on it. I felt eclipsed by the talent and originality of the other people in the group, some of whom had credits to prove their worth: one woman had had a short story broadcast on Radio Four. A man had been shortlisted for the Coates Clarion award.

There was no escape from this dispiriting knowledge. Gone was the safety of lectures in the huge lecture theatre. The creative writing group was only fourteen strong, and we met in small seminar rooms, as often as not adjourning to the pub afterwards. I was tempted to sneak off when we got to the pub stage, but I was afraid of missing something, afraid of what people might be saying behind my back. Everyone knew everyone else's name, and wanted to know everyone else's business. Discussion of people's writings spilled over into discussion of their lives. Only today, I had read out a short story about someone being adopted. One of the other students said, 'Are you adopted, Heather?' Before I could answer, the tutor said, 'You don't have to answer that, Heather. We're here to comment on your story, not your life.' She and my fellow students then proceeded to tear my story apart. The tutor summed up by saying, 'With a bit more work, I really think you could make that into something.'

Eavesdroppers, with its anonymity, was my refuge. I arrived at the prefab at around 11.25 and let myself in. I nodded at Claire, the shift leader, and made brief eye-contact with the two other people I was on with – a middle-aged man who looked like an actor, and a woman of about my age with red hair.

I picked up my work sheets and found a place to sit with a computer that worked and an ashtray. I got rid of sandwich wrappers, crisp packets and apple cores, put on my headphones and got started on a programme about sanctions-busting in South Africa.

The hurricane blew up between about midnight and one. First the prefab started swaying. Then a chunk of metal scaffolding came crashing through a window, missing the red-haired woman by inches. The rest of us dashed over to see if she was all right, which she was. The scaffolding lay at our feet, surrounded by long, sharp shards of glass. Wind was howling through the broken window.

TV screens and computer screens flickered and died. Another window blew in, followed by half a wall. We tried to escape from the prefab and run across the business park to somewhere more substantial, but we were driven back by flying gas cylinders and other objects that you wouldn't want colliding with your face at 60 m.p.h.

We ducked back inside what was left of the prefab and tried to use the phones, but they were dead. The red-haired woman pushed a table against the least insubstantial of the walls and we crawled under it.

We introduced ourselves. The man's name was Francis. The woman was Josephine, Joze for short, pronounced to rhyme with hose. Claire suggested singing songs to keep our spirits up. We sang 'Ten Green Bottles' and 'Bread of Heaven'. Francis had a fine baritone voice, and did beautiful descants.

The wind shrieked around us, picking up anything that got in its way. Tables and chairs toppled over. Televisions and typewriters smashed against wall supports. Bits of roof blew off, revealing a black, boiling sky. We played Twenty Questions, when we could hear ourselves speak, and Call My Bluff and I Spy. We exchanged life stories. Claire talked about her two children. She looked after them in the daytime while her husband worked in local government, and he had them at night. You could see she was wondering whether she would ever see any of them again. Francis mused about the parts he had never played, and probably never would now. Hamlet was one. Claire said he should concentrate on the successes he had had, but he said he couldn't think of any.

Joze said she didn't see why he shouldn't still play Hamlet. He said he was fifty-three years old, that was why. She said so what? It was acting, wasn't it? Francis said, 'Try explaining that to my agent.' Joze said, 'No, you try explaining it to him.'

The wind was building up to one of its climaxes. We clung to the legs of the table to stop it taking off. Above the racket, Francis yelled, 'What do you do in real life, Joze?'

She shouted back, 'I'm trying to set up a business.'

'What sort?'

'Funeral director.'

That was all I needed when I was sure my last hour had come. In gaps between the gusts of wind, Joze tried to explain about how she wanted to change the way the general public thought about funerals, but I didn't want to think about them at all, not now when I was waiting for my life to flash before my eyes. That wasn't going to take long. Perhaps it had already flashed, and I had missed it playing Call My Bluff. What did it amount to? What had I to compare with Francis's three-week run as the alcoholic traffic warden in *Coronation Street*, Claire's children, or Joze's lilac-coloured recyclable coffins? Two failed relationships, two novels that nobody wanted to read and a place on a university course which was starting to look as if I had only got it as a result of an administrative error.

Joze described the time when she had had to fly down to the

south of France to collect the body of an English tourist. The man had known that he was dying, but he had gone in pursuit of a lifelong ambition to watch the Tour de France pass through a particular mountain village in the sunset. She said, 'It's really inspiring – the lengths dying people will go to, to finish their unfinished business.' I didn't feel inspired, and I didn't think the others did either. I think we all wished that Joze would shut up. None of us had the option of going to the south of France, and if we had it wouldn't have been to gawp at some stupid bikes whizzing down a hill, it would have been to save our skins by getting out of this wind. As things were, we could only cower under the flying furniture, thinking of all the things we hadn't done, or had got wrong.

Top of my list was my relationship with Boniface, my loss of him. The trail was cold, or so I had assumed ever since I tried to ring him once from Mum's. At that time I was so miserable that I didn't care about anything except hearing his voice. But his office told me that he no longer worked there; the man at his flat said that he had moved.

I had made determined efforts to forget him. You've heard about some of them: Ronnie was one, others included the burger bar, re-taking my A-levels and reading all those books about solitary women in rooms. Then there had been my attempt to write one. None of them had worked. He was still with me.

But it's true what they say about being close to death: it does concentrate the mind, and allows it to make connections that it might otherwise have missed. The connection was Marjorie. I could find him through her. I didn't know where she lived, but I knew where her late parents' London residence was. I had been there. I guessed she had probably sold it by now, but whoever had bought it would know who they had bought it from. Through them I would find her, and through her I would find him.

That's why, the morning after the hurricane, I extricated

myself from what remained of the Eavesdroppers prefab and limped off in the direction of Chelsea.

I wasn't expecting to find a daughter living there. And Di certainly wasn't expecting me, manic and bedraggled and with a wild look in my eye. I guessed that the only reason she didn't slam the door in my face was because she had been brought up to be kind to those less fortunate than herself.

All I wanted from her was an address or number where I could reach Marjorie, but one look at Di's suspicious expression was enough to let me know that I had better have a good reason. I told her I had once nearly rented this place, and was inquiring whether it was available now for a few weeks as my own place had been damaged in the storm. The sharpness with which Di informed me that it most certainly was *not* available made me realize I had said the wrong thing, and I changed tack: sorry to have bothered her, just thought I'd ask, how *was* her mother, what a nice lady, how lovely it would be to see her again, but we had lost touch, in fact I wasn't even sure that I still had her phone number what with all the stuff I'd lost in the storm. Could Di help me out? No, said Di, looking as if she was about to call the police. I don't blame you, I said, can't be too careful these days can you, do please remember me to her, and look, here's my number, I'll be happy to hear from her any time. And that's how I ended up on Di's kitchen notice-board.

56

'I mean, honestly, Mummy. If you don't like having us here, you only have to say.'

'Don't be silly, dear.'

'You don't have to start moving tenants in on top of us.'

'I'm not moving anybody in.'

'But you admit you know her?' Di made it sound as if knowing Heather Fox was a criminal offence.

'I've met her,' said Marjorie. 'I wouldn't say I knew her.' *I don't want to know her*, she thought. *I don't need to. All I need to know is where she is.*

Her brain was racing. At last she had a hold on Boniface. She had something he wanted: Heather Fox's phone number.

Don't ask her how she knew he wanted it: she *did* know. Call it a woman's intuition. That, and her memories of how he had reacted the first time Heather rejected him, that Christmas when he came to stay, and then a few weeks later when she rejected him for good.

Marjorie knew. She knew more than anyone, because she was the only person to have seen him at both these times, raw and vulnerable. It wasn't a side of himself that he would show to everybody, but he had shown it to her.

His continued love for Heather – secret and unending – explained everything. It explained him having a girlfriend like Orlanda. Orlanda could not be more different from Heather; that was what had attracted him to her. He hoped that she could take his mind off Heather. She hadn't, of course. His mind was still very much on Heather. Marjorie knew this because once, during the early days of their renewed friendship, she had said – casually, purely for the sake of conversation – *Do you ever see that nice girl, Heather? What's she doing these days?* His face had closed down tight. *No idea*, he said, and changed the subject.

He might have no idea, but she had several ideas. The simplest would be to pass the number on. (It would be an excuse to phone him, if nothing else.) But why stop at that? Why not go one better and arrange a lunch date? She would invite Boniface and invite Heather but she would tell neither of them that she was inviting the other. The table would be for two. She herself would not be at the table. She would be hiding behind a bank of flowers. At the crucial moment, she would appear with champagne. The young couple would be eternally grateful to her, and Orlanda would be out on her ear.

Boniface and Heather would invite her to their wedding. She would be godmother to their first child and a regular visitor to their home. It wasn't quite the relationship she had envisaged for herself and Boniface, but, like Lloyd's, it would keep them in touch.

Except that Lloyd's wasn't keeping them in touch. He was supposed to be phoning her to arrange a meeting, to explain about the hurricane, and why she need not worry about it. He had promised. But the days were going by and he was showing no sign of keeping his promise.

Fine. It was up to him. It was his loss, not hers. If he phoned her, he would get Heather back. If not, not.

She decided to phone Heather herself, to establish contact before the girl moved on. The number she had left might belong to some sort of emergency accommodation for victims of storm damage, or the home of a relative, if Heather had relatives. She struck Marjorie as a rather transient sort of person, rootless and disorganized, unable to arrange secure, permanent accommodation for herself. All the more reason, then, for Marjorie to do her bit towards settling her down.

She rang the number. The voice at the other end said, 'Eavesdroppers, may I help you?' Marjorie wondered if it were some kind of night club. Was Heather a hostess – or worse? What would Boniface think of that, she mused grimly.

She asked for Heather. The person at the other end said she wasn't on this shift, but would be in at around midnight. Definitely a night club, then.

Marjorie left her number, and a message for Heather to call back. She was excited. She decided to give Boniface one more chance. She would phone him and ask point-blank for a date when he would meet her to talk about the hurricane. If he agreed, she would give Heather to him. If he did not, he would never know how close he had come to being reunited with his true love.

She dialled the number and was put through.

'Marjorie. You've been on my conscience.'

She said nothing.

'How *are* you?' he gushed.

'Very well. I was hoping you and I could get together soon for a chat.'

'Can't think of anything I'd like more,' he said. 'But unfortunately –'

'No, Boniface. I've had enough of your "but unfortunatelys". I've been asking you for weeks to let me know the extent of my syndicates' exposure to the hurricane –' she had mastered the jargon perfectly '– and I want that information now.'

'You can have it,' he said. 'It's ready for you. And I think you're going to be pleasantly surprised –'

'Splendid. Shall we say next Thursday?'

'Can't, I'm afraid. I'm off to New York.'

'Aren't you the lucky one? When are you coming back?'

He paused before saying, 'I may not be.'

'I beg your –'

'Not for a while,' he said. 'Now, I know what you're think-ing, and believe me, I feel exactly the same, but –' he lowered his voice '– that's the way they do things round here. Someone's been headhunted from our Manhattan office, and my name was first out of the hat to take his place. Mine not to reason why, mine but to pack my pyjamas. Orlanda's doing the letters now to send out to my names. I've been dashing around like a lunatic trying to get things sorted for Neil.'

'Who's Neil?'

'Neil Smith-Stubbs. He's taking over from me. Fine chap. I think you'll like him, and I know he's going to like you. He's not in the office right now, but I happen to know he's not doing anything next Thursday lunchtime, or if he is he can cancel it and take you out for the slap-up meal I was going to give you. He'll tell you everything you want to know.'

57

Dear Mr Smith-Stubbs,
  Kindly accept my resignation from membership of Lloyd's, with immediate effect.
  Yours sincerely,
    Marjorie Fairfax. (Mrs)

The brevity of the letter pleased her. She took it straight to the post. And now she would think of other things. Mince pies for the forthcoming bazaar at Robert's school. Mulch for the garden. The funny noise in the central heating boiler. Stewed apples. Anything.

  A strange man rang up. 'Mrs Fairfax?'

  'Yes?'

  'Neil Smith-Stubbs. Perryer de Park.'

  'Yes.'

  'Just thought I'd give you a call to get acquainted.'

  'Did you not receive my letter, Mr Smith-Stubbs?'

  'Got it in front of me.' The accent was exaggeratedly upper-class, as if he were desperately trying to prove that he was top-drawer. That meant that he was not. He swallowed his pronouns, bit off syllables that didn't interest him. 'Thought I'd better get in touch right away. Say hello before we say goodbye.' Neil Smith-Stubbs let out a squeaky bark which Marjorie took to be laughter. She said nothing.

  'You're not serious, are you?' he said.

  'I most certainly am.'

  'I see. How unfortunate. We knew Bennett had a personal following, particularly among the ladies, but we weren't expecting mass resignations when we sent him off to the States.'

He laughed again, nervously this time, as if he had realized too late that he wasn't being very diplomatic.

She coloured. 'It's nothing to do with that. I made my decision some time ago. I phoned Mr Bennett to tell him about it, and that was when I heard about him going away.'

'Of course. Just joking.'

She was an office joke. She was up there with the dotty duchess. What was she – the horny housewife? '*Have* you had mass resignations?' She hoped so.

'Nope,' he said. 'You're the only one.'

'That's all right then, isn't it?'

'Well, no, it isn't, as a matter of fact, Mrs Fairfax. When can we get together?'

'I'm not sure that I need to get together with you, Mr Smith-Stubbs.'

When he spoke again, he sounded as if he were addressing a very young child. 'Mrs Fairfax, I don't know what sort of explanation Bennett has given you about the way we operate. But you should know that underwriting insurance isn't the sort of thing you can stop and start whenever you feel like it.'

'I don't want to stop and start, Mr Smith-Stubbs. I just want to stop.'

'You could miss out on a major opportunity for growth –'

'I understand that.'

'– and lose a lot of money.'

'Please let me have a note of any charges outstanding.'

'Didn't Bennett tell you that if you're looking for a quick profit, you're wasting your time with us?'

'I'm not looking for a quick anything. I'm resigning.'

'It's not that simple,' he said.

His tone unnerved her. She didn't quite hang up on him, but her goodbye was terse. Her next call was to Rajiv Chaudhery, her accountant. Dear, kind, polite Rajiv. *Professional* Rajiv. She made an appointment and drove to see him.

'It scared me,' she said, meaning the hurricane, as Rajiv

poured tea from the china tea-pot. 'It made me realize the sort of thing that can happen. I've decided to get out before something else does.'

He nodded and passed her cup. She explained that she had informed her agent of her decision. 'A new man,' she said casually. 'The old one's left, I understand. Now it's a Mr Smith-Stubbs. I have to say that I found his attitude rather unfortunate. Perhaps he's new to the work. I won't say he was aggressive, but he seemed to be saying I couldn't resign. Surely that can't be right?'

Rajiv was looking at her with concern. She hoped she wasn't coming across as too emotional. He spread his hands in a simple, calming gesture. 'Marjorie, I want you to stop worrying and leave everything to me.'

If there were any more beautiful words in the English language, it was a long time since she had heard them.

'I will get in touch with this Mr Smith-Stubbs, and tell him that you do not wish to hear from him again.'

She wondered what Rajiv would do if she ran round the desk and kissed him. She held on tight to the seat of her chair.

'All future contact regarding your underwriting affairs is to be conducted through me.'

She frowned. 'But this is what I'm telling you, Rajiv. I don't want any future contact. I don't want any underwriting affairs. I want to get out.'

'I know you do, but –'

' "It's not that simple"?'

'It is,' said Rajiv, 'and it isn't.'

'Go on.'

He pressed his fingertips together. 'If Mr Smith-Stubbs gave you the impression that you could not resign, he cannot have been expressing himself clearly. You are free to resign at any time.'

'Good.'

'What he was probably trying to explain was that resignation cannot be retrospective. It would be effective from January 1st next year, but it would not affect your liability for losses incurred by your syndicates *this* year. Or –' he smiled bravely. 'Let us not be unduly pessimistic. Or your entitlement to profits from them.'

'But you don't think there are going to be any profits?'

'I would not like to say,' said Rajiv. 'Results for 1987 will not be announced until 1990.'

'I have to wait for my ship to come in?'

'So to speak,' said Rajiv.

'I told Boniface only to put me on low-risk syndicates.'

'I am pleased to hear it.'

'So my ship should be all right.'

'Let us hope so.' Rajiv poured more tea. 'Marjorie, may I ask what has caused you to change your mind so suddenly about Lloyd's? Was it simply the hurricane?'

'The hurricane, yes.'

'You see – forgive me if I sound like Mr Smith-Stubbs, but up to a point I must endorse what he said. If you approach underwriting as a short-term investment, and base your de-cisions on individual events rather than long-term trends, you will almost certainly suffer losses. This has been a difficult year for the insurance industry, but signs of improvement are already on the way. A second hurricane is extremely unlikely.'

'So was the first.'

'Indeed. That is the nature of the beast. But you understand the point I was making? If you were to resign now, you could find yourself in the unenviable position of having underwritten a loss-making year, yet not being able to do what everybody else hopes to do, which is to recoup your losses in the profitable years that follow.'

'Are you telling me to stay in?'

'No, Marjorie. I am explaining the alternatives which are open to you, in order that you may make a decision with which you can be comfortable.'

'What would you do, Rajiv?'

'Er –'

'All right, all right. You wouldn't have been such a fool as to get involved in the first place. But if you had, what would you do now?'

'There are no fools in this room, Marjorie. Since you ask, I think that, having joined, I would be inclined to stay in for a while, trade through the difficulties and see if I could not earn back some of what I had lost. Then I would think again.'

'That's what you recommend?'

'It is one of your options.'

'And you would look after everything for me?'

'Yes, indeed.' He smiled his sweet smile.

58

While Marjorie waits for her ship to come in, I'll do what I usually do when there's a hiatus, which is to tell you what was happening to me, insofar as it has some bearing on what was happening to her.

As you've seen, she rang me at Eavesdroppers but I wasn't there, so she left her number. Eavesdroppers was in mid-move at the time, to a new building (bricks and mortar this time, thanks to their insurers) and Marjorie's message got buried under a pile of papers at the bottom of a crate. I didn't get it until the crate was unpacked, in the first week of December.

I rang her at once. At first she seemed unsure of who I was. I reminded her that she had left a message, and she said oh, yes, in a dull, expressionless tone. She said she was sorry but the flat was not available. She sounded as if she wanted to hang up, so I took the bull by the horns. 'Are you still in touch with Boniface Bennett? Do you know how I could contact him?'

'I understand he's living in New York.' She seemed to take a grim satisfaction in saying it. If I had known the background, I would have realized what she was thinking – *I can't have him, and now neither can you*. I pressed for more information and got it out of her that he was working for the Manhattan office of a Lloyd's members' agency called Perryer de Park. The fact that he was still with Lloyd's made me want to scream and bite the carpet. I could have got through to him at any time. All I would have had to do was phone their switchboard and ask.

Now I phoned it and asked for Perryer de Park's New York number. My plan was to phone him from Eavesdroppers. My next shift began at 6 p.m. My evening would be his afternoon. He would be at his desk, and I would be at mine.

At seven o'clock, the shift leader went for supper. I strolled casually over to the phone and started dialling the long New York number. As I reached the fifth digit, the phone let out a loud squawk, followed by a taped message: 'Call barred. Staff may not use this phone for overseas calls.' An ironic cheer went round the office. Obviously I wasn't the first.

I skulked back to my work station. How mean could employers get? All that money from their insurance claim, and they begrudged their staff the odd phone call.

My shift ended at eleven. I was paid in cash as usual and caught a bus to the students' union, where the overseas students' society had a telephone room. It was quite comfortable and private, and you didn't have to feed piles of coins into a slot as the calls were metered and you paid afterwards at a desk.

The caretaker was locking up as I arrived. On the bus going home I wondered if it might be better to write a letter. I drafted various openings in my head.

Dear Boniface, congratulations on your new job.

Dear Boniface, remember me?

Dear Boniface, you know that hurricane –

They all sounded stupid. They would look even more stupid on the page. And what if he didn't write back? I would never know why. Was it what the letter said that had put him off, or was it the fact that I had written to him at all? Had the letter even reached him? I would be setting myself up for a lifetime of torture by unanswered questions. It was a phone call or nothing.

I tried again the following afternoon. An American woman's voice said, 'Perryer de Park, good morning,' in sing-song tones.

'May I speak to Boniface Bennett, please?'

'I'm sorry, caller, he's out of the office right now. May I ask who's calling?'

I slammed the phone down. To let him know that I was calling would be as bad as writing him a letter. I would have revealed myself and he wouldn't have revealed anything. I didn't even know what *out of the office* meant. On the loo, or on his honeymoon? How could I know, if I didn't ask him face to face?

I reviewed my finances: £3.42 in my purse, £47.59 in the building society to last me until the end of term. I thought about ways of getting more – selling my amethyst necklace, or my landlady's furniture. But I liked my amethyst necklace, and I quite liked my landlady. I was already in debt to her. Originally, when I moved in, she had wanted the rent in advance, but now she let me pay in arrears. I could do lots of overtime at Eavesdroppers – but I was already booked in for that, to clear my debts and keep myself going until next term's grant cheque arrived. I couldn't do that if I went to New York. But if I didn't do it, I wouldn't be able to go to New York. I thought about tapping my mother for a loan, or even Ronnie. I reckoned the two of them owed me something, for being so decent and forgiving and for keeping out of their way. *If you two could keep your hands off each other for five minutes, I need some money to go to New York to find my true love, and then you can stop feeling guilty about me.*

And Mum would say, *What, that charmer who nearly set you on fire? You want to go after him? Of course you do. Pass me my cheque book.*

59

It was an ordinary street. It could have been anywhere. The houses were terraced or semi-detached. Some had new front doors and double glazing. Most had net curtains. One or two were for sale.

The gardens were small, inoffensive and orderly, like harshly-disciplined children. There was no rubbish, not even dogshit on the pavement. Everything was neat and tidy, decent and modest; nothing was extravagant or mucky or generous or warm. It was a mean street – exactly the sort of place where I would have expected them to live.

It was early afternoon, but already the light seemed to be draining out of the sky. A cold wind blew. I found the number, walked up the front path and knocked. There was no reply. I knocked again, more loudly. Beyond the bobbled glass of the front door, a white shape moved. The door opened.

'Yes?' she said.

She was in her seventies, grey-haired, wrinkled, dumpy. She wore a floral apron over a grey skirt and blue jersey, and rubber gloves. She started to take the gloves off. Round her neck was a silver chain with a crucifix. The hall behind her was dim and still. The air smelt of meat and two veg, recently cooked. Somewhere a clock was ticking.

'Can I help you?' she said.

'I'm Heather.'

She looked so stunned that for a moment I thought she was going to have a heart attack, which would have been all I needed. I put my hand out to steady her. I touched her arm, or rather the sleeve of her jersey. There wasn't any actual flesh-to-flesh contact, but still it was a shock to feel any part of her body.

'Julia's daughter,' I clarified.

'Yes, yes, of course.'

'I've come to see you.'

'Of course.' She made it sound as if she had always known that I would turn up sooner or later.

She recovered from her heart attack, took out a tissue and dabbed her eyes. 'Let me look at you.' She took her time and seemed satisfied. 'I'd have known you anywhere. You're the image of your mother.' She stood aside to let me follow her into the hall. The walls were cream-coloured. Everything else was brown. 'Dad!' she called. 'Dad!' She didn't seem in the least bit embarrassed about calling him Dad in front of me. I wondered if she did it all the time, and he responded by calling her Mum or Mother. Had they gone on calling each other that in the childless silence of the house after they kicked my mother out?

I think we've done the right thing, Dad.

Oh, yes, Mother. Sometimes you have to be cruel to be kind.

An old man's voice shouted, 'What is it?' from another room. His tone suggested that it had better be something important, otherwise why was she bothering him with it?

'Guess who's here.'

'Why should I guess? Either tell me or not.'

She ushered me into the room. It had a patterned carpet, a television with the racing on, coal-effect fire, *The Lord is my Shepherd* framed on the wall, and two complicated-looking armchairs, the kind you see advertised for people with bad backs.

She turned off the television. 'It's Heather.'

He was bald and wore thick glasses. His trousers were loose and fawn-coloured, and he wore a check shirt and a cardigan. He had a small scab on his chin. He looked at me and I looked at him. I looked at her and she looked at me. She had said she would have known me anywhere, but I wouldn't have recognized either of them. They were just two ordinary old people. They didn't look like me or Mum; they didn't *not* look like me or Mum. They looked like everybody and nobody. They were everybody and nobody. He reached over to the mantelpiece and picked up a snapshot in a silver frame. It showed me and Mum at home, standing in our garden. I was shocked. Madge had taken the photograph when I was about seventeen. I wondered what else they had of mine. He changed his glasses, peered at the photograph, peered at me, then back at the photograph again. Anyone would think it was a recurrent problem for him, having impostors turn up on his doorstep claiming to be his grandchild.

He gave a snort. 'So you've come.'

'Yes.' I felt like adding, *and I can go away again just as easily*, but of course I couldn't.

'You took your time.'

'I don't think you've got any right to say that to me.'

'Ha! You sound like your mother.' There was triumph in his tone, as if he had been deliberately winding me up to sound like her.

'Thanks for the compliment.'

'Now, now, you two.' My grandmother's tone suggested that she had spent most of her life trying to keep him and me from each other's throats. 'Heather's here now, Dad, so let's make her welcome. I'll put the kettle on.'

She headed for the kitchen. I followed. The kitchen was small and neat. There was a prayer on the wall about God blessing this kitchen and his humble servant who worked in it. I tried to imagine growing up in this house. I could understand the urge to rush off and get pregnant.

She took a stainless steel tea-pot off a shelf, then changed her mind, opened a cupboard and brought out a box containing a tea-set with flowers on it.

She said, 'I wish I'd known you were coming.'

'Would you have baked a cake?'

'I would. I've only got a bought one. But it doesn't matter.'

She squeezed my hand. 'Next time I'll push the boat out.' Her wedding ring bit into my flesh. I had only just arrived, and already she was planning the next visit.

She picked up the tray. Her hand shook, so I carried the tray for her. Back in the sitting room, he had been getting out three little tables. He also seemed to have been practising being a genial grandad. 'So, Heather – what have you been up to, eh?'

'I'm studying at the moment,' I said. 'I'm at university.'

'Sociology, eh?'

'No. Why should it be sociology?'

'He thinks that's all they do at university these days. Sociology.'

I drank my tea. 'This is very nice. Is it something special?'

'No, just ordinary,' she said. 'We don't like those funny foreign teas, do we, Dad?'

'You prefer the kind that's grown in England?'

'We do, I think.'

The clock ticked. 'I was wondering . . .'

'How much?' he barked.

I looked at him. 'Pardon?'

'It's money you're after, isn't it?'

'Dad,' she reproached him.

'Don't Dad me. That's what she's come for.'

'It isn't, is it, Heather?'

'I came to see you,' I said.

'And?' he said.

'But Mum did say –'

'What do you want it for, eh? Drugs?'

I didn't answer.

'It's for my education,' I said.

He said, 'I thought you all got grants these days.'

'It's to go to New York.'

'New York!' he exploded. 'I've never been to New York. Mother's never been to New York.'

'It's for a course. It's very important to me. If I don't get the money, I can't go.'

'You hear that, Mother? She needs cash at short notice, so she comes here. We should get one of those machines installed on the front door. She could put her card in and take out what she needs. She wouldn't have to talk to us at all.'

'*Be quiet, Dad.* That isn't the reason you've come, is it, dear? Not the only reason.'

'Of course not,' I said. 'But Mum did tell me that you'd offered to give me, er, £5,000.'

'And that would cover it, would it?' he jeered.

I had nothing to lose. I said calmly, 'Just about.'

'Your mother told us that you didn't want the money,' said my grandmother sorrowfully.

'I may have said that, but I've changed my mind.'

He narrowed his eyes. 'What makes you so sure we haven't changed ours?'

She shushed him. 'Heather, dear, I'm sure we can find a way to help you. But perhaps we'd like to get to know you a little first.'

I realized I ought never to have come here. I ought to have got Mum to ask for the money on my behalf. If they were people of their word, they would have sent it, and gone on thinking of me as someone not quite real. Now that I had made myself real to them, the terms of the deal had been changed.

I remembered an article I had read once about a man who went to a prostitute because he wanted to talk to her. He didn't want to talk dirty or anything, he just wanted to have a conversation with a prostitute. He offered to pay the going rate for her time. She was so revolted by the idea that she charged him double.

I didn't want to charge my grandparents double. I would settle for half. But I had to have something. 'I want to get to know you as well,' I mumbled.

246

He made a scoffing sound. 'Building society cheque all right for you?' He got up out of his chair.

I was too shocked to do anything but nod.

He looked at his watch. 'They're still open. Are you coming with me, or do you want to wait here?'

My grandmother made a sound of protest. He turned on her. 'This is what we always said we'd do – remember, Mother? "She owes us nothing. The debt is all on our side." *You* said that, and I agreed with you. Well, it's time to settle up. Where's my coat?'

She fetched it, and a walking stick. 'Are you coming with me, Heather?' he asked again. 'You might as well. I can drop you off at the station, and you need never come near us again.'

My grandmother was crying. 'I thought we were going to get to know each other.'

'I'll help you wash up,' I said.

'Suit yourself,' he said. 'Want anything from the shops while I'm out, Mother?'

'Some Worcester sauce,' she said. 'We're out of Worcester sauce.'

While we were washing up, my grandmother plied me with questions about my life. She hardly listened to one answer before she wanted to know something else. I told her about my bedsitter (which she insisted on calling my 'digs'), and my course, and about working at Eavesdroppers. She didn't seem to understand what I actually did there, but she liked hearing about it. She asked with a sly look in her eye, whether I had a boyfriend. I told her I was too busy with my studies to bother with anything like that. 'Very sensible,' she said. 'You don't want to go the way your mother went.'

60

He came back with a cheque, which he handed to me folded. He seemed to be daring me to open it and look at it. When I did I saw that it said, 'Pay Heather Fox Five Hundred Pounds Only.'

At first I thought I must have misread. But I counted the noughts and there was no doubt.

I met his eyes. He was daring me to say something. What if I sneaked to my grandmother? Could I count on her to take my side? Or would she respond to my protest by snatching the cheque back and telling me that I was an ungrateful wretch who deserved nothing?

She was smiling happily at the thought of all the bridge-building that was supposedly going on. She saw my expression and looked over my shoulder at the cheque. 'What's this, Dad?'

'It's the maximum you can take out without giving notice,' he said.

I knew he was lying, and he knew I knew. She wasn't sure. 'We'll send her the rest, won't we, Dad?'

'Course we will. If she'll write down her particulars.' He handed me an address book and a pen.

So that was his little game. In return for his ten per cent deposit, he wanted to know where I lived. I wrote the address of the students' union.

Next day, I went to the student travel office. Its windows were full of ads for cheap flights to New York and elsewhere, but by the time the clerk had gone through the ones that were already fully booked, the ones that weren't available at Christmas and the ones you had to arrange at least twenty-eight days in advance, all that was left was a £200 flight going out on 23 December and coming back ten days later on 1 January.

I took it. I also bought a guide book called *New York Cheap*

'N' Cheerful. It didn't make me feel very cheerful: the cheapest hotels it had on offer were around $30 a night. I did the sums. Say £20 a night for accommodation. That would leave me with £100 to keep myself alive. Could you live in New York on £10 a day? You must be able to, I bet lots of people managed on less. It wasn't as if I would be doing anything expensive, apart from looking for Boniface. I didn't know what that would involve, but I knew that I mustn't appear desperate. I must have my own accommodation, and an air of independence. I would take packets of nuts and raisins with me, and other high-energy, non-perishable foodstuffs. I would take *New York Cheap 'N' Cheerful*. It was full of helpful hints about where to go to sell your blood, how to get an illegal job and what to do if you were arrested.

I chose a hotel and phoned across the Atlantic from the union to book a room. The guy at the other end sounded pretty spaced out. He repeated what I said, but I wasn't convinced that he was writing it down or even committing it to memory. I rang international directory enquiries to see if they had Boniface's home address in New York, but he wasn't listed.

I kept an eye on the letter rack in the union, but nothing came. I wasn't surprised. I certainly wasn't disappointed – on the contrary, I thought it was clever of me to have got even £500 out of those two skinflints. I didn't need anything else. I would manage.

My flight left at around midday. I had never flown before. The only other opportunity I had had was four Chistmases ago when I could have gone to Gibraltar. I wondered, if I had gone, how different my life would be now.

I bought duty-free cigarettes, drank my free drink and ate my free meal, all except for the cellophane-wrapped Viennese pastry, which I put in my bag. The woman next to me fell asleep before the steward could remove the trays, so I took her pastry as well, and her cheese and biscuits.

We were due into Newark in the late afternoon, but we were

delayed because of head winds and didn't land until after dark.
A light snow was falling. The New York skyline was high and
glittering and amazing, everything I had ever seen in Woody
Allen movies, or heard sung about by Art Garfunkel or Frank
Sinatra. But it was easy enough for them. When they came
jetting in to New York they would have a fleet of limousines
waiting to whisk them off to their penthouse suites. All I had
was *New York Cheap 'N' Cheerful* and a doubtful booking at
a sleazy-sounding hotel.

The book had already warned me of the terrible things that
could happen to you at the airport, such as being mugged in
the toilet, or inveigled into taking a ride in an unlicensed taxi.
That was if you got that far. You might not. Customs officials
had the power to detain you and search you if they didn't like
the look of you, and immigration could put you straight on a
plane back home. I was starting to wish they would, but they
waved me through.

The address of my hotel was East 35th Street, not too far
from Grand Central Station, where the airport bus went. I
stood in the queue. No one spoke to me. The bus came and I
got a double seat to myself. We raced along a busy freeway
towards the lights of Manhattan. The bus stopped in a dark
street and everyone got off. The air outside the bus was like a
bucket of iced water thrown over me. A snowflake blew into
my eye. Through its sharp, burning crystals I saw the blurred
outline of the station, huge and grey and Gothic, glittering
with frost. Beggars and derelicts huddled on its steps. Hookers
plied their trade. Grand Central Station. I thought what an
amazing name that was – not so much a title, more of a
proclamation. Better than pussy-footing around with semi-
boastful names like Waterloo and Victoria. Grand Central
Station, you better believe it.

I spent $5 on a taxi to my hotel, which turned out to be one
of a terrace of similar establishments, all with flaky paint,

cracked windows mended with sticky tape, and VACANCY signs. I rang the doorbell and was let in by a skinny, ill-looking man who could have doubled as Klaus Kinski in the title role of *Aguirre, Wrath of God*. He made me sign a book, then directed me to my room on the fifth floor. The lift wasn't working, so I walked, dragging my suitcase.

I unlocked the door and entered the room. The carpet had mould on it, the pillowcase was stained, the wallpaper was peeling, the door of the wardrobe had come off its hinge, and there were cigarette ends and pubic hairs in the wash basin. The cold tap dripped at irregular intervals. IN CASE OF FIRE, read the top half of a torn notice. SUCK MY DICK, someone had written across the bottom.

I sat on the bed, ate a Viennese pastry and lit a cigarette. I felt flat and rather lost. Over the past couple of weeks I had thought about nothing but how I was going to get to New York. Now that I was here, I realized that I had no idea of what to do next.

Oh, I knew I had come to look for Boniface, but what was I going to do when I found him? Would he be pleased to see me, or would he be angry or embarrassed? Would he even recognize me? Would I recognize him? Would I even find him? I was mad to have come at Christmas. For all I knew, he had gone away for Christmas – flown back to England to look up old friends.

I spread out the maps at the back of *New York Cheap 'N' Cheerful*. His office was in Lower Manhattan, the financial district. It didn't seem all that far away, but the map had no scale, so it was difficult to be sure. I read the sections on how to use the subway and the buses but it was all too complicated to take in, so I unpacked and went to bed.

I couldn't sleep. My bed stank of old sweat and sperm, my body was confused as to what time it was, and people kept going past my door, talking without bothering to lower their voices. Eventually I nodded off, but woke up with the eerie feeling that there was a man in my room. I couldn't see him, but I seemed to have heard him saying something about honey, calling me Honey. *Honey. Honey, you there?* I leapt out of bed and put the light on. The room was empty, and no one was in the wardrobe. I was seven storeys up and the window was locked. I lit a cigarette, drank water from the tap and got back into bed. I turned the light off and the voice came again, a man's voice outside my door saying, 'Honey. Honey, you there?'

I shot out of bed again and hunted around for a weapon. I found a shoe and a pair of nail-clippers. I brandished them and screeched, 'Go away!' Footsteps receded along the corridor. They didn't come back, so I assumed the man was just someone who had got confused as to where his room was. By now he was probably safely tucked up in bed with Honey, giggling with her about his stupid mistake.

Which was all very well for them, but I was wide awake and worrying. Was Boniface really a batterer? I didn't think he could be a habitual one. Mum said any man could be, they didn't wear badges, but I thought that even without a badge you could probably spot the odd clue. Boniface had only slapped me once, and not very hard at that. He could have slapped me much harder, he could have really hurt me. That was what a real batterer would have done, so obviously Boniface wasn't a real one. What he had done I had to some extent provoked by sitting on the floor with Ronnie eating bread and jam (the very food I had given to Boniface after the first time we made love) and refusing to give Boniface the reassurance that he had a perfect right to, that sitting on the floor was all we had been doing.

I wondered if Boniface would ask again: *was that fellow your lover?* I wouldn't have to give a direct answer. I could just say, *Ronnie? You have to be joking. He's shagging my mum.*

61

One of my last thoughts before finally getting off to sleep was that I would try to get to his office early, catch him on the way in and so avoid having to negotiate with secretaries and receptionists. So I was pretty annoyed when I woke up at around nine.

I leapt out of bed and headed for the shower room that I had spotted last night. It was in keeping with the rest of the hotel – stained enamel, tepid water and plugholes blocked with mucus and hair. But I tried to take no notice and to concentrate instead on scrubbing away the smells of my dirty bed.

Back in my room, I put on clean underclothes and my favourite skirt and jacket – they weren't new, but they would be new to him, and I felt good in them. I headed for the stairs. Down in reception, Klaus Kinski was still on the desk. He started to say something to me, but I had no time to hear it. I went outside and hailed a taxi. I knew I was squandering precious dollars, but I didn't care. I couldn't be bothered fiddling around on the subway, getting lost when I was so close to my journey's end.

I gave the driver the address and settled back to enjoy the journey. My earlier annoyance had passed, and I was full of exhilaration and hope. The driver probably thought I was a high-flying executive, over from England with an important deal to clinch. Perhaps I was.

We drove through midtown Manhattan. Traffic was heavy, but the air was bright and sparkling. Christmas trees were everywhere, and displays in shop windows – nativity scenes, Disney scenes, nativity scenes that looked as if they had been choreographed by Disney. Choirs sang carols, Father Christmases gave out leaflets, people hurried to and fro, carrying parcels, eating fast food. Every other shop seemed to be a burger bar or a pizza place, a Korean delicatessen or a Vietnamese takeaway. Every country America had ever been at war with seemed to have a restaurant in New York.

We reached the financial district, and the driver pointed out which of the dizzying towers of glass was the one I wanted. It had four separate entrances, not all in view of each other, so I wouldn't have been able to lie in wait for Boniface anyway. I ventured towards one of the huge revolving doors and was sucked into the entrance lobby, which was like a miniature town with coffee shops and gift shops and a Christmas tree the size of the one in Trafalgar Square. A plinketty-plunk version of 'Deck the Halls with Boughs of Holly' was playing over loudspeakers. There was an art exhibition, with paintings on loan from the Rijksmuseum in Amsterdam to celebrate the anniversary of some seventeenth-century Dutch explorer arriving in New York.

At the far end of the lobby was a reception desk with a list on the wall behind it of what looked like about five hundred companies. Presumably it said which floors they were on, but you couldn't read the information without going to the desk. People were showing passes, or explaining themselves to the woman at the desk or the security guard with the gun in his belt.

I went up to the desk and said, 'Mr Bennett, please. Perryer de Park.' I tried to sound both casual (I did this sort of thing every day) and brisk (I was used to getting what I wanted, and getting it quickly).

'Your name, please, ma'am?'

I started to say it but I didn't get beyond the first intake of breath before I saw him about twenty yards away, sitting on the terrace of one of the coffee shops with a woman. She had a big blonde hair-do, and wore a mustard-coloured suit over a silk blouse. Her silk-stockinged legs were carefully arranged, not as if she was necessarily flashing them around but as if she knew she could do so if she felt like it, and to some effect. Boniface was showing no interest in her legs. He was going through some documents with her, speaking quietly and sincerely, giving her full eye-contact and businesslike attention, but I wasn't fooled. They had been having breakfast together. That could only mean one thing.

I scuttled away from the reception desk, found a rest room and sat in there for a long time. I wondered why I was such an idiot. What had I imagined – that just because I hadn't got anyone else, he hadn't either?

I emerged from the cubicle, meaning to flee from the building and away from New York for ever. But the woman in the mustard-coloured suit was standing in front of the mirror, combing her hair.

She was older than I had thought from a distance – in her forties, or perhaps even her fifties – but that wasn't much consolation to someone whose boyfriend had recently traded her in for her mother. I looked at her through my eyelashes as I washed my hands. Her skin was still smooth, but there was something artificial about it, as if it had been lifted or peeled or re-upholstered. I wondered if I would be like that when I hit forty or fifty – trying to look young, messing around in the lives of people in their twenties. I hoped I would have more pride.

I left the ladies. I wanted one last look at him, so I glanced in the direction of where he and the woman had been sitting. The table was empty. Half a muffin lay on a plate. A tall glass contained ice cubes, melting in dregs of orange juice. I remembered breakfasts I had enjoyed with him, after nights of love. I spotted him at the till, paying their check. He finished, turned round and saw me.

He did a double-take, and still wasn't quite sure. It was my last chance to run away – or rather to look straight through him and saunter off, leaving him to think he had made a mistake. I couldn't do it. I wanted to, but my feet wouldn't move. My mouth had a will of its own, and smiled. My hand gave a little wave. Realization dawned in his eyes and he walked towards me. He wore a well-cut suit and a shirt that had been freshly pressed – by her? Under his arm was an elegant blue folder with 'Perryer de Park' and a monogram on the front. One look at his face told me that I needn't have worried about how he might react on seeing me. I needn't have feared his annoyance, or hoped for his delight. He wasn't showing either of these things, nor would he. He was too controlled, too well-mannered. He was an Englishman on display who had just spotted a former acquaintance in an unexpected place. He held out his hand and took hold of mine. 'Heather,' he said. 'Well, well, well.'

'Hello, Boniface.'

'What are you *doing* here?'

'I came to see the art exhibition.'

'Oh, the art exhibition.'

'It's really interesting,' I said. 'It's all about this seventeenth-century Dutch explorer who –'

'I know what it's about,' he said. 'We sponsored it.'

The woman in the mustard-coloured suit was at my elbow. 'Boniface, honey, I hate to interrupt.'

Boniface stepped back from me. 'Augusta, the most extraordinary thing has happened.'

'So I see.'

'I've run into an old friend from home.'

'Well, how about that?' Augusta drawled.

'This is Heather Fox. Heather – Augusta Fincham.'

Augusta Fincham gave me a firm, business-like handshake and a bright, white smile. I had never seen so many gleaming teeth in one mouth. 'Good to meet you, Heather.'

'Good to meet *you*.'

'Welcome to New York.' She looked at her watch. 'Boniface, thanks for breakfast, but I have another appointment.'

'Of course. Don't forget this.' He handed her the Perryer de

Park folder. 'See you tomorrow. What time do you want me?'

'We've invited people for around noon.'

'Sounds good,' said Boniface. 'See you then.'

They kissed each other on the cheek and Augusta headed for the exit. He watched her go, then turned back to me. 'I can't believe this. Of all the tower blocks in all of Manhattan, you walk into mine. How *are* you? How have you been? Where are you staying?' Before I could answer, a trilling sound came from his pocket. He took out his mobile phone and spoke into it. 'Bennett. Yes. Yep. Sure. Right. I'm there.' He turned back to me. 'Duty calls.'

'Sure.'

'We must get together and catch up. Tomorrow's Christmas, what are your plans for Saturday?'

'That's Boxing Day, isn't it?'

'Usually is, the day after Christmas. They don't have it here, but I've been telling them they should and I've invited them round to tea at my apartment to show them how it's done. Why don't you come along? You can wear a tea gown and operate the sugar tongs.' His phone was ringing again. 'I said I'm *there*.' He handed me a card with his home address and phone number on it and dashed towards the lifts. Just before the doors closed, he blew me a kiss.

62

I spent the day sightseeing and fighting off a sense of disappointment. I told myself that there was no reason for it. Things were going well. Not perfectly, but when did anything ever go perfectly? Only a fool expects them to go perfectly. They could have been much, much worse. I could easily not have found him, but I *had* found him. My first try, and bingo, here we were, all set up with a date for the day after tomorrow. Not a *date* date, but still.

I had done well, kept my pride intact. I hadn't begged for anything, or said how pleased I was to see him. I hadn't even admitted why I was there. *I came to see the art*. I was an eccentric art-lover, combing the world for seventeenth-century Dutch masterpieces. I was still an outsider.

Even Augusta Fincham was less of a worry than she had at first appeared. All right, he was going to her place tomorrow, but other people would be there.

Evening came, the temperature dropped and darkness gathered. The high buildings, so exhilarating in daylight, became ominous, the walls of a prison, the sides of a maze. Shoppers and business people were gone from the streets, their place taken by more menacing individuals. Still, however inhospitable the streets, the prospect of my hotel room seemed worse. I didn't want to go back there until I was tired enough to sleep. I sat in a café in SoHo, reading a copy of *Village Voice*. I noticed that *House of Games* was showing at the Thalia. I had missed it in London, so this was a chance to catch it. *I saw it in New York*, I could say, if anyone asked.

I enjoyed the film, though I might have enjoyed it more if a couple hadn't been having full sexual intercourse in the row behind me. They finished and so did the film. We came out into darkness; they went one way, I went the other. Sleet was falling. Cars slowed down as they passed me, their drivers taking their time to make their assessment. A man was wrestling with a litter bin. He seemed to be trying to uproot it from the pavement. He yelled and raved. I couldn't work out whether to turn left or right. I stared at him. He stared back. 'You're a *nut*,' he said. His voice was furious, his eyes blazed. 'You're *stoopid*.' I wondered how he knew.

I was lost. I got out my maps, but sleet fell on them, blurring the ink. I went into a cheapish-looking hamburger place, ordered a hamburger and tried once again to get my bearings. The man who had been fighting the litter bin came in and went round the recently vacated tables, helping himself to leftovers. He filled his mouth with cold chips, smeared ketchup on bits of abandoned bun. He washed it all down with dregs of coffee and cola and milkshakes. A woman came back from the loo, found the man eating her food and started to yell at him: 'You asshole, you fucking asshole bum, get your fucking hands off my food.' 'You're a nut,' the man replied. 'You're *stoopid*.' Banana milkshake dribbled through the stubble on his chin. The staff shooed him out into the night and offered the woman customer a replacement meal. I finished my own meal and went back to my hotel.

Klaus Kinski was still on the desk. No wonder he looked so ill, if he never went off duty.

He smiled, showing rotten teeth. 'Hi, honey.'

Something about the way he said *honey* made me pause and look at him. But I decided I must be imagining it.

'You been out on a date?' he asked.

I made a noncommittal sound and headed for the stairs. My room was in the same state of untidiness as I had left it this morning – the bed unmade, clothes all over the floor. I noticed a funny smell, different from the general mustiness and dirt. At first I didn't pay it much attention. It wasn't unpleasant, it was sweetish, some sort of food odour probably, wafting up from the kitchen. I picked my pyjama top off the floor, and then the bottoms. They felt wrong. It seemed ridiculous to think they were too heavy, but I knew how my pyjama bottoms should feel in my hands, and it wasn't like this – heavy, sticky, smelling of something sweet, something that dripped on to my hand. It was honey. Someone had smeared honey on the crotch of my pyjamas. There was another yellow smear on yesterday's knickers. My underwear drawer was sticky with honey. Some-one had been into my sponge bag, taken out my tampons, dipped them in honey and replaced them in the box. There was honey in my bed.

I flung the pyjamas at the wall. The honey left a stain. I bent over the basin and heaved, but nothing came up. I grabbed my handbag and ran down the stairs. The man from the desk was standing near the payphone, grinning. 'Hi, honey.' I ducked out into the street. Snow was falling and I had no coat. I ran towards a row of shops. One of them was a 24-hour delicatessen with a payphone. I got out Boniface's card and dialled his number.

63

The phone rang and rang. He wasn't there. Why should he be there? It was Christmas Eve, he would be out partying. Everyone in New York was partying, apart from me and Klaus Kinski, who I was certain would appear at any minute brandishing the jagged edges of a broken honey jar.

The phone clicked. Against a background of music and voices, a familiar voice said, 'Bennett.'

'It's me. Heather.'

'Hello, sweetie.'

Sweetie, honey.

He said tipsily, 'Fancy you turning up in New York. I hope you're having a cool Yule. We're all having an extremely cool one here, aren't we, folks?' Somebody cheered.

I couldn't say, *I found honey in my knickers.* I couldn't say anything.

He said, 'Are you okay?'

'No!'

'Hang on, I'm going to take this in the other room.' A series of clicks followed. When he spoke again, it was minus the party noise, and minus any hint of flippancy. 'Heather. Listen. Tell me exactly where you are, and what's happened.'

'I don't know where I am,' I wailed. 'In a shop.'

'Ask whoever's serving to come to the phone.'

The man behind the counter came willingly enough, and even more willingly gave Boniface directions for how to get here. He was probably used to having mad people wander into his premises, and relieved that this one at least had someone coming to take her away. He gave me a stool to sit on while I waited, and a can of Coke to drink.

After about half an hour, Boniface came in wearing a sheepskin jacket. Snowflakes clung to his collar and hair. He looked worried. It was almost worth what had happened, to see how worried he looked. He thanked the man behind the counter for looking after me, and gave him five dollars.

'Where's your coat?' he asked me.

'I haven't got one.'

Boniface took off his own coat and put it over my shoulders. He led me outside. He kept looking up and around, like a secret service man guarding the president.

A slinky red car waited at the kerb. He opened the passenger door and I got in. A woman was at the wheel. A girl, I should say. She looked hardly old enough to drive. She had perfect skin, a sweet little snub nose and bright eyes. Her long blonde curls cascaded on to the fur collar of her coat. I couldn't tell whether it was real fur, but I could see that it was expensive. So was her perfume.

'Hi!' she said brightly.

'Hi,' I replied.

Boniface got in the back. 'Heather, this is Petronella Fincham, Augusta's stepdaughter.'

'Oh, right.'

'Petronella very kindly offered to chauffeur me. She reckoned I was too pissed to drive.'

'So you are,' said Petronella, with a pretty little pout. She started the car. 'Where are we going?'

Boniface referred the question to me. 'Do you need to see a doctor, or the police?'

I remembered my mother asking me a similar question once, in relation to him. 'Neither,' I said. 'I just had a bit of a scare, that's all.'

'Come to the party, then,' he said, 'and forget about it.'

Petronella pursed her lips and headed the car south, following signs to Battery Park. We left the streets behind us and drove through trees into an underground car park, where we left the car and got in a lift. It swooshed us up through forty-seven storeys. His apartment was like a larger version of his Dockland pad – ultra-modern, beautifully furnished and bristling with gadgets.

In the pinkish glow of the spotlit sitting room, twenty or thirty people were lolling around on the furniture, or dancing to smoochy numbers by Aretha Franklin and Charlie Rich. Some of them were drinking, some were passing a joint around, some were doing both. A few heads turned to look at me. Their glances weren't unfriendly, more curious. I wondered how much Boniface had told his guests about who I was, and why I was there.

They were too polite to ask anything. Or perhaps they weren't interested. Perhaps Boniface was always having to dash off from his own parties to rescue hysterical Englishwomen from all-night delicatessens. He was talking to Petronella, who was stroking his arm to emphasize a point and sipping a mineral water. A hundred to one she was on a diet. I went over. Boniface said, 'Heather, you look as if a brandy wouldn't do you too much harm.'

I agreed that it wouldn't, and he went off to fetch one.

A tall man of about thirty started talking to Petronella. He had a crew cut and Greek letters on his jacket. He said to me, 'You must be Boniface's friend from London.'

'Yeah, this is Heather,' said Petronella, as if she couldn't understand why anyone would want to know. 'Heather, this is my brother Warren.'

'Hi, Heather,' said Warren. 'Your first time in New York?'

I nodded.

'Then I hope you'll allow me to apologize,' Warren said, 'for whatever's happened to give you a bad first impression.'

'I'm sure your smooth tongue will more than make up for it, Warren,' said Boniface, bringing the drinks.

'I hope you're right, Boniface,' said Warren. 'In my opinion, there are too many disadvantaged individuals on our streets who should be receiving proper support in a therapeutic environment.'

'He means crazies,' said Petronella.

Warren smiled tolerantly. 'Have you been having a good time otherwise, Heather?'

'Great, thanks.' I told him about my sightseeing and about the film I had been to.

His face lit up. 'I'm an admirer of Mamet's work myself.'

Petronella rolled her eyes. 'Don't start him on films. Come on, Warren, it's late. We should be going.'

'I guess,' said Warren. 'We'll see you tomorrow, Boniface. Bring Heather with you, if she'd like to come.'

I didn't know what he was talking about, but I smiled politely. When Boniface came back from seeing them off, I said, 'What did he mean? Bring me where?'

'Augusta and Hector's place out on Long Island. We're invited there for lunch tomorrow.'

'Me?'

'You've made a hit with Warren,' he said. 'He doesn't often meet people who've seen the same films as he has.'

'I don't know,' I said.

'What do you mean, you don't know? Of course you're coming. Warren invited you.'

'I mean . . .' I lowered my voice. 'I don't want to make problems for you and Petronella.'

He laughed scornfully. 'You couldn't make problems for Petrodollar if you tried. She makes all her own problems, and she does it wherever she goes.'

'*What* did you call her?'

'That's one of the politer things she gets called. I can't stand spoilt, stupid little rich girls. I didn't invite her this evening, I invited Warren and she tagged along.' Other guests were leaving. He went to see them off, then came back to me. 'If you come tomorrow, you'll be doing me a big favour – helping to ram it into the vacuous black hole between the ears that passes for Petronella Fincham's brain that I am not interested, with a capital NI. Come on, Heather, be a sport – there are people in New York who would sell their grandmothers for a chance to eat Christmas dinner *chez* Fincham.'

I imagined putting my grandmother on the market. I was about to make a sardonic comment to the effect that I doubted if there would be many offers, when I remembered that without her contribution, and my grandfather's, I wouldn't be here. Their £500 had been just right. If they had given me any more, I would have stayed at a better hotel, and would never have come to the attention of Klaus Kinski and his honeypot. As I thought about my grandparents, I was seized by a strange feeling, one which it took me a while to recognize as affection.

64

After the last guest had left, Boniface put his arms round me and gave me a long, deep kiss. I tried to say something, but he kissed me silent. 'So much to talk about,' he said. 'But I don't want to talk. I want to do this.' He started taking off my clothes. Soon we were in his bedroom making love on the huge bed.

We went on and on, doing everything we used to do, apart from one thing. We didn't talk. In the past, you couldn't stop us talking. In the pauses between doing things, we used to chat and giggle and have little arguments, but now we lay holding each other in silence. I put it down to the profound emotion and intensity of our reunion.

I woke in daylight to find him extricating himself from my arms. It was about 9.30, and his movements were hurried and a touch impatient, as if today were a working day for him. It dawned on me that perhaps it was.

He saw that I was awake and gave me a light kiss. 'Happy Christmas, sweetie.'

'Happy Christmas.'

'Would you mind getting up? I want to be on the road by ten.'

I got out of bed and started picking up my clothes, which lay in little heaps around the floor. My skirt and jacket were creased and generally the worse for wear – not quite the thing for a New York society lunch.

I could see him thinking the same. 'Where's your other stuff?'

The question annoyed me. Where did he *think* it was? 'At my hotel. Covered with honey.'

'Covered with –'

I remembered that he didn't know about the honey. He

didn't know about anything. I wondered if he was regretting having encouraged me to accept Warren Fincham's invitation, and thinking that I would shame him with my tatty clothes. I explained about the honey.

'Jesus,' he said. 'That is so sick.'

'It is, isn't it?'

'I don't understand the way some men behave towards women.'

I laughed. 'You mean why didn't he just ask me out and be done with it?'

'No, but I mean, what did he *think*? That it would make you like him?'

'No. Just notice him.'

'He'd better get used to being noticed,' said Boniface. 'Because I've a good mind to go round there and rearrange his face for him. But not now. First things first, and the first thing is to get you something to wear. We'll ask Cassie.'

'Who's Cassie?'

'A neighbour. Bright girl, writes for *New York Financial Week*, but she's a bit of a shopaholic. Her flat's full of stuff she never wears. We'll tell her you've had your kit stolen.'

I wondered why he didn't want to tell Cassie about the honey. Perhaps he didn't want her to know about the kind of hotel where I had been staying, the kind of people I had been associating with, the kind of person I was.

Cassie was sweet and kind and horrified by what Boniface told her. She seemed to want to take personal responsibility for it, and, like Warren Fincham, said she hoped it wouldn't spoil my visit. As for finding me something to wear at the Finchams', it was all I could do to stop her kitting me out for the rest of my life.

She could have done it, too. Her closet was like a warehouse. You could have held parties in it, once you had pushed aside the rails of coats and jackets, suits, day dresses and evening dresses, blouses, skirts, slacks, shorts, stoles and boas and shawls, sporting things, the shelves of hats, the racks of shoes, the drawers full of accessories and underclothes, some of them still in their bags.

I had never liked second-hand clothes, the strangers' lives that hung around them like a smell, even when there was no smell – but these were something else. The humblest of Cassie's scarves or handbags probably cost more than I spent on clothes in a year. A shopaholic, Boniface had called her. A lot of this stuff she had probably never worn, never would wear. She had just bought it for the thrill of buying. Why shouldn't some of these beautiful things have an outing? Why shouldn't they have it on me? *New York Cheap 'N' Cheerful* called Long Island a millionaires' playground and gave you information on how to get a job as a nanny or a house-sitter, told you which beaches to go to to play spot the celebrity. But I wasn't going there to work or gawp, I was going as a guest. Why shouldn't I look the part? With Cassie's help I chose a short red dress with a black belt, black shoes and black bag and black ear-rings. The moment I put them on, I realized something about expensive clothes. They are better than cheap ones. Because I had never been able to afford expensive clothes, I had kidded myself that they are only expensive because of the label. But now I knew that those labels don't get into those garments by chance. Expensive clothes look better and fit better, even if they haven't been made for you. They feel better, and make you feel better. In my reflection in Cassie's mirror, I looked almost grown up.

We drove out of the city on to the Long Island Expressway. It was a bright, crisp morning with a turquoise sky. The roads were clear of snow, but the fields and woodland on either side had large white patches. We left the skyscrapers behind and started to glimpse the sea between the trees.

He drove fast, anxious not to be late. He seemed distracted, like an actor before a performance or a racehorse before a race. I asked about his new job, and he told me about being a members' agent, signing up wealthy New Yorkers as names. I made interested sounds and tried to ask intelligent questions.

We left the main road and drove three or four miles along a sort of canyon, carved out by a river. We reached a curved lawn the size of a football pitch, with flower beds, hedges cut into complicated shapes and pine trees festooned with fairy lights. The house looked like a stately home, with wings and courtyards and elegant steps.

Boniface whistled through his teeth. 'Not bad, eh?' He started to open the car door.

I grabbed his arm in a panic. 'I don't know anything about these people.'

'What's there to know? She's executive vice-president of one of the oldest banks in New York. He owns half the paper manufacturers in Illinois.'

'But what do I talk to them about?'

'Anything you like.'

A liveried servant appeared and offered to park Boniface's car. He handed over the keys and we walked up the wide white steps towards the front door, which was opened by a maid. Boniface gave our names and the maid took our coats. Augusta appeared, wearing a woollen dress, pearls, her big hair and her big white smile. 'Well, hi, both of you.' She kissed Boniface's cheek and shook my hand. 'I'm so pleased that you could come.'

We followed her into a lounge which was furnished like a set for a Christmas edition of *Dynasty*. About thirty or forty people were standing or sitting around with drinks, looking like actors. I don't mean specific actors, although I did think I had spotted the man who played the art gallery owner in that Woody Allen film about the Hollywood screenwriter who has an affair with the gallery owner's wife; and the oldish man leaning against the mantelpiece bore a striking resemblance to Dean Martin. But that wasn't what caught my eye so much as the air everyone seemed to have of knowing exactly how to stand to show themselves to best advantage, and what expressions to have on their faces, how to hold their drinks and when to take a sip and whether or not to eat a canapé and if so which one and how to eat it elegantly. The women's clothes would have outshone even the contents of Cassie's closet, and the men wore the sort of suits and jackets that you see on world leaders. The men seem to burst out of them, not because they don't fit, they do, they fit perfectly, but because the men are so powerful that mere cloth cannot contain them.

'My husband, Hector,' Augusta was saying. 'Honey, you already know Boniface.'

'Sure.' Hector was the Dean Martin lookalike, with a deep, gravelly voice to match. 'How are you, Boniface?'

'Very well indeed, thank you, sir.'

'And this is Heather Fox, his friend from England.'

Hector took my hand in both his and gazed into my eyes. 'Heather, I'm real pleased that you could be with us today. Welcome to the United States.' He couldn't have been more courtly if he had been the president and I a foreign ambassador.

65

Warren Fincham spotted me with his father and came over to capture me. He gave me an athletic handshake, then launched straight into the life and films of Rainer Werner Fassbinder. It sounded like a prepared lecture, for which he had been searching for an audience. I thought I had seen all Fassbinder's films, but Warren soon set me straight on that. He offered to arrange a private showing for me of Fassbinder's filmed TV series about workers in Germany, *Eight Hours are not a Day*, at his film club in Brooklyn. At first when he talked about *his* film club I thought he meant a film club he belonged to. Only later did it dawn on me that it was the other way round: the film club belonged to him.

Boniface in the meantime was chatting up two very old and bejewelled ladies. From time to time he glanced in my direction to see if I was all right. I was fine. Apart from the fact that I wanted a cigarette but couldn't see anyone else smoking, or any ashtrays, I was having a great time. People accepted me, they didn't know I didn't belong. Warren introduced me to his uncle and aunt. The uncle had recently retired from being chairman of an airline; the wife, who was much younger, worked for a company that built shopping malls. They both seemed to know who Boniface was, and to be interested to meet his friend. They asked what I did and seemed quite surprised when I said I was a student, as if they had assumed I worked in the world of high finance.

If people wanted to make assumptions, they were welcome. I became deliberately vague about my work and background. I enjoyed being mysterious. At lunch, I sat between a man called Alexander, who talked all the time about telecommunications, and a woman called Caroline, who was in real estate. Caroline seemed to know a lot about house prices in London, which was more than I did. She asked me how long I had been in New York, and whether I was having a good time. Everyone seemed to want to know that. I kept saying yes, yes thank you, yes.

Petronella sat at the far end of the table, toying with a salad. She seemed to have adopted a policy of ignoring Boniface and ignoring me. But after the meal, when we all moved to another gorgeous room for coffee, she asked me if I wanted a cigarette. I assumed that meant she was about to give me one, but in fact all she did was take me to a special room where I could indulge my filthy habit.

I followed her out of the house and across a courtyard. The smoking room was a sort of hut, comfortably furnished with deep leather armchairs, beige carpets and lemon-coloured walls. She said, 'Make yourself at home,' and I wondered why she was being so pleasant – whether her stepmother had told her to, or whether she was hoping to hasten my demise by encouraging me to smoke as much as possible.

I lit up. A servant arrived with coffee for us. Petronella handed me a cup. 'Heather, do you mind if I ask you something personal? Are you and Boniface dating?'

'Yes,' I said firmly.

A blush crept up Petronella's delicate neck. I watched her try to hide it. I knew how that felt. For the first time in my life, I was in the presence of a person who was scared of me.

'We used to see each other,' I explained. 'But we sort of drifted apart. And then he came to New York –'

'And you realized how much you missed him?'

'Sort of.'

'It often happens that way.' She sounded old and worldly-wise. 'I hope things turn out real well for you. I guess he told you that he and I dated a few times? When he first came to New York.'

'He mentioned it,' I lied.

'You're not mad?'

'No.'

'I'm not either.' She pronounced it *eether*. Her hands were shaking. 'Could I have one of your cigarettes?'

I was too surprised to do anything but hand over the packet. We smoked in silence for a while.

She said, 'Did he say anything about why we split up?'

I decided to improvise. 'He said you and he weren't suited. He said it was a mutual decision.'

'Yeah.' She nodded several times. 'Right. It was.' There was another pause. Then she said, 'Heather, can I ask you something else?'

'Anything you want.'

'Are you, like, a *name*?'

I couldn't help laughing. 'No way.'

'Boniface says most of his friends are.'

I shrugged.

'I hope you didn't mind me asking?'

'Why should I?'

'Boniface said it's not the done thing in England. To ask, I mean.'

'Are you one?'

'No. He did ask me, though.' She sounded proud.

'But you don't fancy it?'

'I only turned twenty-one in November. I only just got my inheritance.'

'Oh, right.'

'He was kind of – well, I don't want to say pushy, but he kinda went on about it. Get in while you're young, he said, and it'll keep you all your life. Warren's keen. Augusta says it's a good thing, but I don't know. I mean, I don't want to say anything against England, Heather, but I'm an American, and I kinda like the idea of keeping my money here.'

I didn't reply. Petronella Fincham's investment problems were hardly mine. But it amused me to think that I might have happened upon the real reason why Boniface disliked her so intensely – she hadn't succumbed to his blandishments, he hadn't had his way with her.

66

As we drove back towards the city, he said, 'You and Petrodollar seemed to be getting on like a house on fire.'

'I wish you wouldn't call her that. She's okay.'

'If you say so.'

'I didn't realize you'd been out with her.'

He laughed. 'Neither did I.' After a pause, he added, 'She didn't say that, did she? That we "went out"? She must be desperate if she has to count me as one of her scalps.'

I didn't say anything, but he went on as if I had demanded an explanation: 'I'd just arrived in New York. Augusta was giving me a helping hand, introducing me to people. Petrodollar was having her twenty-first birthday party, and I went along. It was hate at first sight, but I sort of felt I had to thank her for the party, so I asked her out to a movie. End of story. Satisfied?'

'I don't have to be satisfied. Your life is your business.'

He looked at me out of the corner of his eye. 'And yours is yours, eh? Is that what you were going to say next?'

'No.'

'I haven't forgotten,' he said, 'what happened last time we saw each other.'

'It's okay.'

'No, it isn't. I behaved like the Beast From 20,000 Fathoms, and you were quite right to tell me to go back there. Believe me, not a day's gone by in the last – how many years has it been?'

'Nearly four.'

'– four years, when I haven't reproached myself. I'm not the sort of chap who hits women.'

'I wasn't very nice to you either,' I said. 'But you know, Ronnie and I –'

'Who?'

'The man you found me with, the man you thought –'

'Oh, Lord, yes, the solicitor. I don't need to know about him, Heather. In fact, I'd rather not. Okay?'

I shrugged. 'Okay.'

'Is there anything you need to know about me?'

I shook my head. I thought how sensible he was, to see that it was better to start afresh than to dig up the past. 'Let's just enjoy you being here,' he said. 'You still haven't told me why you *are* here.'

I said something vague about special-offer student flights; but later on when we were in bed I admitted that I had come looking for him. I told him about the hurricane, and about realizing that if something is important to you, you have to do it because you might never get another chance. I told him about contacting Marjorie, and about going to my grandparents for the fare.

He hooted. 'You actually darkened their door? What are they like?'

I bristled. He was laughing at them, and trying to get me to laugh with him. 'They're okay,' I said. 'They gave me the money, anyway.'

'I don't suppose you gave them much option, did you? I have to admit to a sneaking sympathy for them. There they are minding their own business in their cosy little world, there's a knock at the door and it's you demanding money with menaces.'

'I didn't demand money with menaces.'

'Of course you didn't.' He kissed me. 'You're too sweet for that. Such a sweet girl.' He lay above me, gazing into my eyes. 'How long are you here for?'

'I fly back on January 1st.'

He stroked my hair. 'Will you stay with me until then?'

'I don't want to be in your way,' I said.

'You wouldn't,' he said. 'And you're certainly not going back to that hotel.'

'I could find another one.' I told him about the list in *New York Cheap 'N' Cheerful*.

He rolled off me and shook his head. 'If they're cheap, they won't be cheerful. If the perverts don't get you, the cockroaches will. Stay here, why don't you? I'll be at work most of the time, so I won't be around to bother you. You want to invite a solicitor round for tea, go ahead. Invite the whole firm. But if they charge for their time, you're paying.'

67

Next day was Boxing Day, and Boniface's tea party. The caterers arrived in the morning and set about transforming his bachelor lounge into an Olde Englishe drawing room, with linen napkins and a lace tablecloth, paper doilies, sugar tongs, cake tongs, pastry forks, three silver tea-pots (one for the Earl Grey, one for the Lapsang Souchong, one for the ordinary) and a bone china tea-set. Guests were expected at four o'clock. At three, the caterers started putting out the food – scones, jam, cream, sandwiches cut into triangles, flapjacks, chocolate fingers, meringues, brandy snaps, sponge cake, mince pies and a large Christmas cake with white icing sculpted into mountain peaks and Father Christmas driving his reindeer between them. Music played in the background – Christmas carols from King's College, and something Elizabethan with harpsichords in it.

First to arrive was Cassie, her arms piled high with more clothes that she thought I might like. She was followed by a couple in their thirties called Hal and Celia, who lived near by. Hal was a bond trader, Celia was in personnel management. Also with them was Celia's widowed mother, who was visiting from Kentucky, where she owned a racing stable. Boniface got her in a corner and started chatting her up.

When Celia saw the food she let out a groan of bliss. 'Boniface, you didn't tell us it was going to be a banquet. A cup of tea and some cookies, you said.'

'It's most unlikely that I used the term "cookie", Celia. Where I come from, it's a biscuit.'

'A biscuit is something else,' said Hal.

'Whatever,' said Celia. 'I wasn't expecting all this.'

'I told you I'd give you a taste of an ordinary English afternoon tea.'

'As eaten in homes throughout the United Kingdom, right?'

'Every day,' he said. 'Isn't that so, Heather?'

'Definitely.'

The Finchams arrived. Hector presented Boniface with a bottle. Augusta kissed me on both cheeks and gave me a little parcel containing a silk scarf. Warren told me about a paper he would be giving at an upcoming seminar on the work of François Truffaut. Petronella took photographs of the food with a tiny, expensive camera.

More people turned up – neighbours from the block, friends from Boniface's work, and some people from a country club that he was hoping to join. An elderly couple arrived – grand-parents of someone Boniface had known at school. People made little speeches about how they couldn't possibly eat all that, then settled down to eat it all.

Conversation ranged from work to Christmas to world events, and then to other memorable English tea parties. Harry and Celia had once eaten strawberries and cream on the tea lawn at Wimbledon; Billie Jean King had passed so close that they could have touched her. The grandfather of Boniface's childhood chum had been to a Buckingham Palace garden party in the 1960s and seen Princess Anne in a mini-skirt. You could almost hear the world gasp, he said, at this first officially sanctioned glimpse of royal thigh. Warren had once attended a seminar at the American Institute for Film Studies entitled 'Tea as discourse in British and Japanese Cinema, with particular reference to the works of David Lean and Yasujiro Ozu'.

Boniface told a story about a time at his public school when all the prefects went out to a rugby match and the younger boys invaded their common room and stole and ate their crumpets. The prefects came back early and caught them at it, and they all got caned.

Augusta smiled. 'Including you, Boniface?'

'Lord, yes.' He gave his bum a reminiscent rub.

'Does that still go on?' Augusta inquired.

'I should jolly well hope so. It's an honoured tradition.' I could tell that he was being satirical, but Petronella turned on him.

'I think that's terrible. Hitting little kids, just because some-one once hit you.'

'*Once*! If it was only once, I wouldn't have minded.'

'Happened all the time did it, Boniface?' said Warren, spot-ting an opportunity to wind up his sister. 'Like in Anderson's *If . . .*?'

'Every morning,' said Boniface solemnly. 'Between the cold shower and the run along the cliff. It's what made our nation great.'

At last, Petronella realized she was being laughed at. To hide her annoyance, she got out her camera and started taking more pictures with great concentration.

I poured tea and handed round cakes. People kept congratu-lating me on the food. I gave up explaining that it was nothing to do with me, and just said, 'Thanks.' After the party, when everyone had gone and the caterers were clearing away, Boni-face pulled me on to his lap and thanked me for being such a gracious hostess. Everyone had been charmed by me, he said. He asked if I had made up my mind yet about staying with him. I lay against him, full of cake and cream. I felt like an overfed kitten. I wanted to stay. I said so.

We drove to my hotel to pick up my stuff. Klaus Kinski was nowhere to be seen, and the sheets on my bed had been changed. My honey-smeared underwear and tampons had disappeared. I wondered if Boniface would think I had made the whole thing up. 'It did happen,' I said. He said, 'Of course it did,' and picked up my suitcase. We drove back to Battery Park and I moved in.

And that's really all you need to know about my time in New York – for the purpose of understanding what was shortly to happen to Marjorie, I mean. There is other stuff, but it's about me, and this is her story, not mine. We'll go back to her in the next chapter.

68

She had been trying not to think about it. Most of the time, she succeeded. There was little to remind her. Any correspondence was being fielded by Rajiv.

Now and again her eye might be caught by an item in a newspaper – a plane crash or an oil spill, a fire, extreme weather conditions in a distant part of the world. It always seemed distant. That was a comfort. And she had been told often enough that she should not concern herself about individual events which, serious though they might seem to the people involved, were insignificant in the overall scheme of things.

General trends were what mattered, and she was sure that in that department, everything was fine. If they were not, Rajiv would have told her. There was plenty of time for any little kinks to be ironed out. Under the three-year accounting system, results for 1987 would not be declared until 1990.

So she was quite put out by a letter that reached her in the summer of 1989.

My dear Marjorie,

I am sorry to have to inform you that I have today received notification from Neil Smith-Stubbs of Perryer de Park, of a cash call from one of your syndicates.

The amount is £7,083.87 (seven thousand and eighty-three pounds and eighty-seven pence) and Mr Smith-Stubbs tells me that he will be grateful to receive your remittance within the next twenty-eight days. You may either send it directly to him, or through me, whichever is more convenient.

Once again, my apologies for being the bearer of bad news.

Kind regards,

Yours sincerely,

Rajiv.

She frowned and read it again. She glanced across the break-fast table at Robert, who was going through his own mail, seemingly unaware that anything was amiss.

Nothing was amiss. It was a sunny morning and they were enjoying their grapefruit and coffee in the garden. Roses were in bloom. The dogs were playing on the lawn. A mistake had been made, that was all. A quick phone call would sort things out.

She waved Robert off to work, then phoned Rajiv's office. A secretary informed her that he was in a meeting. She said sharply, 'Will you please ask him to come out of his meeting and speak to me?' There was a cowed silence, and Rajiv was fetched.

'Good morning, Marjorie.'

'Rajiv, what on earth is this?'

'I am sorry?'

Was it possible that he didn't know what she was talking about? How many letters like this did he send out, for heaven's sake? She made her protest. 'The accounting period is three years. This has been dinned into my head until I have become sick of the sound of it. I have only been a member for two and a half years.'

'It is most unfortunate,' said Rajiv. 'It is what is called an advance cash call.'

'It sounds like an advanced swindle to me.' She added a little laugh to show him that she wasn't taking any of this seriously, and to remind herself of the same fact.

Rajiv made a delicate, throat-clearing sound, as if he did not entirely disagree, but was unhappy about having words like *swindle* uttered over his telephone, in case he should be held liable for them.

'Can they do this?' she asked.

'They do it from time to time, when they have had an unusually large number of claims and are expecting more. They need to build up their reserves in order to continue trading. It is a legal requirement.' Rajiv paused. 'To be honest, Marjorie, it does not make a great deal of difference to your position. In some ways, it makes it better than it might otherwise have been.'

'How do you work that out?'

'By asking names to contribute now,' Rajiv explained, 'they save having to borrow more money from the bank, which would of course involve interest charges –'

'So they're doing me a favour.'

'I can see that it might not appear that way to you.'

Marjorie said nothing. Rajiv cleared his throat again. She remembered that he was supposed to be in a meeting. He said, 'If you would care to make an appointment to come and see me, I will be happy to go through the figures with you, and explain the situation in more detail.'

She shook her head, forgetting that he could not see her. She didn't want the details. He had promised to look after everything, and not involve her. Seven thousand pounds, though! He wasn't going to look after that. 'Can't we appeal or something?'

'I have examined Mr Smith-Stubbs' figures, and I can see no grounds to doubt their accuracy.'

'So I have to hand over £7,000? Just like that?'

'Er, £7,083. And 87p.'

'What shall it be – used tenners?'

'I think perhaps a cheque . . .'

'Made payable to whom?'

'Perryer de Park Agencies Limited.'

'I'll put it in the post to you today.'

She heard him smile. 'It is not *that* urgent, Marjorie.'

For her it was. She felt nauseous, as if she had been food-poisoned. She wanted to sick it all up and get it over with.

69

She drove into Eastbourne and went to the building society where she had her instant access account. Her balance was just over £10,000. She liked to keep it that way in order to benefit from the higher tier of interest.

She filled in a withdrawal form for £7,083.87 and handed it to the girl, who said, 'Who did you want the cheque payable to, Mrs Fairfax?'

'I'm sorry?'

The girl passed the form back to her. 'You haven't written the payee's name.'

She wrote, 'Perryer de –', then stopped. What if the girl knew who Perryer de Park Agencies were? It was unlikely that she would, but it could not be ruled out. Marjorie was ashamed of the misfortune that had struck her, and did not want news of it spread along the gossip networks of the south coast. She tore up the form and filled in another. In the space for 'payee', she wrote 'Self'.

She took the building society cheque across the road to the bank and paid it into the current account. Then she went to a coffee shop and ordered a coffee and a fruit scone. She took out her cheque book and wrote a cheque for £7,083.87, payable to Perryer de Park Agencies Ltd. She left her coffee and her half-eaten scone on the table and went next door to a stationer's to buy envelopes. She addressed one to Rajiv and stuck on a second-class stamp (he had said there was no hurry). She inserted the cheque into the envelope and licked the flap. The gum tasted like rotting fish. It stayed on her tongue and spoiled her enjoyment of the rest of the scone.

She didn't bother to add a covering note. Rajiv would know what the cheque was for. After she had posted the envelope, she went for a walk along the sea front and thought of all the other things she could have done with £7,083.87. She could have bought a new car. She could have had a mad splurge on clothes, or gone to a health farm for weeks and weeks. She could have put the money towards her and Robert's retirement, or earmarked it for Caroline's wedding. Not that Caroline was showing any sign of getting married, but Marjorie was sure she would one day. And in any case, putting money aside for an as yet unplanned wedding was a damn sight more sensible than – what exactly *had* she done with it? Where had it gone?

She could have offered it as a bribe to Di and Tony to get them to stop having babies and start looking for a place of their own. She could even have invested it in Tony's business – that bottomless pit. But at least it was a *family* bottomless pit. She could have donated it to ChildPeril – either the general fund or the Shoe Campaign, which was close to her heart. According to a report, thousands of children in Britain were without proper shoes. Marjorie did not know why this information disturbed her so much. She knew already that there was poverty, homelessness, hunger, abuse. These were the reasons why organizations like ChildPeril continued to exist, and why people like her offered their services. Was it really so surprising that children who lacked everything else should also lack shoes, should suffer from bunions and bent toes, chilblains and septic blisters, should turn up at school in flip-flops or bedroom slippers or perhaps not turn up at all because the only serviceable pair of shoes in the family was being worn by a brother or sister? It wasn't surprising at all, but it was shocking in a way that other aspects of poverty – things that one had already thought about and got used to – were not. It was embarrassing, it made your toes curl. Marjorie imagined £7,083.87's worth of children's shoes, brand new, lined up in twos, freshly polished and smelling of leather, and children stepping forward with their mothers to try them on and make their selection. The vision brought tears to her eyes and she reproached herself for her earlier plan to spend the money on herself. She reminded herself that she wasn't spending it; she was working out how she could have spent it if it were not already spent, on nothing.

Robert waved the bank statement aloft. 'What's this?'

'What's what?'

'Seven thousand-odd quid into and out of the joint account in less than a week.'

She froze. She realized what she must have done. Instead of depositing the building society cheque into her private account and paying the cash call from there – and so standing a reasonable chance of keeping the matter private – she had passed it through the household account, the joint account, where Robert must see it.

He was waiting for her explanation. He wasn't angry or upset, just puzzled. 'Have you been laundering drug money for the Mafia or something?'

'It's a bit complicated,' she said.

'I'll say. You could get twenty years.'

'Please don't joke.'

Concern flickered in his eyes. 'Is something wrong?'

Why don't I just tell him? she thought. *I want to tell him. I want him to know. I want him to comfort me and say 'There, there, it doesn't matter, it's the sort of thing that could happen to anyone.' That's the reason why I made the mistake with the cheque. It wasn't a mistake at all.* 'Robert, can we sit down for a moment?'

'Why?'

'So that I can tell you.'

He remained standing and made a winding gesture. 'Can you fast-forward a bit?'

'Darling, you asked a question.'

'I know, but I don't have time for a long answer.' He looked at his watch.

'It's the holidays.'

'I've got a meeting.'

'Go to it then,' she said. 'Go to hell.'

70

He gave her a strange look and left the house. She heard his car drive away. She was miserable all morning. She and Robert never told each other to go to hell. They might get cross with each other, but there were limits. *Go to hell* was outside the limits.

She waited for him to come back from his meeting. But he phoned to say that he was having a pub lunch with a colleague, then going for a round of golf.

She drove into Eastbourne to do her afternoon shift at the ChildPeril shop. Her charity work. Maybe she would feel better about the money if she looked upon it as charity work of a different kind. It was to help people suffering misfortune, wasn't it? Some of it would have gone towards clearing up after that terrible hurricane of a few years ago – a natural disaster in her own country. If it had happened overseas, she wouldn't have thought twice about dropping a few coins into a collecting tin.

Addie Bernard, the shop manageress, remarked that she was looking rather pale, and asked if she would be taking a holiday this year. A holiday was Addie's remedy for everything. She lived from brochure to brochure. She had a fund of information committed to memory about resorts, hotels and optional excursions around the world. Well, there were worse things, Marjorie thought bitterly. The sense of well-being and virtue that had come with her thinking about the money as a donation to a good cause turned into deep irritation at the thought of how easily all this could have been avoided. All it would have taken would have been for Robert to share Addie's passion for holidays, and her ability to spot when Marjorie was a bit down in the dumps. He would have spotted it that Christmas just after her mother died, he would have taken her away for a nice, relaxing holiday, just the two of them, and none of this would have happened.

She would have liked to be able to say all this to Robert – not with a view to blaming him for her own stupidity, but to make him understand. She would have said it that evening if she hadn't put herself in the wrong by telling him to go to hell. As it was, the onus was on her to apologize and keep her problems to herself. And anyway, it wasn't a problem, it was a donation. *Give till it hurts*. Who had said that? She made Robert a special supper, apologized for her earlier quarrel-someness and explained that the £7,000 had gone on estate duty: an extra amount overlooked by the solicitor and the Inland Revenue at the time of settlement. Robert said that if the solicitor and the Inland Revenue had overlooked it, the solicitor and the Inland Revenue should pay it. Marjorie said, 'Very likely,' and soon the two of them were back on their old footing of seeing the funny side of everything.

When, in the spring of 1990, the next cash call arrived, she accepted Rajiv's invitation to his office.

The amount, he explained gently, was £29,004.18.

'I have to pay that?'

'I am afraid so.'

She gave a brave little laugh. 'It is rather a lot.'

'Yes.' He poured tea from the willow pattern china tea-pot into a matching cup. 'It is not the best piece of news I have ever had to give to a client.'

She sipped her tea.

'I knew it would be a shock,' Rajiv went on. 'That is why I suggested that you might like to call in to discuss things in more detail.' He sounded like a doctor giving an unwelcome diagnosis.

'Perhaps there's been a mistake.' She sounded like the patient receiving it.

'I do not think so. Ever since last year's advance call, it has been clear that your results would not be good.'

'You didn't say that at the time.'

'I saw no point. I could have been wrong.'

'What about the others?' she asked.

'I am sorry?'

'You told me once that you had other clients who were, er, names.' She couldn't believe that this archaic, slightly sinister term applied to her.

'That is true.'

'Have their results been better or worse than mine?'

'Marjorie, forgive me, but I cannot discuss my other clients' affairs.'

'I only meant –'

He said, 'I can tell you that these past couple of years have not been good ones for the market, or for the insurance industry generally. I can also tell you that signs of recovery are on the way.'

'You mean I'll get all the money back next year?'

'That is perhaps a little optimistic, but Mr Smith-Stubbs tells me that this year has been quite out of the ordinary – "freakish" is the expression he uses. An unusual number of natural disasters has combined with settlement of some rather large damages claims in the United States. But he expects the er . . .' Rajiv read from a letter '. . . "the natural self-righting mechanisms of the market to reassert themselves in the near future".'

Marjorie looked anxiously into Rajiv's eyes. 'Do you believe him?'

He held her gaze. 'I have no reason not to. It is what many commentators are saying. Would you care to see the figures?' He pushed a little pile of papers across the desk towards her.

She recoiled and moved her hand away. She didn't want anything that Neil Smith-Stubbs had touched to touch her. 'Not now, Rajiv.'

He cleared his throat. 'The balance in your long-term savings account is currently around £30,000 –'

'Fine.' She waved her hand. 'Clean it out. Close it down.'

'I would not advise going that far,' he said. 'You must have some savings.' *Of course I must*, she thought. *To cover up.* 'We could take, say, £15,000 from that account, and raise the rest by selling some shares.'

Daddy's shares. Mummy's savings. Her parents' reproaches hit her like a wave. She gazed round the office in panic. The family photograph on the wall was a new one. There was an additional baby. She must remember to admire the baby and ask its name. Not now, though. 'I can't take money out of the savings account just like that. I have to give ninety days' notice.'

Rajiv nodded. 'Mr Smith-Stubbs is asking for settlement within twenty-eight days. But I am sure he will allow us a little leeway.'

As things turned out, Neil Smith-Stubbs could hardly refuse, since he was asking for leeway of his own. He reported via Rajiv that there had been a clerical error in his calculations: another £1,197 was called for. He was, apparently, deeply apologetic. 'And I,' said Rajiv, 'can only add my regrets to his.'

'Can he do this?' For the second time in three weeks, Marjorie was sitting stiffly in his office, wondering when she would wake. She still hadn't congratulated Rajiv on the new baby.

'I am afraid he can.'

'Double the number he first thought of.'

'It is not quite as bad as that. It is significantly less than before.' Rajiv's voice rose encouragingly. 'Mr Smith-Stubbs thinks we can take this as a hopeful sign.'

'It's not my idea of a hopeful sign.'

'I can understand that.'

71

The next cash call, which came in the spring of 1991, was for just over £20,000. Rajiv sold more shares. Marjorie sold some of her mother's jewellery, replacing it with cheaper versions. Robert did not appear to notice.

She paid a visit to Cheyne Walk. She was rehearsing the tantrum she planned to stage over the neglected state of her parents' antique furniture. She had had enough, she would tell Di. She was going to take the furniture away.

The tantrum didn't take much rehearsing. Daddy's old grandfather clock looked as if attempts had been made to climb it, inside as well as out, using boots and spikes. The oak chest in the hall was being used to store bits of broken computer and maintenance equipment. Coils of wire and the tops of aerosol spray-cans poked out from under the lid. In the sitting room, the once-polished surface of the grand piano was covered with rings. The keys were sticky from chocolate-coated fingers. 'Do you *need* that piano?' asked Marjorie.

Di looked as if she thought it an odd question but was prepared to be a sport and think about it. 'I suppose no one *needs* a piano, Mummy, unless they're a concert pianist. But it's sort of nice to have. Emma thumps away occasionally.'

'But is she learning properly? Are any of them?'

'Mum, to learn the piano properly, you have to be capable of sitting still for more than five minutes. My lot aren't.' Di seemed quite cheerful about it. She cleared a visual display screen off a chair and motioned for Marjorie to sit down. 'Sorry about all the clutter. I keep asking Tony *please* to keep work things at work, but he says there's no room. I say, well, what makes you think there's room *here*?'

'And what does he say to that?'

'He says, "Nag nag nag."' Di mimicked her husband lovingly. 'No, he says as soon as they can move to larger accommodation, there'll be a place for everything and everything in its place. They're angling to take over the lease on the building next door to their present one, but it's a matter of, you know –' Di mimed fingering a wad of notes '– venture capital.'

'I'm sorry, dear, but –'

'Heavens, I didn't mean *you*, Mummy.' Di's face expressed amused and slightly patronizing astonishment that Marjorie should even have thought it. 'I told Tony, "It's out of the question, firstly because Mummy's been more than generous to us already, letting us live here without paying rent or anything, and secondly she's not really a venture capital sort of person." I mean, you're not, are you? You're more, I don't know, gilt edged securities and premium bonds.'

'How well you know me, dear. Now, about the piano –'

'Yes, Mummy.' Di folded her hands like a demure little girl.

'And the grandfather clock, and the chest –'

'What about them?'

'I was thinking of selling them.'

'*Selling Granny's piano?*' Di was aghast.

'Well, it's not fair for you to have everything, is it? There's Caroline to think of.'

Di looked puzzled. 'You mean you're going to sell the piano and give the money to Caroline?'

Marjorie was out of her depth. She struggled back on to safer ground. 'Do you and Tony never think you'd like a place of your own?'

'Of course we do. We dream about it. And then we do the sums, and we say, "dream on".'

A few days later, in the course of a seemingly casual phone call, Caroline said, 'What's this you've been saying to Di about pianos?' Her tone was half-accusing, half-amused; Marjorie could imagine the conversation that had given rise to the question.

'I was thinking of selling Granny's piano, that's all.'

Caroline looked puzzled. 'Di seemed to think you wanted to give it to me. Why would I want a piano? It would take up the whole of my flat.'

'I may have said that,' said Marjorie. 'I didn't want to offend her, but did you notice the state of it? I want it to go somewhere where it'll be treated with respect. If you don't want it, I'll find another home for it.'

'It's only a piano, Mummy. Not a person. It doesn't need to be treated with respect.'

'You know what I mean.'

'Sure I do.' Caroline sighed. 'You and Daddy are obsessed with property. It is possible to live more simply, you know. And by the way, if you want to put some money into Tony's company but you're holding back because it didn't seem fair to me, don't worry.'

'My goodness, you two *did* have a long talk.'

'Mum, I'm not in the business of falling out with my sister over my dead grandparents' money, okay? In fact, I'm not in the business of worrying about money at all.'

She decided to leave the furniture for the time being. Instead, she sold her mother's premium bonds. The numbers never came up anyway. She looked in the local paper to see what jobs were available. She was looking for something she could take in secret. She would pretend that she was working extra hours at ChildPeril, when all the time she would be repairing the ravages in her savings. She lived in dread of a family emergency, something she would be expected to subsidize.

But the rates of pay for shop assistants and breakfast cooks – the only jobs she could imagine herself doing – were too tiny when set against the risk of discovery, which was large. She wished she hadn't sold the premium bonds. They at least provided a chance of salvation, however remote. They gave a reason to look forward to the postman's coming, a glimpse of hope in the darkness of the dread she felt when his van turned into the drive.

Robert found her moving her things out of their bedroom and into the spare room. 'What's this?' he said.

'I'm not sleeping very well,' she said.

'I know you're not. What's wrong?'

'I don't know. Time of life, I expect.' She said it in a funny voice. 'I don't want to disturb you.'

'You'll disturb me a lot more by leaving me to sleep by myself,' he said.

She looked at him in amazement. 'What do you mean?'

'Just because there's no how's-your-father any more, doesn't mean I don't like having you there.'

Tears stung her eyes. *No how's-your-father any more.* He made it sound like warm weather or blossom on the trees – something that just went away. Nothing to do with him, nothing to do with them.

He was looking embarrassed. 'Sleep where you like, love. Why's it called how's-your-father, do you suppose? I'll look it up.' He headed for his study, and his Oxford Dictionary on CD ROM.

72

When the next cash call came (£37,000, in the spring of 1992), she said, 'I can't pay it. I'm bust.'

'You're very far from being bust, Marjorie,' Rajiv soothed. 'You still have your share portfolio.'

'What's left of it.'

'And you still have your late mother's flat. Perhaps it is time for your daughter and her husband to –'

She cut him off. 'What's going on, Rajiv?'

'Do you wish me to explain?'

'I suppose you'd better.'

He spread out the papers. 'Your first agent, Mr er . . .'

'Bennett,' she sighed.

'. . . Mr Bennett placed you on ten syndicates. Five of them are doing fairly well – as well as can be expected, given the current state of the market. They are showing a moderate profit. Nothing to get excited about, but they are keeping their heads above the water. Two are making small losses. Again, nothing excessive – £2,000, £3,000 – the sort of thing that you –' Rajiv corrected himself '– the sort of thing that a properly capitalized name could take in his or her stride. This is not the problem. The problem syndicates are these three down here.' He pointed them out with his pen. Like so much to do with Lloyd's, they had double- or triple-barrelled names: Keighley Bates Syndicate 403, Lancaster Broadley 575, Armstrong Clark Bannister 222 . . . Her eyes started to mist over.

'These are the ones that are giving us the headaches,' said Rajiv.

Us! she thought.

'Why?' she asked. 'What's wrong with them?'

'Perhaps Mr Smith-Stubbs can explain better than I can.'

He handed her a letter. She didn't want Neil Smith-Stubbs's explanation, she wanted Rajiv's; but she knew that she was in no position to argue, so she read the letter.

My Dear Rajiv,

Re: Mrs Marjorie Fairfax
Keighley Bates Syndicate 403
Armstrong Clark Bannister Syndicate 222
Lancaster Broadley Syndicate 575

I am so sorry to be, once again, the bearer of bad news for Mrs Fairfax.

The situation regarding Armstrong Clark Bannister has, as you will see, continued to deteriorate. This is mainly because of ACB's exposure to reinsurance claims arising out of natural disasters and oil-related accidents in the North Sea. Once these claims have passed through the system, we are confident that ACB syndicates will be back on their way towards profitability.

The problems surrounding Keighley Bates are more complex. As I have explained to you on other occasions, Keighley Bates has a long tradition of providing public liability cover for heavy industry and mining companies throughout the world, and in the United States in particular. These companies have been hard hit in recent years by changes in pollution legislation in the US, and also by a rush of personal injury claims from individuals.

What makes the situation particularly galling is that many of these claims – some of which may take many years to settle – are, by the standards of British courts, frivolous and vexatious. Under the 'no win, no fee' system that operates in the States, any individual who ever caught a whiff of something nasty coming out of a factory chimney, and who, twenty or thirty years later, develops a touch of bronchitis, can ring up his lawyer, and, at no risk to himself, issue a writ.

Forgive me for riding my hobby horse, but there is a growing sense of outrage here at Perryer de Park, and throughout the market generally, that while this sort of thing goes on, it is decent, innocent people on this side of the Atlantic like Mrs Fairfax who have to foot the bill, both for the grossly excessive compensation payments which tend to be granted in these cases and for the legal costs of both sides. I know that this must be a time of grave anxiety for her, as it is for all our names. I ask you to pass on my assurances that we are in constant touch with our lawyers in the US, and that we are keeping the situation under review.

If either you or Mrs Fairfax wish to discuss the situation in more detail, please don't hesitate to get in touch.

In the meantime, I shall be pleased to receive Mrs Fairfax's remittance within twenty-eight days.

Kind regards,

Neil.

Rajiv said softly, 'This is a worrying time for you and your husband.'

She looked up from the letter, from the hated signature. 'My husband knows nothing about it.'

'But surely –'

'And you are not to tell him. This is a private matter. Confidential between us, Rajiv. If you ever so much as mention it to Robert, I'll –' she stopped, appalled at the violence of her words. What was she threatening? What could she threaten Rajiv with, and why would she want to threaten him with anything? Gentle, helpful, sorrowful Rajiv was her only friend. He was all that stood between her and Neil Smith-Stubbs.

'He wouldn't understand,' she said.

'I think – forgive me, Marjorie, but I think what I might find hardest to understand, were I in your husband's shoes, is why such a thing should be kept from me.'

'You have no idea, have you?'

She saw that she had embarrassed him. Or perhaps he had embarrassed himself, going beyond his proper professional involvement. 'All I meant to say, Marjorie, was that if my wife were bearing a burden of this magnitude – or any burden at all – I would want to know about it, so that I could bear it with her.'

73

Factory chimneys. Lawyers' costs. *American* lawyers' costs, for heaven's sake. And there she had been, thinking that she was paying to have people's roof tiles put back after the hurricane.

It was almost funny. She could almost laugh. She would laugh when she told Robert. *Darling, I'm afraid I told a little fib about that £7,000 cheque. It wasn't really estate duty, it was the first instalment on a multi-billion-dollar lawsuit that I've got myself involved in.* That was the approach to adopt – exaggerate, and then the truth wouldn't seem so bad.

He might be impressed. He hadn't realized that he had a wife capable of such things. He certainly wouldn't be worried about the financial side. He had always insisted that it was up to her what she did with her inheritance. He might welcome the opportunity to prove that he meant it.

She would tell him – when? Not tonight. Caroline was staying, with her Militant Tendency boyfriend, Don. Don was a nice enough chap, but Marjorie sensed a certain disdain for the bourgeois standards of comfort enjoyed by what he referred to as his outlaws. She didn't fancy discussing her financial affairs in front of him, although Caroline would have to know eventually, she supposed, and might pass the information on.

The two of them would be gone by the weekend. As soon as she was alone with Robert, she would tell all. Own up, confess, make a clean breast of it. So many expressions for the same thing. She would let the cat out of the bag, put her hands up, give the game away. Like the Eskimos having seventy different words for snow because they had so much of the stuff. Did English-speaking people have a lot to confess?

It was a huge relief to have made the decision. She went home feeling positively jaunty. She could even put up with Don lolling in the best armchair, sipping Robert's brandy while he watched the news and sounded off about how there would never be another Labour government in Britain until the party went back to its socialist roots.

'After the break,' said the newsreader, 'why doctors at a practice in the Midlands have started charging for the use of chairs in the waiting room; why a former England cricket captain may have to sell off his collection of autographed bats; and can Brussels bureaucrats change the shape of the Brussels sprout?'

Marjorie went out to the kitchen to make tea. When she came back, a picture of the Lloyd's building filled the screen.

She nearly dropped the tray. It rattled in her hands. Caroline took it from her. 'Seen this, Mummy? A bunch of rich people losing all their money.'

'. . . unlimited liability,' the reporter was saying. 'Now, with the market being hit by losses unprecedented in its 300-year history, many names are discovering to their cost what that term means.'

There was a shot of someone's luxurious country home, and the long drive leading to it. The camera wandered around the spacious grounds, through a water garden, past a tennis court and into the stables where a glossy-flanked hunter was munching hay. There was a sudden stark shot of a For Sale sign.

A face appeared of an oldish man with white hair, kind features and an MCC tie. A caption identified him as 'Sebastian Milford, Former England Cricket Captain. Chairman, Names' Alliance.'

'I've been collecting cricketing memorabilia since I was six years old,' he said. 'Next week, it's all going under the hammer.' He seemed sad but philosophical, as if he had just lost an important match.

'Do you feel bitter?' the interviewer asked.

Sebastian Milford considered the question. 'I'm not bitter about paying my just debts, no. I'm a sporting man.'

'And a rich one,' Don remarked. 'Or at least you were.'

'Sshh, please,' said Marjorie.

'So-rree.'

'. . . formed the Names' Alliance.' Sebastian Milford continued. 'A lot of us are wondering where it's all going to end. We want to know why it's happening now, and why on this grotesque scale. We're asking ourselves if there's something we're not being told.'

Marjorie had a sudden vision of her father, glued to the wireless for *Test Match Special*. However busy he was, he would always stop what he was doing to listen when Milford came in to bat. The warm, gravelly voice of the young John Arlott floated into her mind. *Milford drives it out to the boundary at the Vauxhall End, what a magnificent captain's innings we're seeing this afternoon . . .* She had never grasped the finer points of the game, but she could pick up the excitement. She felt it now.

She wrote to Sebastian Milford c/o the MCC, asking for more information about the Names' Alliance. His reply came after a week. He apologized for the delay. This was a busy time for the Names' Alliance, as he was sure she understood. There had been an encouraging response to the TV report. Some fifty or sixty names, who until now had been alone with their difficulties, had got in touch.

The letter continued:

I enclose a questionnaire for you to consider and, if you have no objection, complete. We are trying to build up an overall picture of what is going on in the market. We need to know to what extent the losses are concentrated on particular syndicates, which members' agencies are involved, and so on.

We also need to know what assurances, if any, were given as to the profitability of the market, or particular syndicates within it, and which individuals gave these assurances.

Please be as detailed as you can, using extra sheets if necessary.

If you need further copies of the questionnaire for friends or family members, I shall be glad to supply them. All information will be treated as confidential.

I look forward to hearing from you.

Sincerely,

Sebastian Milford.

PS: Thank you for your kind comments about my cricketing days. In these troubled times they seem very far off, but letters like yours bring them back to life.

She decided to say nothing to Robert for the time being. Why should she burden him with bad news when good news was on the way?

74

At first the questionnaire seemed straightforward – name, title, address, address for correspondence if different, in what year did you first join Lloyd's? – but it became more difficult. Sebastian Milford wanted to know who had recruited her, and whether that person had applied unreasonable pressure to get her to join. How could she answer that?

She couldn't answer the next few questions either, though for different reasons. They were too technical. They sought information about which syndicates she was on, her profit or loss per syndicate per year, her premium limits, her tax position. She phoned Rajiv and asked him to send her the required information.

'May I ask why?'

'I'm joining an organization.'

'What sort of organization?'

'An alliance,' she said, 'of names.'

'I see.'

'You don't approve?'

'I have not said –'

'You don't need to say, Rajiv. I can tell by the look in your eye.'

'You cannot see the look in my eye.'

'Don't you believe it. Come along, Rajiv. What are you getting at?'

He was quiet for a few moments. 'It is difficult to put into words. But I would urge you to exercise caution.'

'Caution!' It was the funniest thing anyone had said to her for months. 'Or else what? How could things be worse than they are?'

As soon as she had asked the question, she knew she didn't

want the answer. But he gave it. 'You already have your underwriting losses to deal with. Do you really wish to become embroiled in expensive litigation as well?'

'Who's saying anything about litigation?'

'I think you will find that your colleagues in this, er, alliance will want to do more than sit around and say comforting things to one another.'

'So what are you getting at? "Don't rock the boat"?'

'I am saying that my information is that the boat is already being rocked, discreetly and behind the scenes, by people who, forgive me, people who are considerably better equipped than you to rock it to some effect. People with somewhere to swim to if the boat capsizes. Marjorie, what is happening is not some high street business getting into trouble with its creditors. It is a major financial disaster.'

'Tell me about it.'

'Lloyd's is a huge national and international institution, a cornerstone of the City of London. A great many extremely influential people are involved. Landowners, bankers, industrialists, and not just in this country, but –'

'"Financially sophisticated Americans"?'

'Indeed. The ripples reach all round the world. In this country they could have impact on the very system of government.'

'"Think not a million miles from Buckingham Palace"?'

There was a prim silence before Rajiv said, 'I too have heard those rumours. I make no reference to them. What is common knowledge is that a number of members of parliament are involved – cabinet ministers and backbenchers. This in itself raises an interesting problem. If a member of parliament is made bankrupt, he must resign his seat. The government's majority might be put at risk. Do you understand what I am telling you, Marjorie? It is unthinkable that the present situation will be allowed to deteriorate much further, or even continue as it is without there being some kind of, er, intervention. One thing that I have learned as an outsider in this country –'

'Come, come, Rajiv. You're as British as I am.'

'Thank you. I must remember to tell my children that, next time someone shouts "Paki" at them in the street.'

'I am sorry,' she said.

'I too. All I meant to say was that, in my experience, the British upper classes look after their own.'

'But I don't belong to the upper classes!'

'Not strictly speaking, perhaps, but –'

'Not strictly speaking, not unstrictly speaking. I'm a hotelier's daughter, married to a school teacher. That's middle-class, Rajiv. That's as middle-class as you can be. And the upper classes hate the middle classes almost as much as the working classes do. The closest I get to the aristocracy is being condescended to by Olivia and Jake Verlaine. Do you think these blue-blooded landowners and cabinet ministers of yours are going to give a damn what happens to me?'

'Perhaps not personally,' Rajiv conceded. 'But when the rescue vessel arrives for them – as sooner or later it surely will – you may have the opportunity to climb aboard.'

'As long as I've been a good girl in the meantime? Stayed away from the trouble-making element, and paid my cash calls without fuss?'

'That is the impression I have of how these things usually work. And, er, speaking of cash calls –'

'There's been another one?'

'I am afraid so.'

'How much is it this time?'

'You are going to have to brace yourself.'

'I am already braced.'

75

The hotel was in Kensington – huge and new and luxurious. An odd choice, she thought, for people facing financial ruin. A shabby little church hall might have been more appropriate, or a community centre – if a church or community centre would have them. It might prefer not to be associated with them. Lloyd's names were not the week's good cause. You could hardly pick up a paper at the moment without reading about them: whingers and whiners, bad losers, bad sports.

She entered the hotel and looked for some sign that would tell her where to go. She didn't want to have to ask. She didn't even want to be here. She ached with the strength of her desire not to be here. But what choice had she? It was all very well for Rajiv to tell her not to rock the boat. The boat was pitching and tossing already, close to being engulfed by the waves breaking over it. The latest cash call would leave her with no choice but to sell Cheyne Walk – unless some other way out could be found.

She spotted Sebastian Milford making his way towards the lifts. Her heart fluttered. He was shorter than she had expected him to be, but immaculately turned out. He walked with the confident stride of a man for whom getting on in years is no excuse for not keeping fit. He wore flannel trousers and a blazer with a crest on the pocket. His briefcase had seen service.

She followed him into the lift. She didn't see which button he pressed. As the lift rose, a terrible thought occurred to her. Suppose he was staying at the hotel. Suppose he wasn't on his way to the meeting at all, but going to his room, to change or shave. And she was following him.

The lift stopped and he got out. She thought of staying where she was, going up to the top of the building, back down and starting again. But he spoke. 'Names' Alliance?' He did not seem to have any trouble with the words. His matter-of-fact articulation of them made them easier for her to accept and apply to herself. She nodded, and he indicated that he would show her where to go.

'I'm Sebastian Milford.' He thought she didn't know. He took her hand in his famous one. 'I don't think we've met. You are . . . ?'

'Marjorie Fairfax. I wrote to you.'

'Indeed you did. Thank you for your letter, Mrs Fairfax, I was very pleased to receive it. What's the weather like in Shropshire?' He opened a door and stood aside for her to enter a conference room. A woman at a desk just inside the door smiled a greeting at him, but asked to see Marjorie's invitation. Marjorie showed it. The woman said, 'Sorry about that. We don't want to let the press in at this stage.' Fifty or sixty chairs faced a rostrum on which was a table with three rather grander chairs. On the table were three carafes of water and an arrangement of dried flowers.

About half the seats were occupied. People sat in ones and twos and little groups. Some of them seemed to know each other, and chatted. She thought she heard an American accent. Other people sat silently, sunk in gloom. The average age was between forty and fifty, though there were some in their twenties or early thirties, and an old man who looked so frail and wispy that any sudden gust of air might blow him away. He was with a much younger woman – his daughter? His nurse? His mistress? Perhaps she was his accountant. Marjorie wished she could have brought *her* accountant along. He would see that his fears were groundless. This was hardly an assembly of rabble-rousers. It was more like a church congregation, a panel of jurors, a Save Our Countryside pressure group. He would relax and reassure her that she had been right and he had been wrong. She was doing the right thing.

Another advantage of the obvious respectability of the group was that it would make it easier to tell Robert, which she was going to do this evening. But she was only going to tell him about the money, not the affair. The affair she would keep to herself. Why burden him with it? Up until now she had wondered whether she could keep the two things separate; but now she knew she could. She wasn't the only person who had done this daft, mad, crazy thing. Thousands had done it – decent people, clever people, famous people, top people. They hadn't all had affairs with Boniface, had they? Sebastian Milford hadn't. So why should Robert suspect that she had?

People spotted Sebastian Milford and hurried forward to claim him and talk to him, take comfort from him. At the back of the room, a waitress was serving tea and biscuits. Marjorie headed towards her, took a cup of tea and a couple of digestives, and went to sit down. In front of her, a married couple were chatting. For a while they seemed quite cheerful; then they remembered why they were here, and looked glum again. But at least they had each other. Marjorie wondered if they had told their children yet.

Sebastian Milford took his place on the rostrum, flanked by a smaller, rather insipid man and an imperious-looking elderly woman. Sebastian Milford said, 'Thank you all for coming. We have some new faces here this afternoon, as well as old friends. It's a pleasure to see you all; I only wish the circumstances were different.' There were murmurs of agreement. 'Shall we start with the good news or the bad news?' This was obviously a catchphrase of his, and produced some barracking. '*Is* there any good news, Sebastian? The only good news you gave us last time was when you said the bar was open.'

'Don't say the chairman of Lloyd's has done the decent thing and hanged himself,' suggested someone else.

Another voice said, 'We all know who'll get the bill for the rope.'

Sebastian Milford smiled tolerantly and waited. She could see that he had no intention of participating in what he regarded as a tasteless and somewhat undignified attack on a man who was not here to defend himself; but he wasn't going to intervene to stop it. He knew the importance of allowing people to let off steam. He was showing the qualities that had made him captain of England and a leader of men.

76

The bad news was that the situation in the insurance market was continuing to deteriorate. Names on the worst-hit syndicates were receiving calls for hundreds of thousands of pounds. No improvement was in sight.

'What, no light at the end of the tunnel?' asked someone in the audience.

Sebastian Milford smiled his tolerant smile.

'You mean we haven't turned the corner?' said someone else.

'The worst isn't over?'

The tone of the banter was bitter and sardonic. She gathered that everyone was repeating the platitudes that they had heard from their agents. Had she dared to speak, she could have offered the natural self-righting mechanisms of the market.

'Can we have the good news now, please, Sebastian?' said a meek voice.

'By all means.' Sebastian Milford beamed at his unhappy audience. 'The good news is – ourselves. The fact that we are all here this afternoon is the best news that we could possibly have, because it shows that we are a force to be reckoned with. Membership numbers have doubled since our last meeting. Other names' organizations report the same upsurge of interest. The response to our questionnaire has been overwhelming.'

Marjorie didn't feel overwhelmed. She was disappointed in her idol. When he said there was good news, she had thought he meant *really* good news. Getting excited about completed questionnaire forms seemed a bit like the captain of the *Titanic* expecting a round of applause because his passenger lists were up to date.

'The other piece of good news is that we are fortunate to have two very fine speakers here this afternoon. Mr Stephen

Manx, the Names' Alliance solicitor, is going to outline the legal position, but first let me introduce the Duchess of Norby Wick, who describes herself as an amateur Lloyd's-watcher. I am sure we are all very eager to hear what she has to say, amateur or not. In fact, after what we have had to endure from the professionals, I am tempted to say, "Bring on the amateurs." The Duchess is going to provide – and again I must stress that these are her words, not mine – an idiot's guide to what has been going on in the market.'

'Bring on the idiots,' said someone. The Duchess rose to her feet. Marjorie wondered if she was the dotty duchess whose character Boniface had so loved to besmirch. She didn't look dotty, she appeared to be in complete command of herself, and to have addressed a few meetings in her time. Her movements were calm. She had all the time in the world. She gazed round at her audience with a look that was both friendly and assessing. She had white hair, heavy jowls and sharp blue eyes.

'My family have been involved in Lloyd's for almost as long as Lloyd's has existed. It has been a family tradition. Nothing idiotic about *that*: the name Lloyd's used to stand for something. *Uberrima fides* – utmost good faith. I myself joined in the early 1970s, as soon as they decided to admit women. I looked upon it as an honour. It *was* an honour, and my membership has served me well, as I am sure that for many of you, yours has served you well.'

A few people nodded. Others, including Marjorie, did not.

The Duchess said, 'Whatever the newspapers may choose to print about us, I am not one to cry "not fair" just because I am called upon to pay my losses after years of profit. I am sure that you are not either. I would not have any sympathy with you if you were. We all knew the meaning of unlimited liability when we joined.'

There was more nodding.

'I am strictly an amateur observer. You could say that Lloyd's has been my hobby. I read *Lloyd's List* every morning before

I read anything else. I listen to gossip, and I am not backward in coming forward when I have a question to ask. Though I wish I could say that some of our younger agents and underwriters – and my goodness, *aren't* some of them young these days, Sebastian? – were as diligent about answering my questions, as I have been about asking them. At times I have been made to feel like their potty old grandmother who should stick to crocheting and growing roses. Be that as it may, I have reached certain conclusions, some of which I would like to present to you now.

'What we are facing goes beyond the effect of the recent spate of strong winds, plane-crashes, oil-rig explosions, pollution incidents and liability claims. However large and expensive these may be, they are the type of event that the market should be able to absorb and deal with, as it has absorbed and dealt with numerous catastrophes in the past. An insurance institution that cannot take such occurrences in its stride has no business calling itself an insurance institution. *It* is the one that should be crocheting and growing roses.

'An historic institution like Lloyd's would not have been brought to the brink of disaster by these events if, in the years leading up to them, it had been managed with efficiency and professionalism, with probity and honesty and care.'

The emphasis the Duchess placed on the words *probity* and *honesty* and *care* had an edge of pain, as if she were talking about an old friend who had betrayed her. Her wrinkled jowls trembled. Sebastian Milford poured her a glass of water, which she sipped. The solicitor spoke to her behind his hand. She listened to him gravely, then resumed her speech. 'Ladies and gentlemen, I have just been given some legal advice by Mr Manx, for which I am most obliged to him.' Her eyes twinkled. 'He has told me that I had better shut up.' People laughed and shouted, 'Shame!' Mr Manx shook his head and looked cross.

'Forgive me, Mr Manx. That is not what you said at all – I

was just teasing you.' She smiled winsomely – she must have been quite a beauty in her day, Marjorie thought, and a flirt too – but Mr Manx looked as if he was not accustomed to being teased. 'What Mr Manx said was that I must be careful not to state or even imply that Lloyd's itself, or its governing council, or any individual associated with it, has ever behaved inefficiently or unprofessionally, or in a way that suggested a lack of probity, honesty or care. I have been told not to say these things, so of course I will not say them.'

'If you won't, I will,' said a voice. Everyone turned and saw an unshaven man in a grubby raincoat standing up at the back. He was shaking his fist. 'Bunch of crooks, the lot of them. Thieves. Pickpockets. Muggers.'

'Please, sir,' said Mr Manx.

'If I may have your name, sir?' said Sebastian Milford.

'You might as well have it. *They've* taken everything else. You people talk about the profitable years, well some of us haven't had any profitable years. Some of us have been up to our necks in shit from the moment we joined.' He paced up and down.

'Your name, please, sir? There will be time for questions.'

'I've got a question now.'

The Duchess said softly, 'Let us hear the gentleman's question.' She sat down and looked at him with concentration and compassion.

'I've lost my home, I've lost my business. My wife's left me and taken the kids. When I was coming up in the lift, I nearly pressed the button for the top floor so that I could jump off. My question is, why shouldn't I have done that?'

The silence that followed was thick with fear and embarrassment. Even Sebastian Milford was at a loss. Marjorie felt responsible for the silence, but didn't know what to do with it. She felt responsible for the man. She wanted to go to him and tell him he was not alone. But she didn't want to be anywhere near him. She had come to this meeting in a spirit of hope that something might be salvaged. He was in the pit of despair. He might pull her down.

The Duchess spoke softly. 'My dear sir, I am so glad that you did not do that.' She and the man might have been the only people in the room. 'I hope you will put the idea from your mind. We need you here to help us fight.' The man sat down, clasping his head in his hands.

The Duchess resumed her speech, but Marjorie was too upset to give it her full attention. She caught snippets. The Duchess was explaining about something called a reinsurance spiral. Boniface had talked about reinsurance. He had said it was a normal, sensible way of limiting your exposure to risk: you simply shared the risk with other people. It was a good thing. But the Duchess was making it sound like the sort of good thing of which it is possible to have too much – particularly if so much reinsuring was going on that everyone lost track of what was reinsured where, and all the really big, serious risks ended up on a small number of syndicates, and those syndicates were yours.

Some underwriters, the Duchess said, were known throughout the market for being soft touches, for their willingness to sign anything and everything after a good lunch. And some agents were known for bringing hundreds of new, inexperienced, undercapitalized names into the market, and herding them on to doomed syndicates, knowing full well what was to come.

Marjorie stopped listening. When she tuned in again, the Duchess had finished her presentation and had been replaced by Mr Manx, the solicitor. On and on he went about the complex legal issues involved. Marjorie was finding it difficult to breathe in the stuffy room, and was relieved when Mr Manx too sat down.

Sebastian Milford rose to his feet. 'Before we move to questions, I now have a delicate matter to raise. I am extremely sorry to have to remind you that the litigation we are considering will be complex, time-consuming and therefore expensive. We must give ourselves every chance. We owe it to ourselves to make use of the best possible expert witnesses, and to brief skilled and knowledgeable counsel. A fighting fund has been established, and we are looking for contributions of £10,000 per name to cover initial costs. In asking this, I am of course aware of the difficulties that many of you –'

Marjorie's difficulty was that she was about to vomit. She put her hand over her mouth and fled to the ladies'.

77

She locked herself into a cubicle, knelt over the bowl and retched again and again. Nothing came up. She leaned against the wall and wiped sweat from her cold forehead.

Footsteps approached the cubicle. A voice said, 'Hi? Hello? You okay in there?' It was a young girl's voice, American.

'Yes,' said Marjorie weakly. 'Thank you.'

'I got some Alka-Seltzer, if that'd help. You want me to pass it under the door?'

'No, thank you.' It was undignified to talk to a stranger through a locked lavatory door, so she drew back the bolt and stepped out. Facing her was a girl in her twenties with blonde hair and china-doll good looks. 'I had a prawn sandwich for my lunch,' said Marjorie, who had had no lunch. 'Perhaps it wasn't as fresh as it might have been.'

The girl tossed her hair. 'I didn't have a prawn sandwich, but I feel like puking too.' She mimed putting her little pink finger down her throat. 'I couldn't believe that old guy.' She stressed the word *believe* and rolled her eyes.

'He was captain of England.'

'It was just what you people wanted to hear, right? It was just what that poor man at the back wanted to hear. Ten thousand bucks.'

'Pounds.' The fact that Marjorie had been overcome with nausea at Sebastian Milford's cash call, did not mean that she was going to join forces with this girl in implying that there had been anything improper about his issuing it. She had not noticed the girl in the meeting, but presumably she had been there. Was this one of the financially sophisticated Americans? 'It all has to be paid for, dear. Legal advice doesn't come cheap in this country – or in yours, from what I hear.'

'You're not kidding.' The girl looked into Marjorie's face. 'You okay now?'

'Yes, thank you.'

'You want to go get a cup of coffee or something?'

'No, thank you.' The girl was starting to irritate her. She was too synthetic, her display of concern too obviously put on, as if she had read in a book that a good way to make yourself popular is to perform a spontaneous act of kindness in public, and wait for someone to notice. 'I'm going back to the meeting.'

'Better have your credit card handy.'

Marjorie sighed. 'Perhaps a cup of tea wouldn't come amiss.'

They walked towards the lounge. Marjorie's new acquaintance introduced herself as Petronella Fincham from New York City. She said, 'I can't wait to tell my stepmother what that feisty old girl said.'

'The Duchess of Norby Wick.'

'Is that who she is? Is she, like, in line to the throne or anything?'

'I wouldn't like to say.'

They sat at a table and a waiter took their orders – tea for Marjorie, Diet Coke for the girl. A man approached them. 'Excuse me, ladies.' He was short and chunky, like a football referee. 'Did I by any chance see you coming out of the Names' Alliance meeting?'

Petronella flashed a smile. 'Sure.'

The man introduced himself and said he was from the *Sunday Globe*. Ignoring Marjorie completely, he asked Petronella if she would mind if he sat down and asked a few questions.

'Go ahead,' said Petronella.

Marjorie said, 'Are you sure you should, dear? Mr Milford told me that he doesn't think that press coverage would be beneficial at this stage.'

'He didn't tell *me*.' The girl's sweet, steely smile gave an indication of how much notice she would have taken if she *had* been told. She turned back to the reporter. 'What did you want to know?'

He brought out his notebook. 'Is that F-i-n-c-h-a-m?'

'You got it.'

'And are you a name, Patricia? You look a bit young, if I may say so.'

'Thanks, and it's Petronella. No, I'm not, but my dad is, and so's my stepmother and my brother and a whole lot of their friends. My stepmother wanted to be here today, but she couldn't make it, so she sent me instead. She's pretty mad about the whole business. They all are.'

'Can you put a figure on how much they've lost?'

'It's hard to keep track of it. They've been warned not to expect to get out of it for less than a million each.'

'The cash calls are still coming in?'

'They sure are. But they're wasting their time as far as my stepmother's concerned. She says she's an honourable business person and she doesn't mind paying legitimate debts, but this whole thing's been a scam from start to finish. That duchess woman in there –' Petronella nodded towards the conference room – 'was saying pretty much the same.'

'Which duchess would that be?' asked the reporter.

Petronella looked questioningly at Marjorie, who said, 'I've forgotten.'

'I'll show her to you when she comes out,' said Petronella. 'That is one clued-up lady. Augusta's going to love her. Now, what else can I tell you?'

What Petronella told him, or at least a version of it, appeared the following morning in the *Sunday Globe*.

LLOYD'S LUST – Exclusive!
Names take a caning!

Lloyd's Agents 'Used Kinky Sex Sessions
To Lure US Names Into Bonk-ruptcy'

Unscrupulous agents working for the Lloyd's of London insurance market offered perverted sex sessions as an inducement to wealthy American investors, it has been alleged.

Many American and British investors, known as names, are now being forced to pay millions of pounds to shore up the stricken market.

At a protest meeting held in London, wealthy New York socialite and heiress Miss Petronella Fincham (picture, left) told how agents of both sexes 'flirted, flattered and seduced' their way through the upper echelons of Manhattan society in a desperate attempt to raise dollars to fend off the crash that they knew was coming.

VICTIM

'They would turn up at all the best parties,' said Petronella, 26. 'Everyone else was there to enjoy themselves, but you could see that these guys were on the lookout for their next victim.

'The real sharks were the ones who worked for an agency called Perryer de Park. They had only recently opened their New York office, and I guess they were trying to prove themselves. The guys went after all the women, and the girls went after the men. They would chat for a while, then set up private meetings for later.'

SCREWED

Petronella herself had a narrow escape from one of these 'private meetings'.

'A Perryer de Park agent called Boniface Bennett turned up at my 21st birthday party,' she recalled. 'Heaven knows who invited him. I certainly didn't. When he heard that I had just come into my inheritance, he wouldn't leave me alone.

'People say men are only after one thing, well, this guy was after two things.

'I said no to both. I didn't like the way he was coming on to me, like I was for sale or something. Now it seems I made the right decision. I could have been screwed twice over!'

SPONGE CAKE AND CANING

For those who missed out on the glittering evenings with the Manhattan social set, other traps were prepared.

One agent specialized in giving traditional English tea parties at his apartment in New York's fashionable Battery Park district.

'We had Earl Grey tea and cucumber sandwiches,' Petronella recalled. 'And there were pictures of Windsor Castle on the wall.

'Outwardly, it was all oh-so-respectable, but it wasn't long before the conversation turned steamy. The Perryer de Park guys had all been to expensive private schools where discipline was very strict. They talked a lot about caning sessions. No one realized that it was the names who would end up getting caned!'

HOSTESSES

'Girls were flown out from England to act as "hostesses" at these "tea parties",' Petronella recalled.

'One of them called herself Heather Fox. I don't know what her real name was, but she sure was one foxy lady.

'She couldn't wait to get her claws into my brother. He's a sweet, trusting guy, who thinks of nothing but films. He runs a film club with special discount rates for the unemployed. He says it must be bad enough to be unemployed, without having to miss your favourite movies. Now he's had to put the club up for sale.'

PRINCESS DI

'She didn't just go after the guys, either. She did this little-girl-lost act with the women – Orphan Annie meets Princess Di. Then she'd hand them over to Boniface.'

Picture: page 5.

78

I only saw it by chance. I'm not normally a *Globe* reader. An oxymoron, some say.

My jaw dropped as I read it. And even now, as I reread it for the umpteenth time, it's all I can do to stop my mouth hanging open again as I relive the shock.

I've got it in my Marjorie Fairfax file, along with her private papers. There's been no shortage of press coverage of the Lloyd's business. You've probably seen a lot of it. It's varied from weighty analysis on the financial pages ('Lloyd's Of London: What Went Wrong?' 'Property Slump Fear As Names Rush To Put Country Houses On Market') to human interest tales of top people's tailors, restaurants and wine merchants closing down as they run out of customers, or what happened when some latter-day Tom Brown's schooldays came to an abrupt end because his parents couldn't pay the fees. Tragedies have been reported – suicides, family break-ups, alcoholism – and celebrity bankruptcies. There have been jokes too, for example:

Q: How do you make a small fortune at Lloyd's?
A: Start with a large one.

Or, did you hear the one about the Lloyd's name who started begging in the street? He couldn't get the hang of it, he kept asking for £50 to buy himself a square meal. And so on. Even the alternative media have had their say. *Socialist Worker* did an exposé about how posh-voiced names were being treated more politely in social security offices than the usual clientele, and *Spare Rib* ran an editorial saying that what the Lloyd's *débâcle* proved beyond doubt was that if you really want to foul something up, the thing to do is to put white upper-class males in charge of it.

It's been one of those stories that's had something for everybody. But I never expected to see myself featured, particularly not in the *Sunday Globe*, and certainly not in a way that suggested that some of it was my fault.

Picture: page 5. I'm looking at the picture now – a blown-up version of one of the snaps Petronella took at Boniface's tea party in Battery Park in the closing days of 1987. It's a bit grainy, but you can see what's going on. I'm topping up Augusta Fincham's tea-cup. Boniface has a plate of meringues in his hand.

Boniface has his mouth open, as if he's saying something. What he's saying might well relate to the subject of caning. He did talk about caning, there's no denying it. Quite a little conversation got going. I described it in detail for you in Chapter 67. It must have lasted at least forty-five seconds.

Who knows what happened as a result of that conversation? I certainly don't. Forty-eight hours later, I was back in England, and I've been here ever since. So I'm not going to say that they didn't use kinky sex as an inducement. Or even normal sex. How would I know what they used? Though I don't see why they would have bothered. Promised yields of forty, fifty, sixty per cent per annum seem to have been inducement enough for most people. Not to mention the opportunity to let your money work twice.

It's not my problem in any case. My problem is that I am sitting here elbow-deep in newspaper cuttings and Marjorie's letters and notes and accounts, listening to tapes of her voice telling me what happened, and searching my own memories for anything that might back it up, all in the hope that I can make sense of it all – something that you will recognize as sense.

I hope the way I'm doing it isn't too disorientating for you: one minute you're in the third person along with everyone else, the next you're *you*. Maybe it should have been *you* all along: you did this, you did that. But you already know what you did, so what would be the point of that? On the other hand, you don't necessarily know how what you did was perceived by other people, the effect it had on them. I'm trying to tell you about that.

I think I'll stick with a mixture of second- and third-person, if you don't mind. It makes it easier for me to talk to you directly, when that's what I have to do. And when I go back to referring to you in the third person – well, it's not as if you don't know who you are, is it?

79

Speaking of Chapter 67, I realize that I did rather gloss over what led to my hasty departure from New York. It was painful to remember, and it didn't seem relevant. But now I think that perhaps it is relevant. It may be. I'll tell you briefly and let you judge.

You remember Warren Fincham, the film buff? Just before he left the tea party he asked if I would still be around on January 2nd and 3rd, because his cinema club was holding a weekend seminar on Truffaut. 'I'd be glad of your company,' he said. 'And Boniface's too, of course,' he added.

I couldn't imagine Boniface at a gathering of cineastes, but as my flight back was on January 1st, the problem wasn't going to arise, or at least I didn't think it was. I thanked Warren for the thought but told him I couldn't come, and why. He asked which airline I was flying with.

The following day was a Sunday. Boniface and I got up late after a night of love. He cooked bacon and pancakes for brunch, and we were wading through the *New York Times* when the phone rang. He answered and passed it to me.

I was surprised. I wasn't expecting any calls. 'Who is it?'

'Warren.' Boniface put his hand over the receiver and mimicked him. 'Have you seen the latest by Jean-Paul Bidet and Jean-Paul Camembert?'

His mimicry was spot-on as always, but it made me uneasy. It reminded me of what had happened that time when he found me with Ronnie. I put on a matey voice and spoke to Warren. He said he had been talking to a friend of his uncle's, who happened to be president of the airline I was flying with. If I cared to phone the airline's office first thing on Monday morning, they would change my flight to whatever day and time was convenient to me. Could I let Warren know by Tuesday how many tickets he should reserve for the Truffaut?

I said I would and put the phone down. Boniface had gone back to the financial pages. I picked up the news. For a few moments, there was no sound except the rustling of pages. Then, in a voice that seemed as carefully casual as the one I had put on to talk to Warren, Boniface said, 'What was all that about?'

'Nothing much.' I explained about the Truffaut. There was no reaction. 'You're invited too,' I added. 'Warren says he can change my flight.'

Boniface lowered his paper and looked at me strangely. 'What do you mean, change it?'

'If we want to go to the Truffaut, he can fix it for me to fly back afterwards. I mean, if you can stand having me around for a couple more days.' I thought I was joking. After last night, it seemed a safe sort of joke to make. He said nothing, so I laughed lightly and said, 'If not, not.'

'I'm afraid it's not convenient,' he said.

'Fine.' I ought to have left it at that, but of course I didn't. 'What isn't convenient? For you to go to the Truffaut, or for me to stay on?'

'Well, both, really,' he said. 'Or do I mean neither?'

I felt cold. 'Don't ask me what you mean. I never know what you mean.'

'Ah, come on, Heather. Don't be like that.'

'Like what?'

'Sulking.' He pulled me on to his lap. 'Look, sweetie, we've had a marvellous time. Against all the odds, eh? And we can go on having a marvellous time until Friday. But on Friday, you fly back to England. Isn't that what we agreed?'

I didn't think I had agreed to anything. Certainly I had told him that I flew back on Friday, but did that constitute agreeing to something? I hadn't been asked to agree to anything.

The only thing I had agreed to was that we wouldn't talk

about each other's pasts. But what if his past was a present? Augusta and Petronella had turned out to be red herrings, but this might not be.

I got off his lap. 'What else is happening on Friday?'

'How do you mean – what else?'

'That you want me out of the way for.'

He started walking round the room. 'I've got someone coming to stay.'

'Who?'

'A colleague. Someone I've known for years.'

'Man or woman?'

He shrugged. 'Woman.'

'Someone I've met? Someone in New York?'

'She's in London at the moment.'

'What?' I said. 'What? What were you planning to do – drop me off at Departures and then nip over to Arrivals to meet her? That *is* convenient.'

'It's not convenient at all,' he said, 'if it means having conversations like this one. I don't tell Orlanda which flights to take, any more than I tell you.'

'But you sleep with her?'

He didn't answer.

'Do you sleep with her? I want to know.'

'Sometimes,' he said. 'When we feel like it. It's no big deal.' I couldn't tell what it was that was no big deal: sex with Orlanda (in which case I could hang on to the hope that sex with me was a very big deal indeed) or sex in general. But then it hardly mattered. Boniface didn't have to make a big deal about sex. He took what was on offer, he didn't have to go out looking for it. It came flying across the Atlantic looking for him.

80

New York Cheap'N'Cheerful was at the bottom of my suitcase. I had put it there because I wasn't expecting to need it again. I took it out and looked for a hotel. Boniface watched impassively, as if he thought I was just making a gesture. He would see what kind of gesture it was. I selected a hotel, dialled the number and asked if they had a room for the night.

Boniface snatched the receiver out of my hand. 'Don't be so fucking ridiculous.'

'You're the one who's fucking ridiculous if you think I'm going to stay here.' I took the receiver back and booked a room. If the clerk at the other end had heard our exchange, he didn't comment on it. He was probably used to this sort of thing.

Boniface said, 'Let me drive you at least,' but I asked him to call me a cab instead, which he did. He carried my suitcase out and gave the driver money for the fare. He tried to give me money as well, but I threw it on the pavement.

The hotel was a few blocks away from my original one – a similar sort of place, but minus the special brand of room service. I didn't sleep much. In the morning, I phoned the airline and spoke to the person Warren had told me would change my flight. I changed it to the next available – that evening.

I stayed in my room until it was time to go for the airport bus. I dared not go out in case Warren had been notified of my plans and was looking for me. I was aware of how disappointed he would be when he found I had gone, and how mystified too. I knew I was treating him badly, but I couldn't help it. I couldn't help it about Cassie either, Boniface's neighbour who had lent me the clothes. I hadn't returned them or even washed them. I had left them in Boniface's flat, for him to return. Let him explain, was my attitude. Let him have the embarrassment. But I knew he wouldn't be embarrassed. Nothing embarrassed Boniface. He would introduce Orlanda to his friends as he had introduced me, and they would accept her just the same. He might not even need to introduce her, they might know her already. Perhaps she was always in and out of New York, in and out of his flat. They might all have been laughing at me, even Cassie, even Warren. Perhaps that was why Warren had felt free to ask me out. Boniface had told him to help himself.

When I checked in at the airport, I found that I had been upgraded to first-class. I drank free champagne all the way across the Atlantic and arrived at Gatwick in the middle of the night, feeling sick as a dog.

Somehow I got back to my lodgings. The lights in the house were out; everyone was asleep. Just as well, I thought, remembering my unpaid rent. My room was as I had left it the day I went away – the bed unmade, clothes everywhere, left over from not being able to make up my mind what to take with me. I had been too excited to worry about things like unmade beds and unpaid rent. I put coins in the meter and looked through my post – nothing much, circulars and a few cards from people in my university class and an invitation to a party on January 6th from Joze, the woman at Eavesdroppers who ran her own funeral business. Just what I needed – a gathering of undertakers.

I took the cover off my typewriter, fed in some paper and started bashing away. I didn't really know what I was writing. I hadn't got time to read it. At one level it was about Boniface and me, but I disguised our identities. I didn't want to give him the satisfaction of knowing that he was important enough for me to write about. And in any case, there was more to what I was writing than that. It was about the human condition. It was a warning about what happens to outsiders when they put on someone else's clothes and pretend to be insiders. I went on typing until somebody thumped the wall in protest. After that, I wrote by hand. No sense in drawing attention to myself. No one knew where I was, and it seemed sensible to keep it that way. At dawn I went to bed. I lay very still with the light off. I didn't even smoke, though it cost me an effort. When I needed to go to the lavatory, I went on tiptoe, checking first that the coast was clear.

I ate the nuts and raisins that I had taken with me to New York and brought back, and things out of tins from my cupboard. I didn't bother to heat them up. One day I spilled cold mushroom soup on a page of my writing. It smudged the words and made me realize how important spilled food had been in my life. It was almost as important as the clothes thing. The pot of yogurt that Boniface had tripped over at 59, Blondin Gardens, the soup that boiled over that evening when we were reunited after our Gibraltar quarrel, the honey that had been smeared over my clothes in New York. It was all deeply significant. Connections were coming so fast that my arm ached from trying to keep pace. I wrote and wrote. At least, I thought I was writing. Sometimes I would look at a page that I was sure I had written and find nothing there, or else a sort of gibberish. Then I wondered whether I was writing at all, or whether I was having a kind of breakdown. I didn't think I could be, because one of the characteristics of having a breakdown would be that you wouldn't know you were having one. The fact that I was even able to debate it with myself seemed to prove that I was in the clear.

I was nervous of having a breakdown. I didn't know that much about them, but I had a feeling that they were an official sort of thing, something you either had got or you hadn't, like cancer or measles. And there were official treatments that you had to have. You could be forcibly detained in hospital. Psychiatric hospitals I envisaged as terrible, communal places. Everything was done in groups. The aim was to make you turn your back on everything that made you different from other people, and so make you as similar as possible. Once you were similar, you could rejoin the mainstream. In the meantime, they made you sleep in long, locked wards, with other beds only inches away. In the morning, doctors and nurses did the rounds, injecting you with drugs to make you forget the things about you that were different. They would coax information out of you and try to turn it into something else so that they could turn you into someone else. They were like the Mr and Mrs Bloody Perfect of my childhood nightmares, determined to alter my identity, make me forget who I was. I would try to escape but there would be no escape. The doors of the ward were locked. I would spend my days shuffling from one end of the ward to the other, dressed in someone else's clothes. Meals would be served at a long, communal table. Everyone would spill their food, and soon I would spill my own. I would beg for a little table by myself, but they wouldn't let me have one. If I sat by myself, I might sneak off and commit suicide. That was their reasoning, that was their fear. They didn't want suicides spoiling the statistics of their cure rates. I would try to tell them that if there was one sure way of driving me to suicide it was forcing me to join something I didn't want to join, but they wouldn't listen.

81

My landlady came to the door demanding rent. I gave her some dollars on account and she went away, but I knew that she wasn't happy and would be back.

If I could just hold out until next term's grant cheque came, I would be all right. At least, I would if I could persuade my local authority to send it to my lodgings rather than to the university finance office. I couldn't go there. Somebody might see me.

A card arrived from my mother saying welcome home from New York. She thought I had only just got back. I had fooled her as easily as I had fooled everybody else. She said she hoped I had enjoyed my journalism course, and she looked forward to hearing all about it when I had a weekend free to come home.

I got on with my writing. The closing date for the Coates Clarion award was, as always, January 31st. That would be the answer to all my problems. Days passed. I lost track. A letter came from Alice Lott, wanting to know why I hadn't been attending classes. She urged me to call in at her office as soon as possible. I put the letter to one side and thought how ridiculous it was, being expected to interrupt your writing to go and talk to a so-called writer about a so-called writing class.

One day, Joze came round, wanting to know why I hadn't come to her party and why I didn't work at Eavesdroppers any more. She missed seeing me, she said, and so did other people.

I didn't believe her, but I let her in. She was smartly dressed in a dark grey skirt and jacket, and I wondered if she had just come from a funeral or was on her way to one. She looked at me as if she were expecting the next one to be mine. 'Heather, are you all right?'

'Sure.'

'You don't look it.' Her eyes moved from my face to my dressing gown to the room, the overflowing ashtrays, the unmade bed, the piles of papers everywhere, scribbled on, crossed out, annotated, torn in half then stuck together with Sellotape. When she spotted the letter from Alice Lott she more or less forced me into some clothes and drove me to the university.

I was expecting Alice to give me a hard time, but after she had questioned me briefly about the reasons for my absence from class, all she seemed interested in was when I had last eaten a proper meal. I told her I couldn't remember but that I had had lots of soup and nuts and raisins. She asked how much money I had on me. I looked in my pockets and found 30p. She gave me a £5 note and told me to go to the canteen and have the set meal, all three courses. When I had done that, I was to bring her the manuscript that I said I had been working on. If it showed evidence of serious application, she would mark me down as present for the classes I had missed. If not, she was sending me to the dean. From now on, if I wanted to miss classes for any reason other than illness, I must get permission in advance. 'And it won't be given lightly, I assure you, Heather. I won't have people treating this course as a soft option. Why enrol in the first place, if you think you've got nothing to learn? Oh, and by the way, this was in the union letter rack for you. It came during the holidays. One of the porters saw it and thought he'd better keep it safe.' She handed me an envelope. The paper was so flimsy that you could see the magnetic lettering on the cheque it contained. It was from my grandparents – £4,500, posted before Christmas. Alice looked over my shoulder. 'When you've cashed that,' she said, 'you can give me my fiver back.'

Three days after I handed my manuscript to Alice, my mother was on my doorstep. Alice had been so alarmed by my wild ravings that she had sent for her. Of course I didn't realize at the time. It came out later. At the time, all I knew was that Mum seemed to know all my secrets of the past few weeks, and what she didn't know she got out of me.

'I should never have gone,' I sobbed.

'Of course you should. I'd have done the same myself.'

I stared at her through my tears, too surprised to say anything.

'If you get the chance to look these phantoms in the face,' she said, 'you should go for it. Otherwise they grow to ten times their real size, and haunt you for ever.'

She spoke as if from knowledge. I wondered what phantoms she had. I had always been under the impression that when her relationships ended, they did so neatly and conclusively, with a line drawn under them, usually by her. 'How's Ronnie?' I asked.

'He's fine, but we were talking about you. What went wrong in New York?'

I told her about Orlanda, and my decision to flee. She listened quietly – a bit too quietly for my liking. She was sympathetic enough, but I wanted more than that. I wanted anger. I wanted some of the furious indignation that she had expressed on my behalf when Boniface hit me. But this wasn't hitting, it was something which, as far as she was concerned, was a lot less serious. So I got a lot of guff about how awful it must have been for me, and how upset she could see I was, and how time heals all wounds and wounds all heels, but that was it. She wouldn't condemn him. At first I put this down to her relief that he wasn't back in favour or about to become a permanent fixture in my life, but later I realized that the reason why she refused to pass judgement on what he had done was because she might have done the same herself. Imagine it: my mother posted overseas, working in a foreign city. She's expecting a visit from a boyfriend – Ronnie, say – in a couple of weeks, but in the meantime she's living alone and manless in a large and luxurious flat. Out of the blue, one of her exes turns up.

334

She's happy to see him, he's happy to see her. He needs a place to stay. His schedule is such that he'll be gone by the time Ronnie arrives. Would Mum send her ex off to live in a grotty hotel? What do you think?

82

Alice said she thought my novel had potential, which, coming from her, was praise indeed, but it was self-indulgent in places, she said, and too opaque to the outside reader.

I didn't mind it being called opaque, in fact I was quite relieved. It meant that I had not revealed enough, when my fear had been that I had revealed too much. I tried to revise it, but I couldn't get anywhere. I couldn't write it without thinking about Boniface, and thinking about Boniface was too painful.

I didn't tell Alice about it being painful, as that would have brought more brisk comments on self-indulgence. Instead I said I had writer's block. She said 'there's no such thing' and set me a string of assignments. I had to write the opening chapter of a thriller in the style of James Joyce. I had to write sonnets, sestinas, pantoums, limericks, clerihews, haiku. When I handed them in, she said, 'Ready to go back to your novel yet?' If the answer was no, she gave me something else to write, such as a short story consisting of eleven inter-office memoranda, nothing more, nothing less. She made me translate Inland Revenue tax guides into iambic pentameters, and passages from Milton into prose that would win an award from the Plain English campaign.

All of which was child's play compared with my most difficult writing assignment: a letter to my grandparents, thanking them for the cheque. I didn't even know what to call them. I couldn't bring myself to use pet names like Grandma and Grandpa, but 'Dear Mr and Mrs Fox' seemed unnecessarily brutal. If I wanted to be brutal, I could just bank the money and go back to ignoring them, which was probably what they expected. I found a postcard of the Statue of Liberty and wrote, 'Thanks for your generosity, had a great time, best wishes, Heather.'

At Easter they sent me a huge Easter egg, accompanied by a card with fluffy chicks on it, and a rhymed message about how spring brings new life and new hope. I immediately suspected that Mum had been telling them my secrets, but she denied it, so I supposed they must have picked up news of my state of mind on their antennae.

The Easter egg was too big to eat on my own, so I rang Joze and asked if she wanted to share it with me. She had recently bought the lease on a shop, and lived in the flat above it. She was working all hours to pay the money back, but she was on her own when I got there, trying to devise a funeral ceremony for a family who didn't want the traditional church routine for their mother but weren't quite sure what to put in its place. Joze told me how she had talked to different family members and ended up with several diametrically opposed views of the mother's life, beliefs, likes and dislikes. She was trying to pull it all together into a ceremony that would take no longer than fifteen minutes and would offend nobody. It reminded me of one of Alice's fiendish writing exercises, and I sat down with Joze and worked on it with her, drinking coffee and eating bits of Easter egg.

The door opened and a man of about our age came in wearing grubby dungarees and carrying a tray of white flowers. The flowers were gorgeous, delicate and subtle-smelling, but Joze seemed bothered about the dungarees. 'I wish you wouldn't come in here dressed like that.'

'Why on earth not?' the man asked.

'Because I sometimes invite clients up here, that's why. They don't always feel comfortable in the shop. Bereaved people are entitled to a bit of decorum.' Joze was always very protective of her clients.

The man winked at me and said, 'Well, at least they'll know the flowers are real.' Joze introduced him as her brother Tim. He was a market gardener, and had brought some gardenias for a wreath.

I admired the gardenias, and he asked what I did. I told him I was studying English, and he asked if I knew the Dorothy Parker short story about a man who gives gardenias to an ugly woman as a way of mocking her. She misses the mockery because the gardenias are so beautiful that they make her feel beautiful herself. I didn't know it, but I promised to look it up, which I did. I really liked the story, and next time I saw Joze, I asked her to tell him so. She said, 'Tell him yourself.'

'How? I never see him.'

'That's easily solved.' She wrote down his number and gave it to me. She saw me looking suspicious, and put up her hand. 'I know, I know. You're on the rebound. So is he. You're not looking for a relationship. Neither is he. But he fancies you.'

'How do you know?'

'Sisters know.'

'And why doesn't he phone me?'

'Because people on the rebound don't always know what's good for them. They have to be told.'

Tim and I went out for eighteen months. He was a nice guy and we provided mutual comfort and distraction as we extricated ourselves from our separate sorrows. I introduced him to films he didn't know about, and he taught me how to establish a window box that would bloom all the year round. We helped Joze with her funerals, Tim providing flowers, while I was on hand if people wanted help with the words for their ceremonies. When Tim and I split up, shortly after I graduated, it was without rancour. He had been offered a job on the Isle of Mull. We both knew that I wouldn't be going with him.

My friendship with Joze continued, based in part on respect for each other's oddities. At first I thought it was like the old days at school when I used to team up with other loners, faking a partnership for convention's sake. But Joze and I weren't faking. She knew enough about my life to understand about my wariness with people I didn't know; she was wary herself, because of the way some people reacted to the work she did.

She had got into it by chance via a holiday job when she was at school, and had known right away that it was what she wanted to do. Going back to school had been a shock; people gave her funny looks and said things behind her back. They still did.

I admitted that I too had found her profession bizarre, but I was learning to accept it, particularly when I felt I had something to contribute. Joze said people might just as well get used to the idea that they're going to die one day, and then get on with living.

I said, 'Are *you* used to it?' She thought for a long time before admitting that she was as scared as anyone about death, but she hoped that by treating it in a businesslike fashion she was preparing herself to be equally businesslike when her time came.

When she wasn't working, she could have a laugh like anyone else, go out for a drink and a chat about our boyfriends or (more often) lack of same. My memories of Boniface no longer hurt as much as they used to; I felt that I had finally let go of him, which was just as well, because by now the papers were starting to fill up with stuff about Lloyd's. If this had happened at an earlier stage, I don't like to think what it would have done to me. As it was, I was able to read all about it with the same mixture of curiosity, sympathy and – let's admit it – *schadenfreude* that was being felt by the majority of the population – those who weren't involved, anyway.

83

Nige Keston was a freelance journalist in his fifties, who rented an office on the ground floor of a small block near Blackfriars Bridge. I had a part-time job on the second floor, with a PR company that produced promotional materials for over-the-counter medicines. I wrote the leaflets that went inside the packets. If you've ever found such documentation useful in helping you to swallow cough mixture correctly, or insert a suppository without mishap, you have me to thank.

I didn't usually work on Sundays, but there was a backlog and my employers had half-bribed, half-blackmailed me into going in for a few hours. They didn't have to try too hard; I needed the money, and I've never been much of a late sleeper. The alternative to going into work was to spend Sunday morning alone in my one-bedroom rented flat in Camberwell.

Nige Keston lived out of town and used his office as his London base. It gave him prestige, or so he said. Having once made the mistake of looking inside, I doubted it. It also provided somewhere for him to flop when he got drunk and missed his last train home. This was what appeared to have happened on this particular Sunday morning.

I was on my way in with my *Observer* in one hand and a cappuccino from the snack bar across the road in the other, when he poked his head round his door and said, 'Morning, Matron.'

Needless to say, I hadn't the faintest idea what he was talking about. Not that there was anything new about that; he was often a bit vague after a heavy night. He emerged dishevelled and unshaven from his burrow. His shirt was hanging out of his trousers, and he was smoking a roll-up. He was holding a copy of the *Globe* over his bum, as if to protect it. 'Don't spank me, Matron. I've been a good boy.'

'Nige –'

'And I don't want any financial advice, either,' he added. 'The value of units can go down as well as up.' He made a friendly obscene gesture and handed me the *Globe*, which was how I saw the stuff in it about me luring people into Lloyd's with promises of caning parties.

Nige said slyly, 'I always knew you had class.'

'Nige, this is crap.'

'Course it is,' he grinned.

I walked away from him, up the stairs and into my office. Fortunately, I was the only person in. I sat down at one of the computers and took the lid off my cappuccino. The froth had subsided, leaving just a cup of overly milky coffee with a smear of chocolate round the rim.

I lit a cigarette and realized that my hands were shaking. I cursed Petronella Fincham for her cattiness and lies, and wished I had taken the paper off Nige. I didn't want him leering over it. I imagined him doing just that. I imagined the whole nation leering.

What would they be leering at? The exact words and images were fading from my memory, leaving behind only the feeling of being soiled. I ought to get my own copy. At least then I would know the worst. I would need a copy in case there was any come-back. I couldn't imagine what sort of comeback there would be.

I considered going out for a copy, but I didn't want Nige to see me, or to guess that I cared. I tried to put it out of my mind and do some work. Half-way through writing the first draft of a list of circumstances in which it is not advisable to take a particular remedy for travel sickness (during pregnancy, or if you're planning to drive a car or operate heavy machinery, in case you're interested), I became aware that Nige was standing in the doorway.

'Ciggie?'

'Just put one out, thanks, Nige.'

'I've been thinking,' he said. 'The *Globe* business could be a big opportunity.'

'Who for?'

'You, of course.'

'Oh, yeah?'

'I've been having a word with the editor. He's a bit of a mate of mine. He was quite impressed when I told him you were as well.'

I sighed. 'Nige, did you have to?'

''Fraid so, love. That's the business we're in. But don't worry, because in trying to do myself a favour I've actually done you one.'

I waited.

Nige said, 'I told him you didn't work for Lloyd's any more –'

'Nige, I have never –'

'– and that you're by way of being a bit of a scribe. So instead of him doing what I was angling for, which was to commission me to do a profile of you, he said, "Would she write a piece for us?"'

'Me? Write for the *Sunday Globe*?'

'It's not a chance that comes every day, is it?'

I said faintly, 'What sort of piece would it be?'

'"Lloyd's of London, My Part in its Downfall, by Mystery Girl Heather."'

'I haven't had a part in its downfall.'

Nige looked at me as much as to say, *what's that got to do with anything?*

I know what you're thinking: I should have said no there and then, as a matter of principle. You may be right. In fact, you are definitely right. Never mind principle, I would have refused on the grounds of my own self-interest if I had known what the outcome would be.

But I didn't know, did I? All I knew was that when Nige said *it's not a chance that comes every day*, he had hit upon an uncomfortable truth which you too have probably spotted, i.e. that my career was badly in need of a breakthrough. The sum total of my literary achievements since graduating three years ago from the University of South Bermondsey (second-class honours, with a credit for creative writing) were a short story in an arts magazine that didn't pay, another in a women's magazine that did, an occasional column on London life in one of the free magazines that in my youth I used to give away outside Brixton station, and some film reviews in a listings weekly. There was my pharmaceuticals work, and from time to time I would work with Joze on alternative funerals. And then there were the I-was-there books: a book packager hired me to transcribe and edit barely audible tapes of people talking about unusual experiences they had had, such as being fully conscious during major surgery, or being brainwashed by religious cultists whilst on holiday in California. These were then published as 15,000-word slim volumes with sensational titles and pseudonymous authors, retailing on station book-stalls at around £2.50. Shortage of work wasn't the problem – there's usually work for the jobbing hack who isn't too fussy and who can let go of her dream of one day making it on to the Coates Clarion shortlist, or coming to the attention of a national newspaper.

The *Sunday Globe* was a national newspaper. Not the one I would have chosen for my debut, but I was in no position to choose. As Nige said, this could be my big opportunity. One thing could lead to another. And I felt I was entitled to set the record straight.

84

I ought to have smelt a rat when Nige, having said that I was the one being commissioned to write the piece, got out his notebook and said, 'What's the story?'

'I thought I was writing it,' I said.

'You are, but I have to give the guys at the *Globe* some idea of what to expect.'

'Can't I tell them myself?'

'The editor's a busy man, Heather. Now, do you want me to put your proposal to him or not?'

I sighed. 'What do you want to know?'

I knew what he wanted: sleaze, and plenty of it. When I told him that I knew nothing about caning sessions or hostesses, he seemed to lose interest. But he perked up again when I told him that I had once been in a relationship with a Lloyd's agent. As a result, I explained, I knew a bit about how the insurance market worked. I could easily write a background piece. 'Something that respects the *Globe* reader's intelligence.'

'How about an interview?' Nige said. 'With lover boy? What's-he-got-to-say-for-himself-now type of thing?'

I shrugged. 'If the *Globe* wants to fly me to New York . . .'

'Interesting idea, Heather. Tell me more.'

So I told him more.

Next Sunday, the following appeared in the *Globe*.

'I DIDN'T CANE NAMES,' SAYS LLOYD'S GIRL HEATHER

by our special correspondent Nigel Keston

The mystery girl at the heart of the sex scandal surrounding the troubled Lloyd's of London insurance market has denied taking part in caning sessions at afternoon 'tea parties' in New York.

Heather Fox (pictured right, entering her luxury flat in London's fashionable Camberwell district) is the former mistress of Boniface Bennett, a leading light at the now-notorious Perryer de Park members' agency.

Heather said, 'I was deeply in love with Boniface, and I flew to New York to be with him. I would have done anything he wanted to help with his work.'

The 'work' of Perryer de Park consisted of luring investors into a doomed market. Thousands are now facing financial ruin. But, says Heather, 'I only did the things any woman would do – acting as hostess to his friends.

'Boniface was always surrounded by rich, beautiful women. He said they were only clients, but you could see that they fancied him like mad.

'I can't speak for what they got up to in private. But the only sex sessions I took part in were the ones with Boniface. Nice, straight, ordinary sex – no caning!'

I resolved to kill Nige Keston, slowly and painfully. I told Joze this, at the top of my voice.

She was used to dealing with people in states of high emotion, and did her best to calm me down. 'Anyone who knows you will know it's rubbish.'

'What do you mean, rubbish?' I shrieked. 'It says I deny it. That's not rubbish.'

'Yeah, but it's sort of "she denies it, nudge-nudge-wink-wink".'

'Thanks a lot. I feel better now.'

'Why don't you sue them?' Joze suggested.

'With what?'

'Isn't your mother's boyfriend a solicitor?'

I didn't want to involve Ronnie. I didn't even want to sue the *Globe*. Suing would be too businesslike, and I didn't feel businesslike about what had happened. It was too personal for that.

I didn't deserve it. What harm had I ever done Petronella Fincham or Nige Keston? None. So why were they doing this to me? I felt it particularly acutely in Nige's case. Neither of us would claim to be bosom buddies, but in the months that I had worked in that office we had shared a few fags together, a few chats. The sneaky, underhand way that he had gone about getting his story made my gorge rise. The way he must have got the picture was even worse. How had he found out where I lived – by chatting up my boss? Or by following me home?

People who are burgled often say that they feel violated, that they can never again be at ease in their homes. It wasn't quite that bad – the *Globe* photographer hadn't actually been inside the building – but I still felt spied-on as I climbed the steps to the front door, got out my keys and stood in the pose in which I had been captured on camera.

I worried that some pervert who had been titillated by the *Globe* story might try to find me. Joze was reassuring. The *Globe* had stopped short of publishing my address – beyond 'fashionable Camberwell' – and there was nothing distinctive about the building. It was one of thousands of nearly identical, ageing, suburban terraced houses divided into flats that were thick on the ground in fashionable Camberwell and elsewhere.

I was reassured, but not completely. The picture had been taken at a funny angle, and you could just make out a shop on the corner, a trendy jeans mart, whose name, the Camberwell Jean Pool, could easily be looked up in the phone book. If someone wanted to find me, they would know where to start looking. And, as it turned out, somebody did want to find me.

85

It happened on a hot Wednesday afternoon. I was alone in my flat, working on the tapes about the student and the cult, drinking iced tea and wondering whether to apply for a job I had seen advertised in the paper. It involved watching soap operas and writing synopses of what happened in them, for publication in an aficionados' magazine and was quite well paid.

The phone rang. It was Joze. She had some clients coming in, she said – a middle-aged couple whose teenage daughter had just been killed in a road accident. The parents wanted to have some of the daughter's favourite poems read out at the funeral, but they couldn't identify them. They could quote extracts from the poems, but not the whole thing. They didn't know the titles, or the authors. Could I help?

I promised to go round. First I took a shower and changed out of my shorts into something more suitable. I took two large anthologies from my shelves, put them in my shoulder bag and set off.

A car had broken down in the street, and an AA man was lying underneath it. Other cars were having to crawl round. The air was thick with petrol fumes, and everything was in slow motion. My memory of what happened next is also in slow motion.

I made my way to the bus stop, which was outside the Camberwell Jean Pool. I looked in the window at the new season's jeans. I wondered if the girl in the car crash used to wear jeans, and what kind of poetry she had liked. I wondered how her parents could bear what was happening to them. I hoped I would be able to find the poems they wanted.

A middle-aged man was looking at me. I glared back. He

347

was short and fattish, like a former athlete gone to seed. He could have been the Camberwell Jean Pool's favourite customer. He wore denim jeans, tightly belted in an unsuccessful attempt to hold his stomach in, and a white T-shirt. Over his left shoulder was a denim jacket, which he held on to with his finger through the hook in the neck in a way which to me always suggests a vain person. His longish hair was too blond and thick to be natural.

'Excuse me. Is your name Heather Fox?'

I took a few steps away. There were plenty of people about, but that didn't mean they would necessarily come to my aid. I felt the weight of the anthologies in my shoulder bag and wondered how effective they would be as weapons. He pushed his sunglasses up into his hair and crinkled his eyes against the sun. It seemed like a practised gesture, as if he thought it enhanced his looks. 'Julia's daughter, right?'

Mention of her name made me relax a little. He was after her, not me. One of her old Men Against Sexism buddies. Potty, but harmless.

I still hadn't said anything. His face was familiar, and I was trying to place it. He reached inside his jacket and handed me a card. 'Joseph S. Haverstock. Import-Export.' There was a phone number but no address.

I must have put the card in my pocket, because that was where I found it later. At the time I wasn't thinking about the card, I was thinking about him. I had realized who he was. You've probably realized too.

Eighty-odd chapters ago, I sensed that you were wondering why I was going into such detail about my childhood. I told you to bear with me and it would all become clear. And now it has, right?

Haverstock was the name of Mum's first boyfriend – the first one that I was aware of. He was nothing to do with Men Against Sexism, there weren't any men against sexism in his day. Mum didn't know anything about that sort of thing, so she didn't know what she was missing. He practically lived with us for a while, sharing Mum's bed. I hadn't liked that, but I liked the other things: her good moods, the films he took me to, the presents he brought, the outings in his car.

'Remember me?' His voice was gentle and coaxing, as it used to be when he took me for walks in the fields and taught me not to be afraid of cows.

I remembered something else: the day the social security caught us, and what happened after that. My breath started coming in gasps. I felt as if I were drowning as the memories broke over me like waves, huge waves, crashing down till I could barely stay on my feet.

He backed off. 'Sorry, love. I should have thought. This must be a bit of a shock for you.'

Who was he to call me love? Who was he to worry about my being shocked? He had left us, he had *gone away*. He hadn't cared about shocking me then, so why now?

'I was sure it was you in the paper,' he went on. 'So I thought I'd hang around and see if I caught sight of you. I've often wondered how you and Julia were getting on. Does she ever, er, mention me?'

'Mention you?' I was so angry, I could hardly see. 'She makes speeches about you.'

'Eh?'

I could see that he didn't know what I was talking about. He obviously didn't have his finger on the pulse of radical feminism, in the way his successors in my mother's affections were all expected to. He was more a *Globe* reader. Why should he get away with it, why should he not hear the lectures in which he had featured? 'That was when she saw the light,' I told him bitterly. 'The way they tried to make you pay her like a prostitute, even though she wasn't a prostitute or a wife, and you weren't my fath –' my words dried up as I saw the look on his face. To say he flinched would be to overstate the case. It was more a twitch, a tic. I was the one who flinched. I looked again at the card he had given me. Joseph S. Haverstock. The man we got done for cohabiting with wasn't Joseph, he was Stanley. Stan, we used to call him. Maybe that was what the S stood for. That still left the Joseph. I had never called him Joseph, never even known that he was a Joseph. Or a Joe. Joe was someone else. Joe was the name used by my father when he met my mother at the party where I was conceived. The false name, the alias, the pseudonym, the a.k.a. She said it was false. She said she had never seen him again.

'I thought you'd know by now,' he said. 'I thought she'd have told you.'

86

The bus that would have taken me to Joze's was pulling up at the stop. I walked away from it, away from Joe or Stan or whatever his name was. I crossed the road and caught a bus going in the opposite direction, towards the centre of town. I had to see my mother. I needed an explanation of all this.

I don't remember the journey in any detail. I think I went to Liverpool Street and caught a train. Suddenly it was evening, and I was getting off a bus in the middle of the estate where I had done most of my growing-up.

There was a weird, red sunset. Scarlet and pink blobs of light slithered across the roofs of neighbouring houses. The blobs had silvery edges, like the bloodstained mucus you get after a nosebleed. People were out in their gardens, mowing the grass or talking to the people next door. Some of them recognized me, and waved. They didn't know about the blood and the mucus on their roofs.

It wasn't for me to tell them. I walked up our front path and rang the bell. Ronnie came to the door. 'Oh, hi, Heather. Nice to see you.' He stood aside to let me into the house, which was nice of him, considering it wasn't his house. He had moved to the area to be close to Mum, but they kept separate establishments.

I went into the sitting room expecting to see Mum, but she wasn't there. He seemed settled for a quiet night in on his own, catching up on some work. The table was covered with legal papers, and there was a bottle of wine and a single glass. It all looked very cosy.

He appeared in the doorway. 'Er, were we expecting you?'

The domestic *we*. Cosier still. 'Not unless you're clairvoyant. Is Julia around?' I asked.

'She's at ROOOWC, at a meeting.'

'Surprise, surprise.'

'Get yourself a glass,' he said, 'and help yourself to some wine.'

'No, thanks.' My head was spinning enough without alcohol.

'So how are things?' he asked, trying to be genial.

'Okay.' I didn't want to talk to him. I didn't want him to be here. 'Don't let me keep you from your work.'

He bent over his papers. I felt alone, ignored. 'Will she be late?'

He didn't look up. 'Don't know. There's a bit of a crisis on.'

'Surprise surprise again.'

He gave me a look of reproach. 'It's serious. They're practically out of money. They're having to look hard at their priorities.'

'Tell me the old, old story.'

'Heather, she might lose her job. You know how out on a limb she is with some of her ideas.'

'The seven demands.'

'That and other things. Some of them haven't forgiven her yet for what she said at the time of the miners' strike.'

I shrugged. My mother had always been out on a limb. It was where she was most comfortable, and I guessed the ROOOWC women were comfortable with it too, or at least used to it. She had always worked at ROOOWC. What else could she do, where else could she go? ROOOWC was my real father. It was unthinkable that my parents could separate. They might snipe at each other, posture and bluster and throw crockery, but they would never split up.

Ronnie got on with his work. I stubbed out my cigarette before it was finished, and lit another. My stomach was churning, my skin crawling. 'Mind if I put the TV on?' I asked.

'Not at all,' he sighed. 'I'll go upstairs.' He gathered his papers together and picked up his glass of wine. 'There's some salad in the fridge. Help yourself, but leave enough for her.' He went upstairs.

He was still upstairs when she got home, tired and in obvious need of comfort. You could see her expecting comfort as she came into the sitting room: a glass of wine, a cuddle and a listening ear. Instead she saw me sitting there. Nemesis.

'Oh,' she said.

'Sorry for the shock.'

'Not at all. It's nice to see you.'

'Good meeting?'

'Bloody awful, thanks. Where's Ronnie?'

'Upstairs.'

She went to the door as if she was going to call him. I stopped her. 'Guess who I met. My father.'

She spun round, white in the face. 'What do you mean?'

'Stan,' I said. 'Joc. Any other names? I'm losing track.'

She didn't know what to say.

'Mum, why didn't you tell me?' I hated my whining, wheedling tone. 'All these years and you never told me.'

'How did you meet him?' she said. 'Where?'

'Never mind how, never mind where.' The whining and wheedling were gone; I was furious. 'I don't have to explain anything to you. I'm the one who's entitled to explanations.'

Ronnie came in. He kissed her cheek in a way that suggested he would have done a lot more if I hadn't been there. 'Hello, love. Meeting go okay?'

In a tired, stressed voice, she said, 'It was fine. But love, would you mind? Heather and I have something to discuss.'

He looked at me, then back at her. He said slowly, 'Okay. I'll go back up.'

She tipped what remained of his bottle of wine into a glass and drank it in a gulp. She fetched another bottle out of the fridge and opened it. She tried to give me some but I said, 'I don't want wine, for fuck's sake. I want the truth.'

'I *have* told you the truth.' She drained her glass again and started on the one she had poured for me. 'More or less. But you're right, you're entitled to the missing bits.'

She stuck by the story she had always told about my origins. My conception had occurred at a party, with a man who called himself Joe and whom she could not trace afterwards.

Once I was born, she had tried to forget Joe. She had too much else to think about, first with her fight to hang on to me, and then to keep me fed and housed and healthy and educated. She didn't expect to see him again.

But her friend Dorothy Bridgewater – the snobby one who used to visit us but never invited us back to her place – had different ideas. Dorothy made inquiries and eventually found someone who knew someone who had brought a friend to the party. The friend sometimes called himself Joe and sometimes Stan. Mum got in touch with Joe/Stan and told him he was a father.

'What did he say?' I asked, curious in spite of myself.

'At first he didn't believe it. Then I showed him a photograph of you and he did believe it.'

'He's a great one for photographs.'

'He wanted to meet you,' she said. 'And he and I were getting on quite well, so I thought, why not? Only I made him promise not to tell you who he really was until I said he could. He was just to be a friend.'

'Why?'

'Why do you think?' she said. 'I wanted to see if he was going to stick around. I didn't want you finding a father only to lose him again. Which of course is what happened.'

'Oh, so it was all for my good, was it?'

At the sound of my sarcasm, a look of weariness passed across her face. She glanced at the clock. It was nearly midnight. She suppressed a yawn. 'Heather, I've had a terrible day even without this, and this has really thrown me. Could we talk again in the morning?'

'What, so that you have time to get more lies ready?'

She looked as if she would hit me. 'Don't you dare talk to me like that.'

I ducked out of the way and yelled: 'Why didn't you tell me who he was?'

'When? When do you think I should have told you? After he went? I'd already told the social security he couldn't be your dad. Heaven knows what they'd have done to us if they'd found out that he was. You were only four –'

'Five.'

'Five, then. I couldn't trust you not to go blabbing at school.'

'All right, Mum, but you came off benefit, didn't you? You could have told me then.'

'You think I didn't think about it? But it never seemed to be the right time. And your grandparents came back on the scene, and you were so bitter against them, I didn't want to give you something else to be bitter about.' She spread her hands in a gesture that was part pleading, part surrender. 'And anyway, you stopped asking.'

87

She went to bed, and after a while so did I. I stayed awake for a long time, wondering why she was lying to me. It wasn't true that I had stopped asking about my father. I had asked relatively recently.

I could hear the echo of the conversation in my head. My voice was the voice of an adult, not a child. *What was he like?* I asked. She had pretended to think I meant her father. By the time the misunderstanding was cleared up, the subject was changed.

She had done it very deftly. I tried to recall the conversation in more detail and place it in context so that I could challenge her with it in the morning.

It had been shortly after I came back from London, escaping from Boniface that time when he hit me. She had been trying to make me visit my grandparents. I was continuing with my refusal.

The old excuse, then. I was 'bitter' about my grandparents. And it goes without saying that a person who is bitter about her grandparents can't be trusted with the truth about who her father is: that he is a person she used to know, who used to bring her presents and take her to the pictures and show her how to walk through fields of cattle without being afraid of them. A person who one day got sick of all that and went away.

I wasn't bitter about my grandparents any more. We had reached a sort of friendly accommodation – birthday cards, Christmas presents, that sort of thing. The occasional visit when I was in the area. And I had sent her some flowers when she was in hospital recently. We didn't have much in common, but we had come to the realization that I was the only grandchild they were ever likely to have, and they were my only grand-parents. Or so I had assumed. Now it dawned on me that I might have more. Not just grandparents – a whole gang of new relatives.

I imagined them lurking in the shadows, waiting to claim me. I started to shiver and pulled extra covers over myself, even though the night was hot and muggy. In my mind my sinister new relatives became confused with the people I had been on my way to visit at Joze's when all this happened: the couple with the dead daughter. A quiet voice within me told me that I had let them down, let Joze down; but its reproachful whisper was blanked out by my fear. *Just because you've lost your daughter*, I wanted to say to them, *you needn't think you can have me*.

Towards morning, rain began. I woke up at around 7.30 with the windows awash. I could hear from downstairs the sound of Mum and Ronnie having breakfast and the soft, intense hum of a conversation about something important. I wondered what she had told him, how she had told him.

I got dressed and went down. Outside the kitchen door I heard Ronnie say something about, '. . . wait for it to blow over.'

'It won't blow over,' said Mum. 'She'll never forgive me.'

I threw open the door. 'If you must talk about me behind my back, you could keep your voices down.'

Ronnie looked surprised. 'We weren't talking about you.'

'We were talking about my job,' said Mum, who was still in her dressing gown. 'My former job.'

I was speechless.

Ronnie was trying to soothe her. This was typical, he always put her problems before his own. 'Of course it's still your job. They can't sack you just like that. Feelings ran high at the meeting and people said things they didn't mean.'

Mum shook her head. 'They meant it. They want to get rid of me.' She had tears in her eyes. 'They've had the best years of my life and now —' Her voice cracked. She breathed in. 'They passed a resolution saying we've got to scrap the —' she wiggled her fingers to signify inverted commas ' "outdated and backward-looking" Seven Demands Newsletter as an economy measure, and concentrate our resources on environmental campaigns and anti-racism.'

I shrugged.

'Heather, Ronnie, you both know me, be fair. Am I racist? Am I against the environment? Of course I'm not, but that's *not what ROOOWC's about*. It's a *women's* centre. It grew out of sexual politics, it should stay with sexual politics. I said, listen: either men and male institutions oppress women or they don't. If they don't, or if they do but it doesn't matter, fine, let's disband, change our name and take up other causes. But if it does matter, *we've* got to make a priority out of stopping it. If we won't, who will? And if we don't do it by campaigning for our demands — our agreed demands, the few things the women's movement has ever agreed on — how will we do it? Without demands, how do we know what we want? How will we know when we've won? If ROOOWC gives up on the seven demands, I said, it'll be over my dead body. And one of them said —' Mum put on a silly voice '— "I'm sure we all hope it won't come to that, Julia, but if you don't feel able to implement the democratically arrived-at decisions of the collective, perhaps you should stand aside for someone who does." So that's what I'm going to do. We'll see how long it is before they come crawling. "Julia, what's this letter from the Inland Revenue?" "Julia, we're cold and the boiler won't start." "Julia, we keep getting error messages on the computer." ' She left the room. Ronnie made as if to follow her, then decided not to. He closed the door, sat down beside me and looked at me with troubled eyes. 'What's he like?'

'She told you, did she?'

'She hasn't told me much,' he said. 'She told me you met him. When I tried to find out more, I got ROOOWC, ROOOWC,

ROOOWC all night long. So tell me – *what's he like?*'

'I don't know,' I said.

'Come on, Heather, give me a break. We're pals, aren't we?'

'Of course we are, but I only talked to him for two minutes. What do you want to know?'

Ronnie reeled off some questions. 'How old is he? What does he look like? What does he do?'

'He's a bit older than Mum,' I said. 'He looks like a sixties hippie who's been washed up on the shores of the nineties and thinks he's God's gift to women. Tell you what.' I felt around in my pocket and brought out the card Stan had given me. 'If you want to know about him, ring him up and ask him.'

'Import-Export,' Ronnie read. 'What does that mean? Cheap clothes put together by child labour?'

'Or heroin.'

'Or landmines. *Is* he God's gift to women?'

'How would I know?'

Ronnie said gloomily, 'Your mother obviously thought he was once.'

'Did she say that?'

'She didn't have to. She wants to meet up with him.'

'I thought you said she talked about ROOOWC all night.'

'She did. That was part of her denial. She's still in love with him, I can tell.'

I lit a cigarette. With the match still lit, I looked at the card. Ronnie looked at the card and then at the flame and then at me. He passed me the ashtray. Then Mum came in, half-dressed, looking for her own cigarettes. I tried to hide Stan's card, but when Mum saw it and saw what we were trying to do with it, she gave us a dirty look and snatched the card away.

88

It was early afternoon when I reached my grandparents' house. The rain had stopped and he was pottering about in the front garden. He saw me and leaned on his fork. 'Hello, stranger.'

'You always say that.'

He nodded at his roses. 'They've benefited from the rain.' He sounded almost surprised, as if rain were normally a dangerous substance to bring into contact with roses.

'They're lovely.'

'So how are you?' he said. 'Still scribbling?' He made a writing gesture. 'Do you want a cup of tea? Your gran's having her rest.'

'I want to ask you something.'

He did a comedy routine of patting his pockets and finding them empty. 'Where are you off to this time?' It was a regular joke of his, to remind me about the first time I went to see them.

'Nowhere.'

'Come inside.' He took off his muddy shoes and went into the house.

I followed through the shadowy hall and into the spick-and-span little kitchen. The house still made me nervous – this time more so than usual. He stood at the sink, filling the kettle. I said to his back, 'Is there any correspondence?'

'What sort of correspondence?'

'From when you tried to have me adopted.'

He turned round sharply – as sharply as he could manage with his arthritic back. He looked at me for a long moment. 'I thought we'd buried the hatchet.'

'We have,' I said. 'Is there any correspondence?'

He let out a long sigh. 'I don't know. I'd have to ask your gran.'

'Will you ask her, please? I'll make the tea.'

'She's probably asleep. She's not well, your gran.'

'Please ask her.'

He sighed and went upstairs. I heard his voice, and my grandmother's weak one. I wondered if she would ask to see me, ask what I wanted and why I wanted it. Would she listen understandingly and then jolly me out of it? That was what grandparents were supposed to do.

He came back down. 'She says there might be some bits and pieces in the loft.'

'Can we get them?'

'I'm not going up there with my back.'

'I'll go.'

'What do you have to start digging all this up for?'

I didn't answer. I went upstairs. He followed. As I passed my grandmother's room, she called out, 'Heather?'

'Yes?'

'Hello, dear.'

'Hello.'

She didn't say anything else. I wondered if she had fallen asleep, or if she couldn't think of anything else to say. I couldn't either. I stood on a chair under the loft hatch, pulled down the folding ladder and climbed up.

It wasn't so much a loft as a gap under the roof. You couldn't have walked around up there, or even crawled. You would have needed to slither on your belly like a snake, and even then you might get trapped under the rafters. You would be stuck there for ever. There wasn't much there – just a few lampshades and vases and a suitcase.

I brought the suitcase down. My grandfather was waiting at the foot of the ladder. 'We've never been great ones for keeping things.'

'You can say that again. You didn't even want to keep me.'

He made a huffing sound, angry, defensive. We had never talked about this; it wasn't so much a case of burying the hatchet, as never having looked at it. Now his attitude told me that if I insisted on waving the hatchet around, he could do it too.

'That was how it was done in those days,' he said. 'That was the thinking. A clean break.'

I slammed the suitcase down on the kitchen table so hard that the table legs shook. 'And what was *your* thinking?'

'It wasn't for us to think,' he said.

'That's what people said in Nazi Germany.'

'Don't you talk to me about Nazi Germany, young lady. I served my time in the forces.'

I snapped the suitcase open. It was half-full of letters, some handwritten, some typed, some in bundles, some loose. Some looked personal, some were bills.

In a more conciliatory tone, he said, 'You weren't there.'

'And you wish I wasn't here now.'

'You'd never have known the difference.' He snatched the suitcase away from me and tipped its contents all over the table. Some of the letters fell on the floor. He ignored them, rummaging on the table with shaking hands. 'Is this what you're after?' He held out a piece of yellowing paper with a logo showing a child sheltering under a Union Jack and the name of the organization: the National and Colonial Association for Aid to Children of the Destitute. The print had faded and so had the typing. All the *e*s were slightly above the line; the *l*s slightly below it. A spelling error had been corrected with heavy black Xs.

Dear Mr and Mrs Fox,

I have just come from a difficult meeting with your daughter Julia, and I am sorry to have to tell you that she remains recalcitrant and uncooperative. She informs me that she will not sign the papers giving final authorization for the adoption of Heather.

I wonder whether you might consider having one last talk with Julia, using your authority as her parents to urge her to change her mind, for Heather's sake and for her own.

Failing this approach, our only alternative will be to apply to the courts to have Julia declared an unfit mother . . .

My eyes stung. I couldn't read any more. I said, 'Can I take this?' Without waiting for a reply, I folded the letter and put it in my pocket. Then I left the house.

Back in London, I rang up Directory Enquiries but they had never heard of the National and Colonial Association. I went to a number of libraries and looked it up in charity reference books and directories and books on the history of adoption. Eventually I found that it had changed its name to ChildPeril.

I rang their London headquarters, and said, 'I want to talk to someone about adoption.'

The woman at the other end said, 'Do you mean you're interested in adopting?'

'No.'

'You're adopted yourself and you –'

'No.'

There was a short pause before she said, 'What can we do for you, dear?'

'I was *nearly* adopted,' I explained.

'I see.' I noticed a note of caution in her tone which hadn't been there before and which suggested that she thought she had a crazy person on the line.

'You arranged it,' I explained. 'You tried to. Not you personally. The National and um –' I fumbled around for the letter. 'There was this woman who was going to adopt me. She had a house in the country. She was going to give me a pony. I want to find her.'

I realized I was crying. The woman realized it too. She said gently, 'Would you like to come in and talk to somebody, dear?'

89

I walked nervously through the portals of the Pimlico headquarters of ChildPeril and gave my name at the desk. A woman
came to meet me and took me into a little room. She seemed
to have been briefed by her colleague who took my call, and
to know what I wanted, which was a relief. I didn't want to
have to go through it all and risk getting upset again.

She seemed to find it all quite normal and routine. She even
had a printed form to fill in, attached to a clipboard. 'Heather,
may I ask how long it is since you decided to make this search?'

I hesitated before answering. It might be a trick question. If I
said I had only just decided, she might think it was an impulse
thing, and tell me to go away and think about it some more. If,
on the other hand, I told her that my search had occupied my
entire life to date, she might put me down as neurotic, obsessive,
emotionally ill-equipped for the traumas that might lie ahead.

'A while,' I said.

'Would that be years? Months? Weeks?'

I took the middle one. 'Months.' She wrote a note. I said,
'Is that wrong?'

'There's no right and wrong in cases like this, Heather.' Her
voice was soothing. 'There's only what's comfortable and
appropriate for you.'

'Okay.'

'And the other people concerned.'

'You mean Mrs –' I stopped myself, but not in time.

The woman looked at me closely. 'You know her name?'

'I don't know anything about her.'

'But you were about to call her something? Or was that just
a private name you had for her, a pet name?'

'A pet name, yes.'

'Let's talk about you first,' she said. 'Do you know why you made this decision?'

'I've always been curious about her,' I said.

'How long is always?'

'Since I first heard about her, I suppose.'

'And when was that?'

'I overheard my mother talking about her to a friend.'

'What did she say? Can you remember?'

I made a face. I didn't want to go into all this. But the woman was insistent. 'What sorts of things did she say about her? Was she sympathetic? Hostile?'

'Hostile. Very hostile.'

The woman nodded and wrote something down. 'Your adoptive mother was hostile to your birth mother.'

I was surprised – not by the fact of Mrs Bloody Perfect's hostility to Mum, that was only to be expected, but by this woman knowing about it so soon after I made my inquiry. She must have been moving fast, phoning people, looking up files. 'Was she?' I said.

The woman looked puzzled. 'Isn't that what you were saying?'

'I thought it was what *you* were saying.'

I realized then that it wasn't what either of us had been saying.

I tried again. 'Look, my real mother –'

'Heather, we sometimes find it helpful to use the terms "birth mother" and "adoptive mother" rather than "real" mother. It smacks less of value judgements, and it avoids confusion.'

Talking of smacks, I wondered if she knew how close she was to getting one in the mouth. 'I'm talking about the woman who gave birth to me.'

'And who you're trying to find?'

She hadn't been properly briefed at all, she hadn't been listening to me, no one had been listening, we were at cross-purposes.

I spelled it out. 'The person I'm trying to find is the woman who nearly adopted me.'

'Oh, I *see*.' She unclipped the form from her board and replaced it with another one. 'I'm sorry, I misunderstood you. Your foster-mother, you mean? Someone who fostered you with a view to adoption? Can you remember her name?'

'I was never fostered.'

'So who are we talking about?' She was obviously losing patience. Here she was with all these forms, and I didn't fit any of them. I brought out the adoption letter. I didn't like showing something so private to a stranger, but I had no choice. I stabbed at the words *adoptive parents* with my finger. 'These are the people I want to find.'

She thought about it for a while. 'I'm not sure,' she said, 'that we would have records going back that far – particularly for an adoption that never took place. Perhaps in our archive –'

'I want to look in the archive.'

'It's not open to the public,' she said. 'And I'm not sure that it would be our policy in any case to release the sort of information you are looking for. It might be upsetting for the people concerned.'

'I'm one of the people concerned,' I reminded her.

'Of course, but – Heather, would you mind telling me why it's so important to you to find these people? Is there a special reason?'

The question infuriated me. 'You wouldn't ask if there was a special reason if it was the other way round, would you? If I had been adopted and now I was trying to find my real mother, you'd help me, you'd have to because it would be my right. As it is, I don't have any rights.'

'You seem very angry with these people,' she cooed. 'But they must have cared deeply about you to try so hard to adopt you. Don't you think –'

I walked out. She made me sick with her *is there a special reason?* Of course there was, but why should I tell her about finding out who my father was, and finding out that my mother had been in love with him all along?

That was why she had been so adamant about not letting me be adopted: it was nothing to do with me and everything to do with him. I was the only bit of him that she had left.

That was why, after the confrontation with the social security men, she had dragged me into that phone box and pretended she was going to hand me over to Mrs Bloody Perfect. It was the worst punishment she could think of for the worst thing I could have done to her. I had made her realize that she couldn't have him as well as me. She had thought she could, during those idyllic few weeks when the three of us had played happy families together; but the social security men made it clear that it was either/or. And it wasn't even her either/or. The choice had been made for her. She had lost him and was stuck with me. And so she had punished me.

She had loved him then, and gone on loving him. Hence her silence when I was a child – it was nothing to do with me telling tales to the social security, and everything to do with her not wanting to acknowledge how she missed him. She was waiting for him to come back, she would do nothing to break the spell. She wouldn't break it when I was an adolescent either, and that was nothing to do with the supposedly fragile state of my mental balance. She just didn't want to hear me badmouth him the way I used to badmouth her parents. Even when I started to build bridges to them, she had kept quiet. Only once had she come close to being honest: when she talked to me about the phantoms of lost loves, and how the only way of stopping them haunting you was to look them in the face.

Now she was going to, and the irony was that it was all my doing. I had brought her phantom back to her, and she was going to see him, meet him, go out with him. Would she sleep with him? Had he been the Great Fuck of all time, was that the explanation for her free and easy attitude to men over the years – trying to find someone to match him? If he was still up to standard, would she ditch Ronnie and live with him? Marry him, even? She had always said she would never marry anyone, but she was breaking with her feminism: she might do anything. She might decide she wanted a second chance of the life she might have lived.

Two could play at that game. Two could go looking for the life they might have lived. That was why I needed to find Mrs Bloody Perfect.

90

Mum rang up. 'I'm having a party.'

'Great,' I said. 'I hope you enjoy it.'

'I hope *you* do. I'm inviting you.'

'What's the occasion?'

'The occasion,' said my mother, 'is the first day of the rest of my life.'

'What's that supposed to mean?' I asked, as if I didn't know.

'I've been having a good long think about who I am and where I'm going. I'll be fifty soon. I've been taking stock. I've had a talk with Madge and a talk with Ronnie.'

'And?'

'And I've come to the conclusion that this ROOOWC business might be a blessing in disguise.'

I didn't know that I would have put it quite that way, but the timing was certainly convenient. Once, ROOOWC had taken the place of Stan, as the recipient of Mum's passion. Now Stan could take the place of ROOOWC.

She was saying, 'I've never actually sat down and asked myself what I *wanted* to do. I've spent my whole life responding to crises.'

'I thought ROOOWC was what you wanted to do.'

'I didn't *not* want to do it, but I didn't exactly choose it, did I? It chose me. It swept me along. It was great, but it's over. It's another era now, another generation. ROOOWC giveth, ROOOWC taketh away. I'm damned if I'm going to sit around and cry about it.'

'So what are you going to do?'

'Teacher training, I think,' she said. 'I'll need to get some A-levels first, but that's okay. I'll do waitressing or something and study in the evenings. You did it, I can follow in your footsteps. You see, Heather? You're an inspiration to me. You will come to the party, won't you? Bring a friend if you like.'

I ignored the flattery. 'I haven't got any friends.'

'What about what's her name, Joze?'

'Who else is going to be there?'

'Oh, you know, everybody.' She sounded casual, too casual. 'Ronnie. The neighbours. Madge, Patience, anyone else at ROOOWC who's still talking to me.' She reeled off a few more names, then added, as if it were an afterthought, 'And, er, your, er, father. Joe.'

'I thought his name was supposed to be Stan.'

'It is. It's just that I've always thought of him as Joe, I don't know why .'

Because that was what you called him when he was shagging you. Oh Joe, oh Joe, oh Joe. 'What does Ronnie think of this?'

She said lightly, 'I don't think even Ronnie could object to my seeing Joe, er Stan, in a roomful of people. And as Madge says, if he turns out to be a dinosaur or an anorak, I'll have plenty of other people to talk to. And so will you. It seems like a nice, no-strings way to meet him again after all these years. You will come, won't you, Heather?'

Too right I would go. But not on my own.

The idea of asking Joze appealed – or would have appealed, if I hadn't let her down so badly, over the couple with the dead daughter. I couldn't expect her to forgive me, let alone go to a party with me to protect me from my father and my mother.

I would need protection. I wasn't fooled by Mum's talk of dinosaurs or anoraks. She knew he was neither. She wanted him, and this was the party at which she was going to get him. Did she honestly think I was going to stand there on my own and watch her gloating and wallowing in the life she might have lived? No way. I was going to bring the life I might have lived with me to the party.

Come and say hello to your father, Heather.

Of course, Mum. Hi, Dad. May I introduce my other mother? Life with her would have been bloody perfect.

Maybe I could get Mr Bloody Perfect to come too.

The way things were going, I wouldn't get either of them. Time was running out. And I was running out of places to search. I couldn't go back to ChildPeril HQ. I had made a tactical mistake there, revealing what I was after, and perhaps giving the impression that if I located the Bloody Perfects I might go after them with a meat cleaver. I hadn't realized that the organization would be so protective of its failed adoptive parents. It would be on its guard against me. Security would be alerted, as would the switchboard, the archivist, perhaps even the Bloody Perfects themselves.

There had to be another way in. Perhaps if I changed my name and came up with a convincing and respectable reason for needing access to the archive, I might have more luck. I could pretend to be a journalist, or a research student, writing a thesis on the history of British adoption practices.

Which would they prefer – a journalist or a student? I couldn't waste any more time on failed attempts, I had to get it right. I needed advice from someone who knew the organization, who knew how secretive it was and how its systems could be circumvented: someone who would take me in along a different route, both figuratively and perhaps literally, so that I wouldn't bump into the woman I had already spoken to.

I put my brain on search to see if I had ever met anyone who had any connection with ChildPeril. The name Marjorie Fairfax came up. I hadn't spoken to her for years, or even thought about her, but now I seemed to remember her saying that she worked at the ChildPeril shop in Eastbourne. She had spoken about it over lunch – that uncomfortable lunch she and I had with Boniface in 1984, that lunch when (I remembered with a sudden jolt) he was trying to get her to become a name. I hoped he hadn't succeeded.

91

'Dear Diana . . .'

Marjorie crumpled the page and threw it in the waste paper basket. She used her daughter's full name so rarely that to do so now would sound as if she were about to tell her off.

'Dear Di . . .' was friendlier, but it was wrong in a different way: informal, casual, as if what she was about to say didn't matter.

'. . . ana, I am afraid you must prepare yourself for a bit of a shock.' Alarming, perhaps, but justified: it *would* be a shock.

Not too much of one, though, surely, Marjorie hoped. She had dropped enough hints over the years. Di and Tony couldn't have expected to live at Cheyne Walk for ever. It was only intended as a stopgap. She put an upside-down V and added the phrase *and Tony*, then leaned back in her chair and considered how that looked. 'I am afraid you and Tony must prepare for a bit of a shock. I have decided to put the flat on the market with immediate effect and I must therefore ask you to –' She imagined Di flinching as she read, then passing the letter across the breakfast table for Tony to read. Her eyes would signal that he must not say anything in front of the children. Later they would discuss the situation in detail. They would wonder what had brought this on, but would sensibly decide that now was not the time for a post mortem or a confrontation. Marjorie was perfectly within her rights, they would agree. It had been kind of her to let them live in the flat all this time, helping them to find their feet, but now they must join the real world. Tony didn't want to live his whole life beholden to his in-laws. He and Di would be grateful to her for administering a much-needed kick in the pants, forcing them to be independent.

She sighed and gazed out of the window. It was a summer morning in the school holidays; Robert was gardening and throwing sticks for the dogs. He wore ancient cords and a long-sleeved shirt to protect his arms and shoulders from the sun. A floppy white sunhat was pulled down over his eyes. He pushed the hat back to wipe his brow and saw her watching. He lifted the hat in joky salutation and made a little play of examining his watch, lifting a pint to his lips and looking at her quizzically as much as to say *is it time to go to the pub yet?* She smiled and shook her head. It was only 10.20. He shrugged as if in resignation to a life of unremitting toil and went back to tending his runner beans.

Why hadn't she told him yet? And how was she going to tell him now? She tried to imagine telling him. She couldn't envisage how she would do that, the words she would use or where or when she would use them, so she moved instead to his response: the response she would like him to give to the news that she had squandered her inheritance. She would expect him to be shocked and upset, but perhaps more on her behalf than his own. After all, it had been hers all along to squander.

And it wasn't as if he was affected. He still had his salary, his pension arrangements. The house was paid for. Even if the worst came to the worst, they would manage.

But what was the worst, and when would it come? How much longer was this going to go on, how would it end, how could it end? She longed for a cards-on-the-table talk with Rajiv, but she was afraid of what he might say. His most recent communication had been a reminder that interest was accumulating on her unpaid debt at the rate of two per cent per annum above base rate. He also begged regretfully to draw her attention to the outstanding charges for his own professional services.

She dared not ask him anything. She couldn't ask the Names' Alliance either – they too were after her money, a contribution to the legal fund. The word *bankruptcy* floated into her mind. She shooed it out again: she hardly knew what it meant – a ruptured bank? It was something to do with business, she was sure, and not for private individuals.

As if in response to her thoughts, a strange car appeared in the drive, a grey Rover driven by a woman with white hair: the Duchess of Norby Wick, Marjorie realized in alarm. The old lady stepped out of her car, elegant in a summer dress of grey and pink, with a grey jacket. Robert abandoned his gardening and went over to greet her. The dogs were going mad. The Duchess calmed them with the expert hands of one used to dogs, and soothing words. Marjorie didn't give a damn what words she was using on the dogs – what was she saying to Robert? How was she explaining who she was and what she was doing there? What *was* she doing there?

But what did it matter? Since Marjorie had already decided to tell Robert everything – she couldn't not tell him, now that she was about to evict their daughter – the Duchess could say whatever she liked. She couldn't make things worse, and might even make them better, with her engaging manner of speaking and her breadth of knowledge.

Robert called, 'You've got a visitor, darling.'

'Hello,' said Marjorie.

'Good morning, Mrs Fairfax. Kathleen Norby Wick. We met at –'

'Yes, of course.' Now why had she done that – interrupting the Duchess before she could say in front of Robert where they had met? And why was she leading the woman into the house, out of earshot? Why didn't she ask Robert to join them?

The Duchess made a few comments on the weather, and murmured admiringly about the house. Then she got down to business. 'I must apologize for calling unannounced, Mrs Fairfax, but things are moving rather quickly at our end. And as I happened to be in the area I thought I would take a chance on your being in. Our chairman, Sebastian Milford, has asked me to sound you out about something.'

Money, Marjorie supposed. Had there ever been a time when people wanted to talk to her about anything else, when she had thought about anything else? She took the Duchess into the sitting room and offered her a choice of coffee or a drink. The Duchess declined both, saying, 'I mustn't take up too much of your time. Let me get straight to the point.'

The point, it seemed, was the crusades. What they had to do with anything Marjorie could not imagine; but they seemed to be the Duchess's special subject. On and on she went about the arrangements made by knights of old for the management of their estates while they were off fighting the infidel in the Holy Land. 'They might be away for many years,' the Duchess said. 'They might not come back at all. It was important to them to know that their affairs would be properly looked after in their absence.'

'I suppose it would be,' said Marjorie slowly. The woman was obviously dotty after all.

'You may wonder where all this is leading. Bear with me. They appointed trusty stewards to look after everything – some more trusty than others. Human nature in those days was very much as it is now, and our crusading knights were only too aware of the sort of jiggery-pokery that could go on, once their backs were turned. And so they established a body of law to ensure that the stewards and managers handled their affairs for the benefit of their absent employers, rather than their own. Are you with me now?'

'Er –'

'This, Mrs Fairfax, was the origin of the English common law concept of fiduciary duty.' The Duchess could not have looked prouder if she had invented fiduciary duty herself. 'It is this that may turn out to be our salvation. It provides that any person who acts as anyone else's agent must always conduct their business in such a way as to serve the best interests of the person they represent. *Now* do you understand what I am getting at? When we go to court, it will be our case that the Perryer de Park members' agency has been in breach of its fiduciary duty in its handling of its names' affairs – just as surely as if we had all gone overseas to fight for Queen and country, and they had taken the opportunity of our absence to write forged cheques on our bank accounts.'

'I'm sorry,' said Marjorie. 'I know it's only right that everyone should pay their share, but I can't.'

'I haven't come here to talk about finance, Mrs Fairfax. Not at this stage.'

Marjorie relaxed a little. 'What, then?'

'The Names' Alliance,' said the Duchess, 'now has nearly five hundred members. Obviously we can't all go to court at once; and even if we could, some of us would have a better chance of success than others. We want to start with a case that we feel sure we can win. A case that will establish useful precedents, and perhaps encourage Perryer de Park to settle other cases out of court.'

'A test case, you mean?' Marjorie felt uneasy using legal jargon, but wanted to contribute something.

'Exactly, Mrs Fairfax.' The Duchess beamed. 'And what I have come to ask you today is whether you will consider *being* one of our test cases?'

Marjorie closed her eyes. She didn't want this, she didn't want any of it. She wanted her old life back. 'I don't understand.'

'I don't blame you, and of course we are not asking for a decision now. You will have many questions, and so will we. But on the basis of the information provided on your questionnaire, our legal advisors feel that you are exactly the sort of person who will win the sympathy of the court. Because you didn't really know what you were doing, did you? New to underwriting, inexperienced, undercapitalized, you were obviously someone whose interests would be best served by your being shepherded towards the low-risk end of the market.

Instead, you were placed on some of the worst-performing syndicates the market has ever seen. Your profits have been negligible, your losses are huge and continuing. Continuing, that is, unless our lawyers can obtain an injunction restraining Perryer de Park from sending out any more cash calls –'

Marjorie hardly dared believe what she was hearing. 'No more cash calls? Is that what you said?'

The Duchess smiled. 'I am guaranteeing nothing. But if the court were to find that Perryer de Park had been negligent, they might even find that calls which were sent out in the past were improper and unlawful and that there was no obligation on the names to pay them. All or part of the money could be returned, together with compensation and –'

'What do I have to do?'

The Duchess patted her hand. 'Hold your horses, Mrs Fairfax. It is a serious step, one which I am sure you will want to talk over with your husband and your own advisors before finally committing yourself. We are in the process of setting up a meeting, and I would like to take some alternative dates from you. In the meantime, though, the most useful thing you can do is to start gathering information together. Your questionnaire was helpful, but we need more. We will need every shred of correspondence that you have ever received from anyone connected with Perryer de Park. We need any notes that you may have made after meetings, whether formal or informal, and any notes that you can make now, remembering what was said. Don't worry that we might not think it important; everything is important. These people we are dealing with are clever devils. They know how to half-say something, how to give a verbal undertaking which sounds convincing but which they believe cannot be held against them when it turns out to be riddled with mendacity. So please remember everything that was said to you, the name of the person who said it, and the way in which it was said. Every nuance, every lift of the eyebrow, every turn of phrase.'

92

Marjorie walked with the Duchess to her car. The Duchess gave her a card with her telephone number on it, and asked Marjorie to get in touch as soon as she had made a decision. 'Do please try and make it sooner rather than later, Mrs Fairfax. You know what they say in American police dramas – "Let's do it to them before they do it to us."'

'I'll bear that in mind.' Marjorie watched the Duchess drive away.

Robert came over. 'Who was that?'

'Nobody,' she said quickly. 'Just a friend.'

'Is it time to go to the pub yet?'

She imagined wandering down the road with him, to the Rose & Crown. She remembered all the times in their marriage when they had done just that, with nothing more serious on their minds than whether they were going to have a cheese ploughman's or a jumbo sausage with French bread. This time would be different – for her, anyway. He could remain carefree for a little longer. They would sit outside the pub under a parasol advertising Harp Lager; he would drink a pint of the local bitter, she a tomato juice or perhaps a sherry. They would watch the hikers make their way up the footpath towards the South Downs Way, and slowly, carefully, and without becoming over-emotional, she would tell him everything.

Everything?

It was the Duchess who wanted to be told everything. *Every nuance, Mrs Fairfax. Every lift of the eyebrows. Every turn of phrase.*

Every turn of phrase?

You'd be insuring the toothbrush-holder in the captain's bog. I bore for England on unlimited liability.

Marjorie had never envisaged going into that sort of detail with Robert. It would look too suspicious, wouldn't it, if she remembered whole conversations?

That was . . . unexpected.

I wish it happened more often.

Was that the sort of thing the Duchess wanted? Did she expect Marjorie to stand up in court and describe the lunches she and Boniface had had together, the intimate conversations about love and family and bereavement, the winter's afternoon when they had cruised down the Thames on a ferry, eating liqueur chocolates to keep out the cold, the time when she had gone to his flat and . . .

Pulled him. That was the word young people used: they talked about *pulling* each other. *I pulled him, Your Honour.* It sounded rather jolly, like the tug o' war at the Fristendean summer fête. It hadn't sounded jolly on the pages of the *Sunday Globe*. There, Boniface's sex life had been presented as squalid and sick, as a scam, a cheat, a trick, a lure. The women on the receiving end were desperate dupes who had submitted to perverted practices and been screwed twice over. She shuddered as she remembered the agony of first reading that report, the shame, the fear that Robert might see it – not that he was a regular *Globe* reader, but he was always buying odd publications and cutting them up for media studies projects. It would have been just her luck if he had bought this one, recognized the name and put two and two together.

That anxiety had passed – she thought it had. Now here it was again. If the Duchess needed to know about everything that had passed between her and Boniface, did not Robert need to know too? And didn't he need to know immediately, not months hence in some public court room, with tabloid journalists scribbling in their notebooks?

At the moment, all he seemed to want to know was whether she was coming to the pub. She said, 'You'll have to go without me. I'm due at the shop.'

He looked puzzled. 'Tomorrow's your day, not today.'

'Someone's ill, I've been asked to do an extra shift.' She turned her back to hide her blushing face, and started walking towards the house. 'That's what the, er, that's what Kathleen came round to tell me.' She waited for him to call after her, *what are you talking about, she said she was from the Names' Alliance, what is the Names' Alliance, what's going on?* But he said nothing, just let her go. She drove into Eastbourne and walked on the pier. Sunbeams danced on the water; children played and swam. She entered the amusement arcade and looked in her purse. She was short of cash, she would need to go to the bank – if there was anything left at the bank. She had stopped trying to keep track. She found a pound coin in the bottom of her handbag, took it to the desk and exchanged it for 10ps. She fed them one by one into the Silver Falls, but the silver did not fall for her.

She drove to the ChildPeril shop. She would make some excuse to Addie Bernard about needing to use the office phone. A personal matter, she would say, something she didn't want Robert to overhear, something to do with his birthday. Naturally she would pay for the call.

But Addie was out, at a conference. The fort was being held by a newish volunteer called Sheila, whose deferential manner suggested that she viewed Marjorie as a person of some standing in the organization. Sheila did not demur when Marjorie walked purposefully into the office and closed the door.

She dialled the Duchess's number, but there was no reply. Still out rallying the faint-hearted, Marjorie supposed. She drummed her fingers on the table. *Why does it have to be me?* she wondered bitterly. *Why can't someone else be the test case and leave me to benefit from the out-of-court settlement?*

Sheila came in without knocking, looking for a new receipt book. It took her rather a long time to find it, and Marjorie was glad she was not talking to the Duchess, for what would Sheila have overheard? She wondered how soon she could get rid of her. She went out into the main shop and tried to find things to help Sheila with. There was a dearth of customers, probably because of the fine weather; but there was a suitcase of donated clothes to sort out. Some of them were quite smelly and had to go straight in the back, to be sent for dry cleaning.

'Would you mind taking them round?' Marjorie asked. 'There's no need to come back.'

'You mean you're going to close early?' Sheila looked shocked.

'No, no, but I've got a bit of paperwork to do, so I can lock up. It seems a shame to keep you indoors in this lovely weather.'

Sheila still seemed reluctant. 'Do you want me to do the till?'

'I think I can manage the till, my dear,' said Marjorie, in the icy tones of a very important person to a very unimportant one. Sheila fled; Marjorie watched her disappear down the street, then locked the door, and put up the CLOSED sign. Then she went into the office and picked up the phone.

This time the Duchess was in. Marjorie got straight to the point. 'I don't think I'm the person you're looking for.'

'Won't you allow us to be the judges of that?' The Duchess's voice was kind and coaxing, as it had been when she spoke to the man at the meeting who had threatened to commit suicide. 'If you would just provide us with the information I have asked for – or as much of it as you –'

Marjorie gripped the phone. 'That's the whole point. You've got me wrong. You want me to say I was tricked into joining. I wasn't. You want me to say I didn't understand about un-limited liability. I did. Boniface explained it all to me, he –' she wouldn't say *bored for England*. That was his joke for her, not for anybody else. And she had never been bored in his company. She had been enchanted.

'Of *course* you understood, Mrs Fairfax,' the Duchess crooned. 'It was *because* you fully understood the seriousness of your obligations as a name that you asked only to be placed on low-risk syndicates. Perryer de Park disregarded that instruction. That will be our case.'

Marjorie swallowed hard. Her eyes darted round the stuffy little office, looking for a means of escape. Posters solicited support for the forthcoming ChildPeril flag day, and a campaign about teenage runaways. Perhaps the teenage runaways had a point, spotting their escape route and taking it. She had thought she had found one – coming up with the perfect argument for being left out of the test case. But the Duchess was having none of it.

'Did you say "Boniface"?' the Duchess enquired. 'Would that be – forgive me, I don't have your file in front of me – would that be Mr Boniface Bennett? Was he your agent?'

The sound of his name made her shiver. It could still do that. 'Only at the beginning. Then he went off to New York and left me to the tender mercies of a Mr Smith-Stubbs. That's when all the trouble started.' Marjorie thought of something else. 'We wouldn't be suing Boniface – er, individual agents personally, would we?' She couldn't confront him in court.

'*Sue* Boniface Bennett?' The Duchess's tone was caustic and incredulous. 'We'd have to catch him first. Things got too hot for him in New York, and our latest information is that he was last seen boarding a plane for Singapore, passing himself off as a derivatives trader. If we get out of this, Mrs Fairfax – *when* we get out of it – my advice to you is to steer clear of the derivatives market.'

'I will.'

'To answer your question, our action would be against the agency as a whole, but there is a risk that Mr Bennett's very special contribution will come out during cross-examination, especially if the Perryer de Park counsel is of a mischievous turn of mind, and feels that it would be a useful line of argument to suggest our case is frivolous – sour grapes, a woman scorned, that sort of thing. I don't know whether you are aware of the suggestions that have appeared in the gutter press that Mr Bennett had – how shall we put it? – a way with the ladies, and used it to full effect?'

'Did he?'

'When recruiting ladies, particularly those who were young and fair of face, he was in the habit of offering a little more than a sixty per cent return per annum and tax benefits – if you take my meaning.'

'Well.'

'The press would enjoy nothing more than to be able to make links between our court action, much of which will be rather dry and technical, and Mr Bennett's other activities. But we don't want sleaze and sordidness distracting attention from the seriousness of our case. Too much is at stake. We must all be seen to be respectable and above reproach. That is why I am so sure that you would make a first-class plaintiff.'

93

The Duchess went on talking, but Marjorie did not hear what she said. She was deafened by the fizz of hatred in her blood, hot, white, metallic.

There had been times when she had thought she hated Boniface. She had definitely hated Neil Smith-Stubbs, and Petronella Fincham, and Orlanda and that other girlfriend of Boniface's, Heather Fox. But those hatreds were as nothing compared with what she now felt for the Duchess, for her casual assumption that she, Marjorie Fairfax, had not been and could never have been of more than financial interest to the young bloods of Perryer de Park.

She felt like saying, *Just because you're past it, you cow, don't assume everyone else is*, and then describing what had happened. What wouldn't Marjorie give to see the Duchess's face, to hear her reporting back to the legal team about Marjorie's unexpected transgression? They would have to begin their search anew. How annoying for them. It wasn't enough for Marjorie. She wanted to be much, much more than annoying. She wanted to kill the Duchess and her condescending cronies. Failing that, she wanted to hurt them in such a way that they would stay hurt, humiliate them as she felt humiliated. She wanted to wreck their chances. To do that, she must wait until the case came to court and then choose her moment to announce then that she – yes, even she – had been mistress to the No. 1 ladies' man of the London insurance market.

In the meantime, she would play along. She would allow herself to be persuaded to pursue the case, but only gradually and with difficulty. She put on a display of caution. 'Isn't that very risky? What if we lose? What about costs?'

'You already know what the cost has been to you of not

fighting, Mrs Fairfax. But of course if you want to go on receiving cash calls –'

'You make it sound as if I have a choice.'

'Oh, you have a choice.'

'I do?' Marjorie was no longer acting. 'Tell me . . .'

The Duchess sighed. 'You may find that if you go to Perryer de Park with your cap in one hand and evidence in the other that your coffers are finally bare, they will be quite accommodating. They won't hound you into bankruptcy – what would be the point, since by then you would have nothing?'

'When you say "nothing" . . .'

'Mrs Fairfax, you are talking to the wrong person. If you want to submit yourself to the tender mercies of the Perryer de Park Names Special Circumstances Committee, I cannot stop you. I have no definite information, but I understand that what happens is that they would visit your house, value it, and value everything it contains – paintings, jewellery, carpets, every household appliance, every stick of furniture. They would want details of your income, and your husband's income, and any pension arrangements the two of you may have. They –'

'Just a minute. This is nothing to do with Robert. He's not involved.'

'Of course, and they would not have any claim on property held in his name alone. But their attitude is that, since you and he share a household, his income must be taken into account in assessing your assets.'

'That's outrageous.'

'Did I say I was defending it? They would also want to know about any gifts of money you have made over the last few years, and loans, including private loans. The loans would have to be repaid, and the gifts would be investigated to check that they were not simply an attempt to conceal assets. This could mean questioning your friends and relatives, checking the bona fides of charities that you give to, and so on. Once they have decided what you are worth, they will help themselves to as much as they consider appropriate, and that will be the final settlement. For your part, you will be left with enough to acquire a small home to replace your present one, and live modestly in it with what remains of your possessions. I have not so far been able to ascertain what they mean by "modestly". It may mean a standard of living slightly better than that enjoyed by social security beneficiaries; then again it may not. Those who have entered into these arrangements have been required to sign an undertaking not to reveal the details to third parties. They have also had to agree not to take legal action at a later date, and they are barred from receiving compensation from any settlement that may be reached in the meantime. But at least they know that there will be no more cash calls. They can stop dreading the sound of the postman; the nightmare is over. For some people that makes it all worthwhile – though I must say, Mrs Fairfax, I had believed that you were made of sterner stuff.'

Marjorie got off the phone and pulled down the Venetian blind on the shop door. One of the slats was broken, so someone could peep in. She must be quick.

She went into the back room and found the suitcase that had been brought in this afternoon with a batch of clothes. It was just the right size, but the clothes were mainly men's. She tipped them out on to the floor and carried the case into the main shop. A sour, damp smell came from the case. She put shoes in first, a nice pair of grey Hush Puppies, only slightly scuffed. She chose a couple of skirts, and some blouses and a dress. There was no time to try things on for size, so she went by the labels and hoped for the best. She realized she was taking only cotton things; it would be winter soon and she could not rely on there being central heating where she was going. She took a pair of thick winter slacks off the rail, examined them, peered into the crotch and sniffed. They seemed clean enough, but the woolly fabric scratched her nose – she was sweating, and couldn't believe that in a matter of weeks summer would be over and she would be grateful for this thick, harsh material against her flesh. She put the slacks in the suitcase and looked for a coat. She chose a dark blue sensible one. There was no room in the case, so she put it on and moved on to kitchen things – plates, cutlery and an oven-proof casserole. It was a lovely casserole, nearly new, but it took up a lot of space in the suitcase and what was the point of an oven-proof casserole when you might not have an oven? She might have to share a gas ring. She had heard of that, and read about it in ChildPeril reports: people struggling to cook for a family on a single gas ring, shared with other families. But she would be on her own, so she would be all right. She had always fancied herself as a good cook – now would be the chance to put herself to the test, because a really good cook could cook anywhere. Hadn't they had a book in stock once, about how you could prepare a three-course meal in a single saucepan? *The Pauper's Cook Book*, something like that? They might still have it. Sweating in her winter coat, she went to the books section and checked. It wasn't there, they must have sold it. Either that or someone had stolen it. Before she worked at ChildPeril she would never have believed that people would shoplift from charity shops, but they did. Perhaps they needed to. They probably felt terrible about it, and meant to pay it back one day. She advanced on the till, which still contained the day's takings. Pity it had been such a slow day. If she was going to do this, she might as well do it properly. She opened the till and started to transfer its contents to the pockets of the coat. Something made her stop and stare at the door. She felt she was being watched. She was. She was being watched by me.

94

At first, when she saw two eyes peering at her through the gap in the blind, she thought it must be Sheila, the volunteer helper whom she had sent home.

Sweating in the stolen coat, its pockets laden with cash from the till, Marjorie worked out what must have happened. Sheila had come back for something. She had spotted Marjorie helping herself to the shop's stock and takings. Any second now, she would be off to report the matter to the police – or, worse, Addie Bernard.

All Marjorie could think of was how to prevent this happening. She opened the door of the shop, dragged Sheila-alias-me inside and locked the door.

That's how it happened. I understand that, now that she's explained. But at the time I was quite shocked. It's not what you expect – walking up to the door of a respectable charity shop, and being bundled inside.

It reminded me of that scene in Zinnemann's *The Nun's Story* when the nun, played by Audrey Hepburn, is working in an asylum as a nurse, and one of the women patients drags her into a padded cell. In the struggle, the nun's headdress comes off and you see her shaven head. And what with the strangeness of that and all the grunting and screaming and clacking of rosary beads, you begin to lose track of which of these two women is mad and which is supposed to be normal.

I thought I was normal. I thought what I was doing – looking for Mrs Bloody Perfect so that I could take her to Mum's party – was perfectly sensible. I thought it was quite resourceful of me to come down to Eastbourne to find the only person I knew who had connections with the organization.

It hadn't occurred to me that Marjorie might *be* Mrs Bloody

Perfect. But as her fingers gripped my wrist and the door of the shop closed behind me, I realized I had walked into her trap.

It must be her. She was of the right age and the right background. She looked right – the permed grey hair, the linen frock, the flat-heeled shoes, the pillar-of-the-community overcoat worn even at the height of summer. This was the sort of person that the sort of person who used to be allowed to adopt would turn into in late middle age. I seemed to remember her saying that she had two daughters, but that proved nothing. She hadn't categorically stated that she gave birth to them. Not personally. They might have been taken away from a woman or women less able to stick up for themselves than Mum had been. The adoption people might have handed them over to Marjorie to make up to her for not getting me.

Now she had got me as well.

She had realized that I wasn't Sheila, but she couldn't work out who I was. She knew me from somewhere, but where? She looked at me with frantic eyes.

I in the meantime was taking in the nightmarish quality of the place where she had lured me, where I had lured myself – a shop full of second-hand clothes. The air was thick with the stink of them – dry cleaning fluid over old sweat, made worse by the heat of the day and the poor ventilation. It was the smell of my childhood, the actual childhood I had had with Mum, not the one I would have had with Mrs Bloody Perfect. Mrs Bloody Perfect wouldn't have expected me to wear old clothes. She would have taken pride in kitting me out in new ones. So what was she doing selling old ones to other people?

She seemed to decide where she had seen me before: I must be a customer, probably a regular. She saw herself manhandling me, and was stricken with embarrassment. She let go of my wrist as if she had never touched it, and said pleasantly, 'May I help you?'

She was playing for time, trying to work out how the hell

she was going to get out of this. So was I. I said, 'I thought you stayed open until five.'

Marjorie said in polite, customer-is-always-right tones, 'We do normally. But we sometimes close early in the summer when we're short-staffed. Do please have a look round, I'm just, er, sorting out some stock.' She took off the coat as if it were the most normal thing in the world for her to be wearing it. She was unready for its weight, and dropped it. Coins poured from the pockets and rolled all over the floor. She looked at them in horror, but I wasn't interested in the money. All I wanted was to get out. As she bent to pick up the coins, I feigned interest in the clothes and edged towards the door. I noted a summer dress made of lilac-coloured Crimplene, two brides-maids' frocks, a beige cardigan. I glanced at the books, mainly Mills & Boon and thrillers, and kitchenware – a tea-set with a handwritten note admitting that two of the cups were cracked, and a complete set of kitchen knives. I wondered how sharp they were.

I reached the door and turned the handle. It was locked, of course. I had forgotten that. I said, 'Could you let me out, please?' I was trying to sound firm and assertive but my voice was high-pitched and squeaky from fear. 'I've got friends waiting for me.'

She said, 'Don't I know you?' I spun round. She was still on her knees, like a person doing penance. She said, 'It's Heather, isn't it? Heather Fox.' Her tone was embittered and wondering, like the person in a thriller who says *so YOU were the murderer all along!* She got up and started to walk towards me, stiff-legged from kneeling. I tried to believe that she was coming to unlock the door, but I didn't think she was. Her face was contorted with fury and terror. Her voice came out as a hiss. 'Did *he* send you?'

I didn't have to think for long to work out who she meant. Who else did we have in common? But I wasn't concerned about him, I was concerned about the kitchen knives. Could I get to them, could I defend myself with them? Or would she take them off me, use them against me? Nobody knew where I was. 'I'm looking for the archive –'

'Are you his errand girl as well as his tart?' She was hissing in my face. I caught a little spray of spit, and a whiff of sourness on her breath. I recognized the sourness – I get it myself sometimes, in the corners of my mouth, when I'm scared or confused or stressed out. I had it then. I wondered if she could smell my sourness as I could smell hers, I wondered if she was aware of the strange fact that the tastes in our mouths were the same.

I said, 'I don't know what you're talking about.'

'I've read about you in the papers.'

'They made that up.'

She waved my words away with a gesture of contempt. 'I don't know how girls like you live with yourselves.'

'I didn't –'

She wasn't interested in my denial. She was looking at me with sly triumph in her eyes. 'He was *my* lover too, you know.'

In your dreams, I thought. But I feigned belief and interest. 'Really? When?' It seemed like a safer topic of conversation than the previous one.

And that was how I started to hear about it – by encouraging her to talk and keep talking, as an alternative to what I was sure she wanted to do which was to kill me.

I didn't get the whole story there and then, obviously. But that's when I got the broad outline – in between her bouts of weeping and anger.

I don't know why she chose me as confidante. Lack of alternatives was one reason, I suppose. I was both an acquaintance and near-stranger, which is a good combination, and I already knew some of the people involved in the story, which cut down on the need for complicated background explanations.

The timing helped as well. She needed somebody to talk to,

and I was there. If nothing else, she needed practice, and I don't just mean for giving her testimony in court. I mean for telling you, Robert.

You might think I've got an incredible cheek to be doing this. We've never laid eyes on each other, and here I am telling you the most personal things about your life and your wife and your marriage.

So let me make it clear that I'm only recounting this story as it was recounted to me. I've tidied it up a bit, but you know. I'm strictly the messenger, so don't shoot me. I'm not telling you what to do with the message.

How would I tell you? I'm not a Lloyd's name, or married to one, or ever likely to be either. I'm just the scribe, the jobbing hack who picked up the commission.

It was shortly after you rang. It was about 7.30 p.m. I had been incarcerated with Marjorie for nearly three hours, listening to her story. Sometimes she ranted, sometimes she wept. Sometimes she just talked, calm to the point of objectivity, as if all this had happened to a friend of a friend.

She was slumped in a chair; I was sitting on the floor with my back against a wall, defying the No Smoking signs. The shadows of the summer evening were lengthening; the air was smoky and stagnant and over-warm. You in the meantime were wondering what had happened to your dinner.

I was relieved to hear the phone. It reminded me that there was a world outside, one that I might eventually escape to; and it made a change from Marjorie's voice.

She picked up the receiver. I guessed at once who she was talking to. I could tell from her tone – intimate, familiar and yet somehow evasive, as if keeping something hidden from you was a habit she had got into.

She made some excuse about a stock-taking exercise that was going on longer than expected, and said she and the others would be going for a Chinese afterwards. A girls' night out, she said gaily. She gave you what struck me as over-detailed instructions about taking something out of the freezer and putting it into the microwave, and told you not to wait up. She said goodbye and put the phone down.

She stood with her back to me, as if too exhausted to turn round. 'Where was I?'

I couldn't remember. I didn't care. I was half-asleep myself, and had heard enough. I didn't want any of this, I wanted to be alone, I wanted to go home. But I was still locked in and she still had the key. 'How's he taking it?' I asked.

She turned slowly and looked at me. 'He doesn't know.'

I couldn't believe my ears. 'What – none of it?'

'I told him it was estate duty. '

'He can't still think that.'

'I don't know what he thinks.'

'You've got to tell him,' I said. 'You'll go mad if you don't.'

'I'll do that anyway,' she said.

I shrugged. 'You don't have to.'

'I'm mad now.' She pointed at the money on the floor. 'Look what I was about to do.' She picked up a pound coin with one hand, a 5op with the other. 'Pathetic, isn't it? But I was all sct to take it.' Her eyes filled with tears. 'Drop in the ocean. What difference would it have made?'

'What *would* make a difference?' I didn't expect a sensible answer to a question that I had only asked as part of my strategy of keeping her talking while I worked out how I could get away from her, but she considered the question before saying slowly, 'It would make a difference if Robert knew. If I could talk to him about it.'

'What's stopping you?'

'He doesn't know,' she wailed.

'I get it.' I was starting to lose patience. 'You can't talk to him because he doesn't know, you won't talk to him until he does know, but he won't know unless you talk to him.'

Her eyes narrowed. The tears had dried, the mad glint was back. 'If you're so clever,' she said, '*you* tell him.'

'Me?'

'Borrow my car.' She fumbled in her handbag and flung a set of keys at me. 'I'll give you directions. Go there, tell him I sent you. Don't tell him where I am, but tell him everything I've just told you. Then come back here and tell me what he said.'

95

That's not quite how I've done it, obviously. I couldn't drive her car, I haven't got a licence. And I didn't fancy the idea of coming face to face with a strange man in a strange house and giving him news like that.

It was none of my business anyway. My business was to get out of that shop. She had thrown me a set of keys. They were car keys not door keys, but keys were keys. They showed the way her mind was working.

I picked them up and sauntered towards the door as if I had agreed to do what she asked and took it for granted that she was going to open the door and let me out.

Which she did. The evening air was cool and fragrant. Seagulls cried through the twilight. Restaurants were open, and pubs. We walked round the corner and she pointed out a car. 'Follow the main road out past Safeway's,' she was saying. 'Then go left at the lights –'

I wondered why I didn't just run for it. I doubted that she would be able to catch me. But out in the open, she seemed so pathetic. She wasn't Mrs Bloody Perfect any more, on the lookout for defenceless babies to adopt. If anyone was in need of adoption, she was the one.

She was waiting for me to get into the car. It was time to come clean. I said, 'I don't drive.' I waited for her anger, her enraged accusation that I had misled her. But she just let out a long sigh, closed her eyes and leaned against a lamp post, as if overwhelmed by this latest betrayal.

To lighten the moment, I added, 'Boniface tried to teach me once, but I was hopeless.'

'I don't suppose he minded,' she said.

'What do you mean?'

'I expect it was one of the few occasions he was allowed to tell you what to do.'

'Maybe.'

'You were the only one he ever really loved,' she said.

I was startled, and wondered what she meant. I feigned indifference. 'Yeah? Me and all the others.'

'I was one of the others. He didn't love *me*.'

'You never know,' I said. 'Um, what did you mean exactly? About me being the only –'

'I didn't mean anything.'

A young couple went by, hand in hand, slightly drunk. They had to walk between us, and cast curious glances into our intense faces. Marjorie glared back, with the air of someone who believes that everyone in the world is happy apart from herself. She said to me, 'I suppose you might as well be on your way.'

I wanted to know what she had meant about Boniface. Had he talked to her about me? How recently? In the course of her monologue, she had said something about him being in Singapore, but only vaguely, in passing, as if it were something she had heard from somebody else. Who else? Whom did she know who knew where he was? Whereabouts in Singapore? 'I could write it for you,' I offered.

'Write what?'

'Everything you've told me. I could write it down – I'd need a bit more information – tidy it up a bit, and you could give it to Robert. It might help, you know, to get the conversation started.'

She looked at me closely. For the first time, I saw something in her eyes that resembled hope. 'Would you do that?'

'It's the sort of thing I do.'

'Will you do it now?'

'Not now this minute.'

'Why not?'

'Because I'm tired,' I said. 'And I need my stuff.'

'What stuff?'

'Pens, notebooks. My word-processor. I could go home now and get started, on the basis of what you've told me. If I needed to know anything more I could ring you up, and –'

'I can't wait that long,' she said. 'It has to be now.' She snatched the car keys out of my hand, opened the passenger door and pushed me inside. I was too surprised to resist. Soon we were out on a dual carriageway, speeding towards Hastings.

I asked several times where we were going and why, but she was deep in her own thoughts and did not reply. I remembered the opportunity I had had to escape. I had thrown it away.

She pulled off the road towards a vast out-of-town shopping centre. Floodlights and a packed car park indicated that this was its night for late opening. We got out of the car. It was another chance for me to get away, but I followed her like a dog on a lead, into an electrical goods superstore. She took a trolley and strode past the washing machines and the micro-wave ovens to the computers. There were rows and rows of them; she told me to choose any one I wanted. It was clear from her manner that she intended to pay, so I picked out a state-of-the-art model that Joze used in her business and which I had long coveted. She told me to put it in the trolley. 'What else do you need?' she asked. 'Disks?' I chose the word-processing package that I used at home, and a box of floppies. She took it from me. 'I think these are the same ones as Robert uses.' She seemed quite excited. 'When you've written it, I can load it all into his machine as a surprise. There's nothing like having something pop up on a screen for making him take notice of it.' We headed for the checkout.

I felt a pang of conscience and said, 'Marjorie, are you sure about this?'

'What, the money?' She waved her credit card gaily in the air. 'I might as well make the most of this while I still have it.' She paid for everything and we wheeled the trolley out into the clammy night air. By now it was getting on for ten o'clock, but she was indefatigable, driving around looking for a shop that sold pens and paper. We found an off-licence-cum-newsagent's, and stocked up. I could have done with a bottle of something as well, but it seemed best not to put the idea into her head; she was high as a kite already. We returned to the car and drove back to the main road. I had no idea where we were or where we were going, but after a few miles we saw a sign for a hotel and turned towards it. It was one of those businessmen's hotels that you see advertised, where the rooms are the same all over the world, and where you can send a fax or hire a secretary at any hour of the day or night. Marjorie stopped outside Reception and told me to wait. She came back with a key and drove to a row of little chalets. She unlocked one and indicated that I was to carry the computer inside. She followed with the disks and the notebooks. She closed the door and surveyed the room – the two large beds, luxury bathroom, TV, cocktail bar, the writing desk with the power point close by. She seemed satisfied, and so was I. I wanted to do nothing more energetic than sink into the bath and then lie in bed watching television, but she was already taking the computer out of its box.

I took it from her, I didn't want her to break it. I plugged it in and loaded the software. 'All set for the morning,' I said firmly. She looked disappointed, but I managed to convince her that I needed to be alone to think about what she had already told me, and the best way of writing it. In the morning, we would start afresh.

She went away with an air of such reluctance that I wondered if she thought I would do a runner, and take the computer with me. I guessed she might book herself into the chalet opposite so that she could keep an eye on me, but when I looked out of the window her car had gone.

I ordered cheeseburger and chips from room service, helped myself to a whisky and soda and lay on the bed with my glass in one hand and the TV remote control in the other. I flicked through the channels and thought how far I had come, from 59, Blondin Gardens to this.

96

I've been thinking about you a lot, and wondering how you feel. I've been wondering how I might feel if I came home one day and found that the person I had been living with for more than thirty years had imported a strange file into my computer telling me that they had lost all the family money, and that the family home might be next to go, along with the more valuable of its contents. And that the only way out of this mess was a choice between abject surrender of what remained of our possessions and our material comfort, or else a court case which could end up costing us even more money, could involve embarrassing revelations, and whose outcome was far from certain.

I don't think I would be too thrilled about it, to be honest. I'd be even less thrilled if the file went on to reveal that this situation had been building up for years, and I hadn't been allowed to know anything about it. I might take the view that if it wasn't my business before, it wasn't my business now. It certainly wasn't up to me to solve it. I might decide to pack a few treasured possessions and get out while the going was good.

What I'm saying, Robert, is that I'm not without sympathy for your plight. Not without sympathy at all. But where will that get us, eh? Nowhere. I'd better get on and do what I'm being paid to do, or rather what I'm not being paid to do. Still, I'm getting a nice break in a luxury hotel, and if I play my cards right she'll probably let me keep the computer.

I didn't play them right that first morning. I was still asleep when she came round. Mind you, it was only five o'clock. I heard a knock on my chalet door, rolled out of bed, pulled on

the hotel dressing gown and fumbled with the door handle. I
was half-expecting to see Boniface extricating himself from a
yogurt pot. That's how sleepy I still was, that's how intensely
she had got to me, with her talk of me being the only one he
ever loved. I wondered what had made her say that. I wondered
what he was doing in Singapore.

She stood on the path, fidgeting miserably in the beautiful
summer dawn. Birds twittered overhead. She had changed
her clothes, otherwise I might have thought that she hadn't
been home. She had the same air of desperate preoccupation
as she had had the night before, the same manic energy. Behind her was her car, with two rather elderly red setters in
the back. She said conspiratorially, 'I told Robert I was taking
them for an early morning walk.' She handed me a small tape-
recorder. 'I've brought you this, I can't expect you to remember everything I say, I'm such a chatterbox. How's it
going?'

'Fine.' I stifled a yawn. 'Er, fine.'

She walked past me into the chalet and saw the unmade bed,
the blank computer screen, the remains of last night's meal.
She gave me a look of reproach, and said, 'Can I read what
you've written so far?'

'Not really,' I said. 'It's in rather a raw state.'

'But I want to see how it's going.'

'I can't do it with you breathing down my neck, okay?'

She stepped back as if I had hit her. I skulked guiltily into
the bathroom, had a quick wash and got dressed. I resolved
then to pull my finger out, to do my best and furthermore
to be nice to her while I did it. She didn't need me bullying
her, telling her off. She was going to get enough of that from
you.

Maybe you won't tell her off. Maybe instead you'll put your
arm round her and say *there, there*, and *poor you* and *never
mind*, and *don't worry, we'll manage*. Maybe you'll realize

that there's no point in wasting your breath on reproaches. She's heard them all before, after all – from herself.

You might decide to concentrate instead on keeping her spirits up and helping her to make the right decision about whether to give in or go to court. To do that, you're going to have to make up your mind what you feel about her affair with Boniface, if you call it an affair. It doesn't sound much like one to me. To me it sounds more like a single rather joyless episode, embarrassing rather than erotic, but if that's all she was getting . . . I don't want to think about that. I had to think about it to write those scenes, but I don't want to think about it any more. I'm no stranger to long periods without sex, but at least I still have prospects, or so I like to kid myself. I'm not thirty yet, I'm not grey yet or wrinkled, my flesh is still firm. I don't want to think about how it feels to be fifty and have no partner, or to have one who doesn't want you. Come to that, I don't want to think about how it feels to have a partner who *does* want you, but you don't want them. You used to, but now that has all died in you. I don't want to give space in my head to those sorts of predicament. It would be indecent, like speculating on the sex life of your parents.

Speaking of the sex life of my parents, round about my fifth night in the hotel I realized that I was missing Mum's first-day-of-the-rest-of-her-life party.

I could remember thinking that I wouldn't go. I could remember thinking that I would go and make a scene. But it had never been on my agenda that I would *forget* to go.

It was getting on for midnight. Marjorie had been with me for most of the day, speaking into the tape-recorder, running little errands to fetch me cigarettes or documents or stationery or newspapers; or pacing up and down, thinking up excuses to make to you about why she was spending so much time away from home, and why she found it so difficult to talk to you when she was in it. Laryngitis I think was the current one.

Now she had gone and I was alone in the chalet. I imagined Mum's party in full swing. I dialled her number. At the other end someone picked up the phone, and I heard party noises. Madge Kennedy's voice said tipsily, 'Hi, there.'

'Hello, Madge.'

'Heather! We were wondering where you had got to.'

'I can't make the party,' I said. 'I've got a rush job on.'

'Sounds exciting. Do you want to speak to Julia?'

I had thought I would, but now I had lost my nerve. 'No need,' I said. 'Just pass the message on, would you, Madge? Tell her I hope it goes well, and I'll phone her during the week.'

'Okay,' said Madge. 'I probably wouldn't be able to tear her away anyway.'

'Tear her away from what?' I asked, thinking I knew.

'Your mother,' said Madge, 'is currently addressing a rapt audience on the future of the women's movement.' She paused to swig at her drink. 'The *reculer pour mieux sauter* model.'

'The – ?'

'Don't make me say it again, Heather, I'm pissed.'

'No, but –'

'Here's how it goes,' said Madge. 'Feminism has lost its way. Nothing new about that. It's trying to do too much, she says. It's carrying banners proclaiming Women Against All Bad Things And In Favour Of All Good Things, and they're too heavy. It's going to collapse under the strain. When that happens, who shall we see striding out through the dust and smoke of the battlefield, bearing the standard of the seven demands, but Julia Fox. She'll set up the standard and see who rallies.'

'Is that what she's doing now?'

'No, no, that's for the future.' Madge took another swig and cleared her throat. 'The historical moment is not yet.'

'But they're rapt?'

Madge considered. 'Some of them look rapt-ish, you know how your mum can talk.' She lowered her voice. 'Your dad doesn't look very rapt, he looks totally bemused, he hasn't the faintest idea what she's on about. He even made a crack about bra-burning, and couldn't understand why everyone looked the other way. *Bra-burning.* Where's he *been*?'

'I don't know, I don't care, and I wish you wouldn't call him that.'

'Sorry,' said Madge. 'But I keep losing track of what his name is.'

'Is she ignoring him?'

'Not exactly.' Madge tried to be fair. 'Not in a nasty way. I mean, they were all kissy-kissy when he got here, and I thought, oh Lord, here we go, and poor old Ronnie was shifting from foot to foot. But then it was like – I don't know, once they'd done the how-amazing-to-see-you-again stuff and the you-haven't-changed-a-bit routine, they hadn't got all that much to say to each other. He asked after you and she asked after his kids – his other kids, I should say –'

'What other kids?'

'Seven, I think he said,' said Madge. 'And another one on the way from his current wife. His previous two divorced him.' She sniffed. 'Can't say I'm surprised.'

'I'm picking up that you don't like him very much, Madge.'

'Put it this way, I've sort of got used over the years to not having men fondle my bum the first time I meet them or even at all and it's a bit of a surprise when I run into one who does, particularly in Julia's house. But there you go, I don't suppose we'll be seeing much of him, he's off back to Singapore next week.'

'Singap –'

'He's based there half the year, his wife's Chinese, he commutes. He's got some sort of import–export business – clothes and shoes and textiles. For which read sweated labour, no doubt.' She lowered her voice. 'I think he's leaving, it's finally dawned on him that this is one party he can't be life and soul of. Shit, he's kissing everyone. What shall I do?'

'What would you normally do?'

'I can't do that to your dad.' She went away from the phone and I heard her say charmingly, 'Leaving already, Joe? Yes, it was nice meeting you too. I hope so. Oh, thank you, we'd love to.'

When she came back, I mimicked her: ' "Oh, thank you, Joe, we'd love to." '

'I was being polite.'

'You'd love to what?'

'Any friend of Julia's is a friend of his apparently, and if Patience and I ever happen to find ourselves in Singapore we must be sure and go and stay with him and his wife in their mansion overlooking Serangoon Harbour.'

97

I thought and I wrote and I went to bed. I couldn't sleep, I was too busy thinking – not just about Marjorie and her story but about me and mine.

Nothing new about that, I hear you scoff. *You've been thinking about your own story all along, even though you've been pretending to tell Marjorie's.*

That's not entirely fair. I've had to include some parts of my story in order to throw light on Marjorie's. But all right, I admit it, in places I have gone a bit over the top, hijacking her story and turning it into mine.

But it's no more than she would have done to me, is it? She and you, if you had adopted me, if you had been Mr and Mrs Bloody Perfect. That's what adoption is – taking over someone else's story, and turning it into your own.

You're not the Bloody Perfects. I know that now; or at least, I know there's no more reason it should be you, than why it should be any other of the thousands of fiftysomething couples I've passed on the street in my life, or the ones I've never laid eyes on.

It doesn't matter, in any case. It doesn't matter where they are or who they are because I know they can't get me. They never could, because my mother was strong and brave and tough, and then as now she didn't care whom she infuriated, whom she outraged, as long as she clung on tight to what was important, which in those days meant me. The Bloody Perfects can't adopt me because I've adopted them, in the form of you and Marjorie, Marjorie in particular. She was at rock-bottom that day when I found her in the shop – ready to steal and run away and do all sorts of mad things that would have solved nothing and would only have made her feel worse. I stopped her and talked to her and let her talk to me, and now I'm doing what I can to help, the only thing I'm capable of – telling her story to you. And you're sitting there, almost at the end of reading it.

I phoned Joze and apologized for not turning up to help her clients choose poems for their daughter's funeral. She was quite cold at first, so I explained about finding my father, and what a shock it had been. She said gruffly, 'I'm sure. They'd just lost their daughter, that was quite a shock too.'

'I know,' I said. 'I'm sorry.'

'I tell you this, Heather – if you ever do anything like that again, the only funeral you'll need to worry about choosing poems for will be your own.'

I knew then that she had forgiven me, so I said, 'Joze, how would you fancy a holiday in Singapore?'

'Singap –'

'The fares are on me, to show you how sorry I am.'

'Well, thanks, but – are you feeling quite well?'

'Never better.'

She promised to think about it, though I could tell she thought I was mad. But I'm not. I'll raise the money for the fares by selling the computer. Singapore sounds like a nice place, I'd like to go there.

It's a big place too, but so is New York, and I found him there. I've got a few clues to go on. Marjorie let slip that it was the dotty duchess who told her about him being in Singapore, the Duchess of Norby Wick. I'll look her up in *Burke's Peerage* and drop her a line, see how much more she knows.

My father might be able to provide other leads. There's probably no special reason why one slightly iffy English businessman based in Singapore should know another; on the other hand, there's no special reason why he shouldn't. For all I know, they drink in the same bars, they're members of the same club.

And even if they're not – well, it'll be a chance to see a bit of the world. We can stay at my dad's place, it's the least he can do to put me and my friend up for a while.

I wonder if he ever has his other kids to stay – my half-brothers and half-sisters. I wonder what they're like, whether they look like me, think like me. I wonder what they think of him. And there's another one on the way. By the time I get there, it might be born: a beautiful little half-Chinese baby, related to me. I wonder what they'll call her.

If things don't work out, if all these new flesh-and-blood relatives get me down and scare me and give me the creeps the way the old, unreal, shadowy ones did, I'll be able to escape with Joze. Or even with Boniface, if I find him, if I still feel the same about him, if Marjorie is right that I'm the only one he ever loved, and if he hasn't turned into an anorak in the meantime.

An anorak or a crook. Are Marjorie and all those other names victims of crookery, or was it just their hard luck that they were in the wrong place at the wrong time, blithely believing in their divine right to cash in on clairvoyance and the forces of fate? It's not for me to say, though maybe one day Boniface will tell me how much he knew. I'd like to think that in his case it wasn't actual dishonesty that was to blame so much as the fact that he never quite managed to get to grips with *Principles of Underwriting*; maybe he really did think he was only putting Marjorie down to insure the toothbrush-holder in the captain's bog. But it's not my problem, it's a matter for the courts. There are quite a few cases in the pipeline, and the issues are complex, so it could be months or even years before judgement is reached, which is a pity, because it means I'm not going to be able to end this with a nice neat court scene with jubilation or disappointment as the case may be. That'll come later, it'll be in all the papers. But it's not the court's verdict that's the point, really, is it, Robert? I don't mean it's not important; obviously it's very important, it's going to have a major impact on your long-term future, and Marjorie's, not to mention those of Di and Tony and their unfortunate kids; but this isn't about the long-term future, it's about the next five minutes, the time in which you're going to stop staring at your computer and get up from your chair, rubbing your eyes perhaps, and stretching your limbs after sitting still for such a long time. And then you're going to go and look for Marjorie, who's waiting alone somewhere in this house where you've lived all your married life but which you may be about to lose. She may be trembling a little, or crying, or else deathly calm in the realization that at last you *know*. And now that you know, the ending is whatever you're going to say to her, so say it.